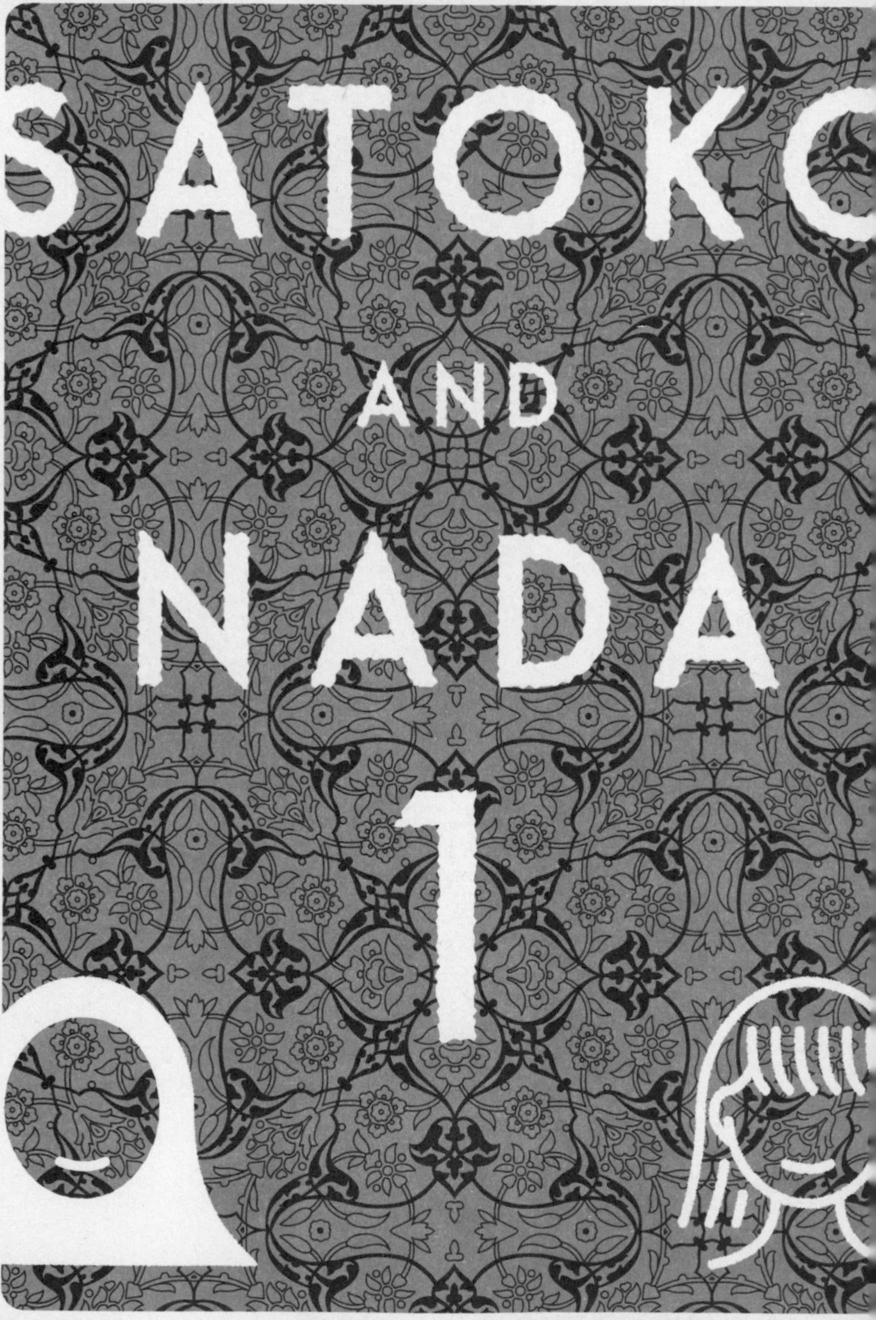
SATOKO
AND
NADA
1

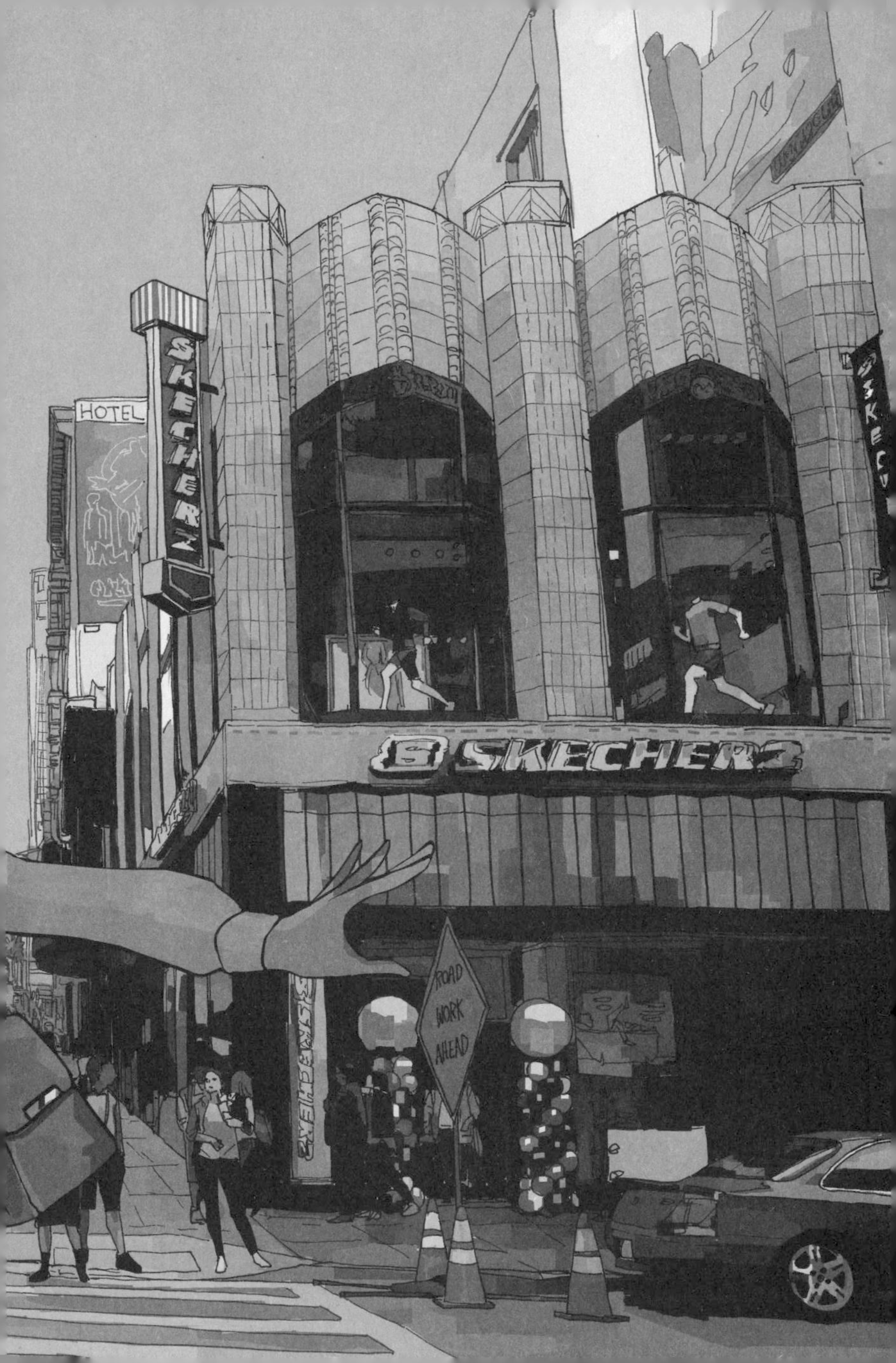
HOTEL
SKECHERS
SKECHERS
ROAD WORK AHEAD

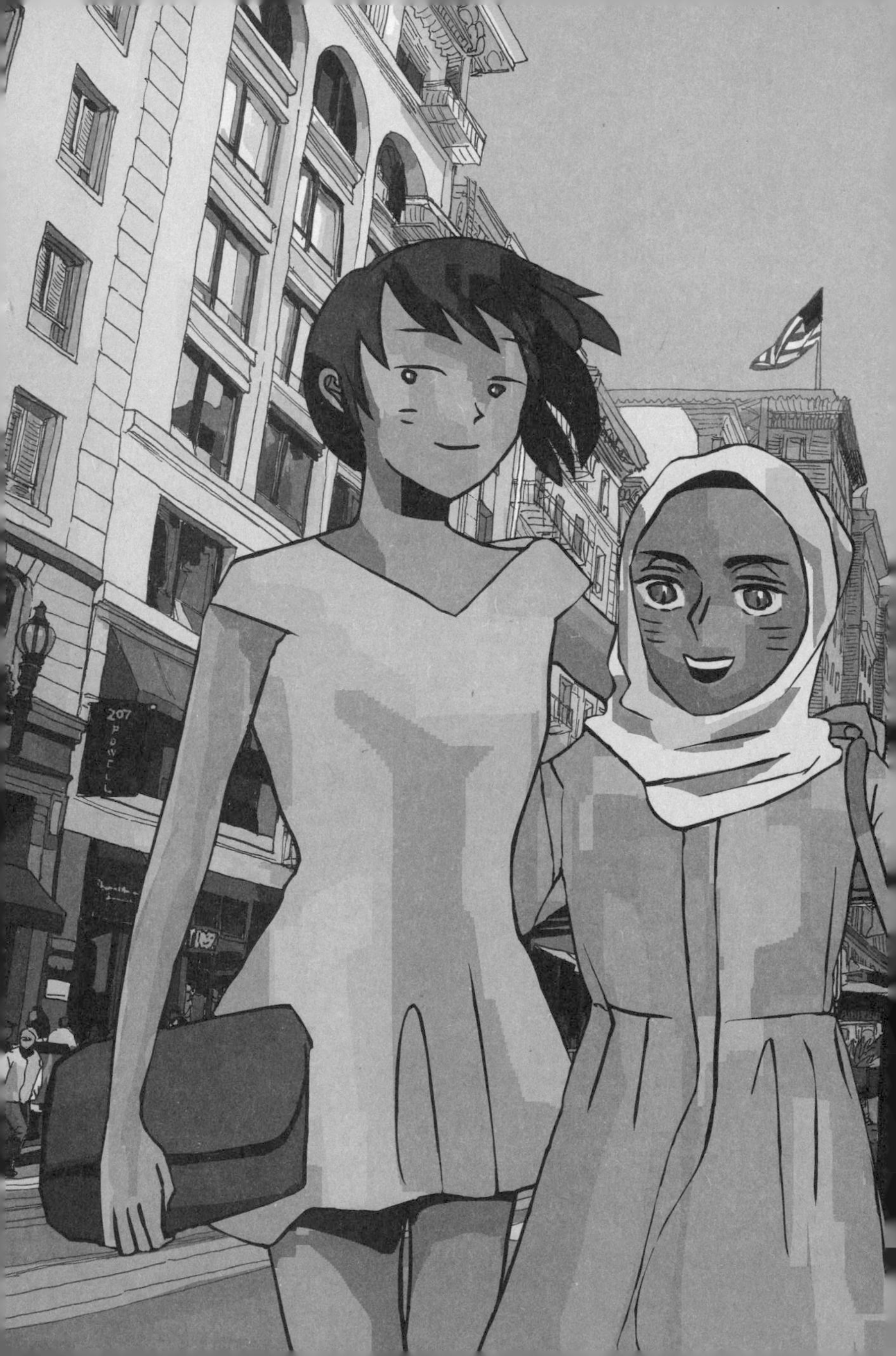
207
POWELL

THEIR FIRST MEETING

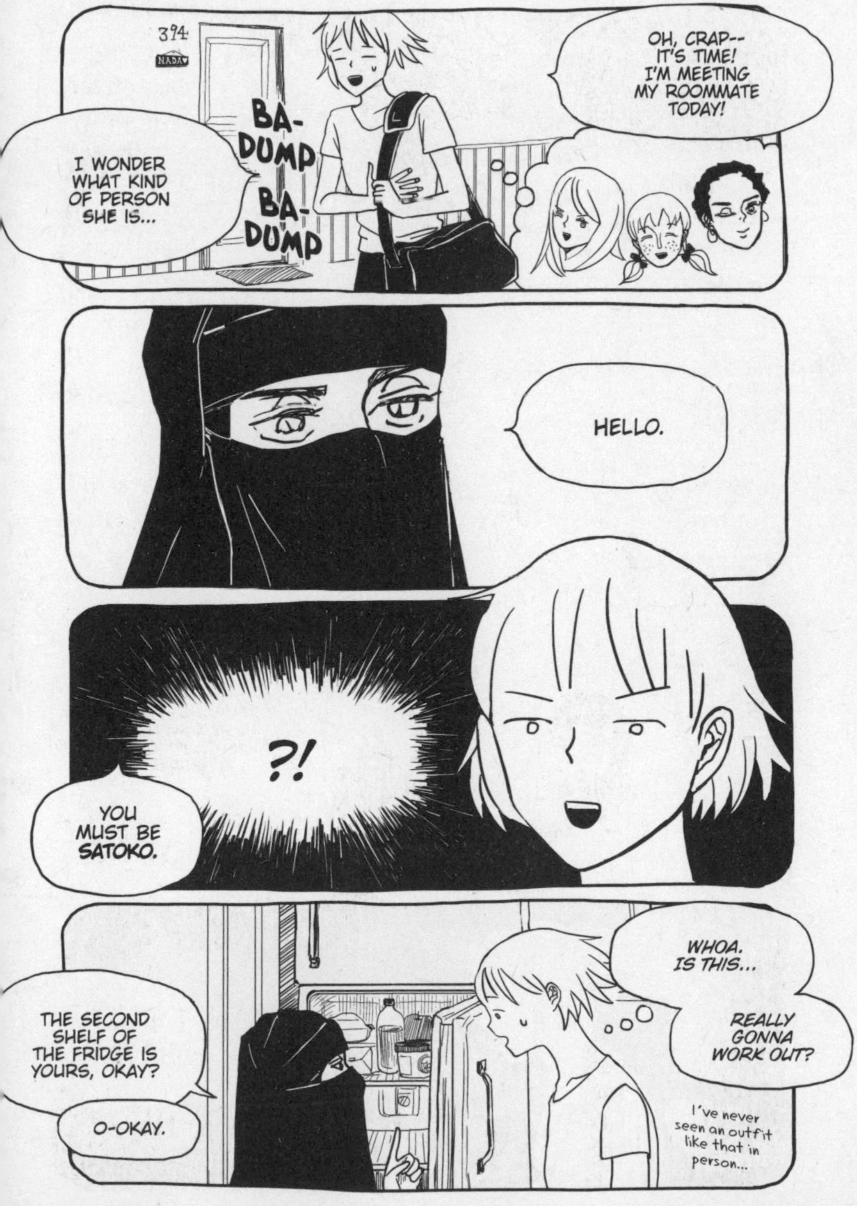

OH, CRAP-- IT'S TIME! I'M MEETING MY ROOMMATE TODAY!
NADA
BA-DUMP BA-DUMP
I WONDER WHAT KIND OF PERSON SHE IS...
HELLO.
?!
YOU MUST BE SATOKO.
WHOA. IS THIS...
REALLY GONNA WORK OUT?
I've never seen an outfit like that in person...
THE SECOND SHELF OF THE FRIDGE IS YOURS, OKAY?
O-OKAY.

SELFIE

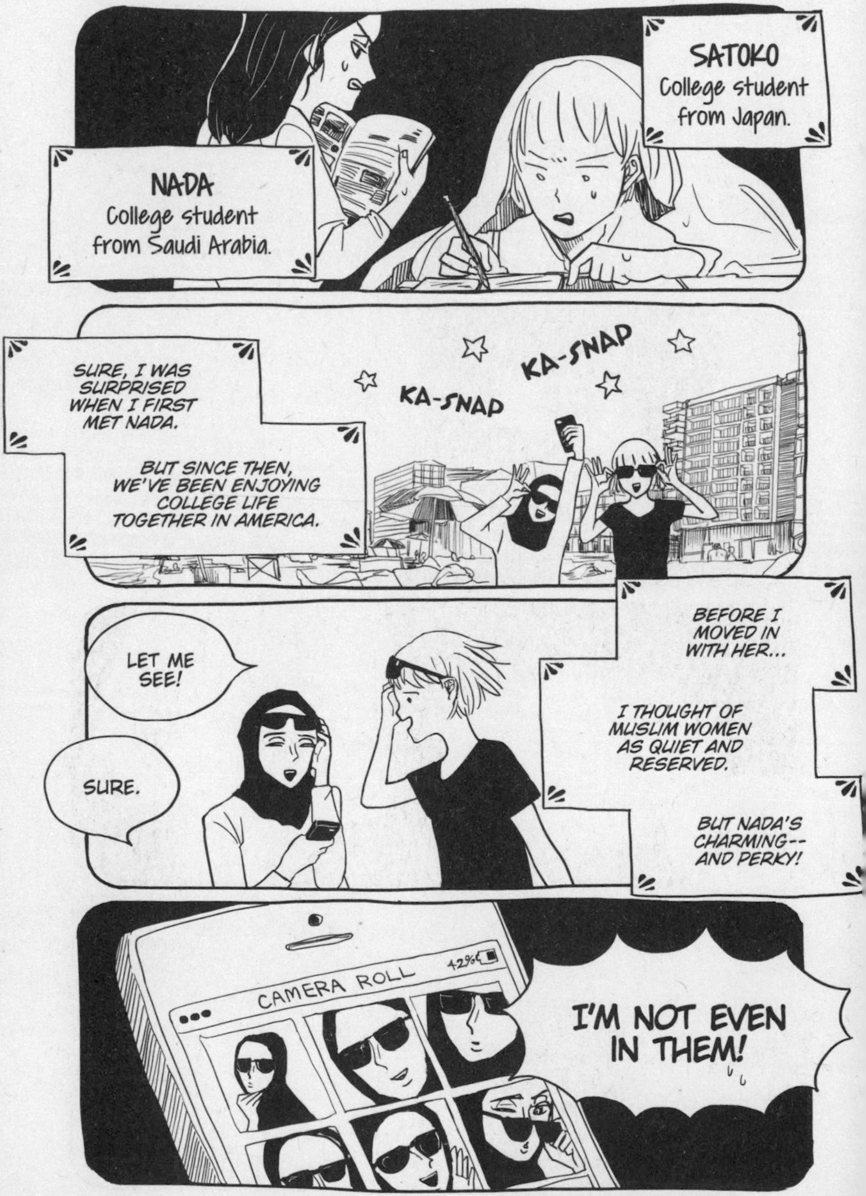

SATOKO
College student from Japan.
NADA
College student from Saudi Arabia.
KA-SNAP
KA-SNAP
SURE, I WAS SURPRISED WHEN I FIRST MET NADA.
BUT SINCE THEN, WE'VE BEEN ENJOYING COLLEGE LIFE TOGETHER IN AMERICA.
BEFORE I MOVED IN WITH HER...
I THOUGHT OF MUSLIM WOMEN AS QUIET AND RESERVED.
BUT NADA'S CHARMING--AND PERKY!
LET ME SEE!
SURE.
I'M NOT EVEN IN THEM!
42%
CAMERA ROLL

A MAIDEN'S HAIR

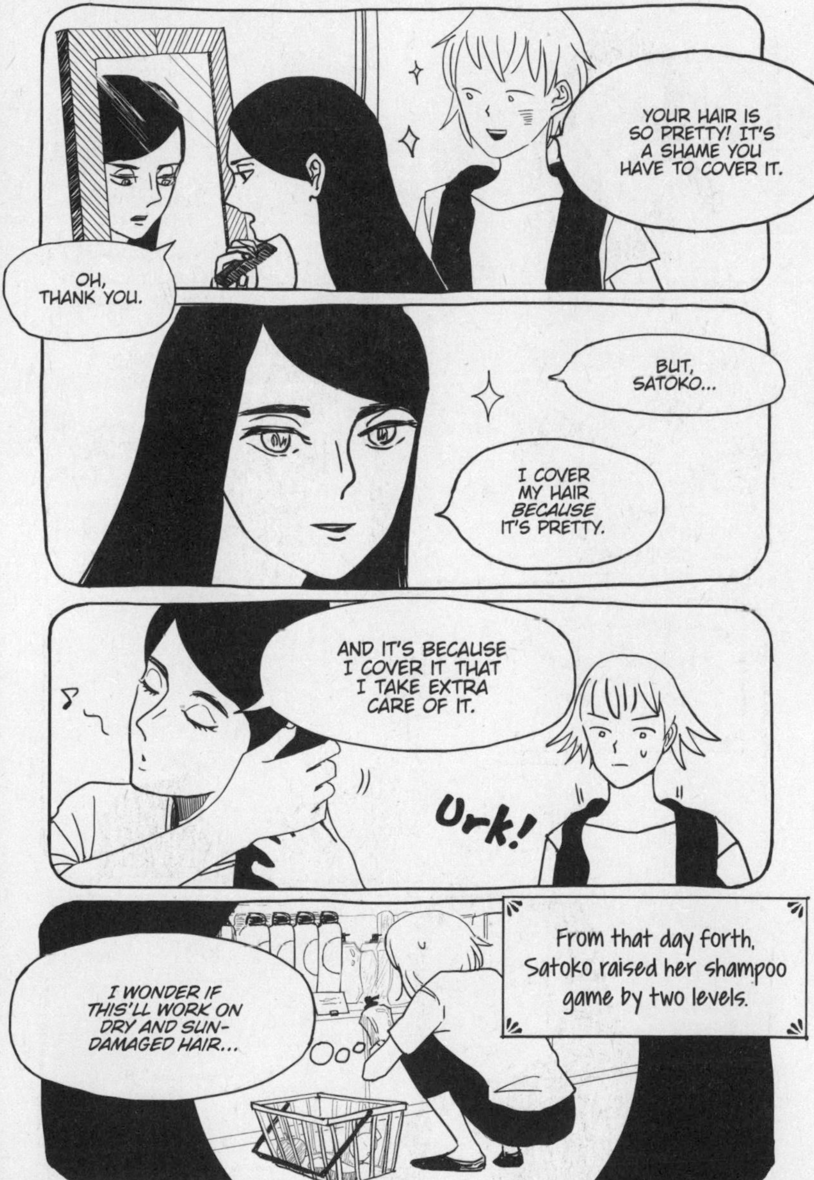
YOUR HAIR IS SO PRETTY! IT'S A SHAME YOU HAVE TO COVER IT.
OH, THANK YOU.
BUT, SATOKO...
I COVER MY HAIR *BECAUSE* IT'S PRETTY.
AND IT'S BECAUSE I COVER IT THAT I TAKE EXTRA CARE OF IT.
Urk!
From that day forth, Satoko raised her shampoo game by two levels.
I WONDER IF THIS'LL WORK ON DRY AND SUN-DAMAGED HAIR...

MISS FASHIONABLE

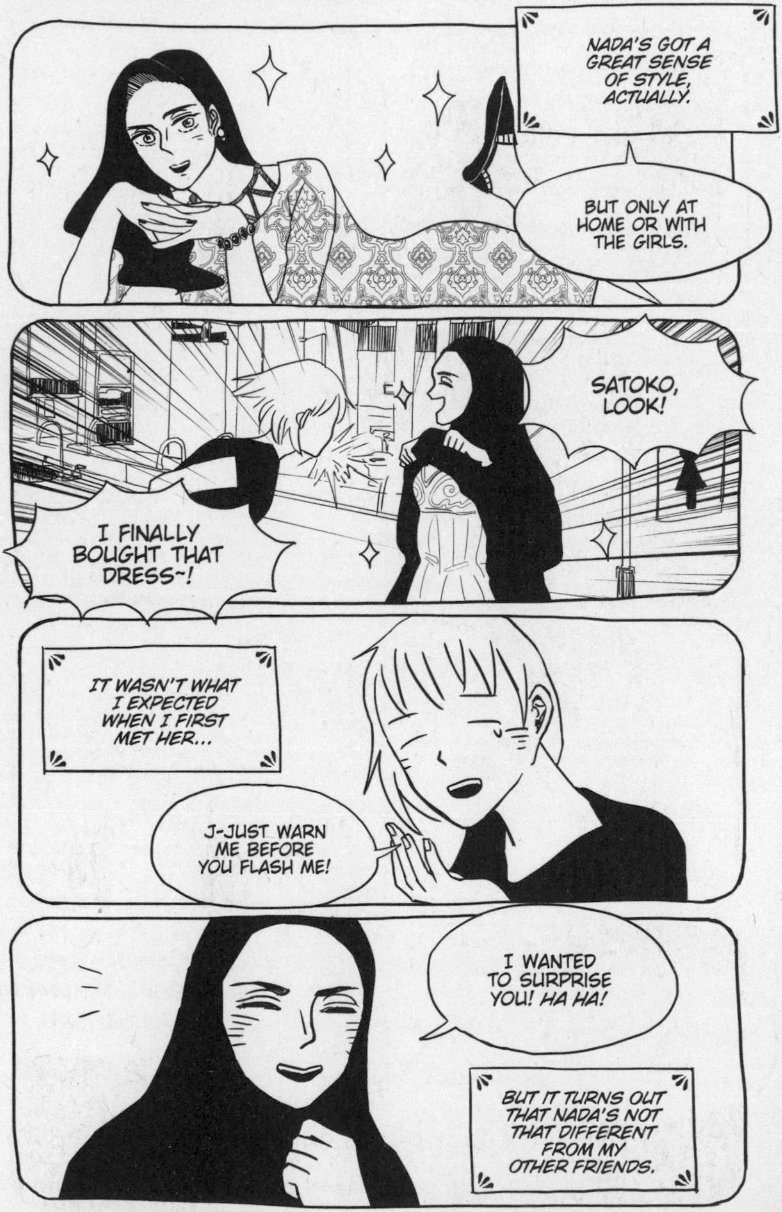
NADA'S GOT A GREAT SENSE OF STYLE, ACTUALLY.
BUT ONLY AT HOME OR WITH THE GIRLS.
SATOKO, LOOK!
I FINALLY BOUGHT THAT DRESS~!
IT WASN'T WHAT I EXPECTED WHEN I FIRST MET HER...
J-JUST WARN ME BEFORE YOU FLASH ME!
I WANTED TO SURPRISE YOU! HA HA!
BUT IT TURNS OUT THAT NADA'S NOT THAT DIFFERENT FROM MY OTHER FRIENDS.

LIKE THAT?

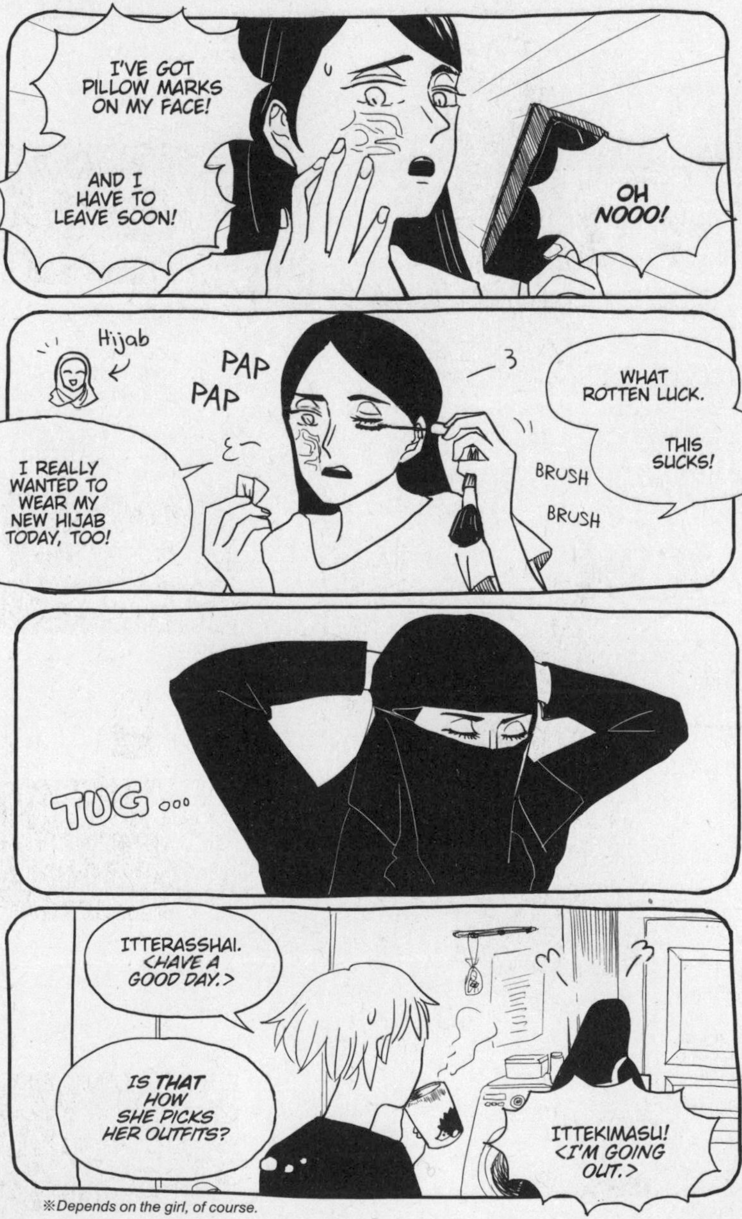
I'VE GOT PILLOW MARKS ON MY FACE!
OH NOOO!
AND I HAVE TO LEAVE SOON!
WHAT ROTTEN LUCK.
THIS SUCKS!
BRUSH
BRUSH
PAP
PAP
Hijab
I REALLY WANTED TO WEAR MY NEW HIJAB TODAY, TOO!
TUG...
ITTEKIMASU! <I'M GOING OUT.>
ITTERASSHAI. <HAVE A GOOD DAY.>
IS THAT HOW SHE PICKS HER OUTFITS?

※*Depends on the girl, of course.*

VEILS

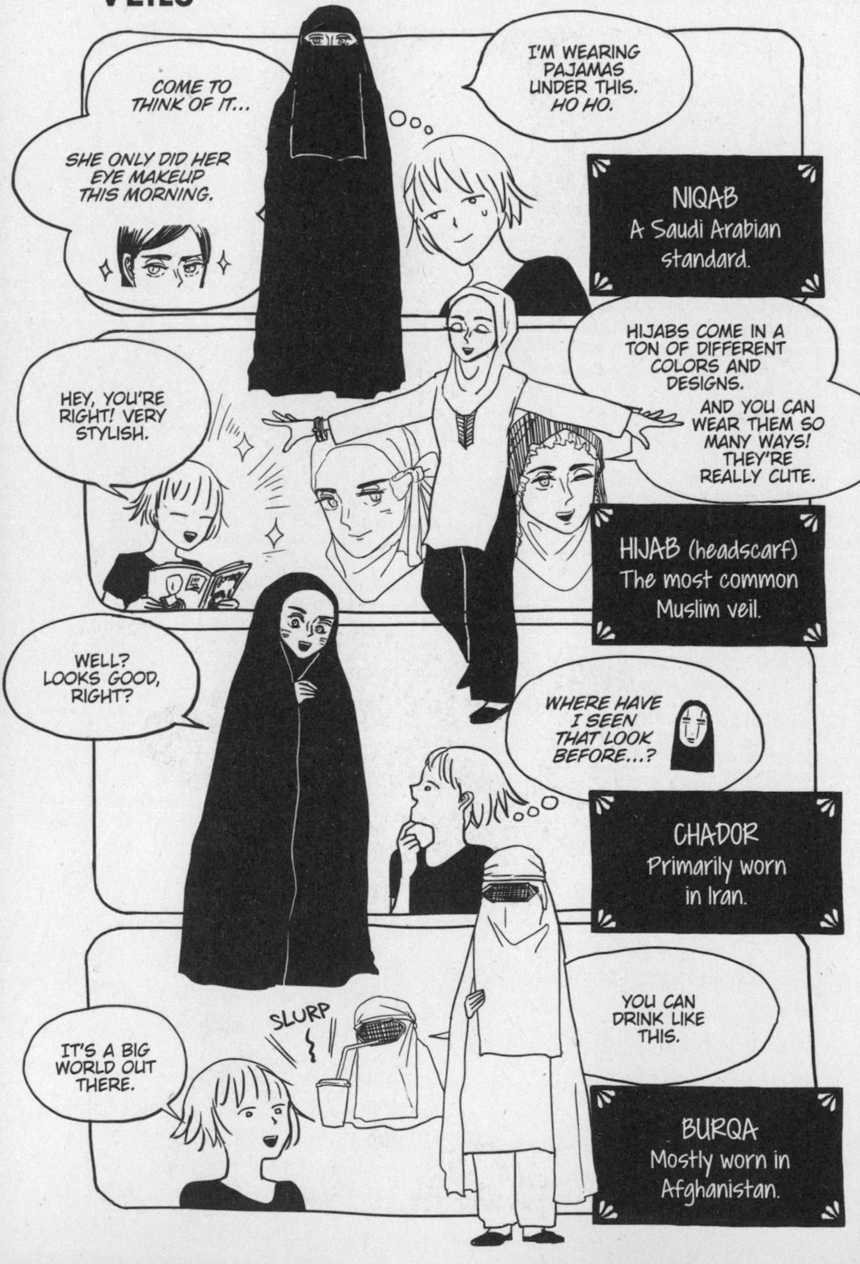

I'M WEARING PAJAMAS UNDER THIS. HO HO.
COME TO THINK OF IT...
SHE ONLY DID HER EYE MAKEUP THIS MORNING.
NIQAB
A Saudi Arabian standard.
HIJABS COME IN A TON OF DIFFERENT COLORS AND DESIGNS.
AND YOU CAN WEAR THEM SO MANY WAYS! THEY'RE REALLY CUTE.
HEY, YOU'RE RIGHT! VERY STYLISH.
HIJAB (headscarf)
The most common Muslim veil.
WELL? LOOKS GOOD, RIGHT?
WHERE HAVE I SEEN THAT LOOK BEFORE...?
CHADOR
Primarily worn in Iran.
YOU CAN DRINK LIKE THIS.
SLURP
IT'S A BIG WORLD OUT THERE.
BURQA
Mostly worn in Afghanistan.

NAMES

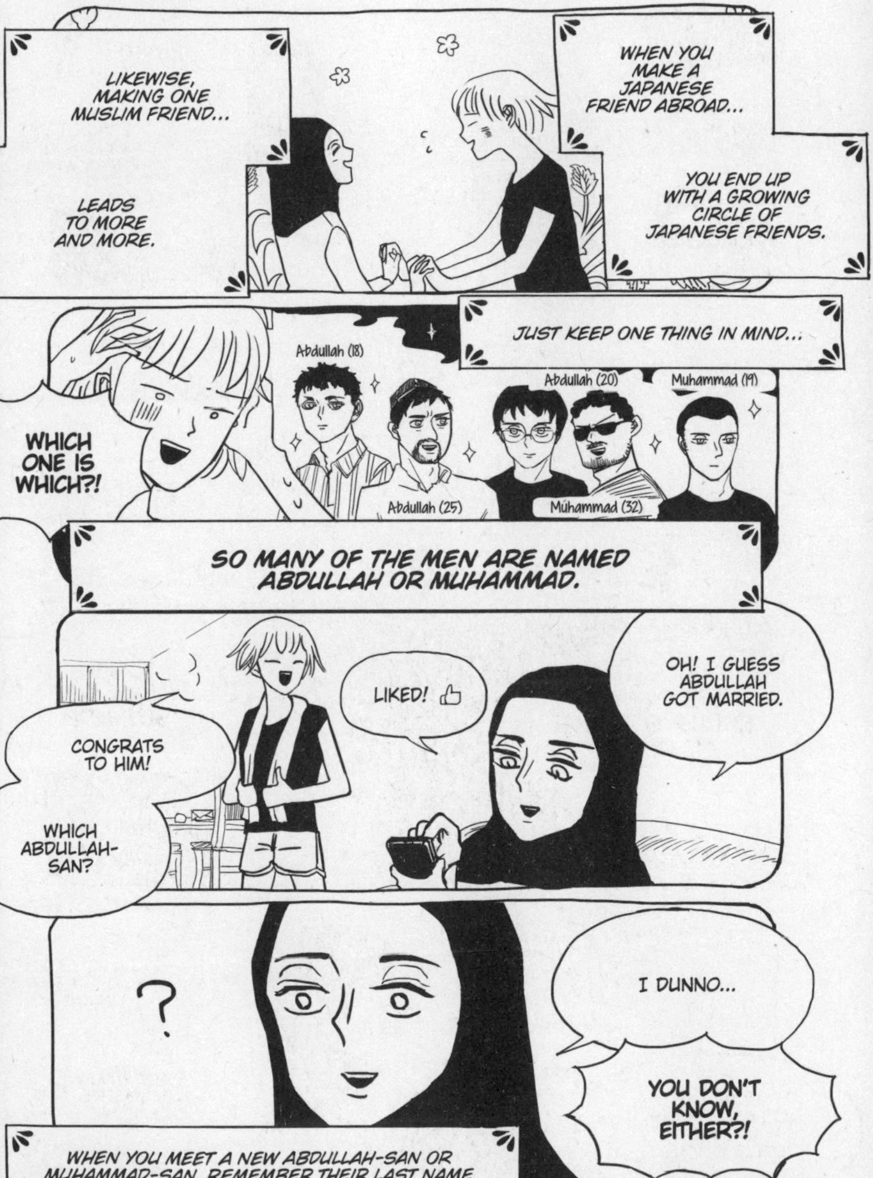

WHEN YOU MAKE A JAPANESE FRIEND ABROAD...
YOU END UP WITH A GROWING CIRCLE OF JAPANESE FRIENDS.
LIKEWISE, MAKING ONE MUSLIM FRIEND...
LEADS TO MORE AND MORE.
JUST KEEP ONE THING IN MIND...
Muhammad (19)
Abdullah (20)
Muhammad (32)
Abdullah (25)
Abdullah (18)
WHICH ONE IS WHICH?!
SO MANY OF THE MEN ARE NAMED ABDULLAH OR MUHAMMAD.
OH! I GUESS ABDULLAH GOT MARRIED.
LIKED!
CONGRATS TO HIM!
WHICH ABDULLAH-SAN?
I DUNNO...
YOU DON'T KNOW, EITHER?!
?
WHEN YOU MEET A NEW ABDULLAH-SAN OR MUHAMMAD-SAN, REMEMBER THEIR LAST NAME OR UNIQUE TRAITS--BECAUSE YOU'LL NEED 'EM.

RAMADAN

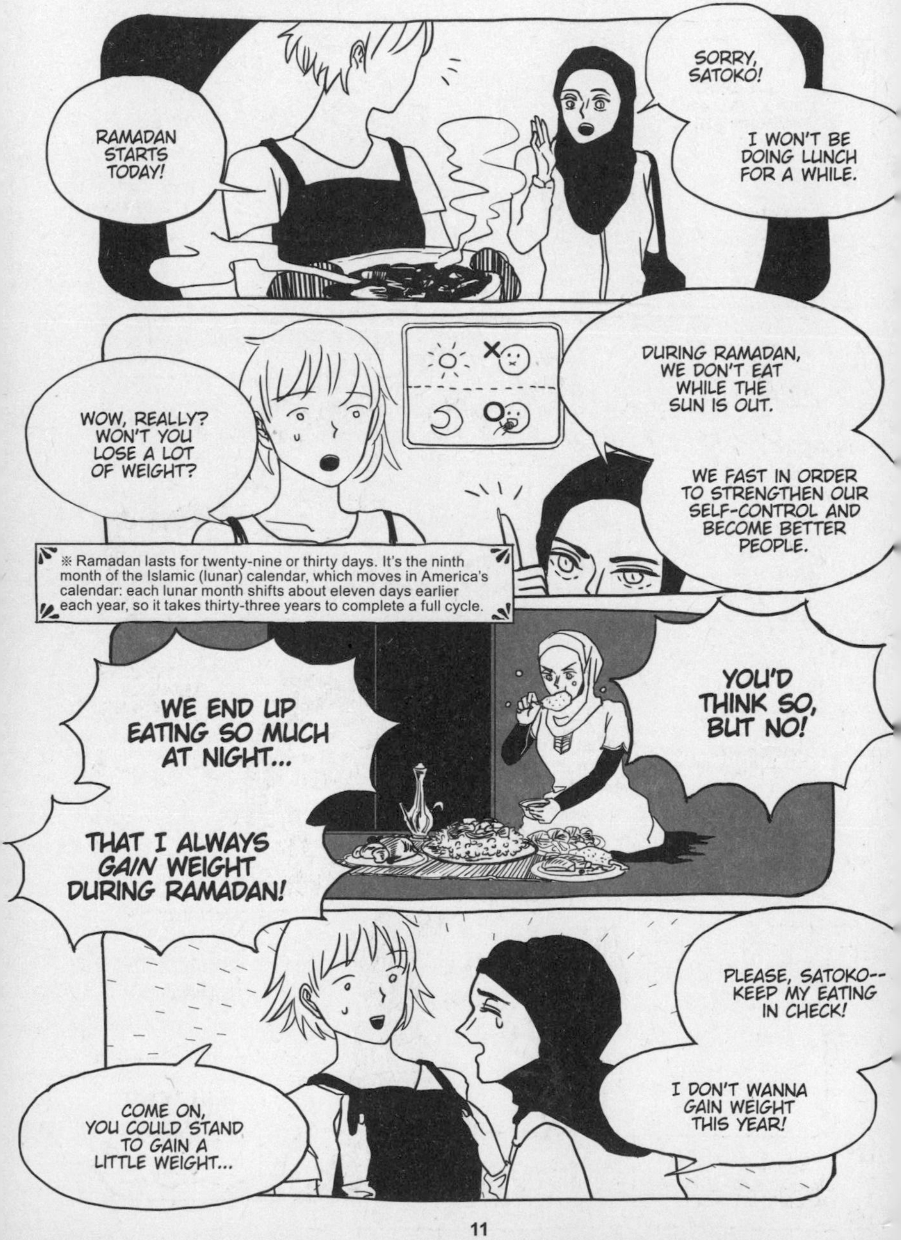
SORRY, SATOKO!
I WON'T BE DOING LUNCH FOR A WHILE.
RAMADAN STARTS TODAY!
DURING RAMADAN, WE DON'T EAT WHILE THE SUN IS OUT.
WE FAST IN ORDER TO STRENGTHEN OUR SELF-CONTROL AND BECOME BETTER PEOPLE.
WOW, REALLY? WON'T YOU LOSE A LOT OF WEIGHT?
※ Ramadan lasts for twenty-nine or thirty days. It's the ninth month of the Islamic (lunar) calendar, which moves in America's calendar: each lunar month shifts about eleven days earlier each year, so it takes thirty-three years to complete a full cycle.
YOU'D THINK SO, BUT NO!
WE END UP EATING SO MUCH AT NIGHT...
THAT I ALWAYS GAIN WEIGHT DURING RAMADAN!
PLEASE, SATOKO-- KEEP MY EATING IN CHECK!
I DON'T WANNA GAIN WEIGHT THIS YEAR!
COME ON, YOU COULD STAND TO GAIN A LITTLE WEIGHT...

TEMPERATURE DIFFERENCE

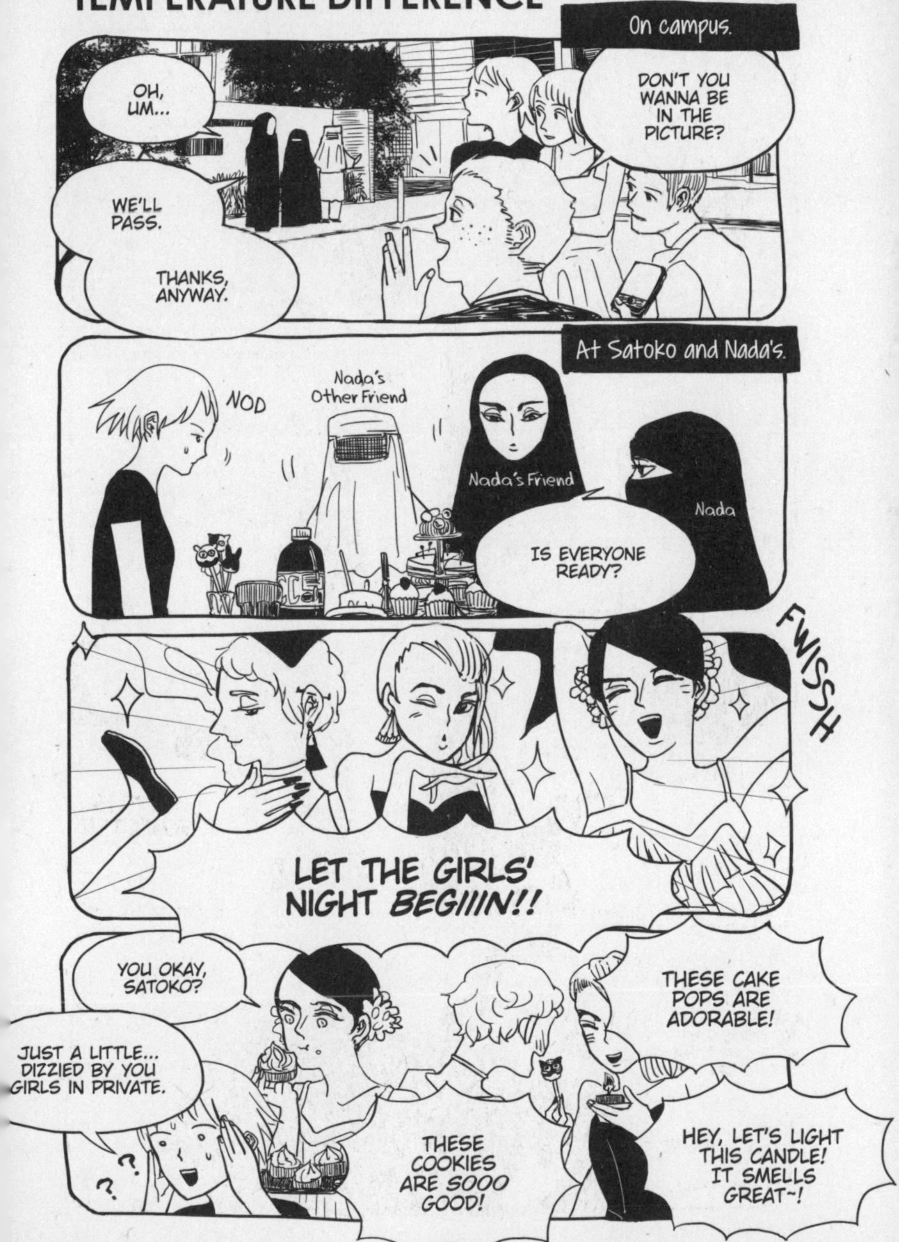
On campus.
DON'T YOU WANNA BE IN THE PICTURE?
OH, UM...
WE'LL PASS.
THANKS, ANYWAY.
At Satoko and Nada's.
Nada
IS EVERYONE READY?
Nada's Friend
Nada's Other Friend
NOD
FWISSH
LET THE GIRLS' NIGHT BEGIIIN!!
THESE CAKE POPS ARE ADORABLE!
HEY, LET'S LIGHT THIS CANDLE! IT SMELLS GREAT~!
THESE COOKIES ARE SOOO GOOD!
YOU OKAY, SATOKO?
JUST A LITTLE... DIZZIED BY YOU GIRLS IN PRIVATE.
? ?

ONE PIECE

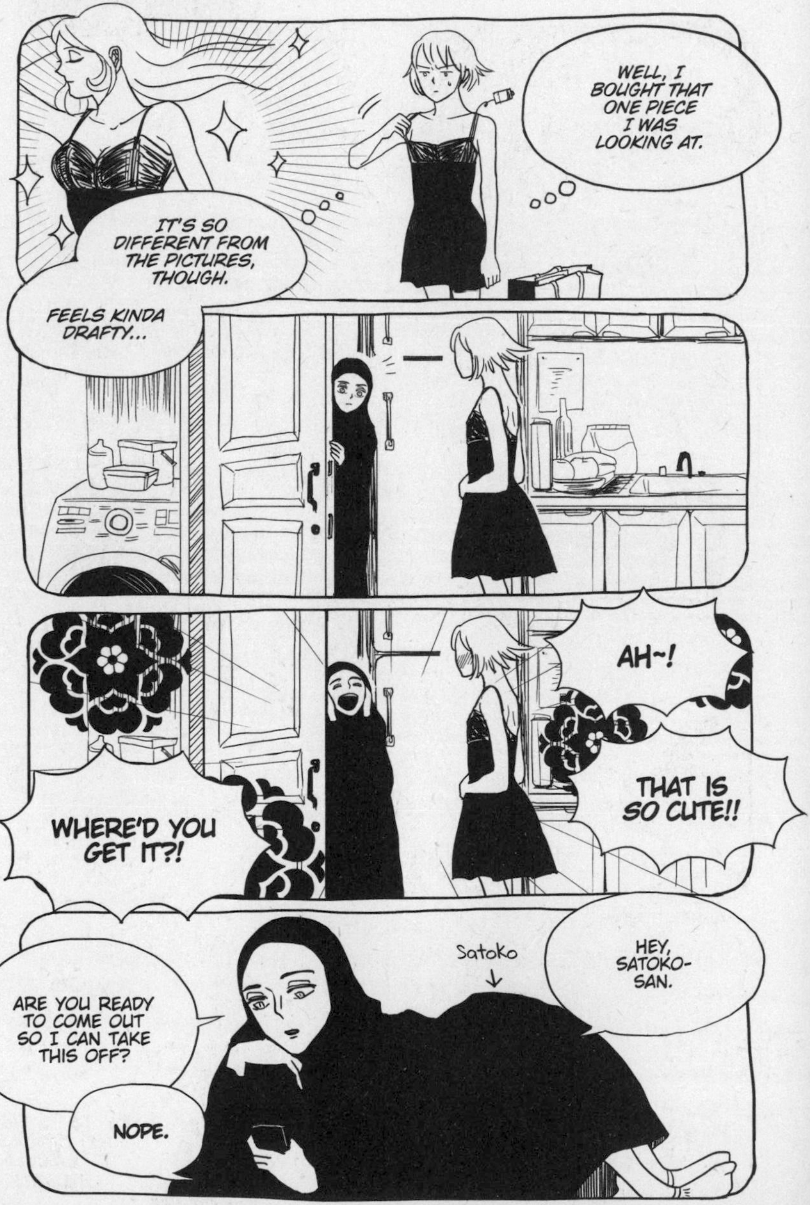
WELL, I BOUGHT THAT ONE PIECE I WAS LOOKING AT.
IT'S SO DIFFERENT FROM THE PICTURES, THOUGH.
FEELS KINDA DRAFTY...
AH~!
THAT IS SO CUTE!!
WHERE'D YOU GET IT?!
HEY, SATOKO-SAN.
Satoko
ARE YOU READY TO COME OUT SO I CAN TAKE THIS OFF?
NOPE.

LITTLE STAB

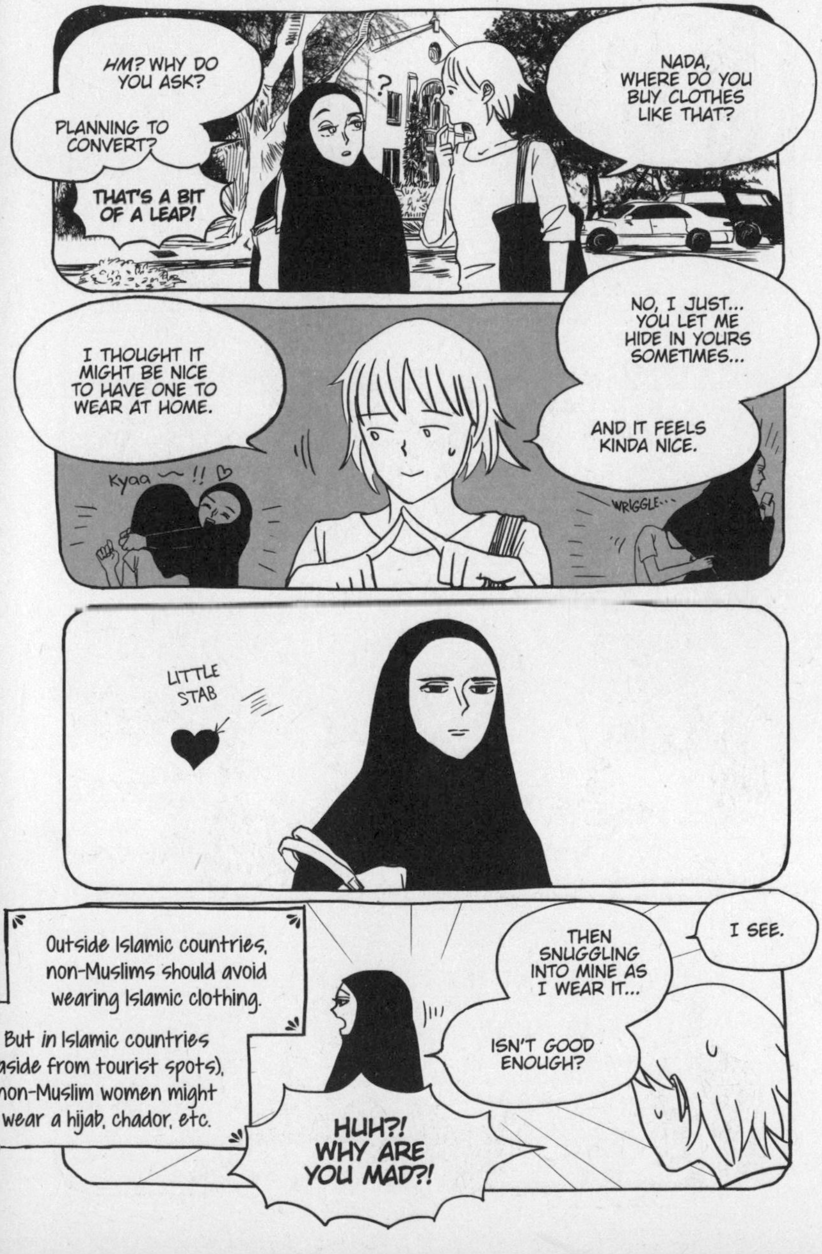

NADA, WHERE DO YOU BUY CLOTHES LIKE THAT?
HM? WHY DO YOU ASK?
PLANNING TO CONVERT?
THAT'S A BIT OF A LEAP!
NO, I JUST... YOU LET ME HIDE IN YOURS SOMETIMES...
AND IT FEELS KINDA NICE.
WRIGGLE...
I THOUGHT IT MIGHT BE NICE TO HAVE ONE TO WEAR AT HOME.
Kyaa~!! ♡
LITTLE STAB
I SEE.
THEN SNUGGLING INTO MINE AS I WEAR IT...
ISN'T GOOD ENOUGH?
HUH?! WHY ARE YOU MAD?!
Outside Islamic countries, non-Muslims should avoid wearing Islamic clothing.
But in Islamic countries (aside from tourist spots), non-Muslim women might wear a hijab, chador, etc.

LIKE CELEBRITIES

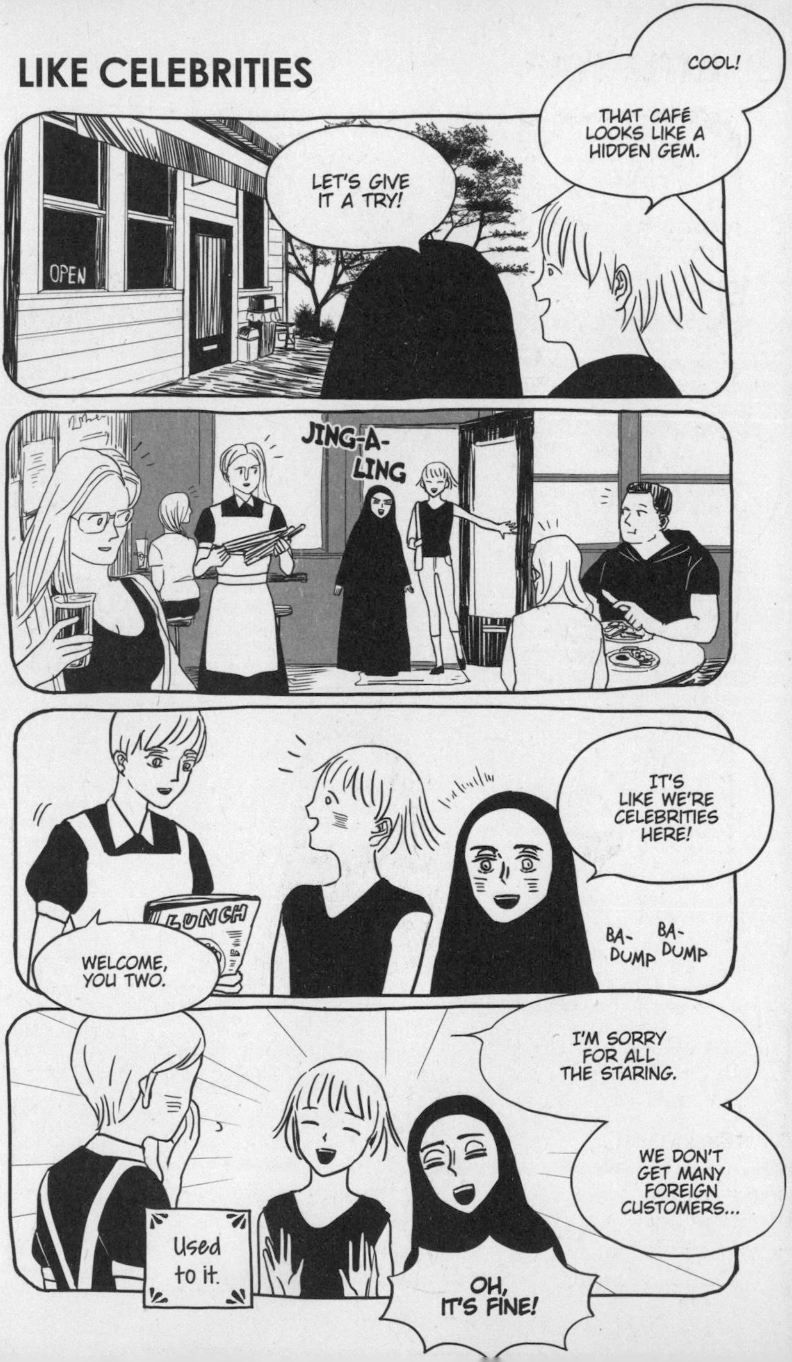

COOL!
THAT CAFÉ LOOKS LIKE A HIDDEN GEM.
LET'S GIVE IT A TRY!
OPEN
JING-A-LING
IT'S LIKE WE'RE CELEBRITIES HERE!
BA-DUMP BA-DUMP
LUNCH
WELCOME, YOU TWO.
I'M SORRY FOR ALL THE STARING.
WE DON'T GET MANY FOREIGN CUSTOMERS...
OH, IT'S FINE!
Used to it.

PRIDE

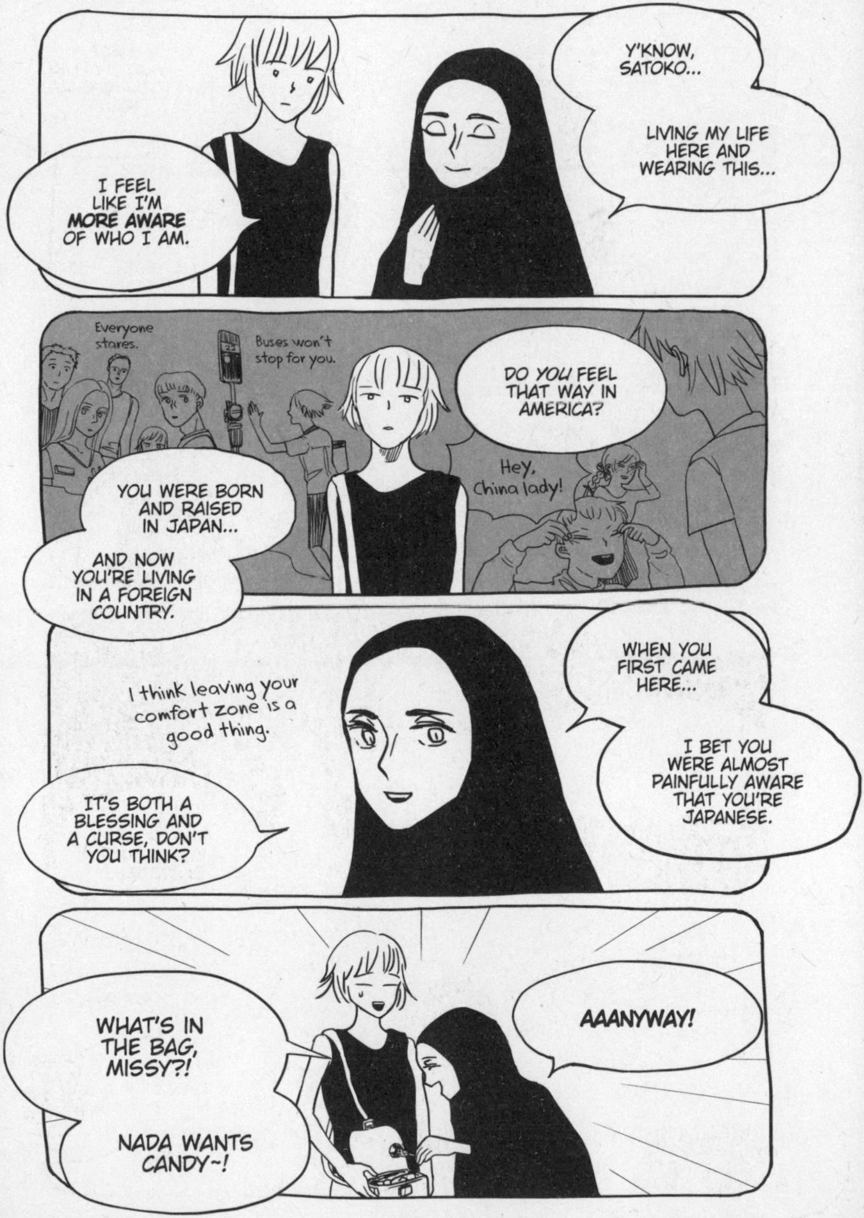

Y'KNOW, SATOKO...
LIVING MY LIFE HERE AND WEARING THIS...
I FEEL LIKE I'M **MORE AWARE** OF WHO I AM.
DO *YOU* FEEL THAT WAY IN AMERICA?
Hey, China lady!
Buses won't stop for you.
Everyone stares.
YOU WERE BORN AND RAISED IN JAPAN...
AND NOW YOU'RE LIVING IN A FOREIGN COUNTRY.
WHEN YOU FIRST CAME HERE...
I BET YOU WERE ALMOST PAINFULLY AWARE THAT YOU'RE JAPANESE.
I think leaving your comfort zone is a good thing.
IT'S BOTH A BLESSING AND A CURSE, DON'T YOU THINK?
AAANYWAY!
WHAT'S IN THE BAG, MISSY?!
NADA WANTS CANDY~!

CHOICE

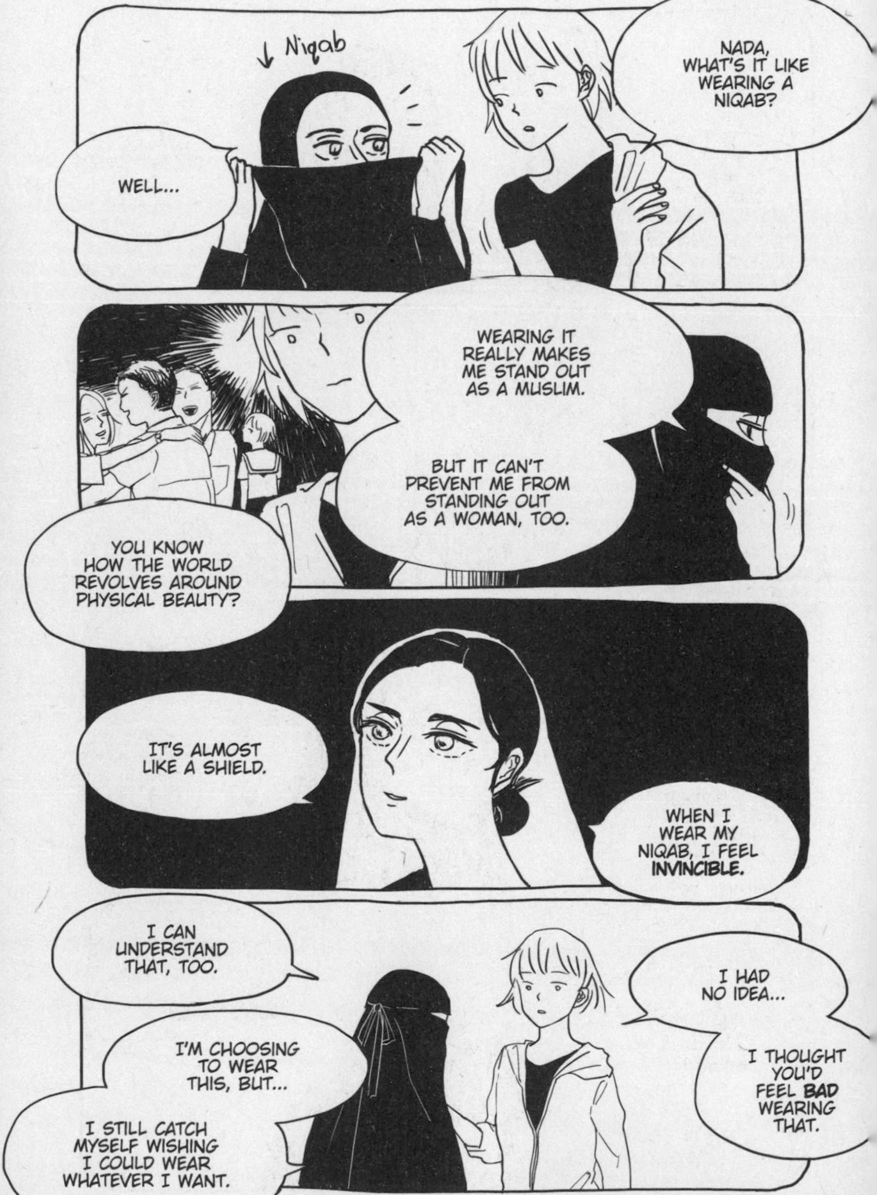
NADA, WHAT'S IT LIKE WEARING A NIQAB?
↓ Niqab
WELL...
WEARING IT REALLY MAKES ME STAND OUT AS A MUSLIM.
BUT IT CAN'T PREVENT ME FROM STANDING OUT AS A WOMAN, TOO.
YOU KNOW HOW THE WORLD REVOLVES AROUND PHYSICAL BEAUTY?
IT'S ALMOST LIKE A SHIELD.
WHEN I WEAR MY NIQAB, I FEEL **INVINCIBLE.**
I HAD NO IDEA...
I THOUGHT YOU'D FEEL **BAD** WEARING THAT.
I CAN UNDERSTAND THAT, TOO.
I'M CHOOSING TO WEAR THIS, BUT...
I STILL CATCH MYSELF WISHING I COULD WEAR WHATEVER I WANT.

IMPOSSIBLE

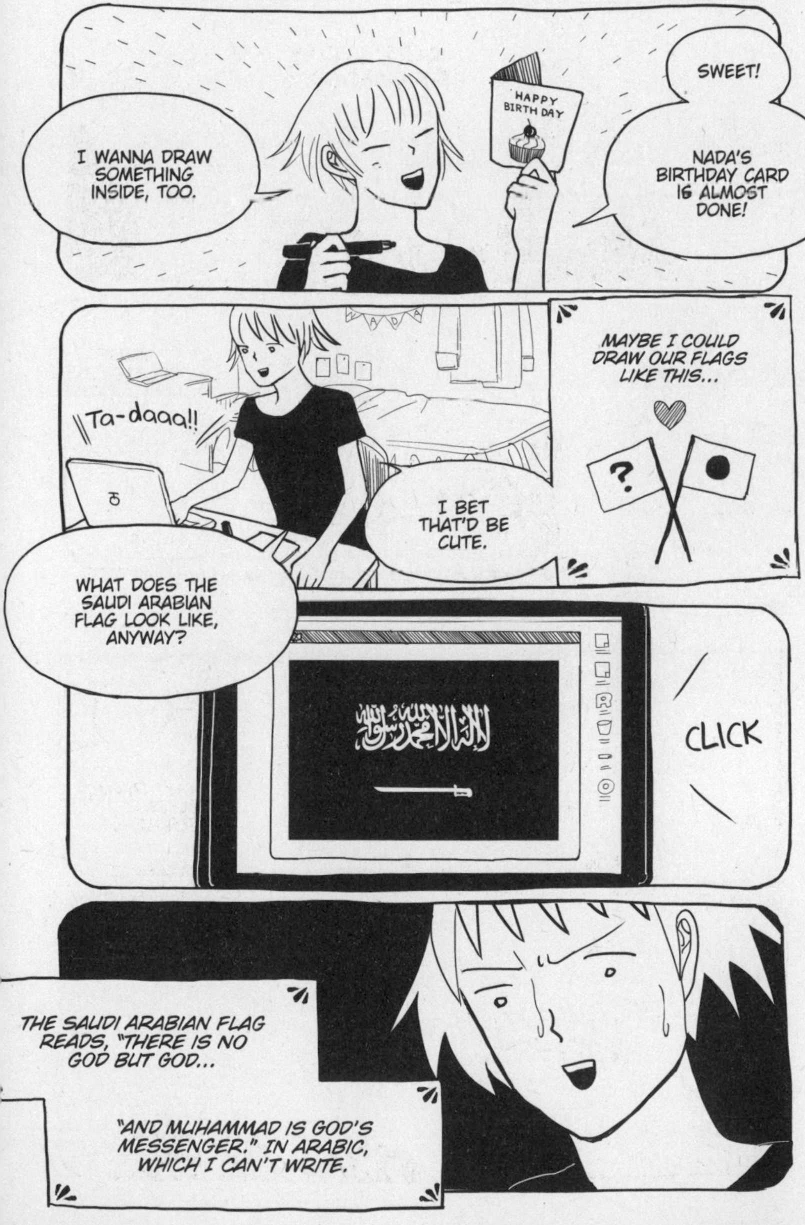

SWEET!
NADA'S BIRTHDAY CARD IS ALMOST DONE!
HAPPY BIRTH DAY
I WANNA DRAW SOMETHING INSIDE, TOO.
MAYBE I COULD DRAW OUR FLAGS LIKE THIS...
?
I BET THAT'D BE CUTE.
Ta-daaa!!
WHAT DOES THE SAUDI ARABIAN FLAG LOOK LIKE, ANYWAY?
CLICK
THE SAUDI ARABIAN FLAG READS, "THERE IS NO GOD BUT GOD...
"AND MUHAMMAD IS GOD'S MESSENGER." IN ARABIC, WHICH I CAN'T WRITE.

BIRTHDAY

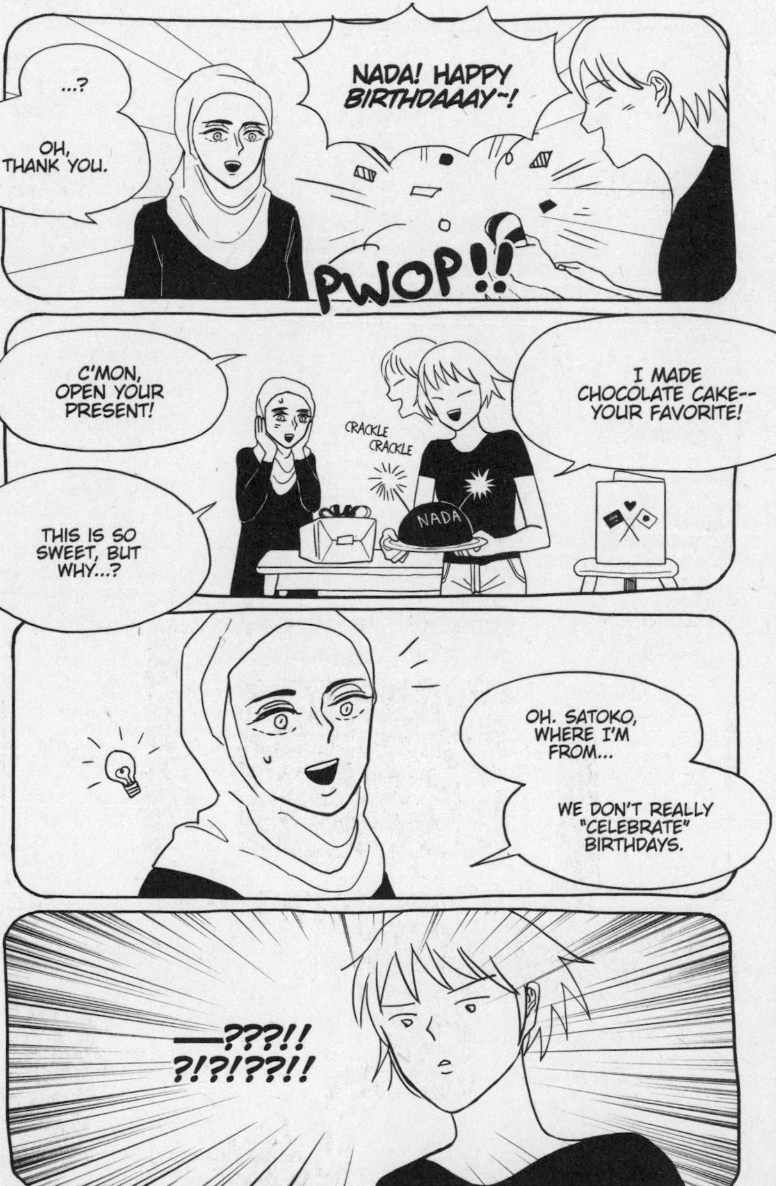
NADA! HAPPY BIRTHDAAAY~!
PWOP!!
...?
OH, THANK YOU.
I MADE CHOCOLATE CAKE-- YOUR FAVORITE!
NADA
CRACKLE CRACKLE
C'MON, OPEN YOUR PRESENT!
THIS IS SO SWEET, BUT WHY...?
OH. SATOKO, WHERE I'M FROM...
WE DON'T REALLY "CELEBRATE" BIRTHDAYS.
—???!! ?!?!??!!

BIRTHDAY 2

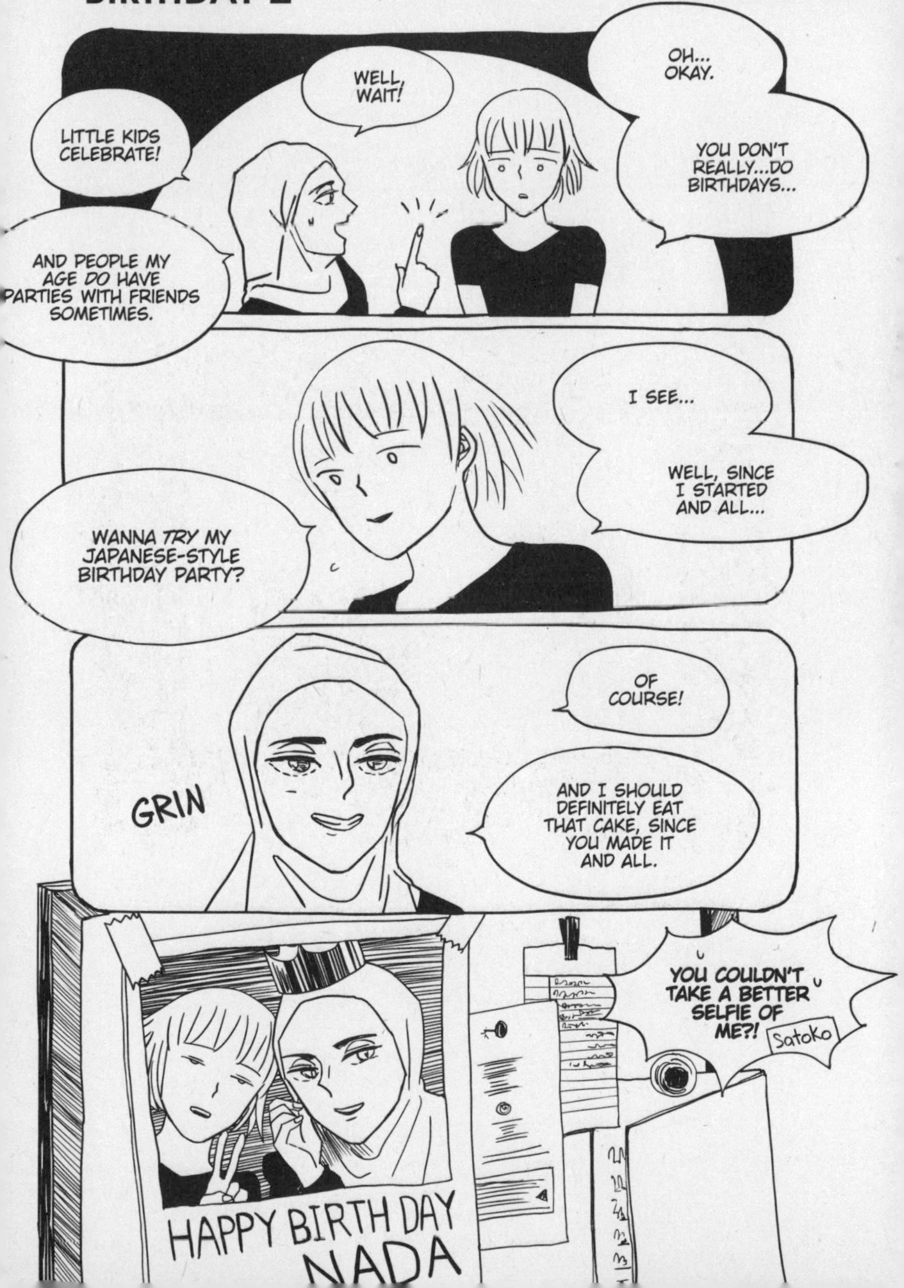
OH... OKAY.
YOU DON'T REALLY...DO BIRTHDAYS...
WELL, WAIT!
LITTLE KIDS CELEBRATE!
AND PEOPLE MY AGE *DO* HAVE PARTIES WITH FRIENDS SOMETIMES.
I SEE...
WELL, SINCE I STARTED AND ALL...
WANNA *TRY* MY JAPANESE-STYLE BIRTHDAY PARTY?
OF COURSE!
AND I SHOULD DEFINITELY EAT THAT CAKE, SINCE YOU MADE IT AND ALL.
GRIN
YOU COULDN'T TAKE A BETTER SELFIE OF ME?!
Satoko
HAPPY BIRTH DAY NADA

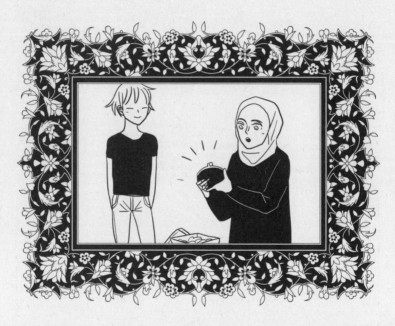

SATOKO AND NADA

Presented by Yupechika

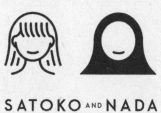

SATOKO AND NADA

Presented by Yupechika

DRIVE

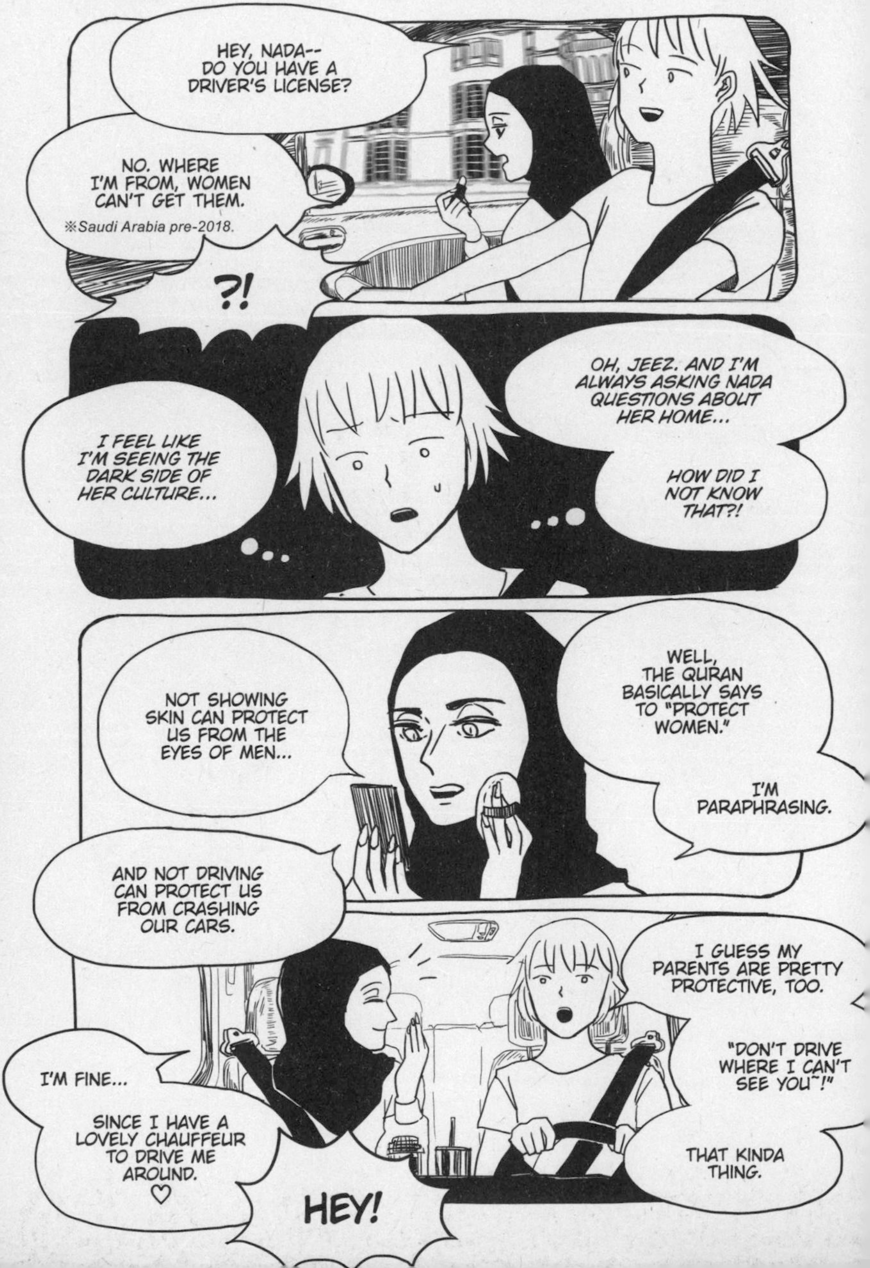
HEY, NADA-- DO YOU HAVE A DRIVER'S LICENSE?
NO. WHERE I'M FROM, WOMEN CAN'T GET THEM.
※Saudi Arabia pre-2018.
?!
OH, JEEZ. AND I'M ALWAYS ASKING NADA QUESTIONS ABOUT HER HOME...
HOW DID I NOT KNOW THAT?!
I FEEL LIKE I'M SEEING THE DARK SIDE OF HER CULTURE...
WELL, THE QURAN BASICALLY SAYS TO "PROTECT WOMEN."
I'M PARAPHRASING.
NOT SHOWING SKIN CAN PROTECT US FROM THE EYES OF MEN...
AND NOT DRIVING CAN PROTECT US FROM CRASHING OUR CARS.
I GUESS MY PARENTS ARE PRETTY PROTECTIVE, TOO.
"DON'T DRIVE WHERE I CAN'T SEE YOU~!"
THAT KINDA THING.
I'M FINE...
SINCE I HAVE A LOVELY CHAUFFEUR TO DRIVE ME AROUND. ♡
HEY!

LICENSE

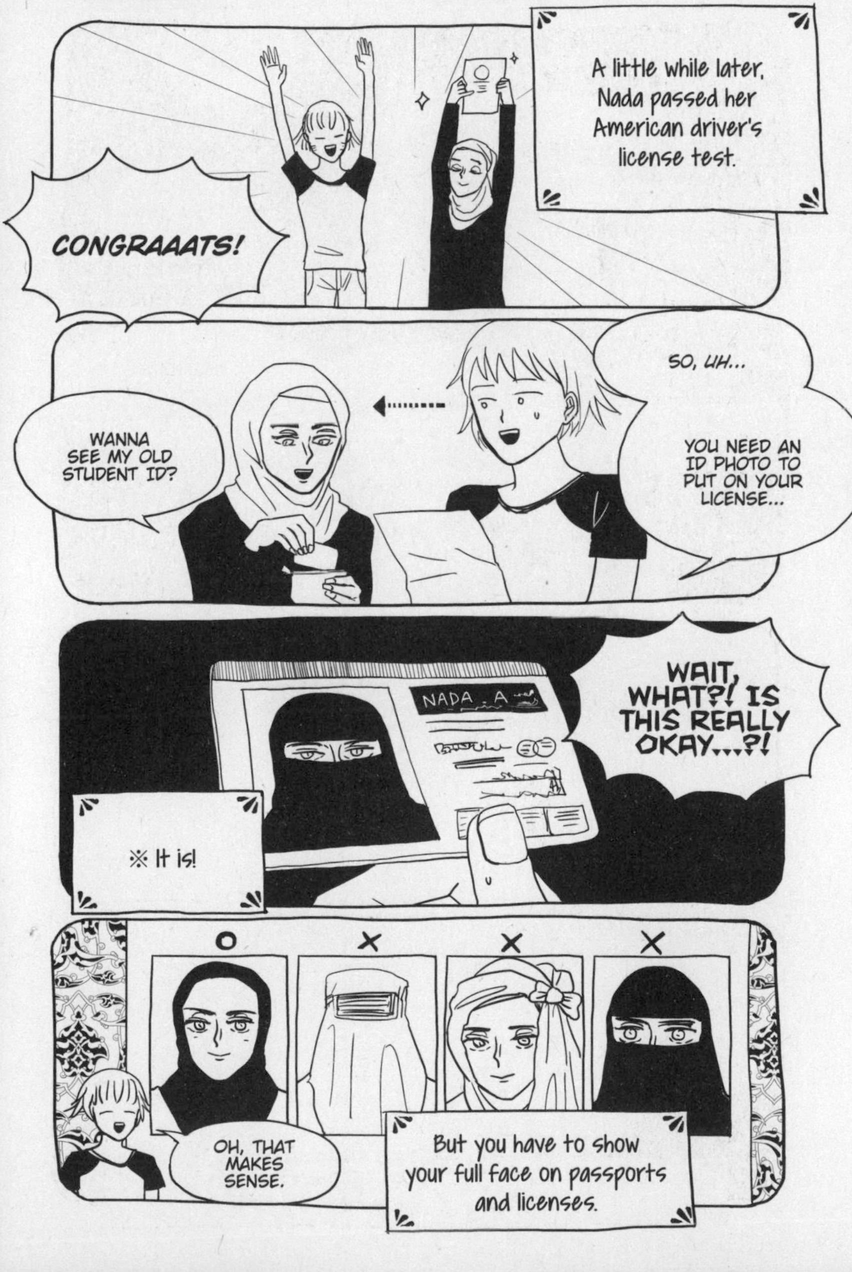
A little while later, Nada passed her American driver's license test.
CONGRAAATS!
SO, UH...
YOU NEED AN ID PHOTO TO PUT ON YOUR LICENSE...
WANNA SEE MY OLD STUDENT ID?
WAIT, WHAT?! IS THIS REALLY OKAY...?!
NADA A
※ It is!
But you have to show your full face on passports and licenses.
OH, THAT MAKES SENSE.

¯_(ツ)_/¯

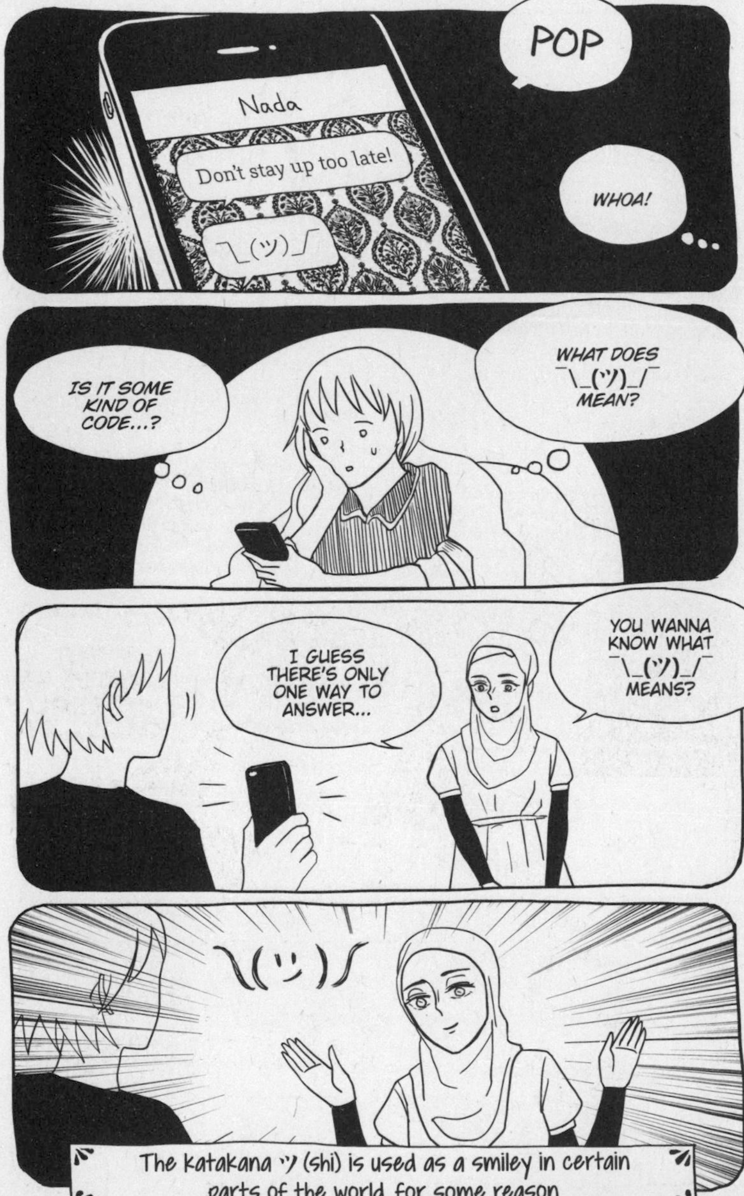
POP
WHOA!
Nada
Don't stay up too late!
¯_(ツ)_/¯
WHAT DOES ¯_(ツ)_/¯ MEAN?
IS IT SOME KIND OF CODE...?
YOU WANNA KNOW WHAT ¯_(ツ)_/¯ MEANS?
I GUESS THERE'S ONLY ONE WAY TO ANSWER...
The katakana ツ (shi) is used as a smiley in certain parts of the world, for some reason.

SHE CUTS IT CLOSE

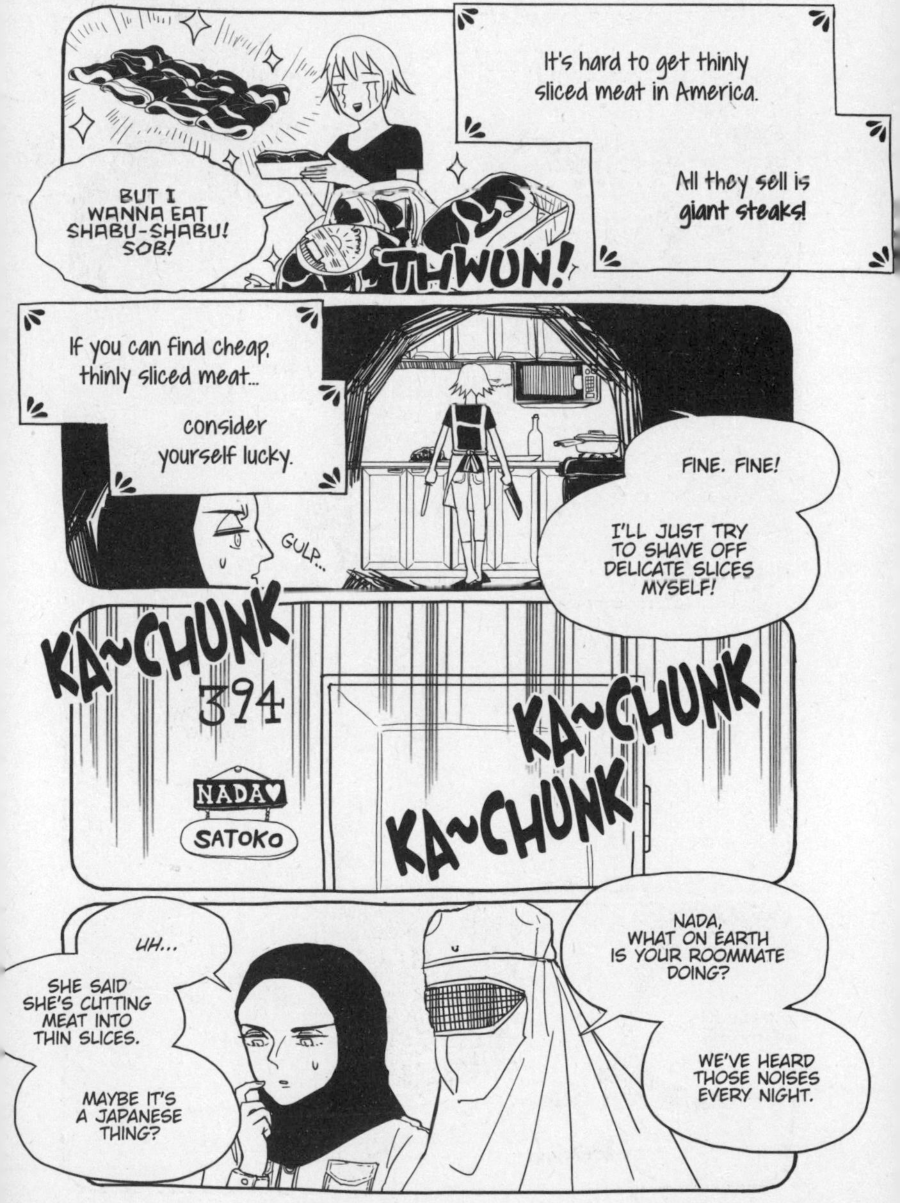
It's hard to get thinly sliced meat in America.
All they sell is giant steaks!
BUT I WANNA EAT SHABU-SHABU! SOB!
THWUN!
FINE. FINE!
I'LL JUST TRY TO SHAVE OFF DELICATE SLICES MYSELF!
If you can find cheap, thinly sliced meat...
consider yourself lucky.
GULP...
KA~CHUNK
KA~CHUNK
KA~CHUNK
394
NADA♥
SATOKO
NADA, WHAT ON EARTH IS YOUR ROOMMATE DOING?
WE'VE HEARD THOSE NOISES EVERY NIGHT.
UH...
SHE SAID SHE'S CUTTING MEAT INTO THIN SLICES.
MAYBE IT'S A JAPANESE THING?

LUCKY

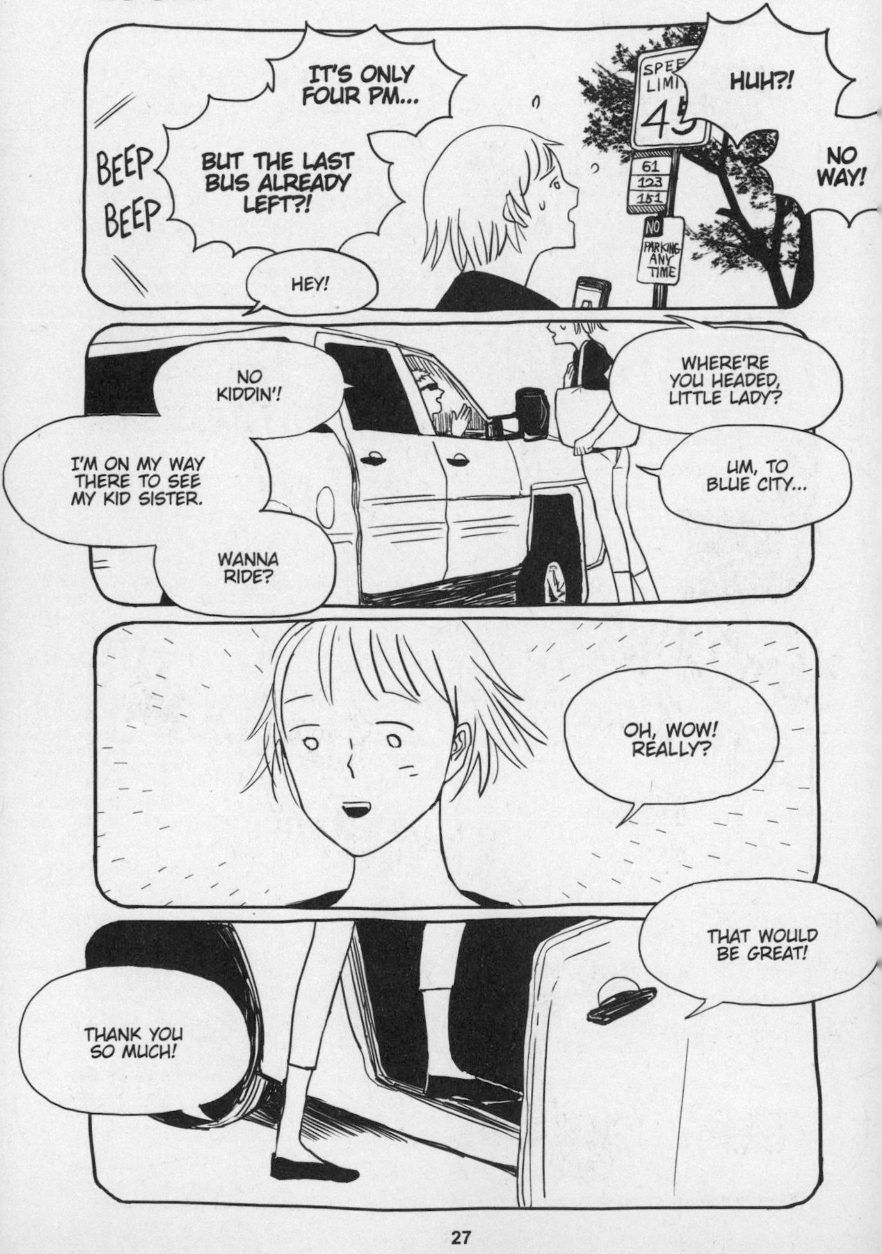
HUH?!
NO WAY!
61
123
151
NO PARKING ANY TIME
IT'S ONLY FOUR PM...
BUT THE LAST BUS ALREADY LEFT?!
BEEP BEEP
HEY!
WHERE'RE YOU HEADED, LITTLE LADY?
UM, TO BLUE CITY...
NO KIDDIN'!
I'M ON MY WAY THERE TO SEE MY KID SISTER.
WANNA RIDE?
OH, WOW! REALLY?
THAT WOULD BE GREAT!
THANK YOU SO MUCH!

BAD VIBES

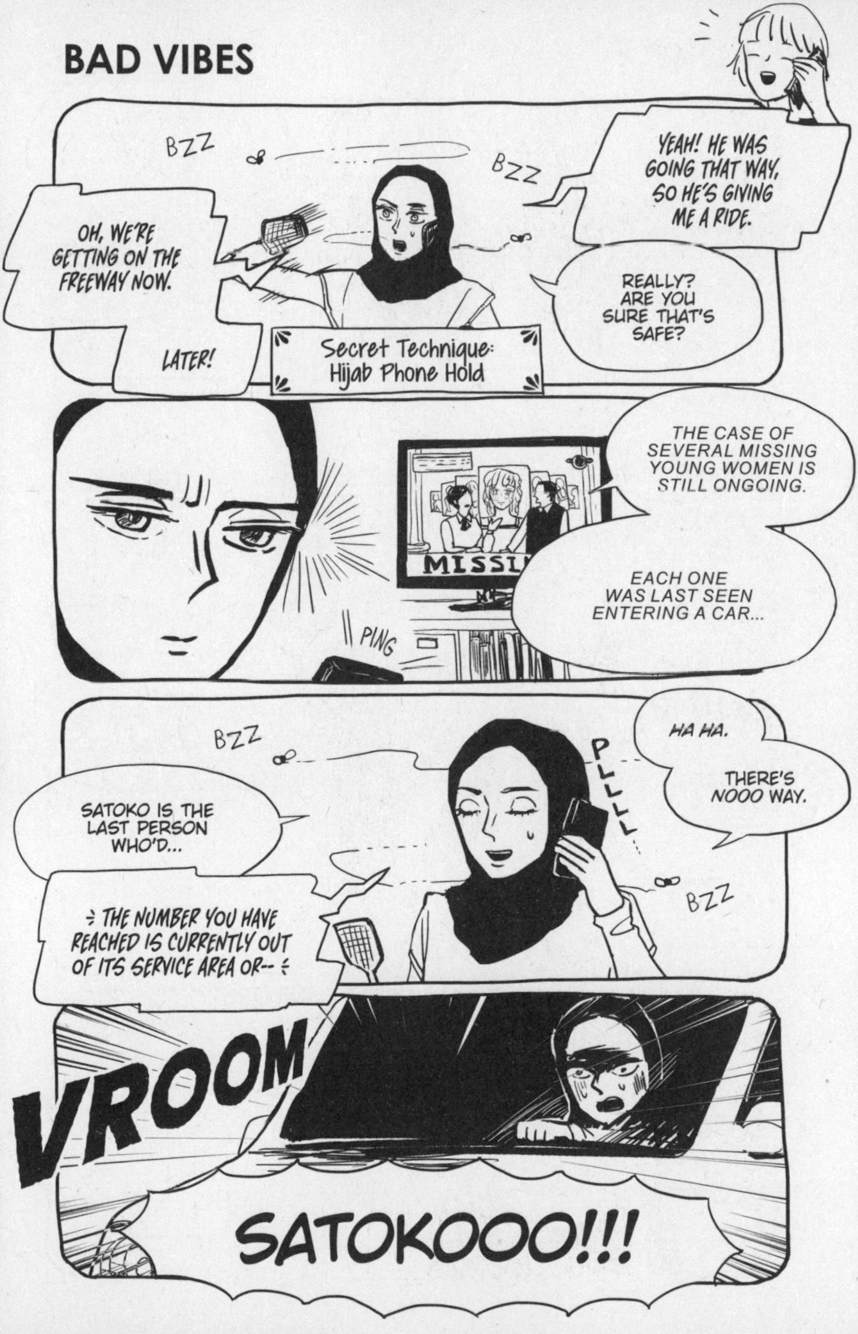
YEAH! HE WAS GOING THAT WAY, SO HE'S GIVING ME A RIDE.
BZZ
BZZ
OH, WE'RE GETTING ON THE FREEWAY NOW.
REALLY? ARE YOU SURE THAT'S SAFE?
Secret Technique: Hijab Phone Hold
LATER!
THE CASE OF SEVERAL MISSING YOUNG WOMEN IS STILL ONGOING.
EACH ONE WAS LAST SEEN ENTERING A CAR...
MISSI
PING
HA HA.
THERE'S NOOO WAY.
PLLLL
BZZ
BZZ
SATOKO IS THE LAST PERSON WHO'D...
THE NUMBER YOU HAVE REACHED IS CURRENTLY OUT OF ITS SERVICE AREA OR--
VROOM
SATOKOOO!!!

TROUBLE

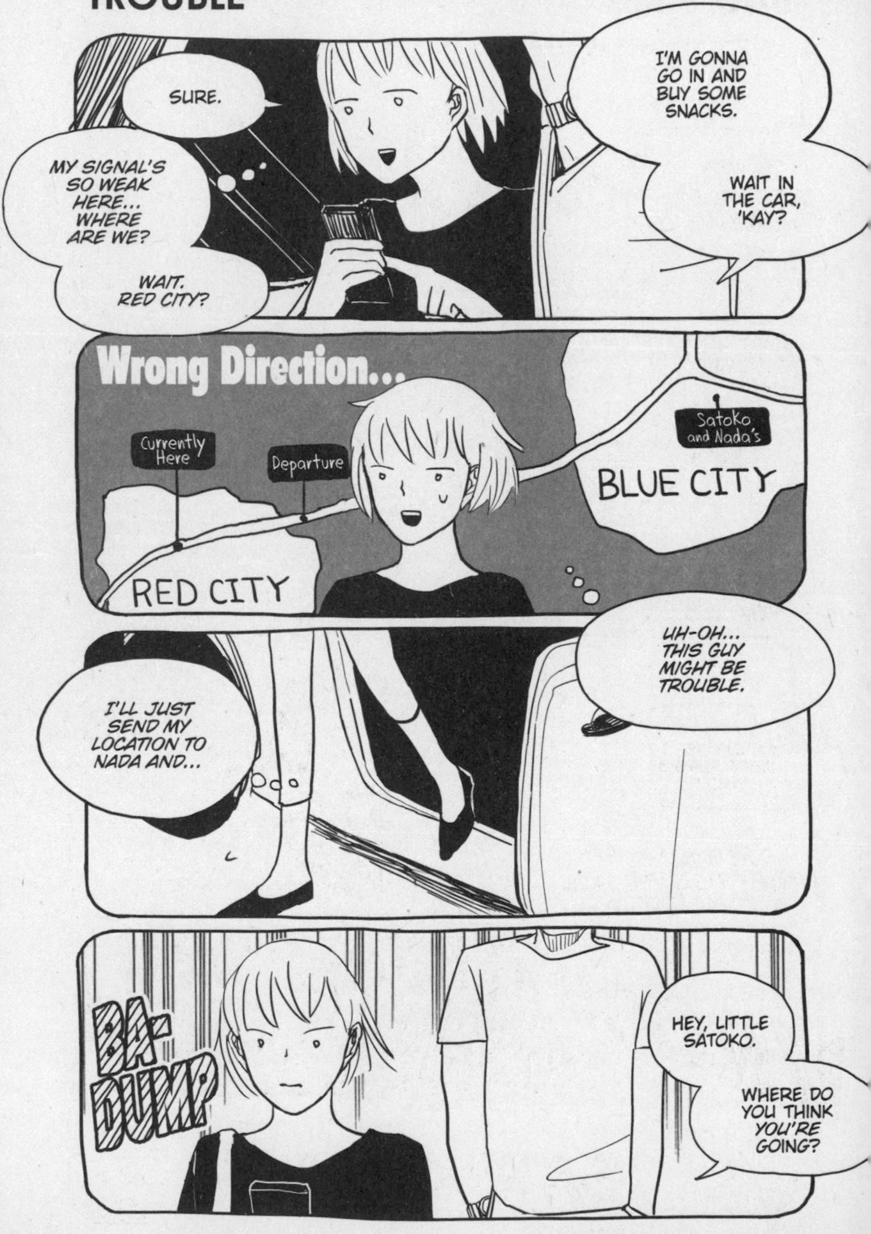

I'M GONNA GO IN AND BUY SOME SNACKS.
WAIT IN THE CAR, 'KAY?
SURE.
MY SIGNAL'S SO WEAK HERE... WHERE ARE WE?
WAIT. RED CITY?
Wrong Direction...
Satoko and Nada's
BLUE CITY
Departure
Currently Here
RED CITY
UH-OH... THIS GUY MIGHT BE TROUBLE.
I'LL JUST SEND MY LOCATION TO NADA AND...
HEY, LITTLE SATOKO.
WHERE DO YOU THINK YOU'RE GOING?
BA-DUMP

BIG TROUBLE

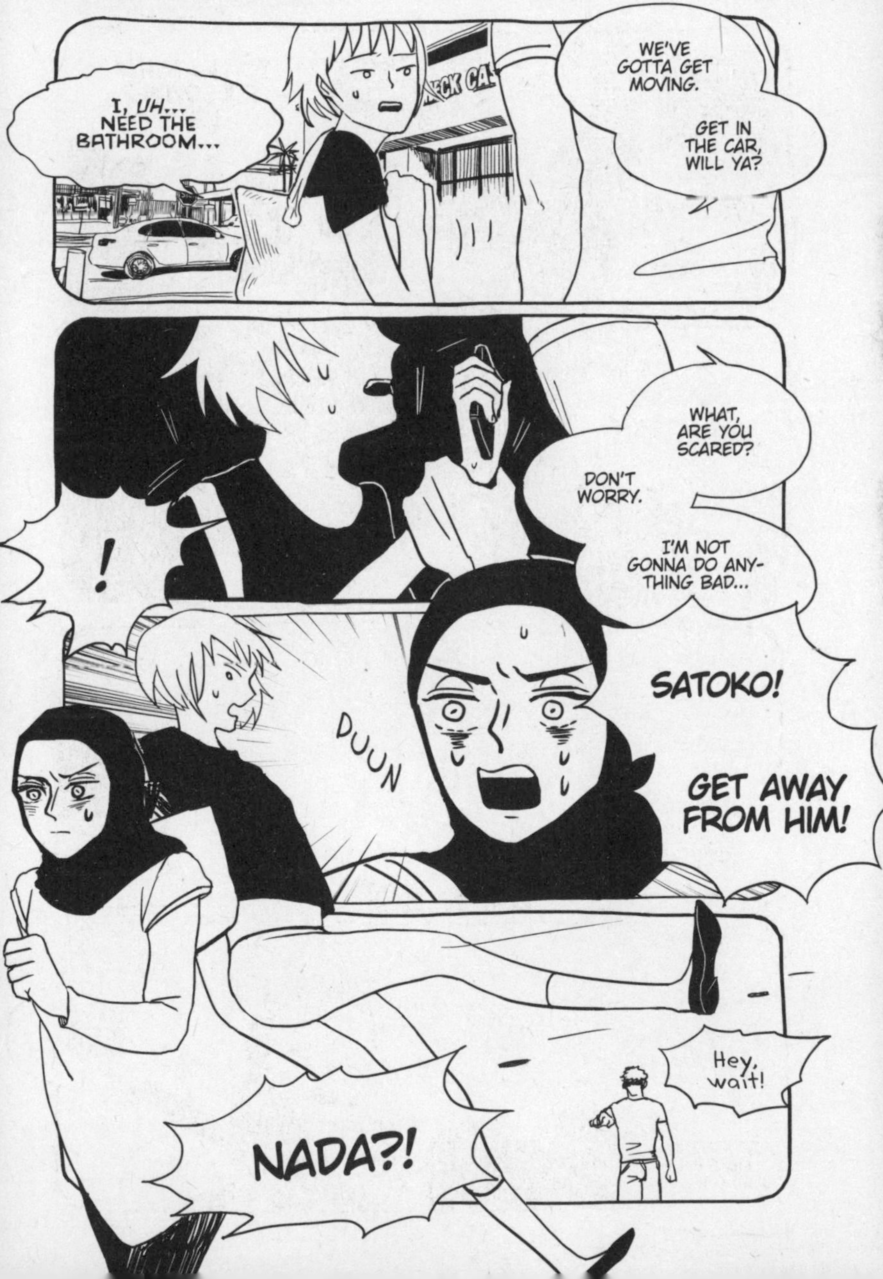
WE'VE GOTTA GET MOVING.
GET IN THE CAR, WILL YA?
I, UH... NEED THE BATHROOM...
WHAT, ARE YOU SCARED?
DON'T WORRY.
I'M NOT GONNA DO ANY-THING BAD...
!
SATOKO!
GET AWAY FROM HIM!
DUUN
Hey, wait!
NADA?!

CALM DOWN

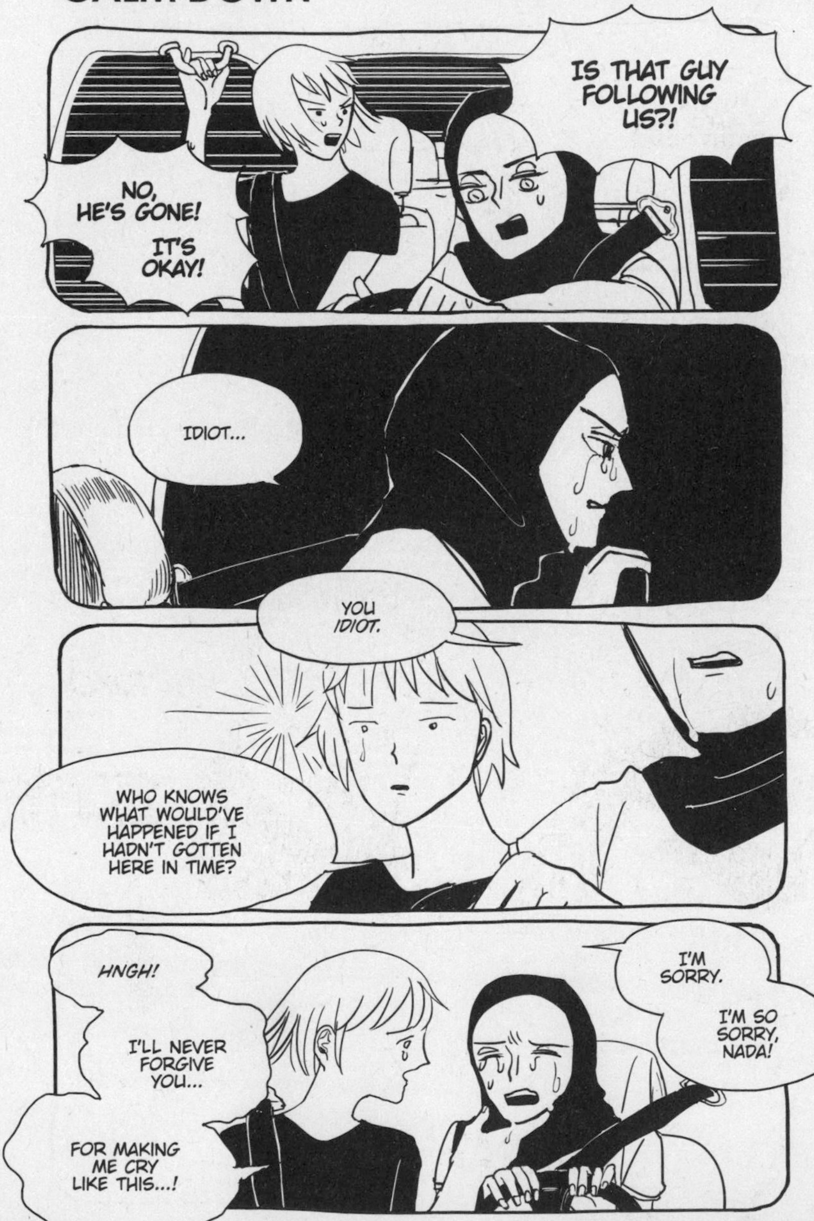
IS THAT GUY FOLLOWING US?!
NO, HE'S GONE!
IT'S OKAY!
IDIOT...
YOU IDIOT.
WHO KNOWS WHAT WOULD'VE HAPPENED IF I HADN'T GOTTEN HERE IN TIME?
I'M SORRY.
I'M SO SORRY, NADA!
HNGH!
I'LL NEVER FORGIVE YOU...
FOR MAKING ME CRY LIKE THIS...!

GUARD

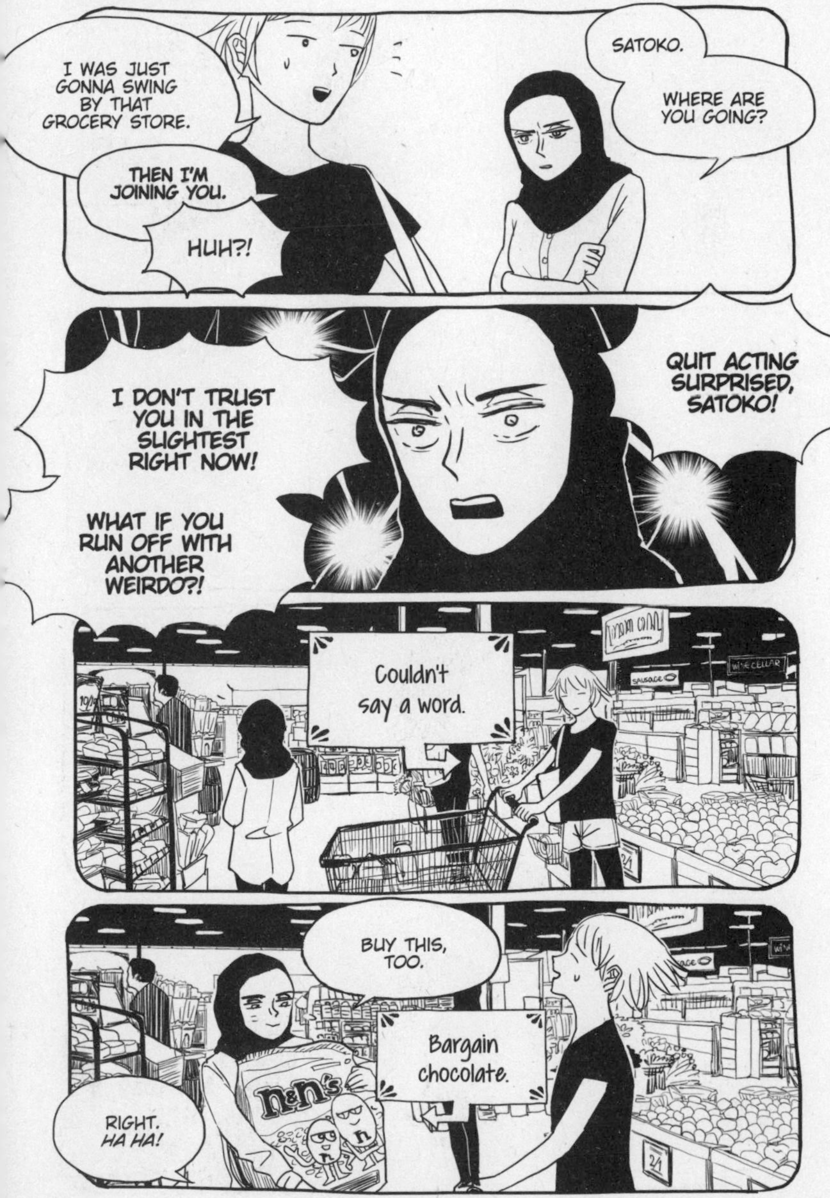
SATOKO.
WHERE ARE YOU GOING?
I WAS JUST GONNA SWING BY THAT GROCERY STORE.
THEN I'M JOINING YOU.
HUH?!
QUIT ACTING SURPRISED, SATOKO!
I DON'T TRUST YOU IN THE SLIGHTEST RIGHT NOW!
WHAT IF YOU RUN OFF WITH ANOTHER WEIRDO?!
SAUSAGE
Couldn't say a word.
BUY THIS, TOO.
Bargain chocolate.
n&n's
RIGHT. *HA HA!*

YOU

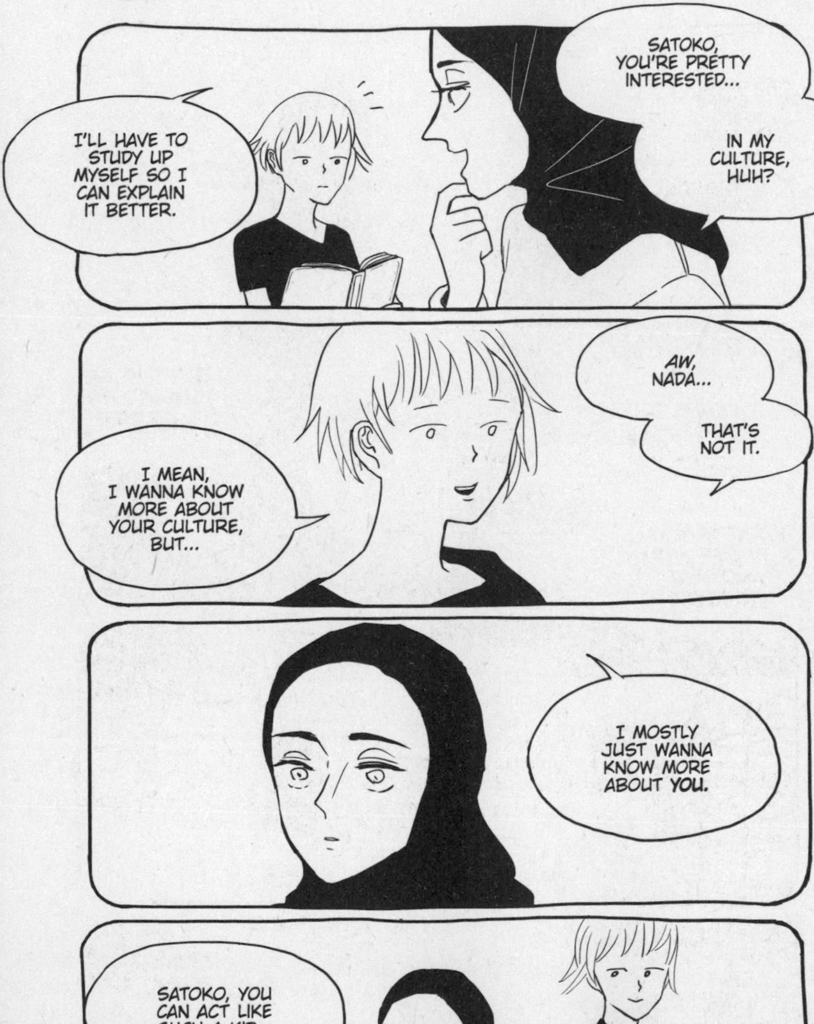
SATOKO, YOU'RE PRETTY INTERESTED...
IN MY CULTURE, HUH?
I'LL HAVE TO STUDY UP MYSELF SO I CAN EXPLAIN IT BETTER.
AW, NADA...
THAT'S NOT IT.
I MEAN, I WANNA KNOW MORE ABOUT YOUR CULTURE, BUT...
I MOSTLY JUST WANNA KNOW MORE ABOUT YOU.
SATOKO, YOU CAN ACT LIKE SUCH A KID...
BUT THEN YOU GO AND SAY SOMETHING THAT MAKES MY HEART SKIP A BEAT!

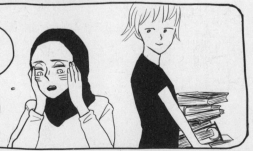

THE TWO OF US

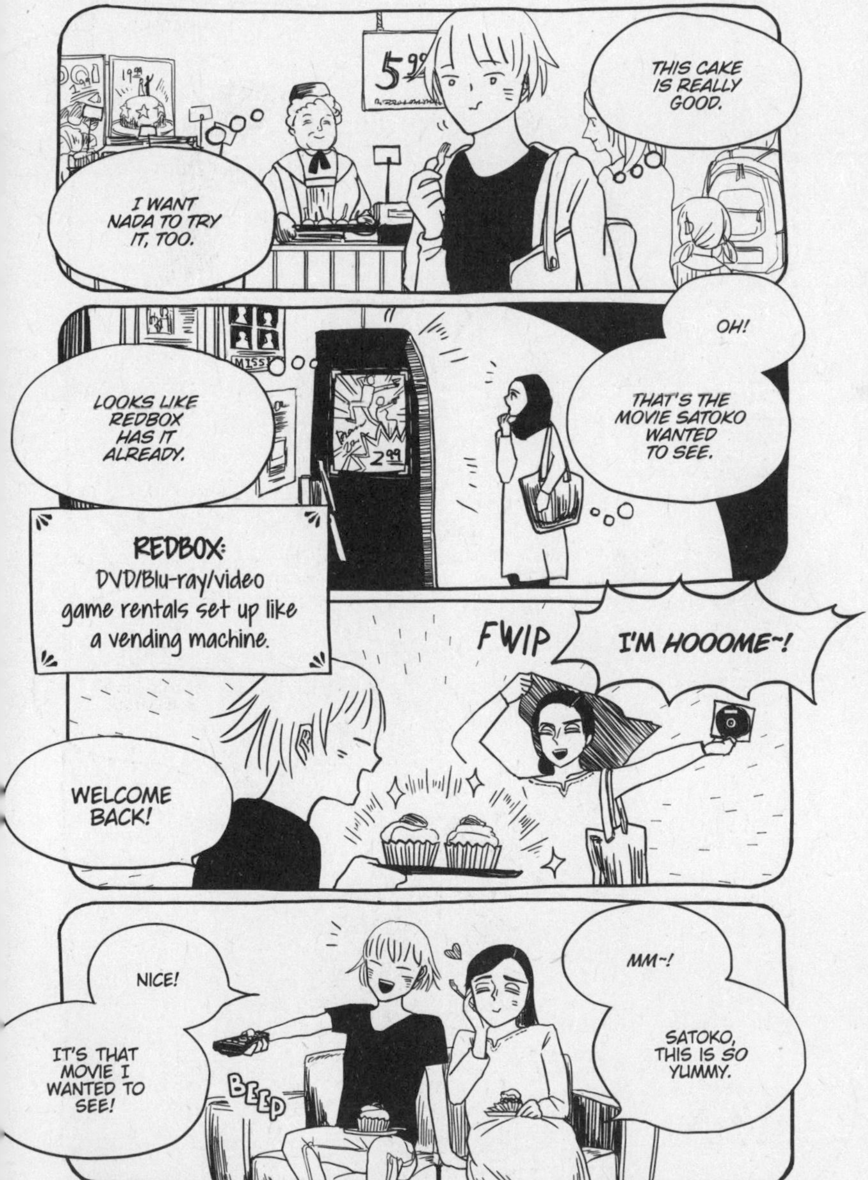
THIS CAKE IS REALLY GOOD.
I WANT NADA TO TRY IT, TOO.
OH!
THAT'S THE MOVIE SATOKO WANTED TO SEE.
LOOKS LIKE REDBOX HAS IT ALREADY.
REDBOX: DVD/Blu-ray/video game rentals set up like a vending machine.
I'M HOOOME~!
FWIP
WELCOME BACK!
MM~!
SATOKO, THIS IS SO YUMMY.
NICE!
IT'S THAT MOVIE I WANTED TO SEE!
BEEP

FOREVER

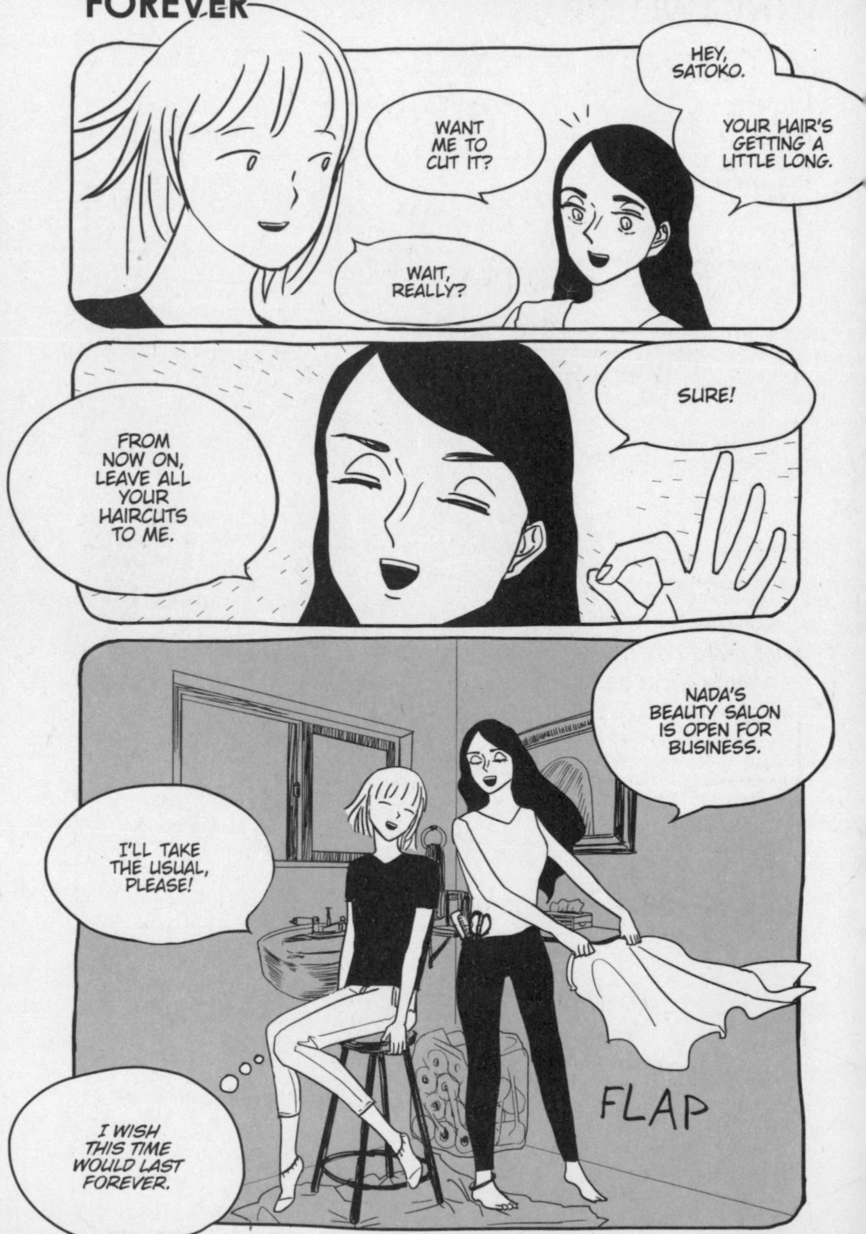
HEY, SATOKO.
YOUR HAIR'S GETTING A LITTLE LONG.
WANT ME TO CUT IT?
WAIT, REALLY?
SURE!
FROM NOW ON, LEAVE ALL YOUR HAIRCUTS TO ME.
NADA'S BEAUTY SALON IS OPEN FOR BUSINESS.
I'LL TAKE THE USUAL, PLEASE!
FLAP
I WISH THIS TIME WOULD LAST FOREVER.

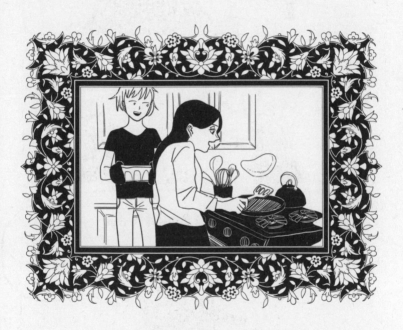

SATOKO AND NADA

Presented by Yupechika

REINTRODUCTION

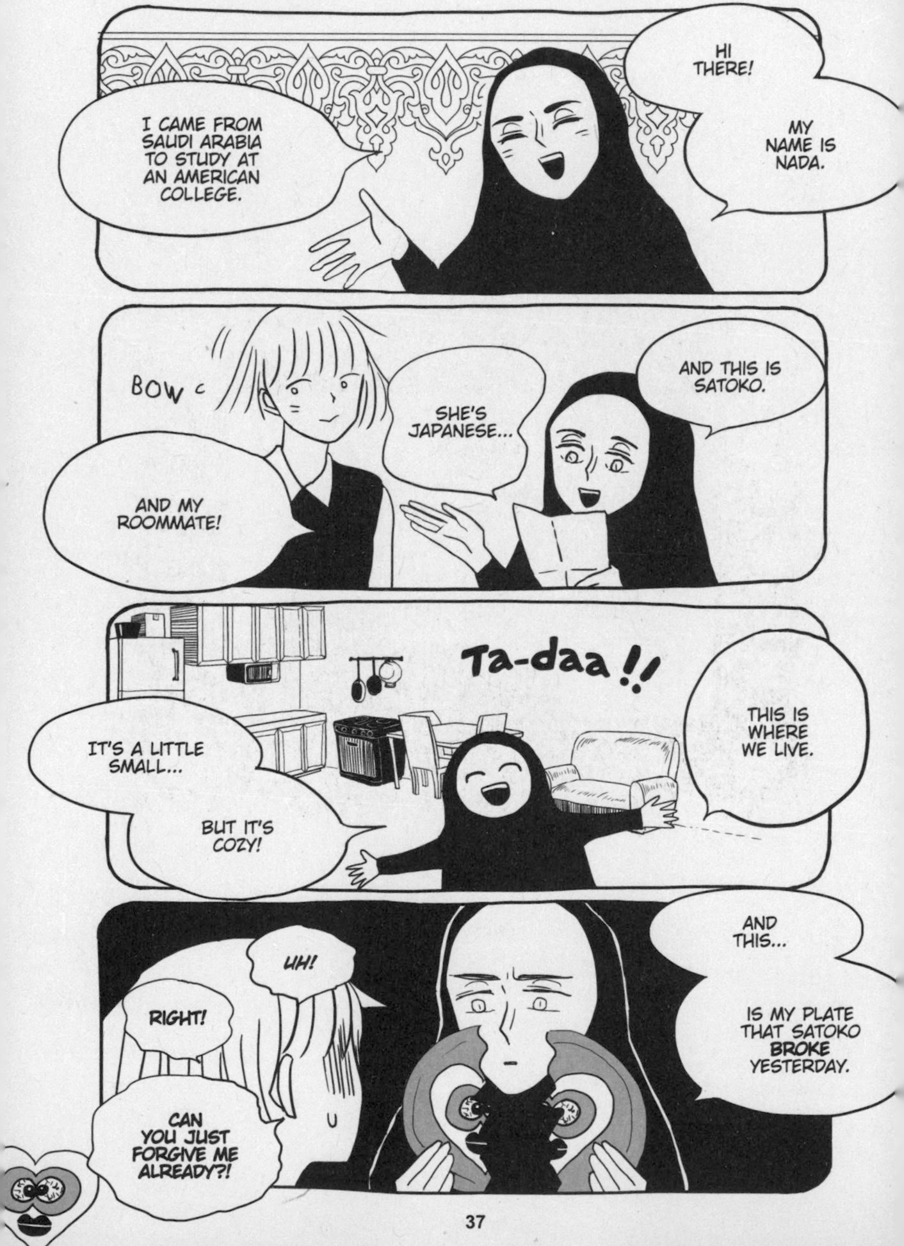
HI THERE!
MY NAME IS NADA.
I CAME FROM SAUDI ARABIA TO STUDY AT AN AMERICAN COLLEGE.
AND THIS IS SATOKO.
SHE'S JAPANESE...
AND MY ROOMMATE!
BOW
THIS IS WHERE WE LIVE.
Ta-daa!!
IT'S A LITTLE SMALL...
BUT IT'S COZY!
AND THIS...
IS MY PLATE THAT SATOKO **BROKE** YESTERDAY.
UH!
RIGHT!
CAN YOU JUST FORGIVE ME ALREADY?!

ONIGIRI

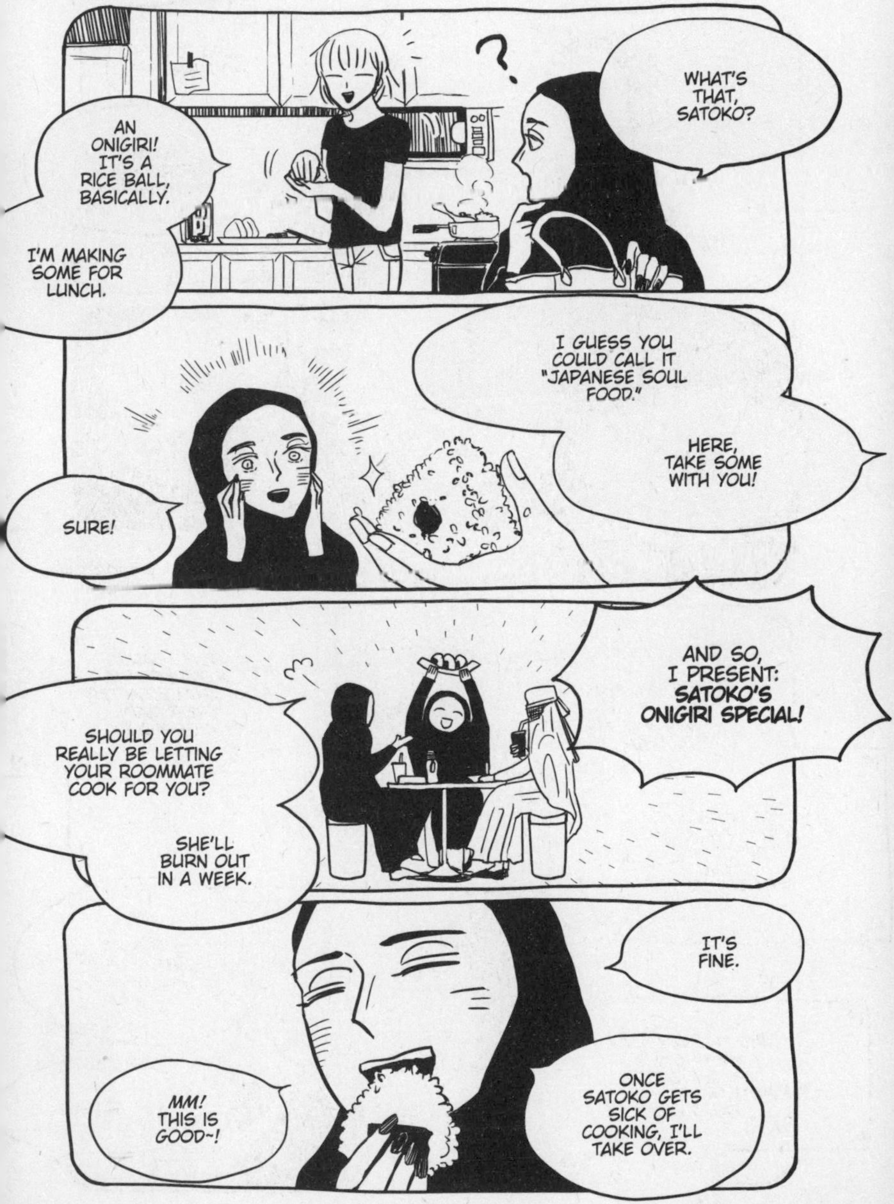

WHAT'S THAT, SATOKO?
AN ONIGIRI! IT'S A RICE BALL, BASICALLY.
I'M MAKING SOME FOR LUNCH.
I GUESS YOU COULD CALL IT "JAPANESE SOUL FOOD."
HERE, TAKE SOME WITH YOU!
SURE!
AND SO, I PRESENT: **SATOKO'S ONIGIRI SPECIAL!**
SHOULD YOU REALLY BE LETTING YOUR ROOMMATE COOK FOR YOU?
SHE'LL BURN OUT IN A WEEK.
IT'S FINE.
ONCE SATOKO GETS SICK OF COOKING, I'LL TAKE OVER.
MM! THIS IS GOOD~!

POTATOES

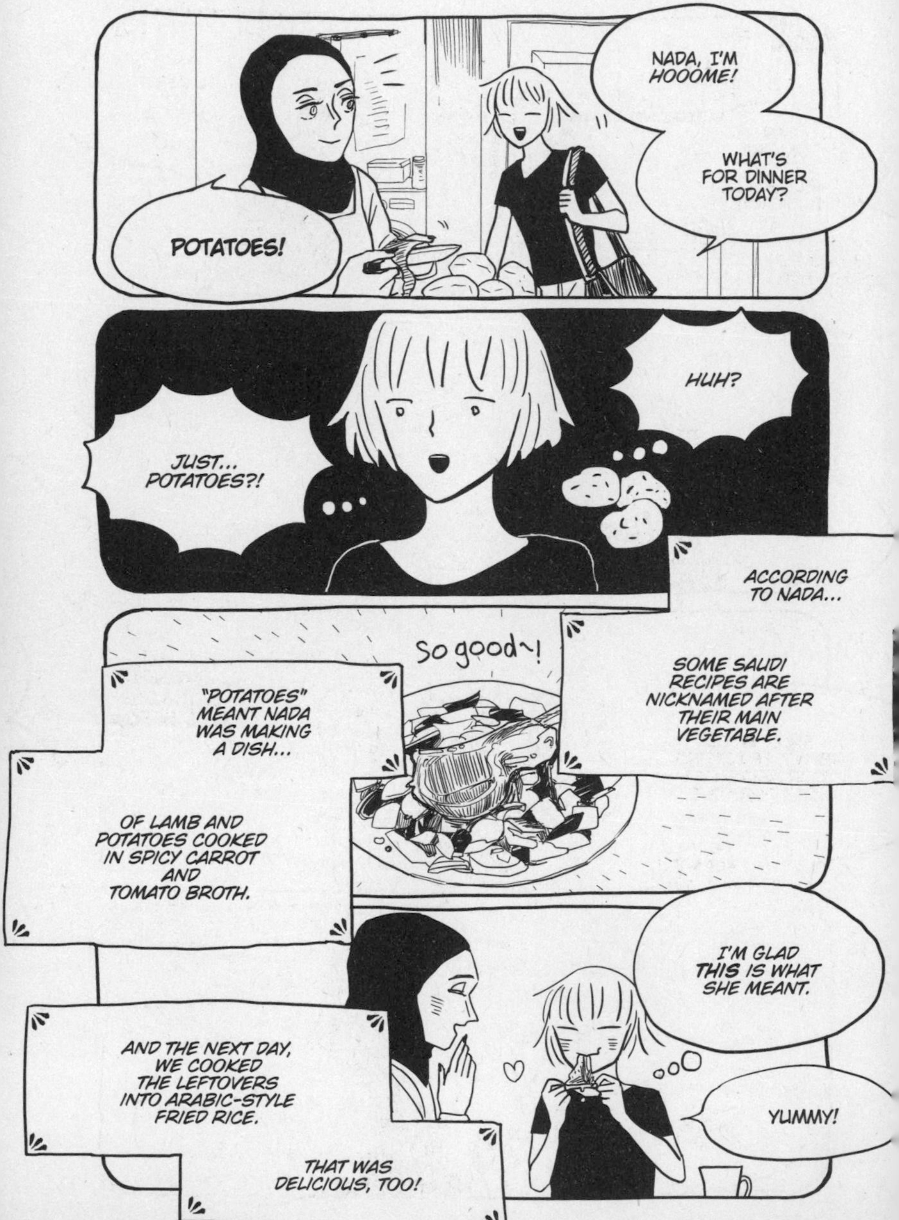

NADA, I'M HOOOME!
WHAT'S FOR DINNER TODAY?
POTATOES!
HUH?
JUST... POTATOES?!
ACCORDING TO NADA...
SOME SAUDI RECIPES ARE NICKNAMED AFTER THEIR MAIN VEGETABLE.
So good~!
"POTATOES" MEANT NADA WAS MAKING A DISH...
OF LAMB AND POTATOES COOKED IN SPICY CARROT AND TOMATO BROTH.
I'M GLAD THIS IS WHAT SHE MEANT.
YUMMY!
AND THE NEXT DAY, WE COOKED THE LEFTOVERS INTO ARABIC-STYLE FRIED RICE.
THAT WAS DELICIOUS, TOO!

BUILDING TRUST

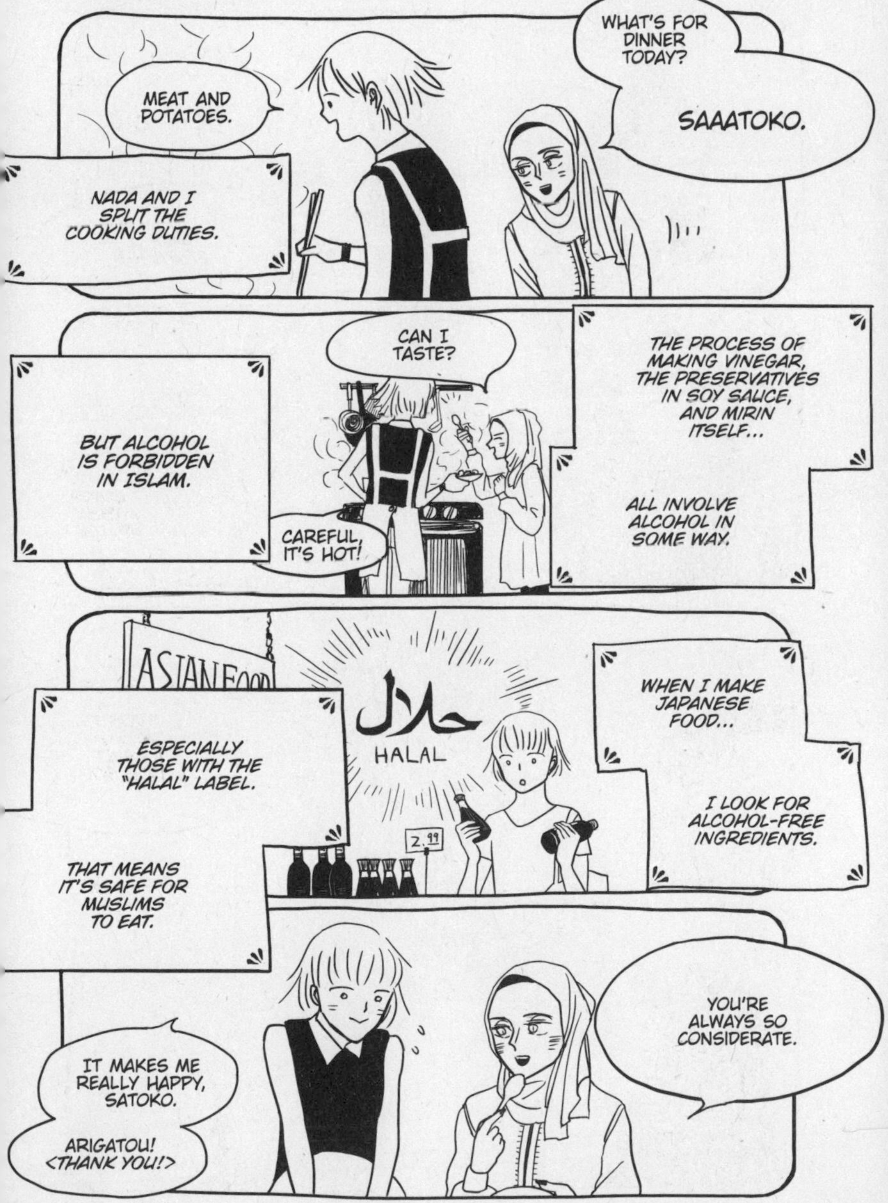

WHAT'S FOR DINNER TODAY?
SAAATOKO.
MEAT AND POTATOES.
NADA AND I SPLIT THE COOKING DUTIES.
THE PROCESS OF MAKING VINEGAR, THE PRESERVATIVES IN SOY SAUCE, AND MIRIN ITSELF...
ALL INVOLVE ALCOHOL IN SOME WAY.
CAN I TASTE?
CAREFUL, IT'S HOT!
BUT ALCOHOL IS FORBIDDEN IN ISLAM.
WHEN I MAKE JAPANESE FOOD...
I LOOK FOR ALCOHOL-FREE INGREDIENTS.
حلال
HALAL
2.99
ASIAN FOOD
ESPECIALLY THOSE WITH THE "HALAL" LABEL.
THAT MEANS IT'S SAFE FOR MUSLIMS TO EAT.
YOU'RE ALWAYS SO CONSIDERATE.
IT MAKES ME REALLY HAPPY, SATOKO.
ARIGATOU! <THANK YOU!>

PRAYER

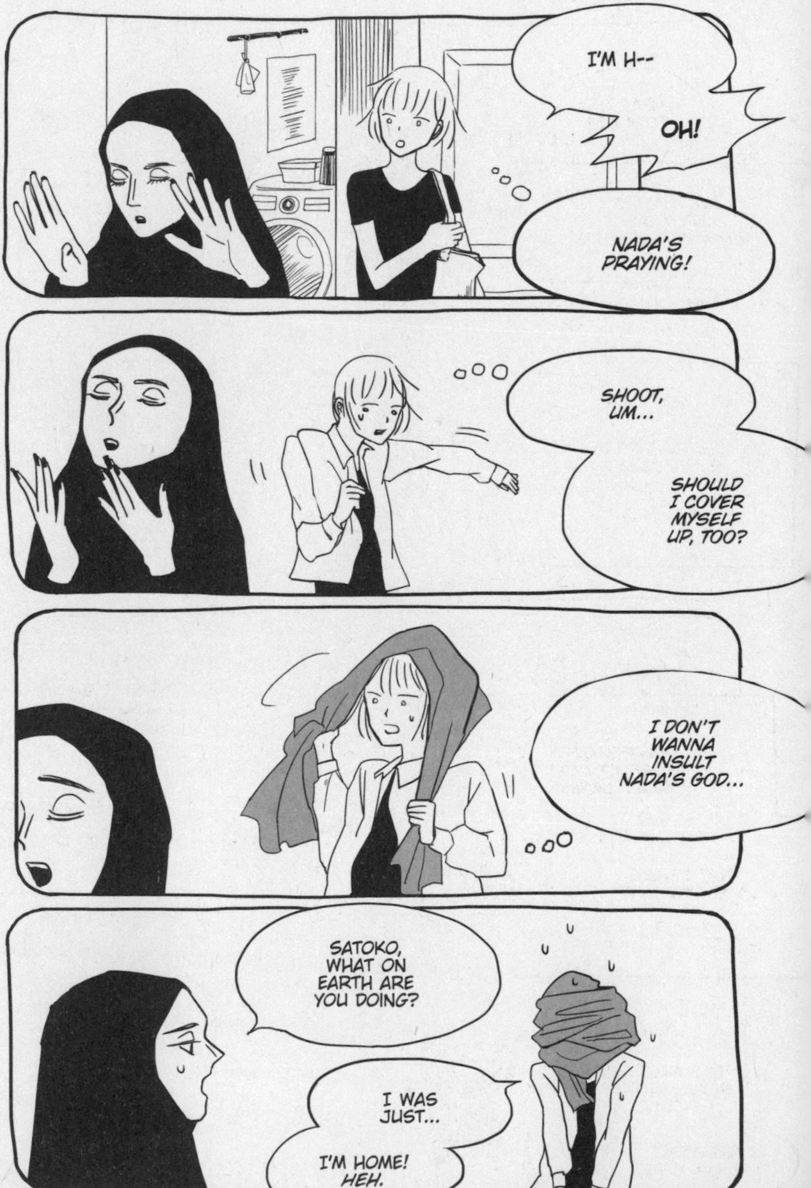
I'M H--
OH!
NADA'S PRAYING!
SHOOT, UM...
SHOULD I COVER MYSELF UP, TOO?
I DON'T WANNA INSULT NADA'S GOD...
SATOKO, WHAT ON EARTH ARE YOU DOING?
I WAS JUST...
I'M HOME! HEH.

DURING PRAYER TIME

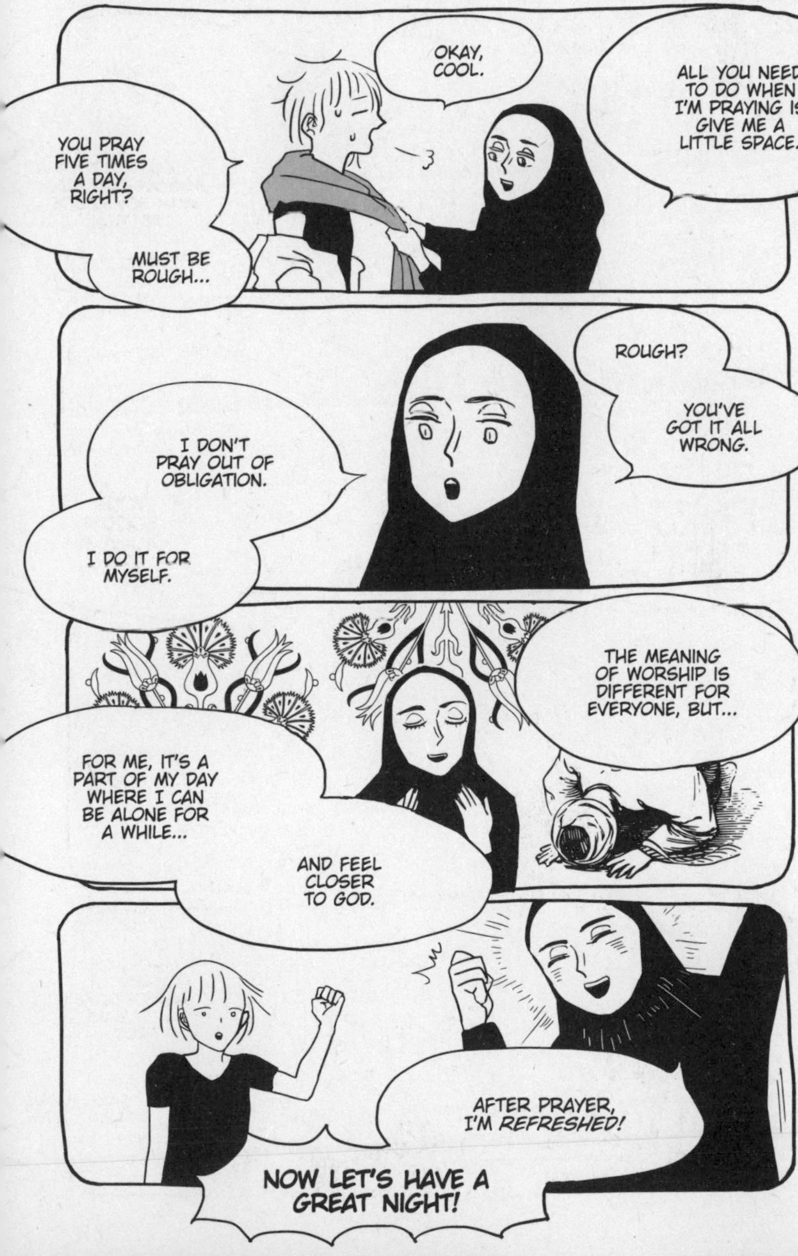
ALL YOU NEED TO DO WHEN I'M PRAYING IS GIVE ME A LITTLE SPACE.
OKAY, COOL.
YOU PRAY FIVE TIMES A DAY, RIGHT?
MUST BE ROUGH...
ROUGH?
YOU'VE GOT IT ALL WRONG.
I DON'T PRAY OUT OF OBLIGATION.
I DO IT FOR MYSELF.
THE MEANING OF WORSHIP IS DIFFERENT FOR EVERYONE, BUT...
FOR ME, IT'S A PART OF MY DAY WHERE I CAN BE ALONE FOR A WHILE...
AND FEEL CLOSER TO GOD.
AFTER PRAYER, I'M *REFRESHED!*
NOW LET'S HAVE A GREAT NIGHT!

GETTING HEATED

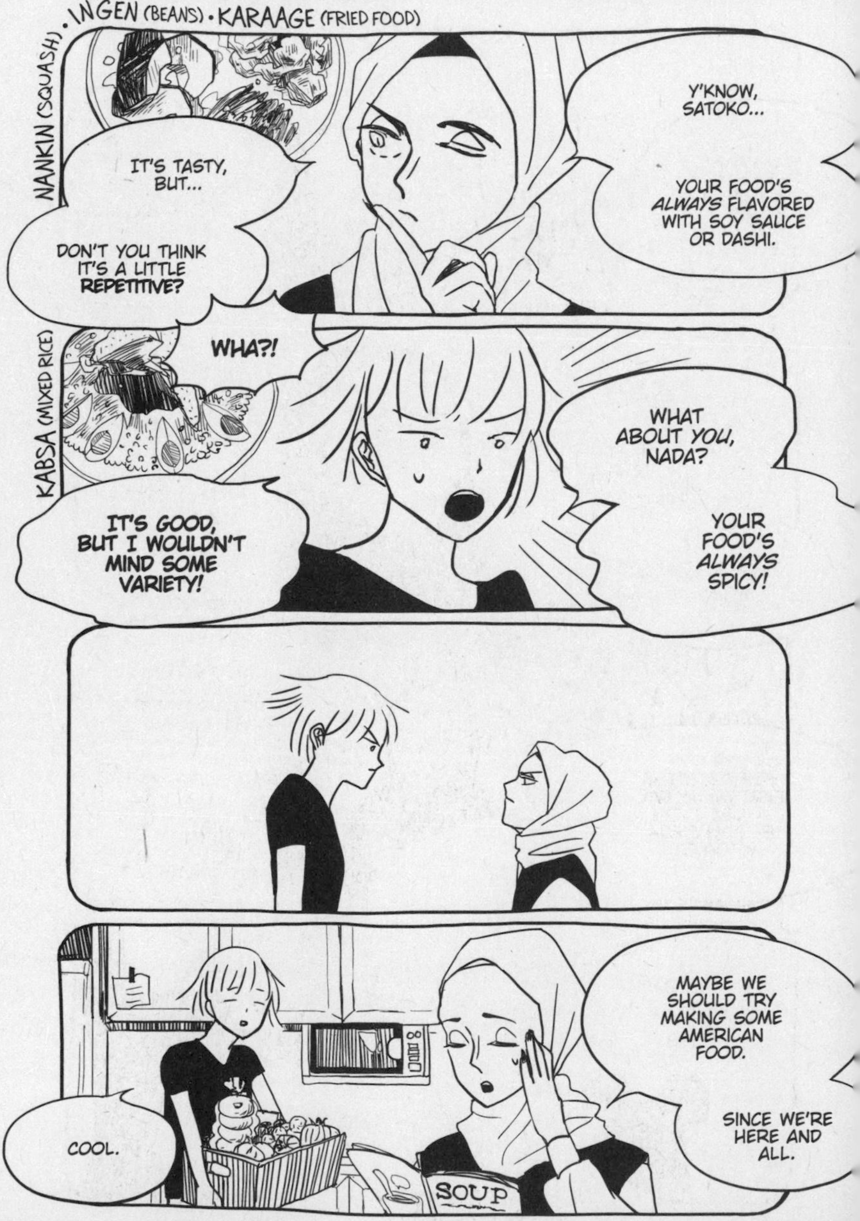

NANKIN (SQUASH) • INGEN (BEANS) • KARAAGE (FRIED FOOD)
Y'KNOW, SATOKO...
YOUR FOOD'S ALWAYS FLAVORED WITH SOY SAUCE OR DASHI.
IT'S TASTY, BUT...
DON'T YOU THINK IT'S A LITTLE REPETITIVE?
KABSA (MIXED RICE)
WHAT ABOUT YOU, NADA?
YOUR FOOD'S ALWAYS SPICY!
WHA?!
IT'S GOOD, BUT I WOULDN'T MIND SOME VARIETY!
MAYBE WE SHOULD TRY MAKING SOME AMERICAN FOOD.
SINCE WE'RE HERE AND ALL.
COOL.
SOUP

EXCEPTION

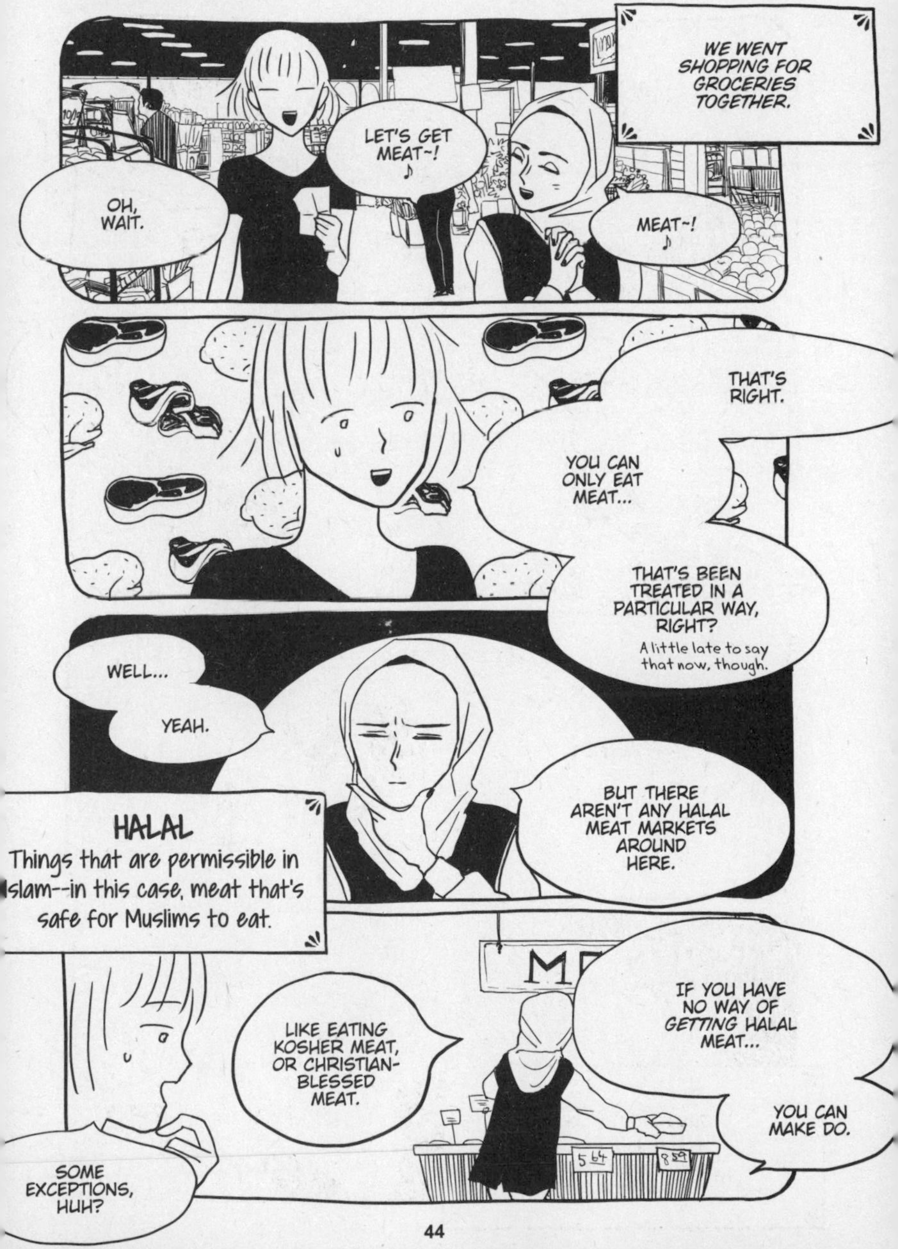
WE WENT SHOPPING FOR GROCERIES TOGETHER.
LET'S GET MEAT~! ♪
MEAT~! ♪
OH, WAIT.
THAT'S RIGHT.
YOU CAN ONLY EAT MEAT...
THAT'S BEEN TREATED IN A PARTICULAR WAY, RIGHT? A little late to say that now, though.
WELL...
YEAH.
BUT THERE AREN'T ANY HALAL MEAT MARKETS AROUND HERE.
HALAL
Things that are permissible in Islam--in this case, meat that's safe for Muslims to eat.
IF YOU HAVE NO WAY OF GETTING HALAL MEAT...
YOU CAN MAKE DO.
LIKE EATING KOSHER MEAT, OR CHRISTIAN-BLESSED MEAT.
SOME EXCEPTIONS, HUH?

CHICKEN SOUP

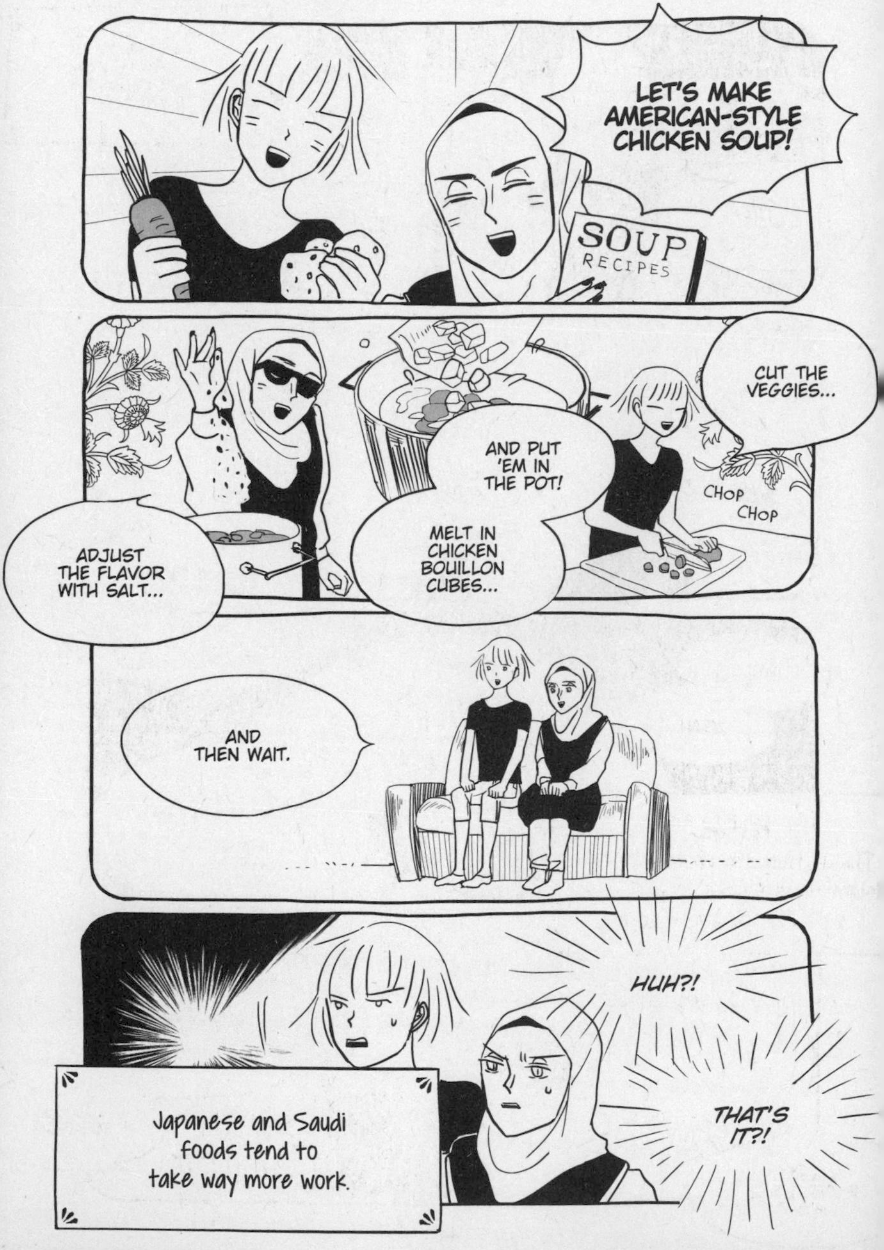
LET'S MAKE AMERICAN-STYLE CHICKEN SOUP!
SOUP RECIPES
CUT THE VEGGIES...
CHOP CHOP
AND PUT 'EM IN THE POT!
MELT IN CHICKEN BOUILLON CUBES...
ADJUST THE FLAVOR WITH SALT...
AND THEN WAIT.
HUH?!
THAT'S IT?!
Japanese and Saudi foods tend to take way more work.

FINISHED

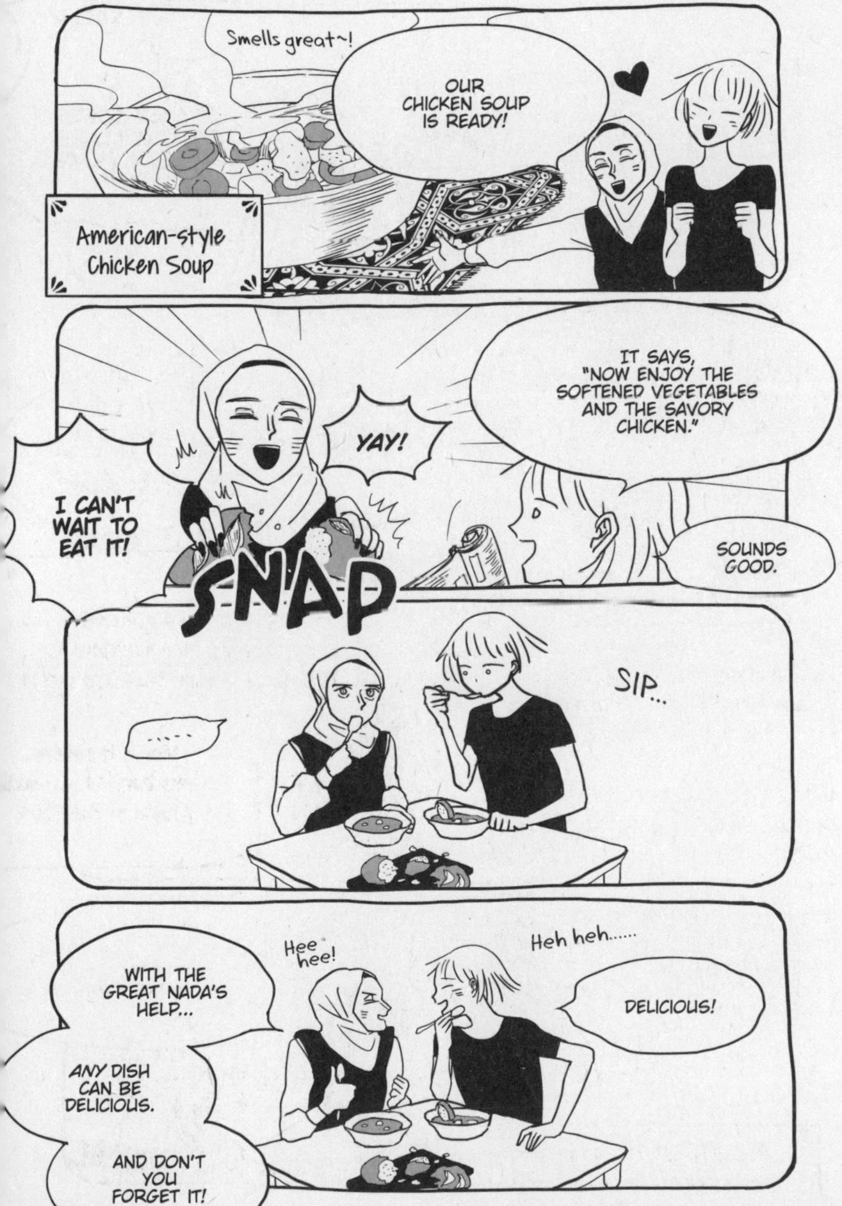
OUR CHICKEN SOUP IS READY!
Smells great~!
American-style Chicken Soup
IT SAYS, "NOW ENJOY THE SOFTENED VEGETABLES AND THE SAVORY CHICKEN."
SOUNDS GOOD.
YAY!
I CAN'T WAIT TO EAT IT!
SNAP
SIP...
......
Heh heh......
DELICIOUS!
Hee hee!
WITH THE GREAT NADA'S HELP...
ANY DISH CAN BE DELICIOUS.
AND DON'T YOU FORGET IT!

MOVIE THEATER

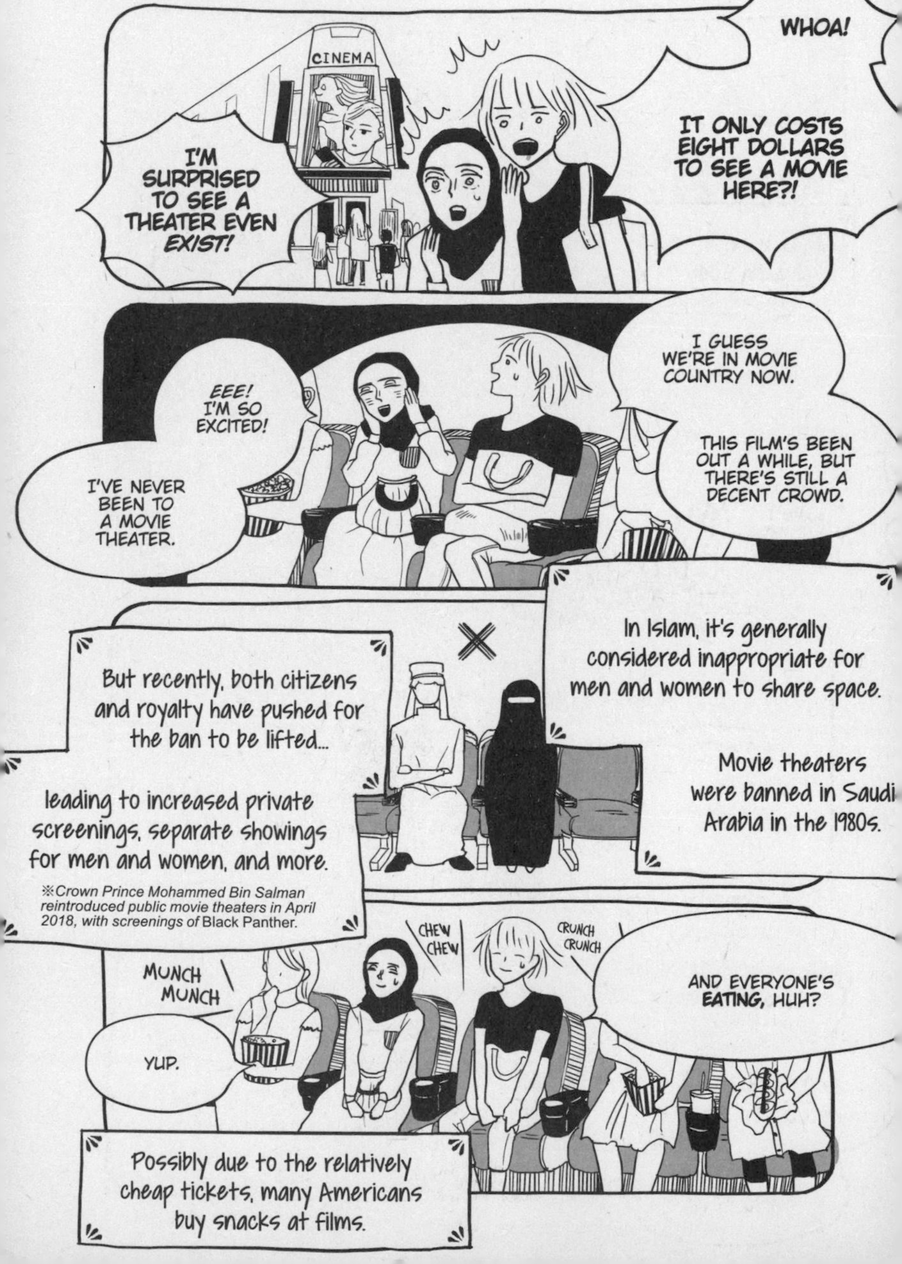
WHOA!
IT ONLY COSTS EIGHT DOLLARS TO SEE A MOVIE HERE?!
CINEMA
I'M SURPRISED TO SEE A THEATER EVEN *EXIST!*
I GUESS WE'RE IN MOVIE COUNTRY NOW.
THIS FILM'S BEEN OUT A WHILE, BUT THERE'S STILL A DECENT CROWD.
EEE! I'M SO EXCITED!
I'VE NEVER BEEN TO A MOVIE THEATER.
In Islam, it's generally considered inappropriate for men and women to share space.
Movie theaters were banned in Saudi Arabia in the 1980s.
But recently, both citizens and royalty have pushed for the ban to be lifted...
leading to increased private screenings, separate showings for men and women, and more.
※Crown Prince Mohammed Bin Salman reintroduced public movie theaters in April 2018, with screenings of Black Panther.
CRUNCH CRUNCH
AND EVERYONE'S **EATING**, HUH?
CHEW CHEW
MUNCH MUNCH
YUP.
Possibly due to the relatively cheap tickets, many Americans buy snacks at films.

POPCORN

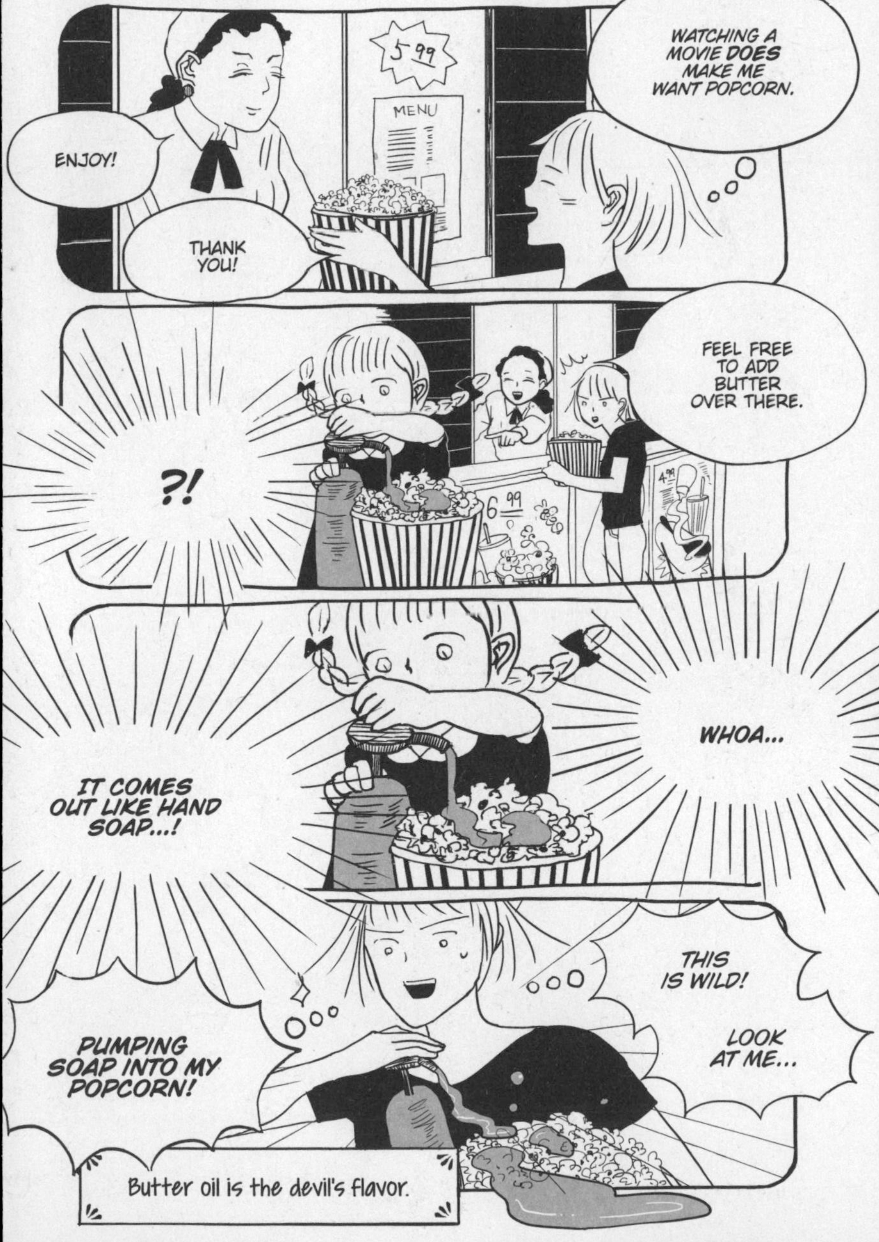

WATCHING A MOVIE DOES MAKE ME WANT POPCORN.
MENU
ENJOY!
THANK YOU!
FEEL FREE TO ADD BUTTER OVER THERE.
?!
WHOA...
IT COMES OUT LIKE HAND SOAP...!
THIS IS WILD!
LOOK AT ME...
PUMPING SOAP INTO MY POPCORN!
Butter oil is the devil's flavor.

FOR MYSELF

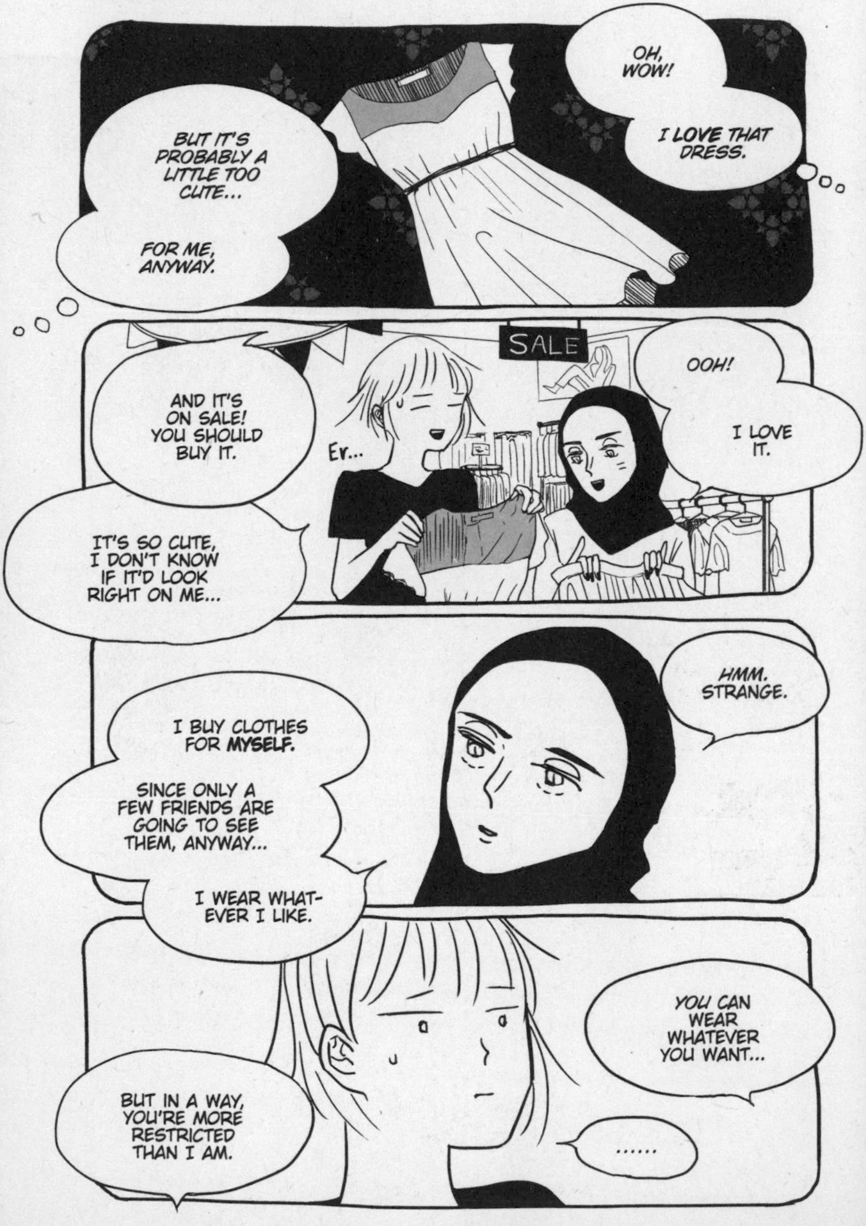
OH, WOW! I LOVE THAT DRESS.
BUT IT'S PROBABLY A LITTLE TOO CUTE...
FOR ME, ANYWAY.
SALE
OOH!
I LOVE IT.
AND IT'S ON SALE! YOU SHOULD BUY IT.
Er...
IT'S SO CUTE, I DON'T KNOW IF IT'D LOOK RIGHT ON ME...
HMM. STRANGE.
I BUY CLOTHES FOR MYSELF.
SINCE ONLY A FEW FRIENDS ARE GOING TO SEE THEM, ANYWAY...
I WEAR WHATEVER I LIKE.
YOU CAN WEAR WHATEVER YOU WANT...
......
BUT IN A WAY, YOU'RE MORE RESTRICTED THAN I AM.

UNDERWEAR

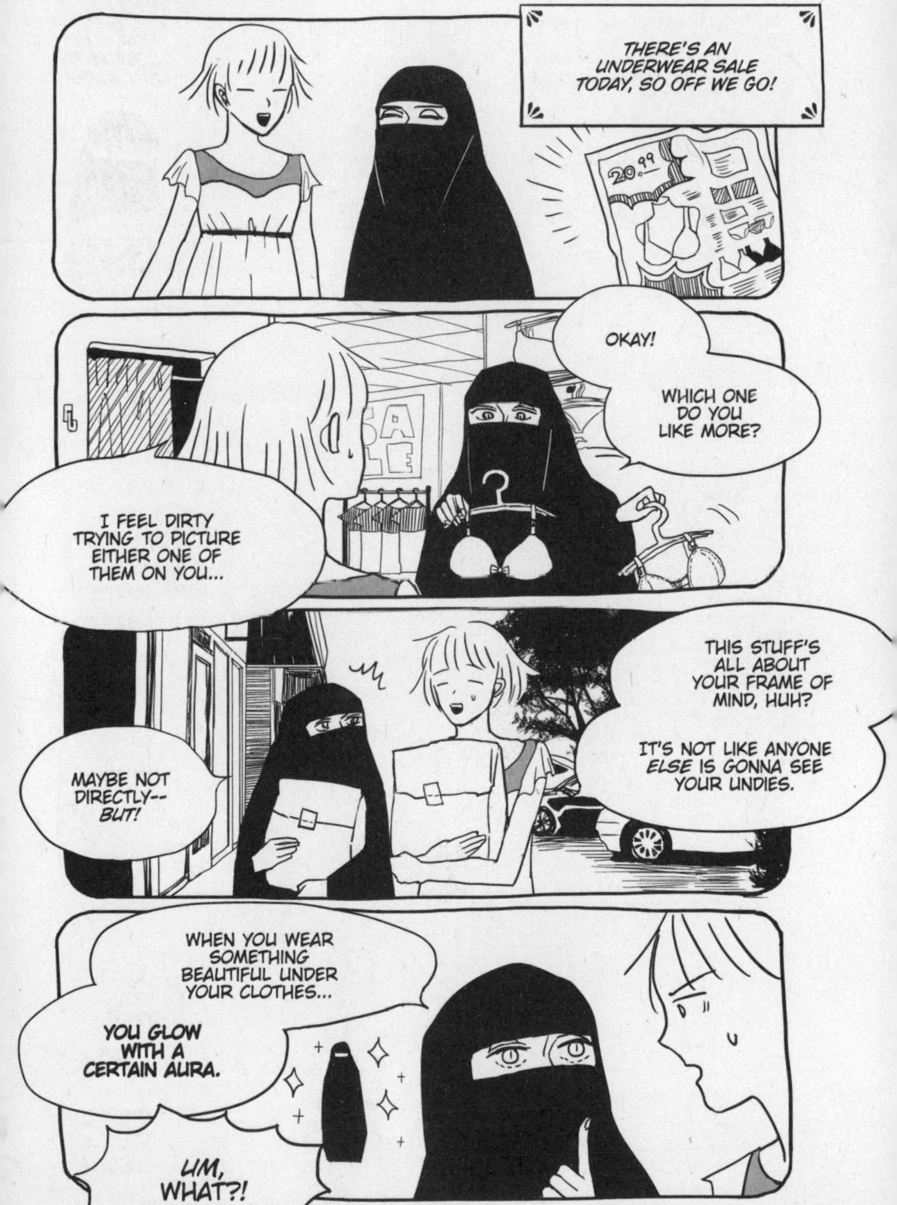

THERE'S AN UNDERWEAR SALE TODAY, SO OFF WE GO!
20.99
OKAY!
WHICH ONE DO YOU LIKE MORE?
I FEEL DIRTY TRYING TO PICTURE EITHER ONE OF THEM ON YOU...
THIS STUFF'S ALL ABOUT YOUR FRAME OF MIND, HUH?
IT'S NOT LIKE ANYONE *ELSE* IS GONNA SEE YOUR UNDIES.
MAYBE NOT DIRECTLY-- *BUT!*
WHEN YOU WEAR SOMETHING BEAUTIFUL UNDER YOUR CLOTHES...
YOU GLOW WITH A CERTAIN AURA.
UM, WHAT?!

AURA

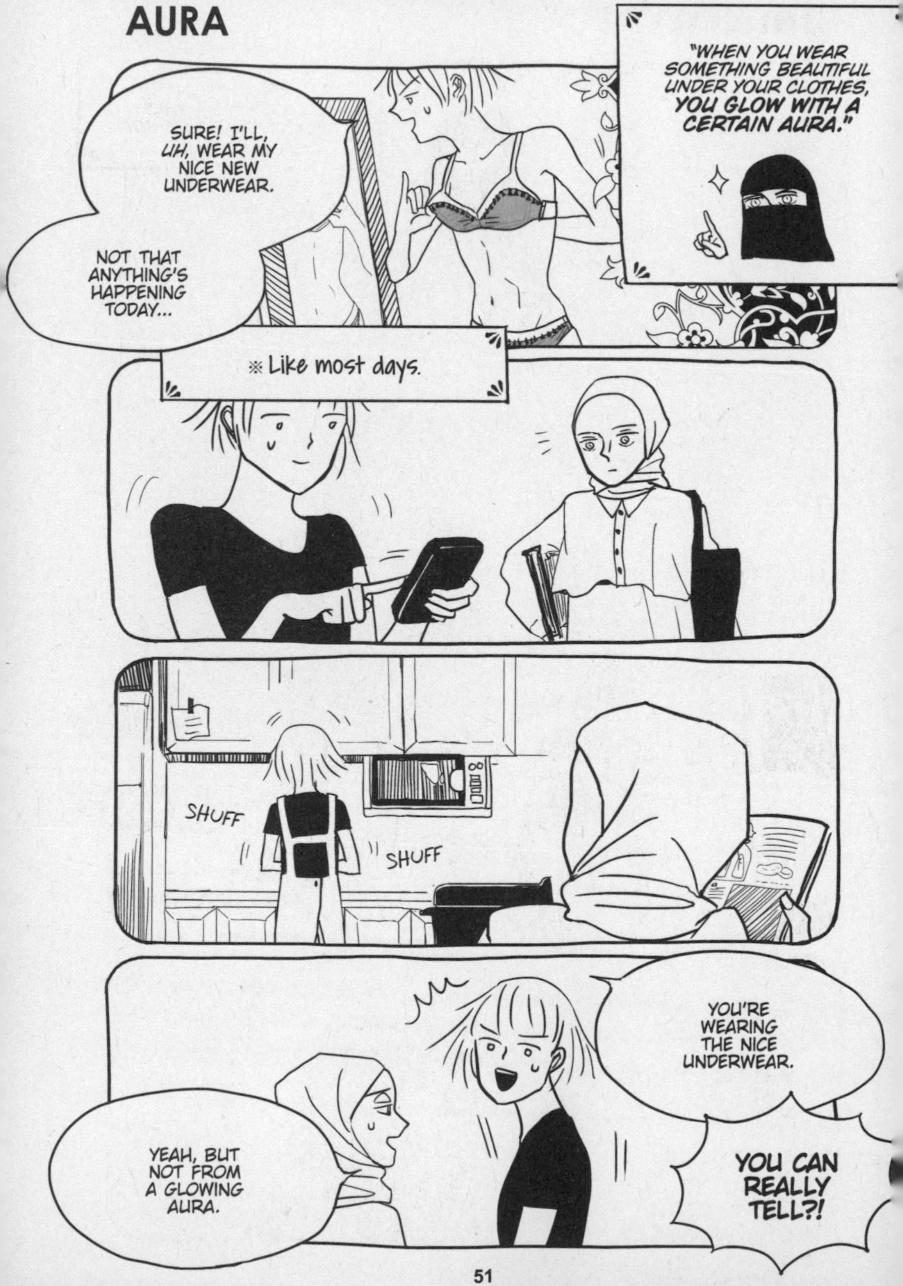
"WHEN YOU WEAR SOMETHING BEAUTIFUL UNDER YOUR CLOTHES, **YOU GLOW WITH A CERTAIN AURA.**"
SURE! I'LL, *UH*, WEAR MY NICE NEW UNDERWEAR.
NOT THAT ANYTHING'S HAPPENING TODAY...
※ Like most days.
SHUFF
SHUFF
YOU'RE WEARING THE NICE UNDERWEAR.
YOU CAN REALLY TELL?!
YEAH, BUT NOT FROM A GLOWING AURA.

CAT EARS

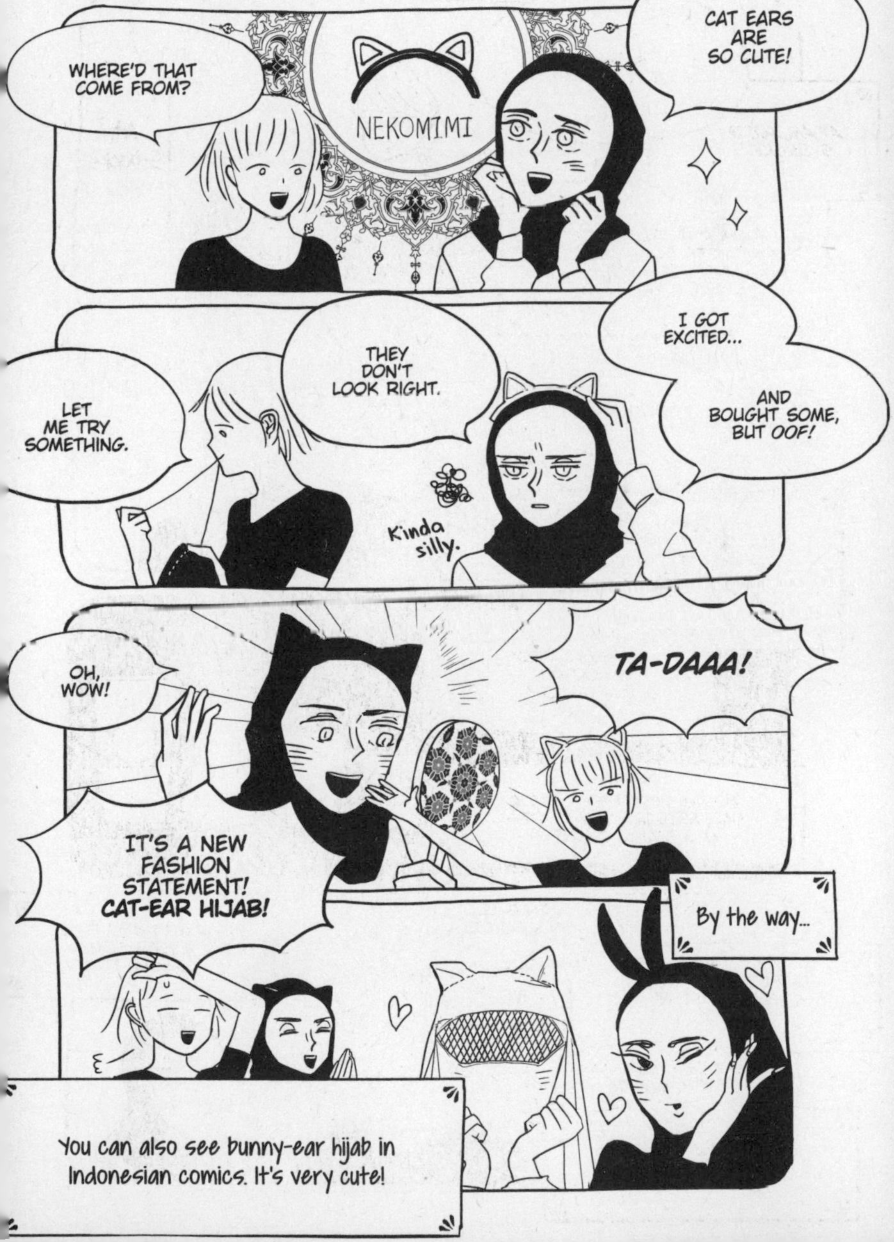
CAT EARS ARE SO CUTE!
WHERE'D THAT COME FROM?
NEKOMIMI
I GOT EXCITED...
AND BOUGHT SOME, BUT OOF!
THEY DON'T LOOK RIGHT.
Kinda silly.
LET ME TRY SOMETHING.
TA-DAAA!
OH, WOW!
IT'S A NEW FASHION STATEMENT! CAT-EAR HIJAB!
By the way...
You can also see bunny-ear hijab in Indonesian comics. It's very cute!

COFFEE SHOP

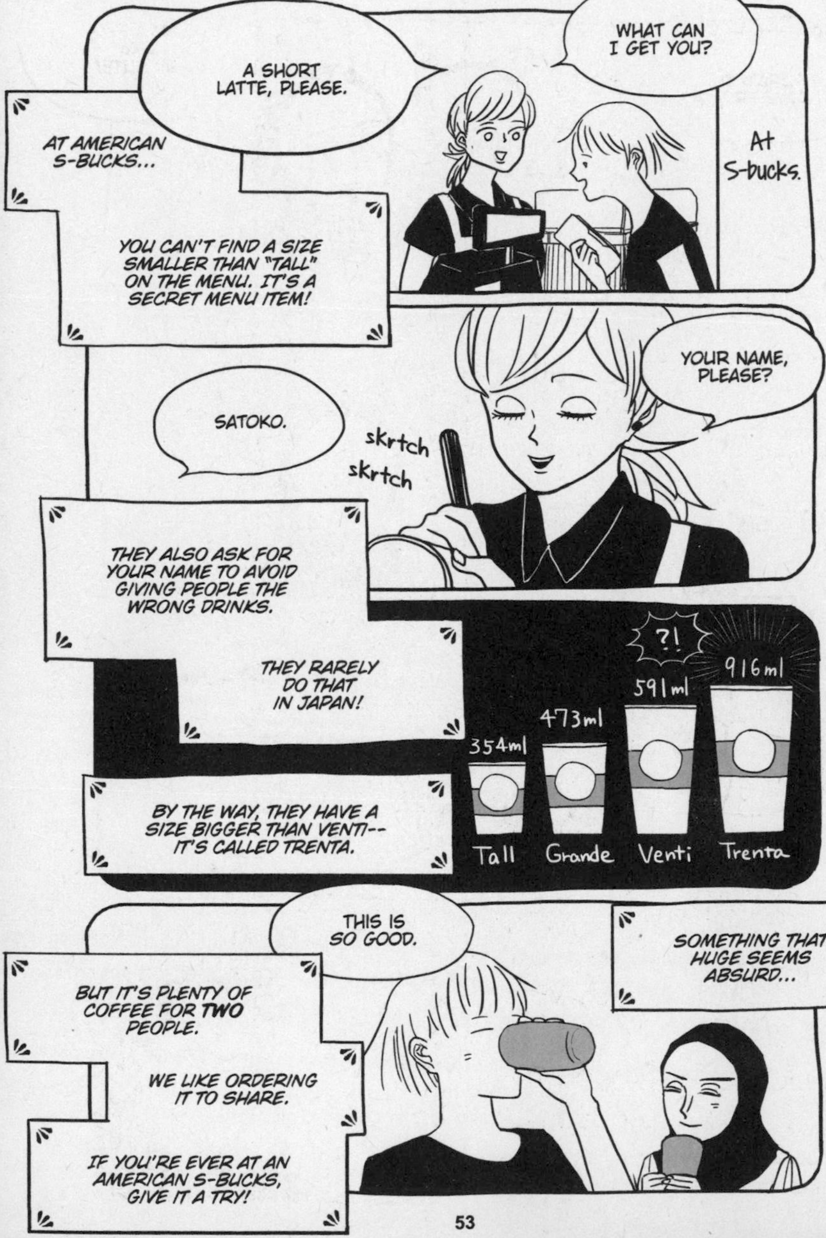
At S-bucks.
WHAT CAN I GET YOU?
A SHORT LATTE, PLEASE.
AT AMERICAN S-BUCKS...
YOU CAN'T FIND A SIZE SMALLER THAN "TALL" ON THE MENU. IT'S A SECRET MENU ITEM!
YOUR NAME, PLEASE?
skrtch
skrtch
SATOKO.
THEY ALSO ASK FOR YOUR NAME TO AVOID GIVING PEOPLE THE WRONG DRINKS.
THEY RARELY DO THAT IN JAPAN!
?!
916ml
591ml
473ml
354ml
Tall
Grande
Venti
Trenta
BY THE WAY, THEY HAVE A SIZE BIGGER THAN VENTI-- IT'S CALLED TRENTA.
SOMETHING THAT HUGE SEEMS ABSURD...
THIS IS SO GOOD.
BUT IT'S PLENTY OF COFFEE FOR **TWO** PEOPLE.
WE LIKE ORDERING IT TO SHARE.
IF YOU'RE EVER AT AN AMERICAN S-BUCKS, GIVE IT A TRY!

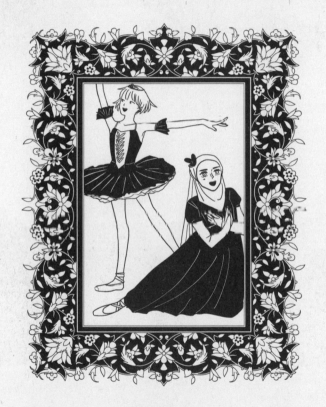

SATOKO AND NADA

Presented by Yupechika

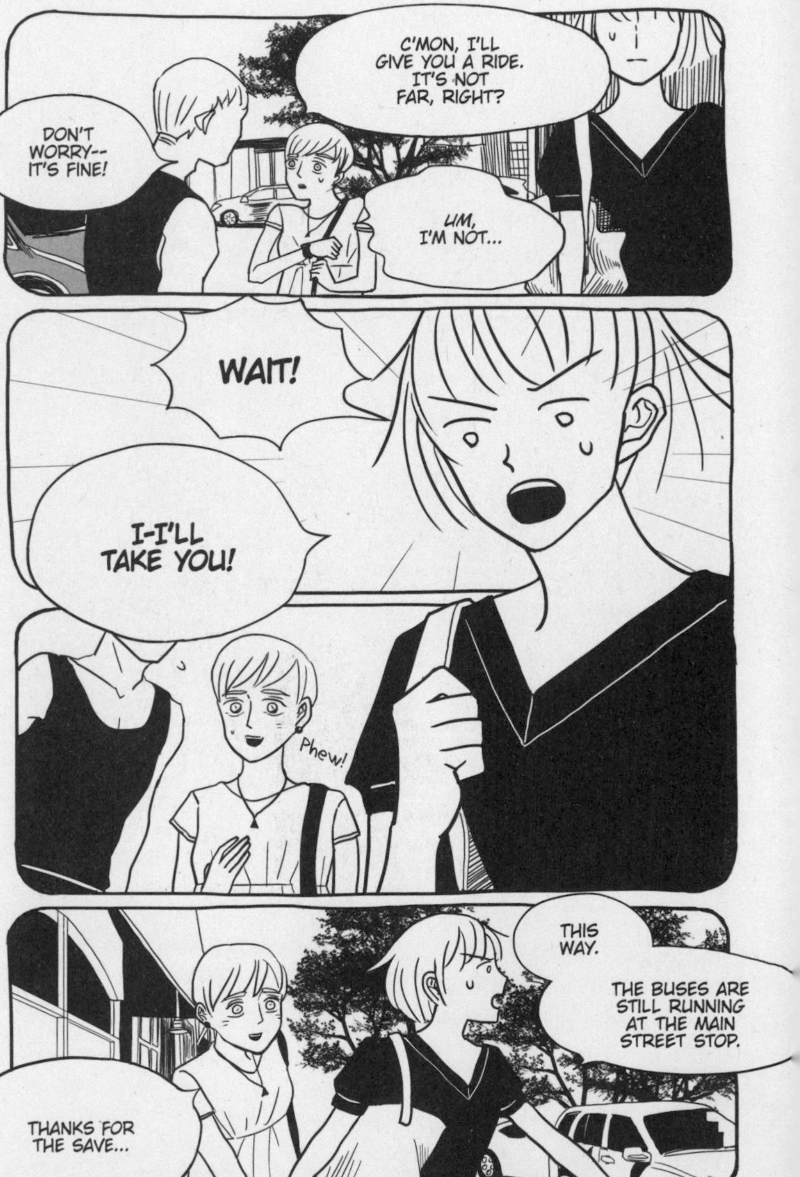
C'MON, I'LL GIVE YOU A RIDE. IT'S NOT FAR, RIGHT?
UM, I'M NOT...
DON'T WORRY-- IT'S FINE!
WAIT!
I-I'LL TAKE YOU!
Phew!
THIS WAY.
THE BUSES ARE STILL RUNNING AT THE MAIN STREET STOP.
THANKS FOR THE SAVE...

SPARKLY

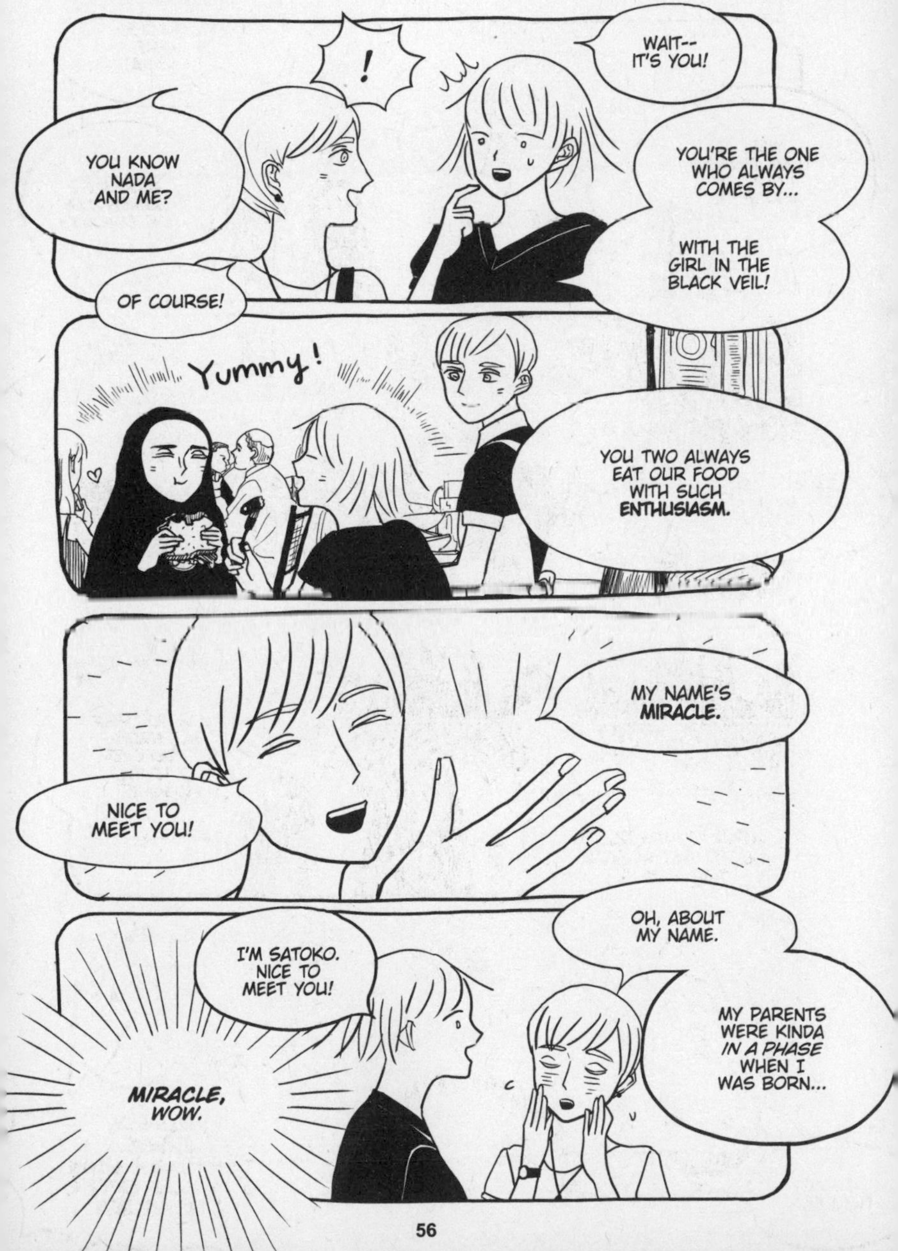
WAIT--
IT'S YOU!
!
YOU KNOW NADA AND ME?
OF COURSE!
YOU'RE THE ONE WHO ALWAYS COMES BY...
WITH THE GIRL IN THE BLACK VEIL!
YOU TWO ALWAYS EAT OUR FOOD WITH SUCH **ENTHUSIASM.**
Yummy!
MY NAME'S **MIRACLE.**
NICE TO MEET YOU!
I'M SATOKO. NICE TO MEET YOU!
OH, ABOUT MY NAME.
MY PARENTS WERE KINDA *IN A PHASE* WHEN I WAS BORN...
MIRACLE, WOW.

CHURCH

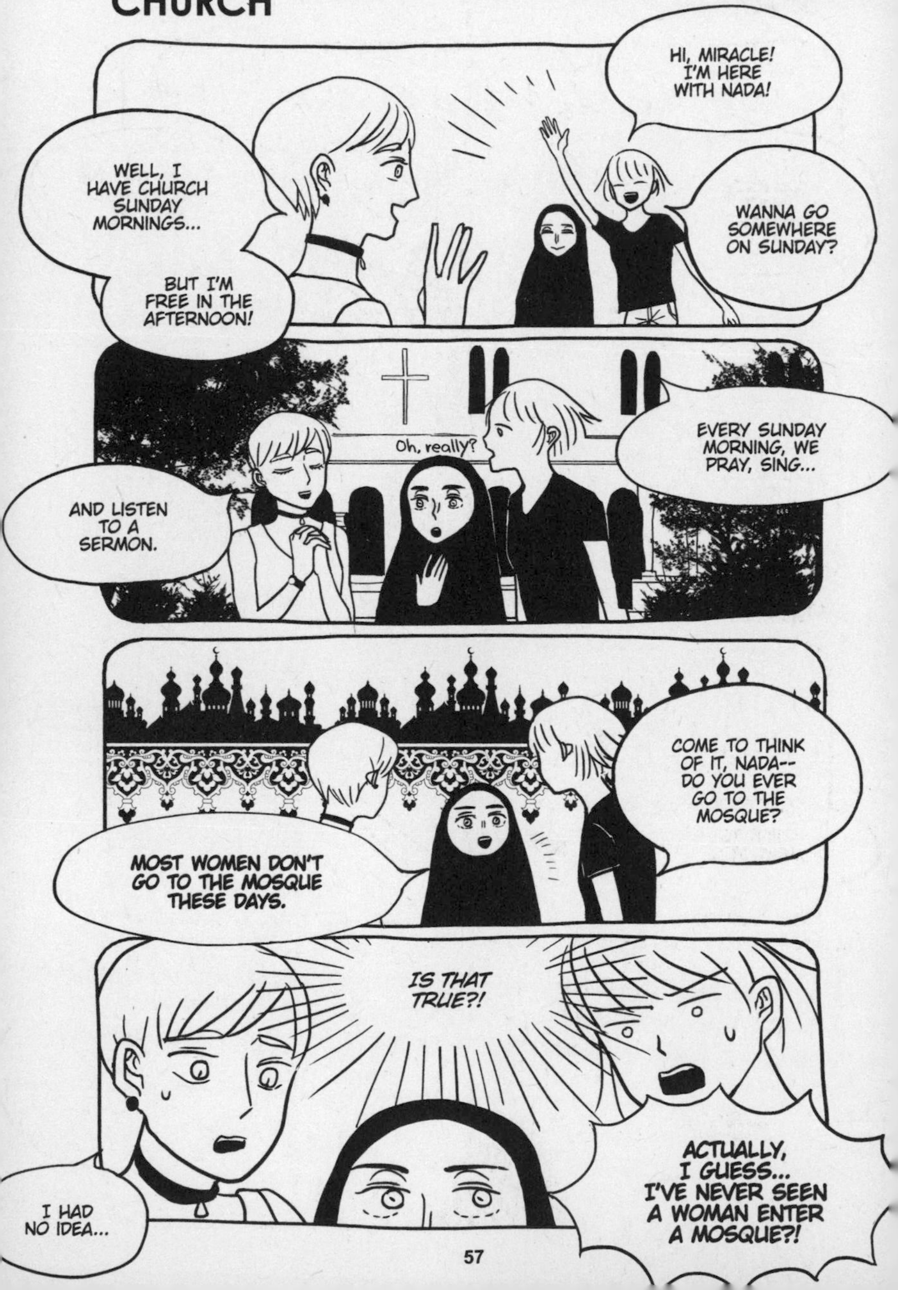

HI, MIRACLE! I'M HERE WITH NADA!
WANNA GO SOMEWHERE ON SUNDAY?
WELL, I HAVE CHURCH SUNDAY MORNINGS...
BUT I'M FREE IN THE AFTERNOON!
EVERY SUNDAY MORNING, WE PRAY, SING...
Oh, really?
AND LISTEN TO A SERMON.
COME TO THINK OF IT, NADA-- DO YOU EVER GO TO THE MOSQUE?
MOST WOMEN DON'T GO TO THE MOSQUE THESE DAYS.
IS THAT TRUE?!
ACTUALLY, I GUESS... I'VE NEVER SEEN A WOMAN ENTER A MOSQUE?!
I HAD NO IDEA...

MOSQUE

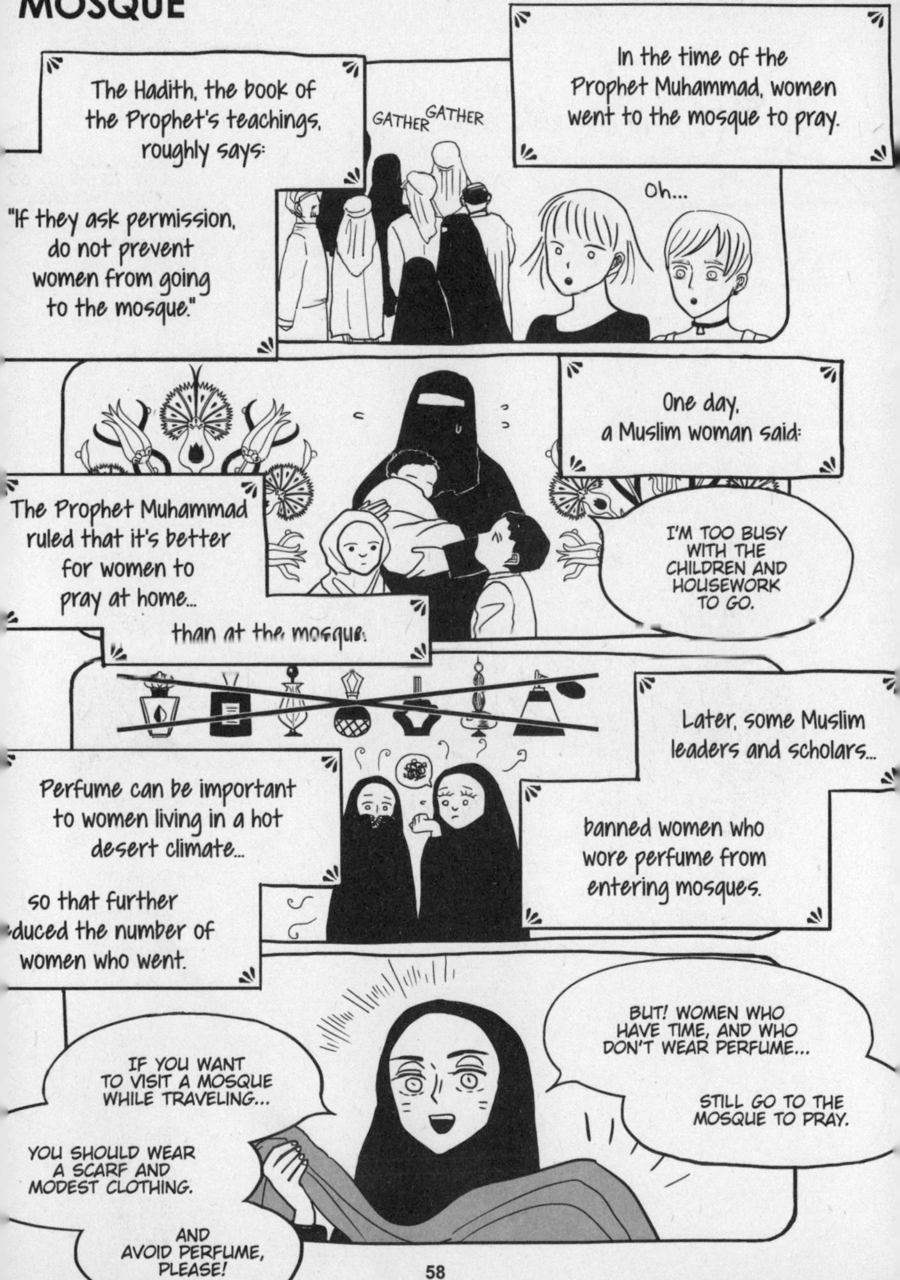

In the time of the Prophet Muhammad, women went to the mosque to pray.
Oh...
GATHER GATHER
The Hadith, the book of the Prophet's teachings, roughly says:
"If they ask permission, do not prevent women from going to the mosque."
One day, a Muslim woman said:
I'M TOO BUSY WITH THE CHILDREN AND HOUSEWORK TO GO.
The Prophet Muhammad ruled that it's better for women to pray at home...
than at the mosque.
Later, some Muslim leaders and scholars...
banned women who wore perfume from entering mosques.
Perfume can be important to women living in a hot desert climate...
so that further
duced the number of women who went.
BUT! WOMEN WHO HAVE TIME, AND WHO DON'T WEAR PERFUME...
STILL GO TO THE MOSQUE TO PRAY.
IF YOU WANT TO VISIT A MOSQUE WHILE TRAVELING...
YOU SHOULD WEAR A SCARF AND MODEST CLOTHING.
AND AVOID PERFUME, PLEASE!

MOSQUE 2

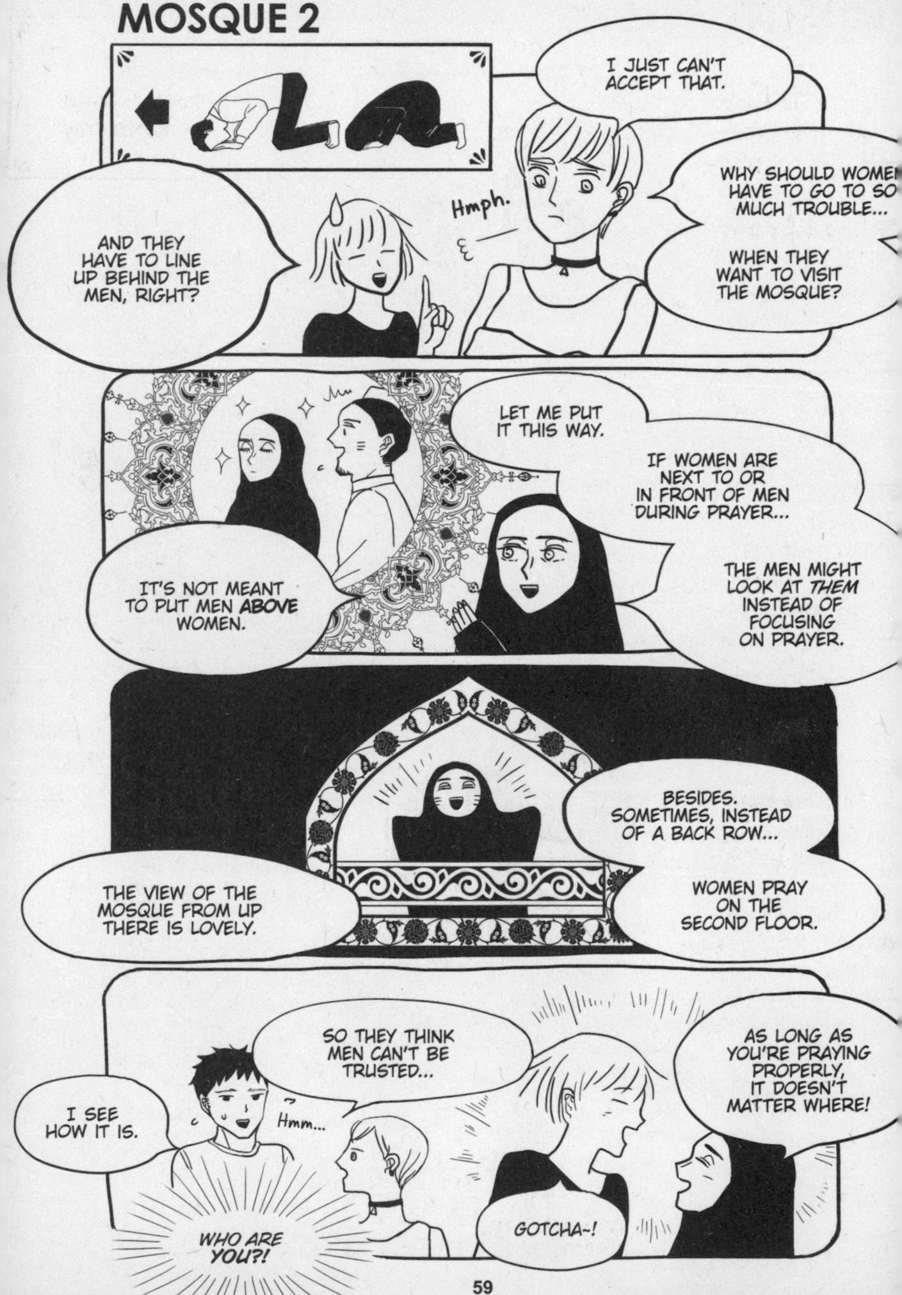

I JUST CAN'T ACCEPT THAT.
WHY SHOULD WOME HAVE TO GO TO SO MUCH TROUBLE...
WHEN THEY WANT TO VISIT THE MOSQUE?
Hmph.
AND THEY HAVE TO LINE UP BEHIND THE MEN, RIGHT?
LET ME PUT IT THIS WAY.
IF WOMEN ARE NEXT TO OR IN FRONT OF MEN DURING PRAYER...
THE MEN MIGHT LOOK AT *THEM* INSTEAD OF FOCUSING ON PRAYER.
IT'S NOT MEANT TO PUT MEN **ABOVE** WOMEN.
BESIDES. SOMETIMES, INSTEAD OF A BACK ROW...
WOMEN PRAY ON THE SECOND FLOOR.
THE VIEW OF THE MOSQUE FROM UP THERE IS LOVELY.
AS LONG AS YOU'RE PRAYING PROPERLY, IT DOESN'T MATTER WHERE!
GOTCHA~!
SO THEY THINK MEN CAN'T BE TRUSTED...
Hmm...
I SEE HOW IT IS.
WHO ARE *YOU*?!

KEVIN-KUN

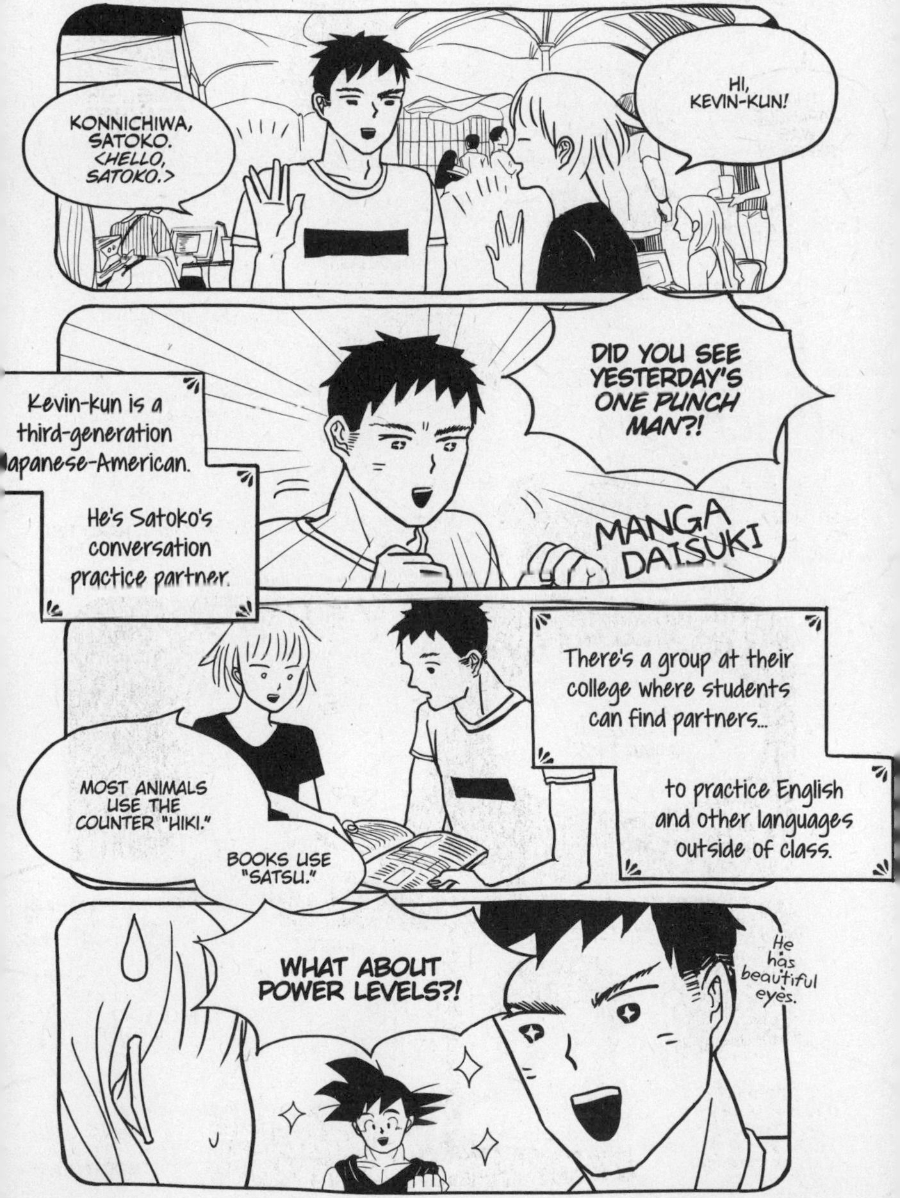
HI, KEVIN-KUN!
KONNICHIWA, SATOKO. <HELLO, SATOKO.>
DID YOU SEE YESTERDAY'S ONE PUNCH MAN?!
MANGA DAISUKI
Kevin-kun is a third-generation Japanese-American.
He's Satoko's conversation practice partner.
There's a group at their college where students can find partners...
to practice English and other languages outside of class.
MOST ANIMALS USE THE COUNTER "HIKI."
BOOKS USE "SATSU."
He has beautiful eyes.
WHAT ABOUT POWER LEVELS?!

KEVIN-KUN 2

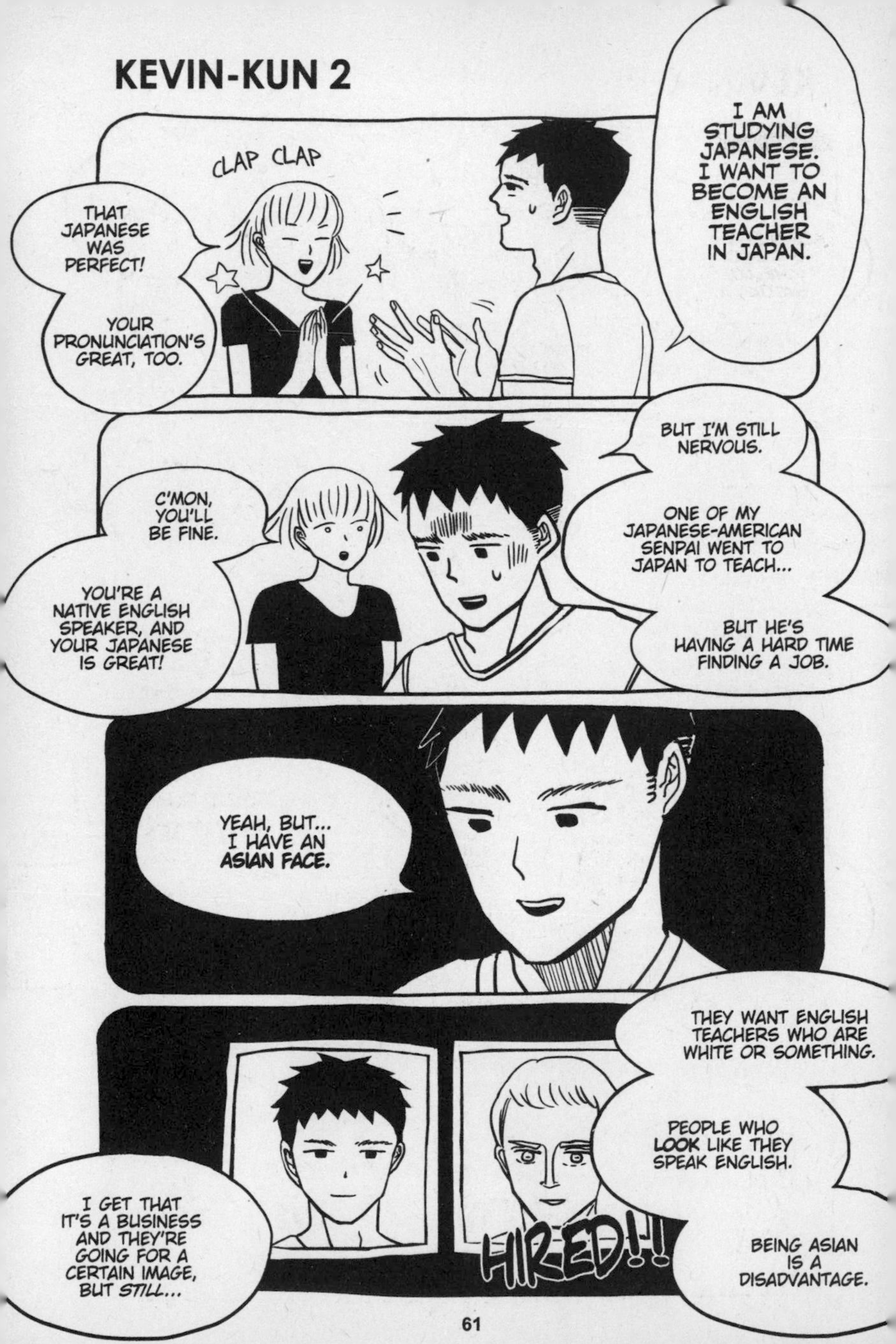
I AM STUDYING JAPANESE. I WANT TO BECOME AN ENGLISH TEACHER IN JAPAN.
CLAP CLAP
THAT JAPANESE WAS PERFECT!
YOUR PRONUNCIATION'S GREAT, TOO.
BUT I'M STILL NERVOUS.
C'MON, YOU'LL BE FINE.
YOU'RE A NATIVE ENGLISH SPEAKER, AND YOUR JAPANESE IS GREAT!
ONE OF MY JAPANESE-AMERICAN SENPAI WENT TO JAPAN TO TEACH...
BUT HE'S HAVING A HARD TIME FINDING A JOB.
YEAH, BUT... I HAVE AN ASIAN FACE.
THEY WANT ENGLISH TEACHERS WHO ARE WHITE OR SOMETHING.
PEOPLE WHO LOOK LIKE THEY SPEAK ENGLISH.
HIRED!!
BEING ASIAN IS A DISADVANTAGE.
I GET THAT IT'S A BUSINESS AND THEY'RE GOING FOR A CERTAIN IMAGE, BUT STILL...

RESUME

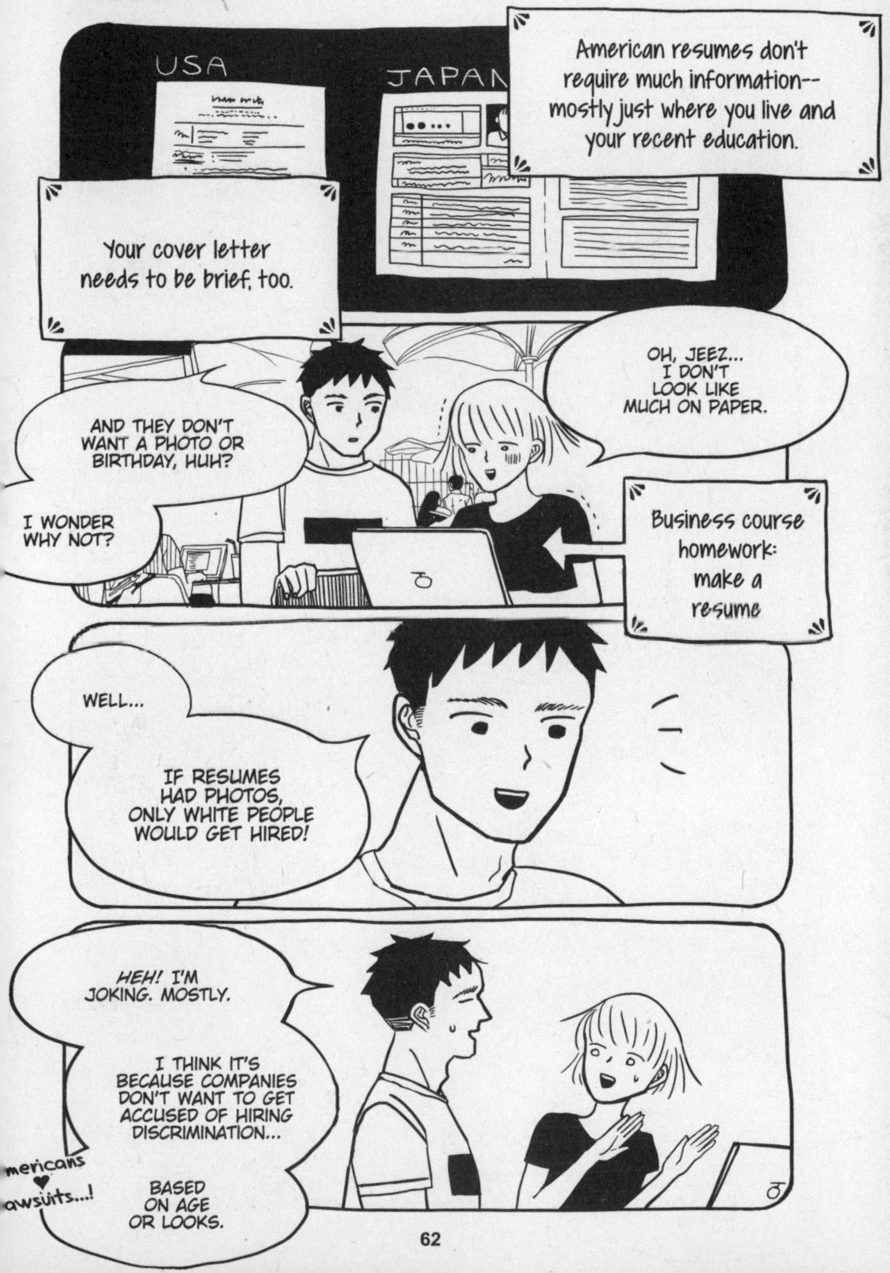
USA
JAPAN
American resumes don't require much information--mostly just where you live and your recent education.
Your cover letter needs to be brief, too.
OH, JEEZ... I DON'T LOOK LIKE MUCH ON PAPER.
AND THEY DON'T WANT A PHOTO OR BIRTHDAY, HUH?
I WONDER WHY NOT?
Business course homework: make a resume
WELL...
IF RESUMES HAD PHOTOS, ONLY WHITE PEOPLE WOULD GET HIRED!
HEH! I'M JOKING. MOSTLY.
I THINK IT'S BECAUSE COMPANIES DON'T WANT TO GET ACCUSED OF HIRING DISCRIMINATION...
BASED ON AGE OR LOOKS.
mericans ♥ awsuits...!

DREAM

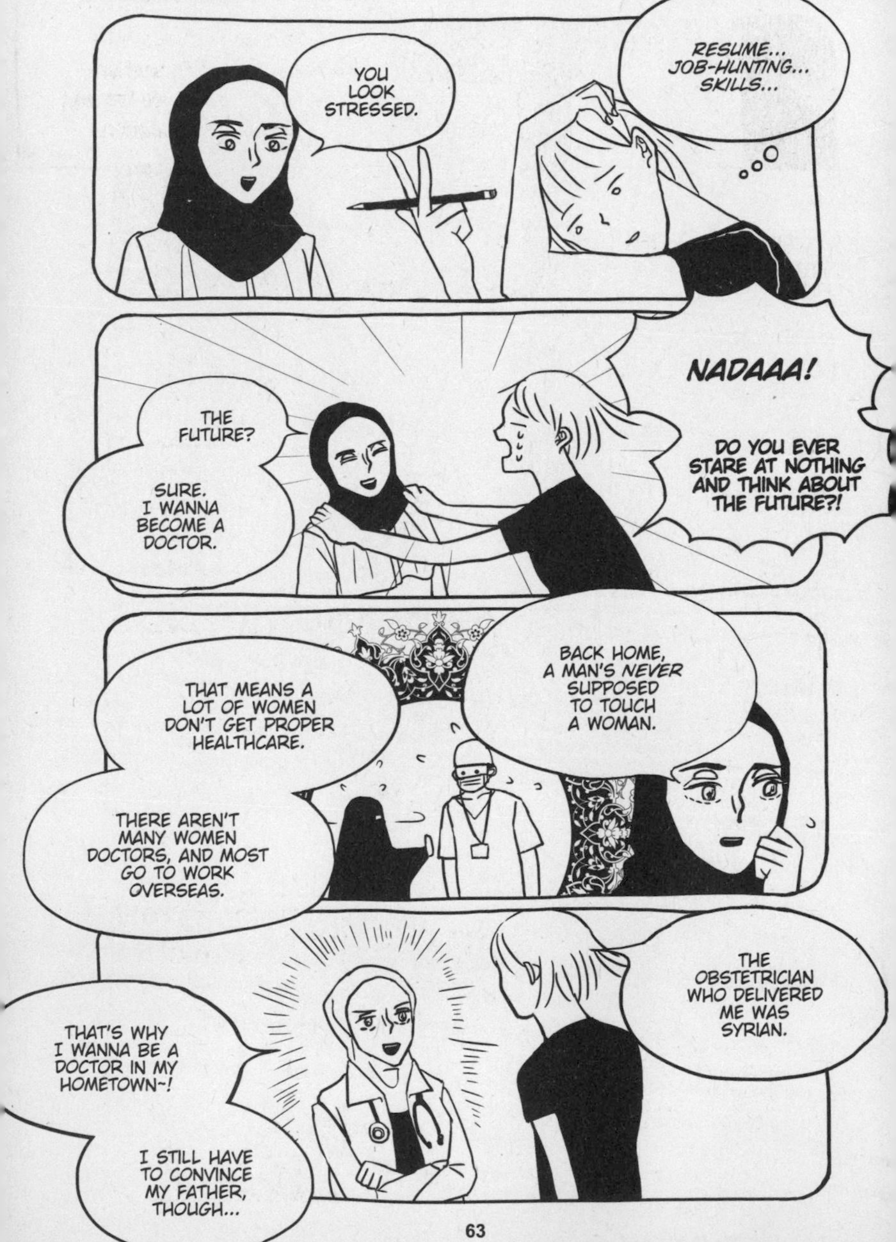

RESUME... JOB-HUNTING... SKILLS...
YOU LOOK STRESSED.
NADAAA!
DO YOU EVER STARE AT NOTHING AND THINK ABOUT THE FUTURE?!
THE FUTURE?
SURE. I WANNA BECOME A DOCTOR.
BACK HOME, A MAN'S *NEVER* SUPPOSED TO TOUCH A WOMAN.
THAT MEANS A LOT OF WOMEN DON'T GET PROPER HEALTHCARE.
THERE AREN'T MANY WOMEN DOCTORS, AND MOST GO TO WORK OVERSEAS.
THE OBSTETRICIAN WHO DELIVERED ME WAS SYRIAN.
THAT'S WHY I WANNA BE A DOCTOR IN MY HOMETOWN~!
I STILL HAVE TO CONVINCE MY FATHER, THOUGH...

SATOKO'S STRENGTHS

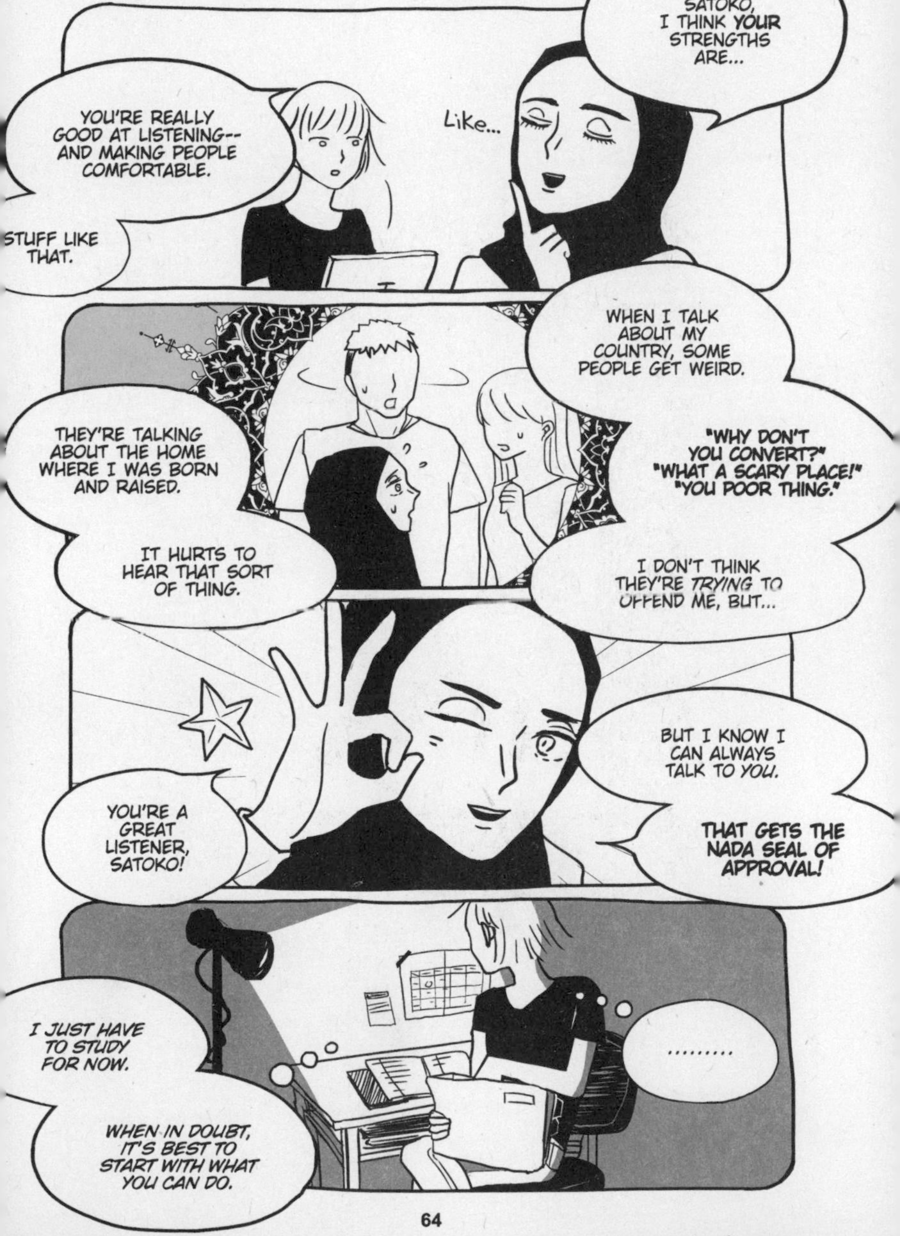

SATOKO, I THINK *YOUR* STRENGTHS ARE...
Like...
YOU'RE REALLY GOOD AT LISTENING-- AND MAKING PEOPLE COMFORTABLE.
STUFF LIKE THAT.
WHEN I TALK ABOUT MY COUNTRY, SOME PEOPLE GET WEIRD.
"WHY DON'T YOU CONVERT?" "WHAT A SCARY PLACE!" "YOU POOR THING."
THEY'RE TALKING ABOUT THE HOME WHERE I WAS BORN AND RAISED.
I DON'T THINK THEY'RE *TRYING* TO OFFEND ME, BUT...
IT HURTS TO HEAR THAT SORT OF THING.
BUT I KNOW I CAN ALWAYS TALK TO *YOU*.
YOU'RE A GREAT LISTENER, SATOKO!
THAT GETS THE NADA SEAL OF APPROVAL!
....
I JUST HAVE TO STUDY FOR NOW.
WHEN IN DOUBT, IT'S BEST TO START WITH WHAT YOU CAN DO.

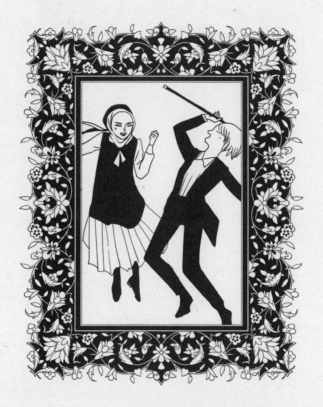

SATOKO AND NADA

Presented by Yupechika

SATOKO'S RELIGION

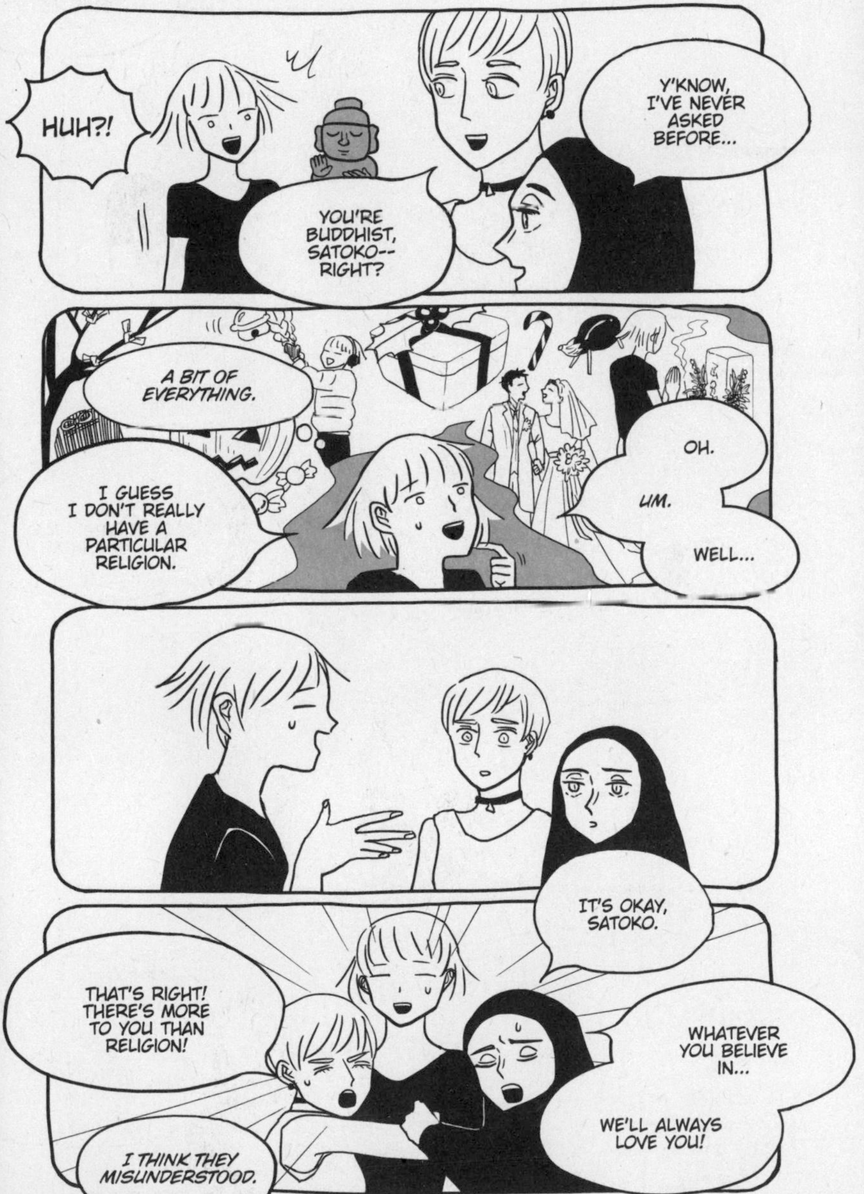
Y'KNOW, I'VE NEVER ASKED BEFORE...
YOU'RE BUDDHIST, SATOKO-- RIGHT?
HUH?!
OH.
UM.
WELL...
A BIT OF EVERYTHING.
I GUESS I DON'T REALLY HAVE A PARTICULAR RELIGION.
IT'S OKAY, SATOKO.
WHATEVER YOU BELIEVE IN...
WE'LL ALWAYS LOVE YOU!
THAT'S RIGHT! THERE'S MORE TO YOU THAN RELIGION!
I THINK THEY MISUNDERSTOOD.

A COUNTRY OF MANY GODS

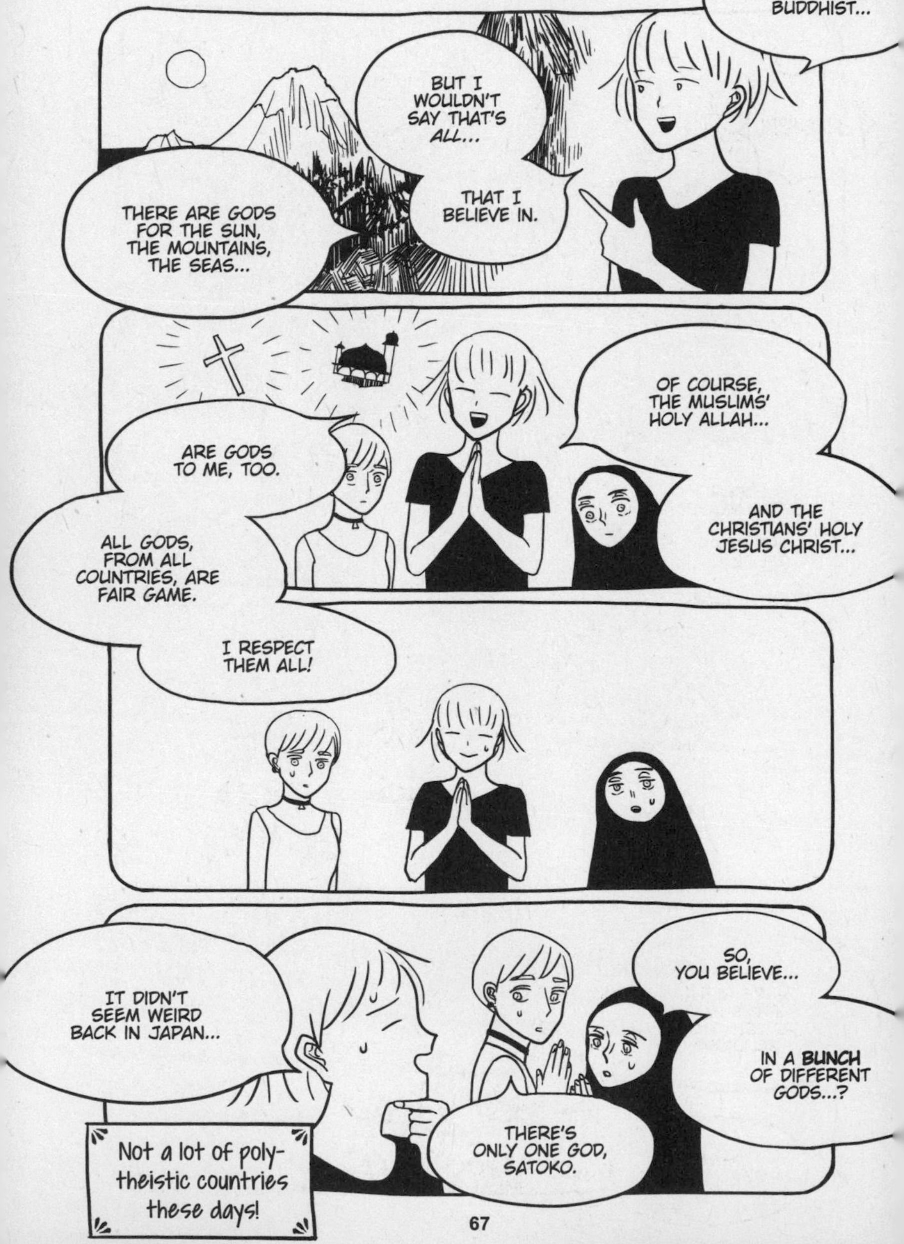
I'M TECHNICALLY BUDDHIST...
BUT I WOULDN'T SAY THAT'S ALL...
THAT I BELIEVE IN.
THERE ARE GODS FOR THE SUN, THE MOUNTAINS, THE SEAS...
OF COURSE, THE MUSLIMS' HOLY ALLAH...
AND THE CHRISTIANS' HOLY JESUS CHRIST...
ARE GODS TO ME, TOO.
ALL GODS, FROM ALL COUNTRIES, ARE FAIR GAME.
I RESPECT THEM ALL!
SO, YOU BELIEVE...
IN A BUNCH OF DIFFERENT GODS...?
THERE'S ONLY ONE GOD, SATOKO.
IT DIDN'T SEEM WEIRD BACK IN JAPAN...
Not a lot of polytheistic countries these days!

SOCIAL MEDIA DEBUT

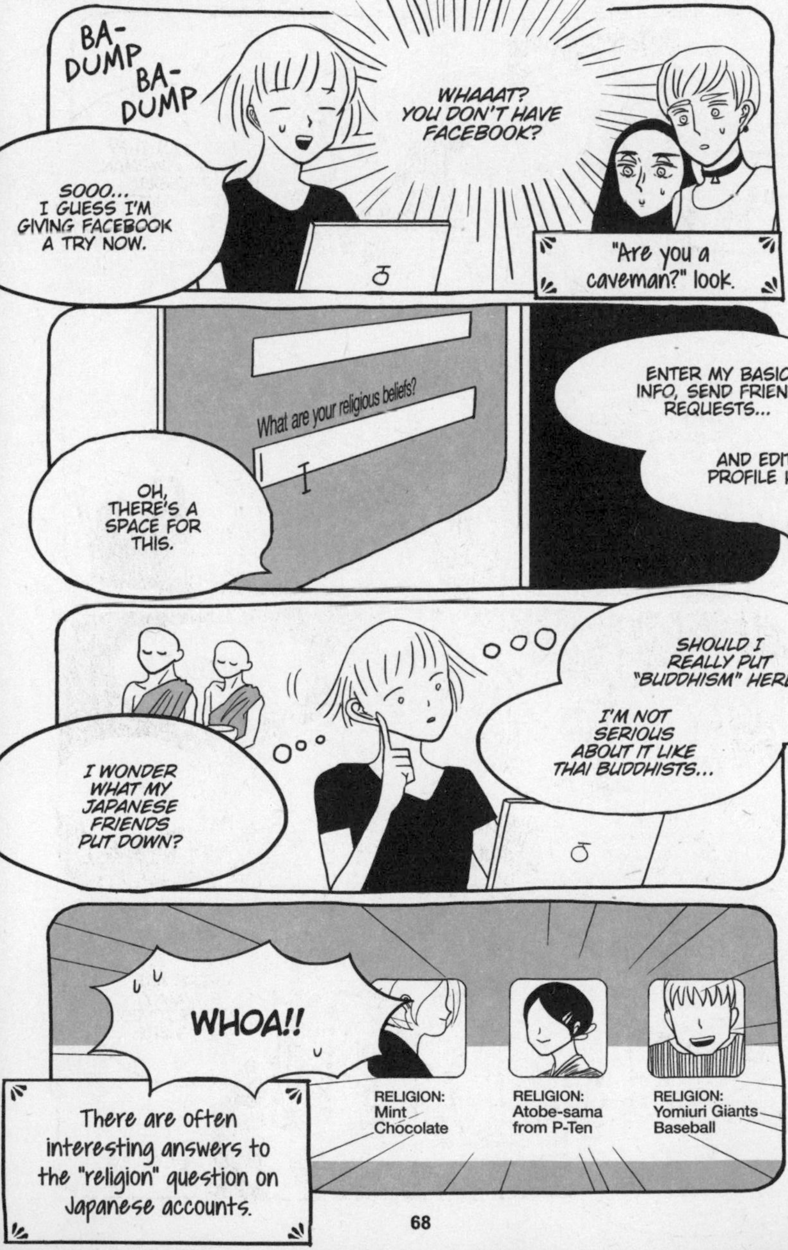
WHAAAT? YOU DON'T HAVE FACEBOOK?
"Are you a caveman?" look.
BA-DUMP BA-DUMP
SOOO... I GUESS I'M GIVING FACEBOOK A TRY NOW.
ENTER MY BASIC INFO, SEND FRIEND REQUESTS...
AND EDIT MY PROFILE HERE.
What are your religious beliefs?
OH, THERE'S A SPACE FOR THIS.
SHOULD I REALLY PUT "BUDDHISM" HERE?
I'M NOT SERIOUS ABOUT IT LIKE THAI BUDDHISTS...
I WONDER WHAT MY JAPANESE FRIENDS PUT DOWN?
WHOA!!
RELIGION: Yomiuri Giants Baseball
RELIGION: Atobe-sama from P-Ten
RELIGION: Mint Chocolate
There are often interesting answers to the "religion" question on Japanese accounts.

PERSPECTIVES

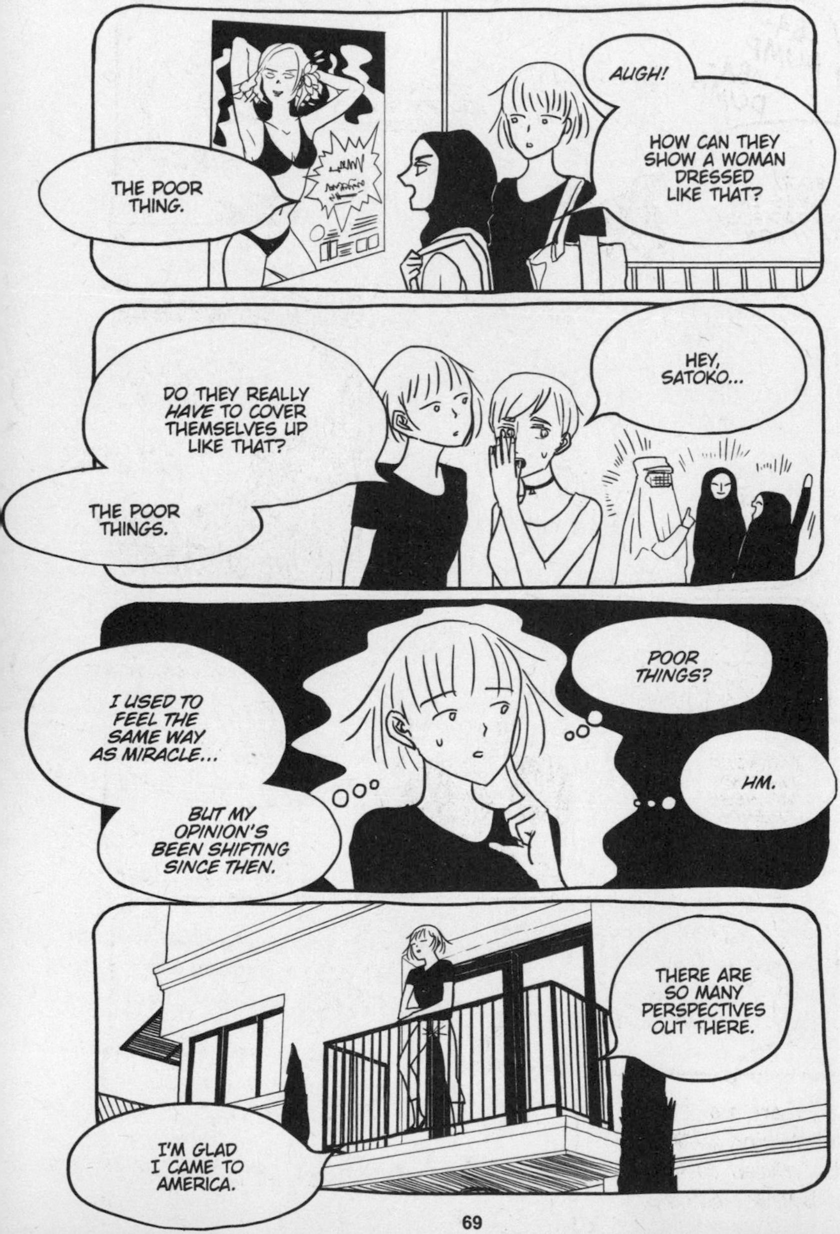
AUGH!
HOW CAN THEY SHOW A WOMAN DRESSED LIKE THAT?
THE POOR THING.
HEY, SATOKO...
DO THEY REALLY *HAVE* TO COVER THEMSELVES UP LIKE THAT?
THE POOR THINGS.
POOR THINGS?
HM.
I USED TO FEEL THE SAME WAY AS MIRACLE...
BUT MY OPINION'S BEEN SHIFTING SINCE THEN.
THERE ARE SO MANY PERSPECTIVES OUT THERE.
I'M GLAD I CAME TO AMERICA.

EXERCISE, ARE YOU SERIOUS?!

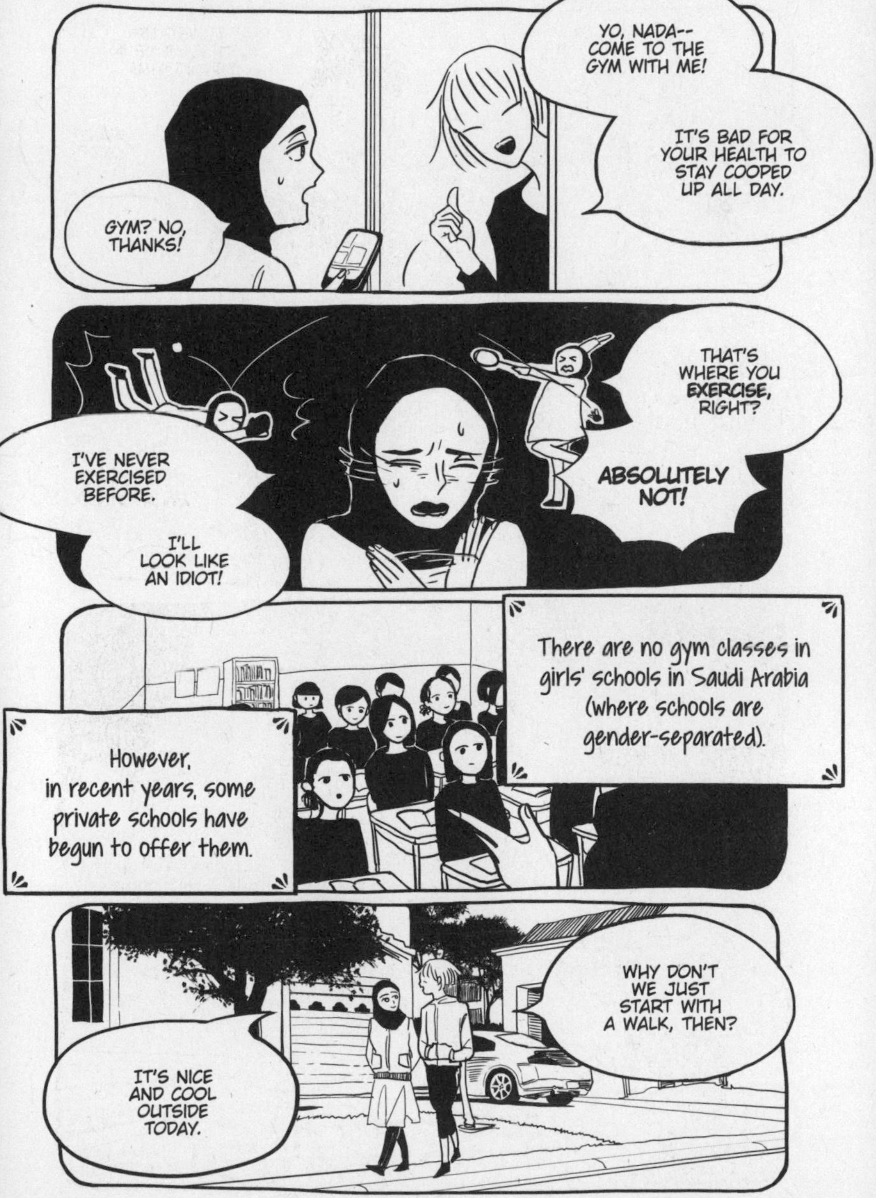
YO, NADA-- COME TO THE GYM WITH ME!
IT'S BAD FOR YOUR HEALTH TO STAY COOPED UP ALL DAY.
GYM? NO, THANKS!
THAT'S WHERE YOU EXERCISE, RIGHT?
ABSOLUTELY NOT!
I'VE NEVER EXERCISED BEFORE.
I'LL LOOK LIKE AN IDIOT!
There are no gym classes in girls' schools in Saudi Arabia (where schools are gender-separated).
However, in recent years, some private schools have begun to offer them.
WHY DON'T WE JUST START WITH A WALK, THEN?
IT'S NICE AND COOL OUTSIDE TODAY.

RAMUNE

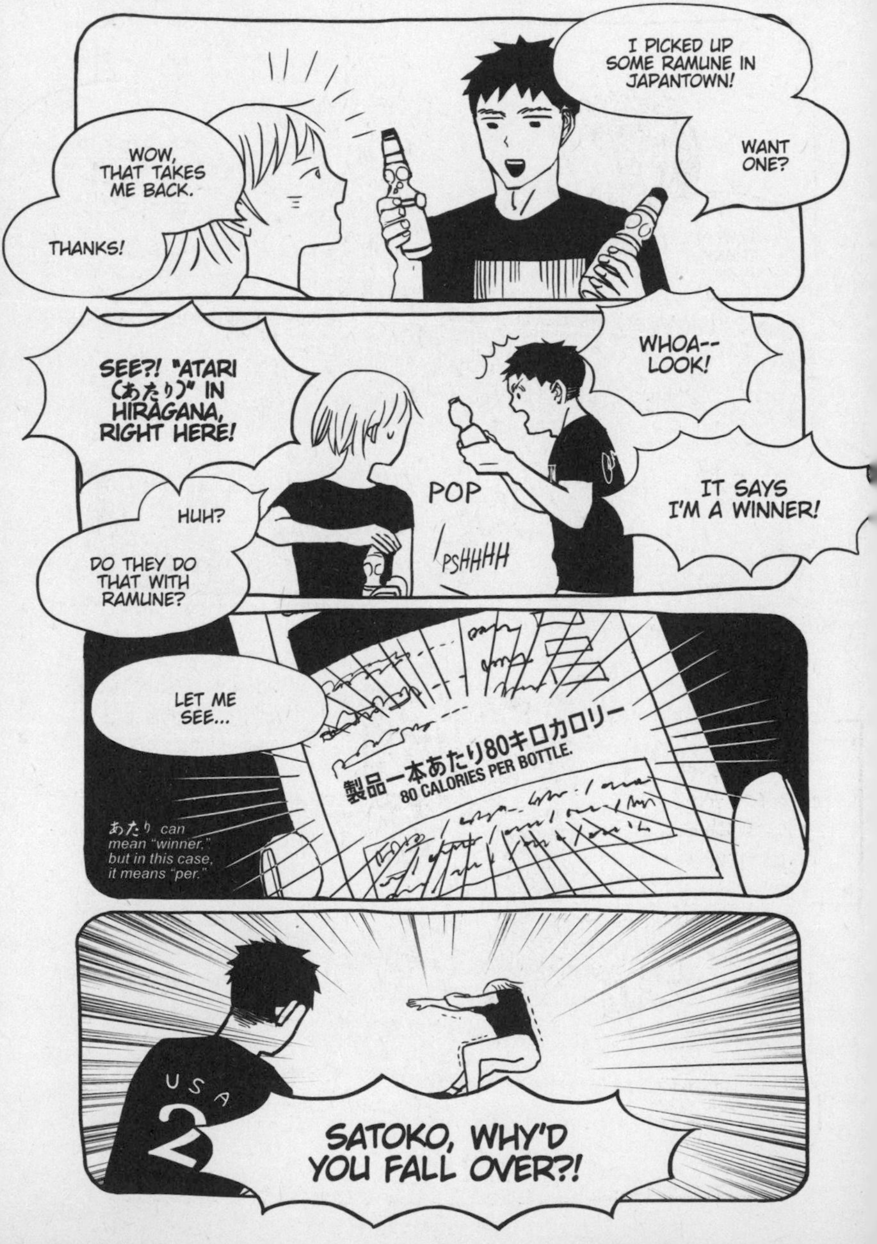

I PICKED UP SOME RAMUNE IN JAPANTOWN!
WANT ONE?
WOW, THAT TAKES ME BACK.
THANKS!
WHOA-- LOOK!
IT SAYS I'M A WINNER!
SEE?! "ATARI (あたり)" IN HIRAGANA, RIGHT HERE!
POP
PSHHHH
HUH?
DO THEY DO THAT WITH RAMUNE?
製品一本あたり80キロカロリー
80 CALORIES PER BOTTLE.
LET ME SEE...
あたり can mean "winner," but in this case, it means "per."
USA 2
SATOKO, WHY'D YOU FALL OVER?!

ALCOHOL

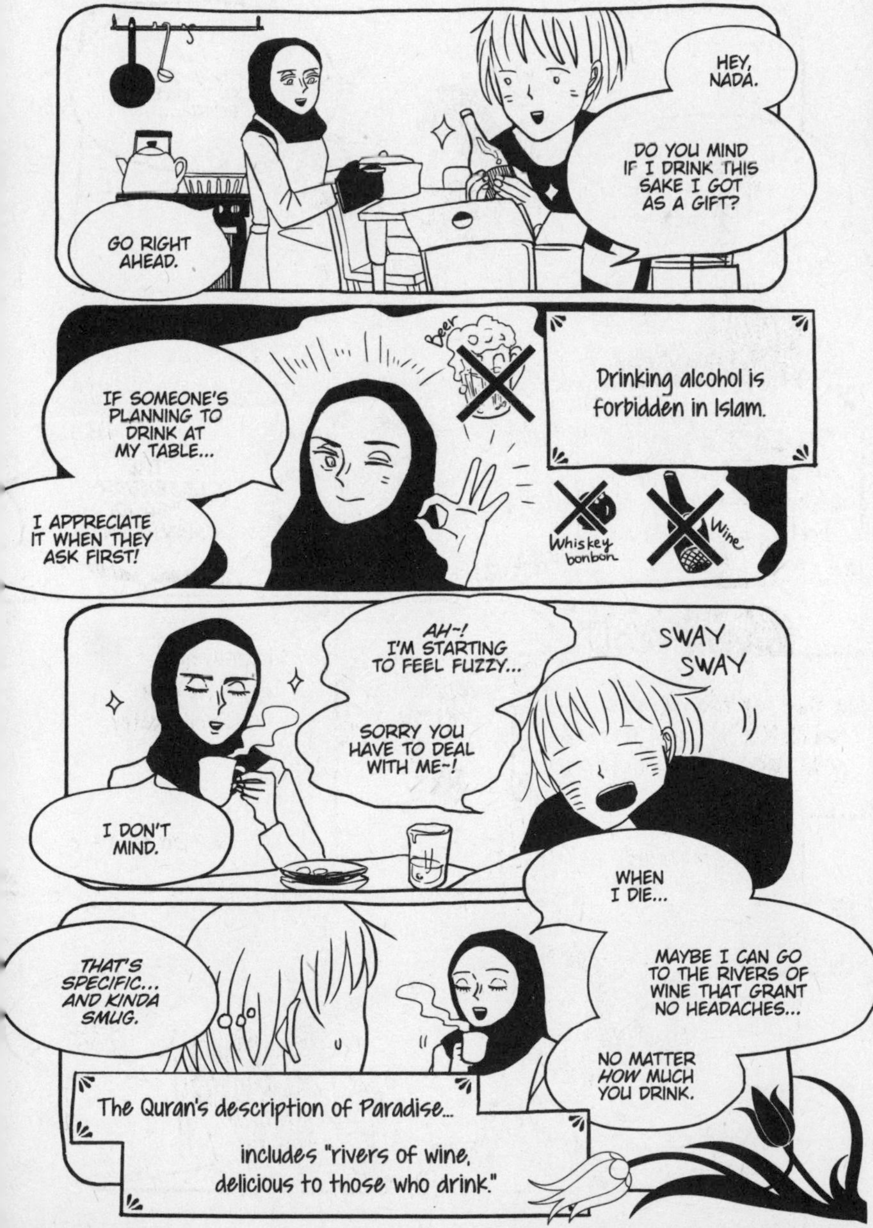
HEY, NADA.
DO YOU MIND IF I DRINK THIS SAKE I GOT AS A GIFT?
GO RIGHT AHEAD.
Drinking alcohol is forbidden in Islam.
Beer
Whiskey bonbon
Wine
IF SOMEONE'S PLANNING TO DRINK AT MY TABLE...
I APPRECIATE IT WHEN THEY ASK FIRST!
SWAY SWAY
AH~! I'M STARTING TO FEEL FUZZY...
SORRY YOU HAVE TO DEAL WITH ME~!
I DON'T MIND.
WHEN I DIE...
MAYBE I CAN GO TO THE RIVERS OF WINE THAT GRANT NO HEADACHES...
NO MATTER HOW MUCH YOU DRINK.
THAT'S SPECIFIC... AND KINDA SMUG.
The Quran's description of Paradise...
includes "rivers of wine, delicious to those who drink."

SAUDI CHAMPAGNE

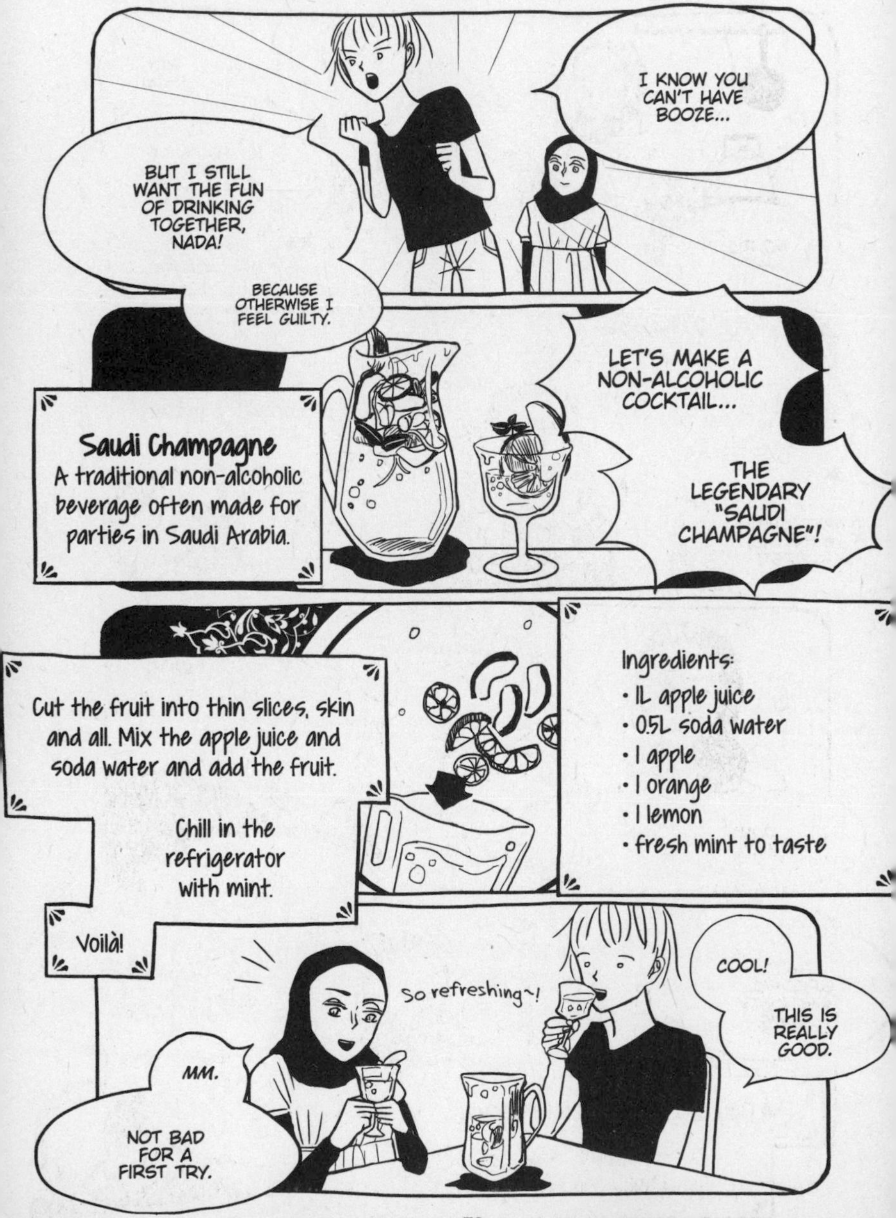

I KNOW YOU CAN'T HAVE BOOZE...
BUT I STILL WANT THE FUN OF DRINKING TOGETHER, NADA!
BECAUSE OTHERWISE I FEEL GUILTY.
LET'S MAKE A NON-ALCOHOLIC COCKTAIL...
THE LEGENDARY "SAUDI CHAMPAGNE"!
Saudi Champagne
A traditional non-alcoholic beverage often made for parties in Saudi Arabia.
Ingredients:
• 1L apple juice
• 0.5L soda water
• 1 apple
• 1 orange
• 1 lemon
• fresh mint to taste
Cut the fruit into thin slices, skin and all. Mix the apple juice and soda water and add the fruit.
Chill in the refrigerator with mint.
Voilà!
COOL!
THIS IS REALLY GOOD.
So refreshing~!
MM.
NOT BAD FOR A FIRST TRY.

CAKE

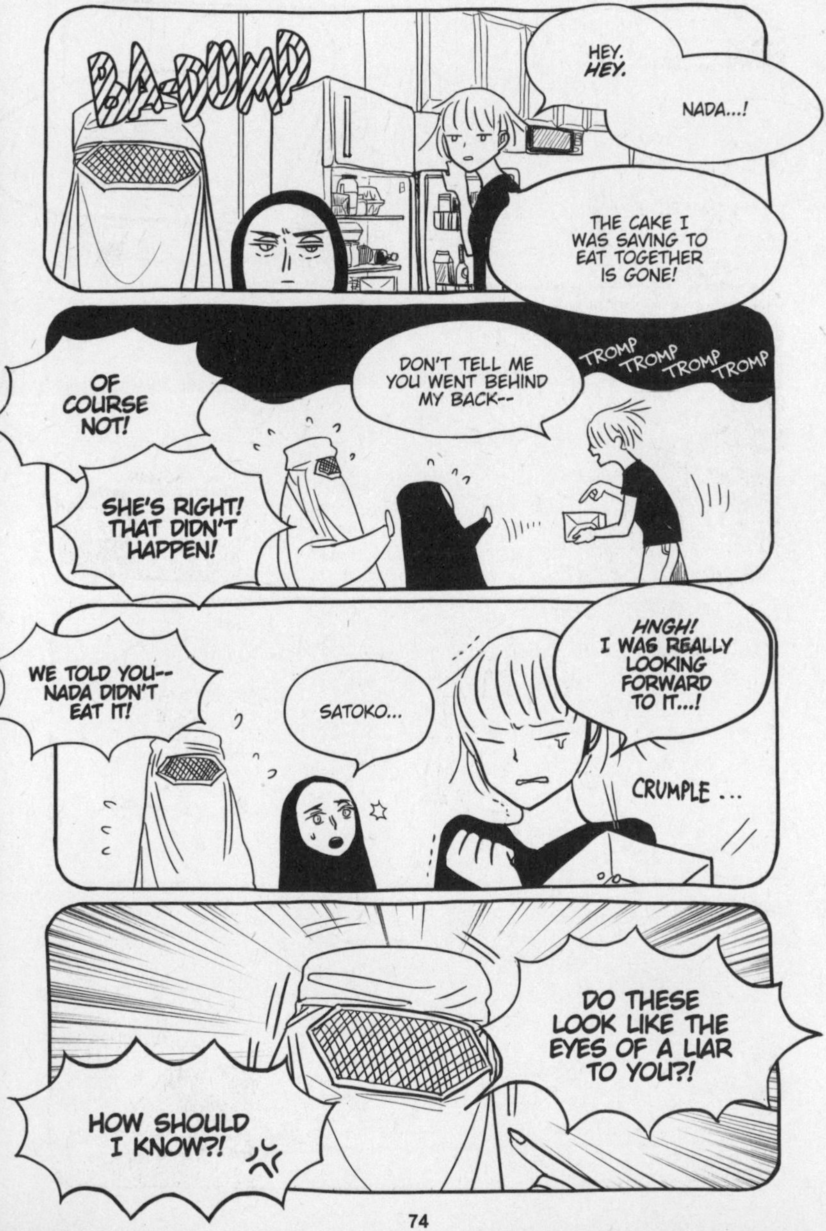

HEY. *HEY.* NADA...!
THE CAKE I WAS SAVING TO EAT TOGETHER IS GONE!
BA-DUMP
TROMP TROMP TROMP TROMP
DON'T TELL ME YOU WENT BEHIND MY BACK--
OF COURSE NOT!
SHE'S RIGHT! THAT DIDN'T HAPPEN!
HNGH! I WAS REALLY LOOKING FORWARD TO IT...!
CRUMPLE ...
SATOKO...
WE TOLD YOU-- NADA DIDN'T EAT IT!
DO THESE LOOK LIKE THE EYES OF A LIAR TO YOU?!
HOW SHOULD I KNOW?!

SORRY

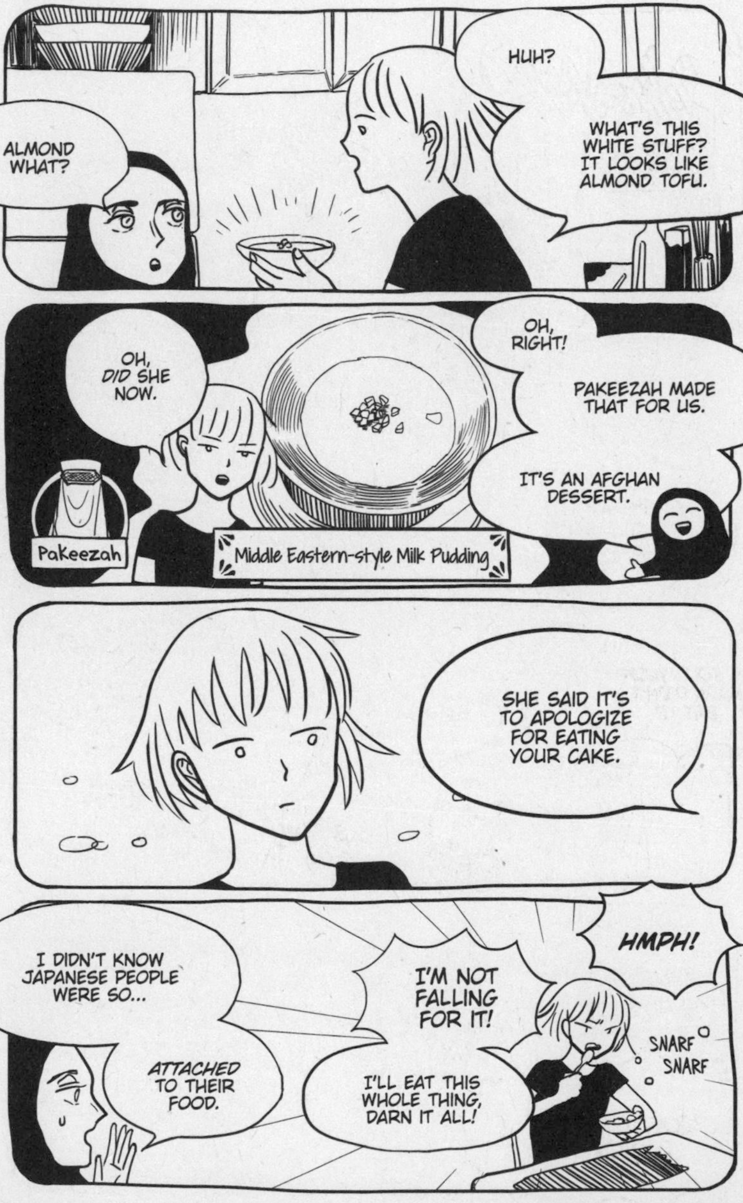

HUH?
WHAT'S THIS WHITE STUFF? IT LOOKS LIKE ALMOND TOFU.
ALMOND WHAT?
OH, RIGHT!
PAKEEZAH MADE THAT FOR US.
IT'S AN AFGHAN DESSERT.
OH, *DID* SHE NOW.
Middle Eastern-style Milk Pudding
Pakeezah
SHE SAID IT'S TO APOLOGIZE FOR EATING YOUR CAKE.
HMPH!
I'M NOT FALLING FOR IT!
SNARF SNARF
I'LL EAT THIS WHOLE THING, DARN IT ALL!
I DIDN'T KNOW JAPANESE PEOPLE WERE SO...
ATTACHED TO THEIR FOOD.

ARABIC DESSERT ♥

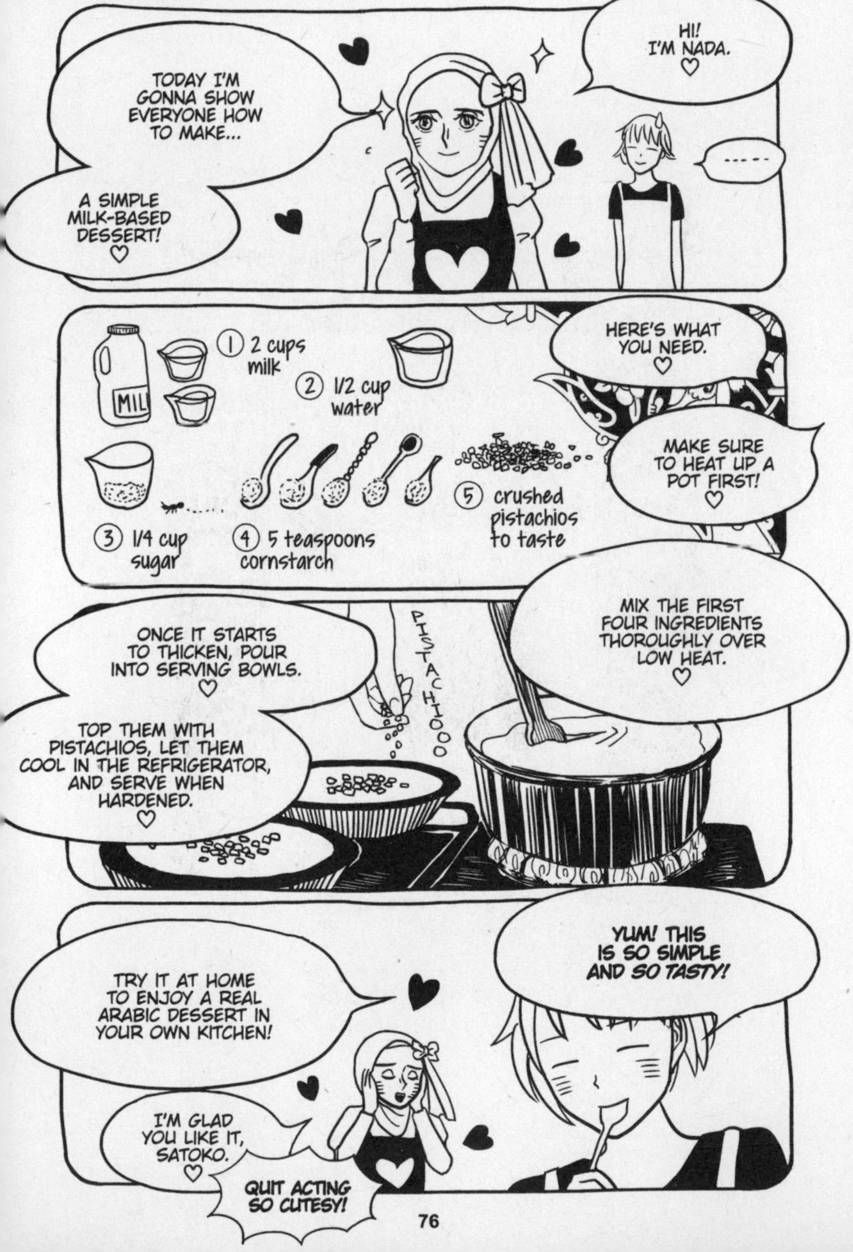
HI! I'M NADA. ♡
....
TODAY I'M GONNA SHOW EVERYONE HOW TO MAKE...
A SIMPLE MILK-BASED DESSERT! ♡
HERE'S WHAT YOU NEED. ♡
MAKE SURE TO HEAT UP A POT FIRST! ♡
① 2 cups milk
MIL
② 1/2 cup water
③ 1/4 cup sugar
④ 5 teaspoons cornstarch
⑤ crushed pistachios to taste
MIX THE FIRST FOUR INGREDIENTS THOROUGHLY OVER LOW HEAT. ♡
PISTACHIO
ONCE IT STARTS TO THICKEN, POUR INTO SERVING BOWLS. ♡
TOP THEM WITH PISTACHIOS, LET THEM COOL IN THE REFRIGERATOR, AND SERVE WHEN HARDENED. ♡
YUM! THIS IS SO SIMPLE AND SO TASTY!
TRY IT AT HOME TO ENJOY A REAL ARABIC DESSERT IN YOUR OWN KITCHEN!
I'M GLAD YOU LIKE IT, SATOKO. ♡
QUIT ACTING SO CUTESY!

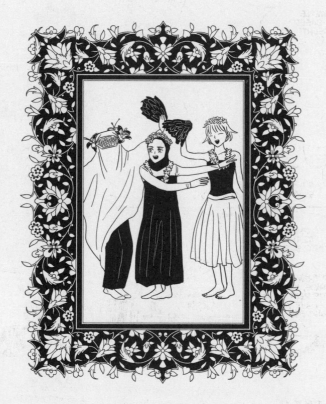

SATOKO AND NADA

Presented by Yupechika

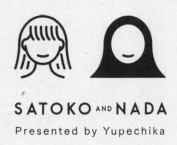

SATOKO AND NADA

Presented by Yupechika

HOMESICK

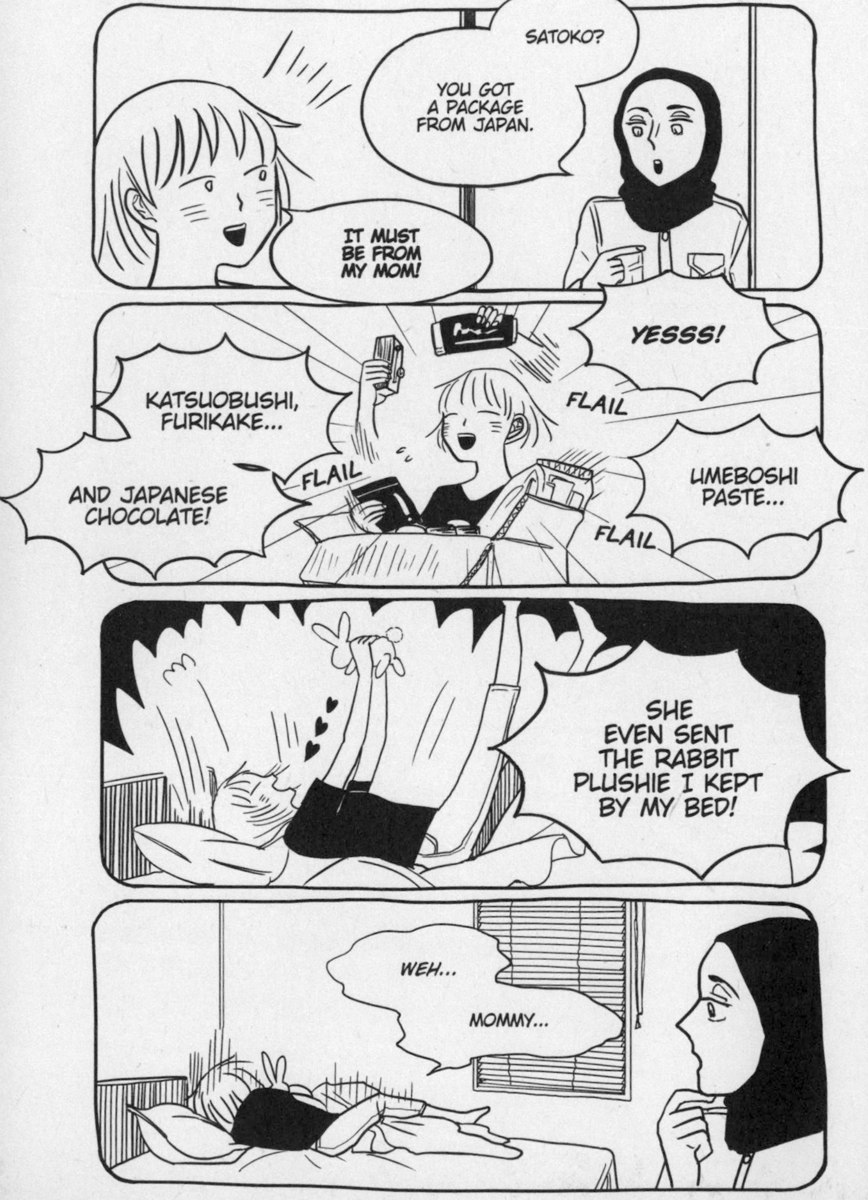
SATOKO?
YOU GOT A PACKAGE FROM JAPAN.
IT MUST BE FROM MY MOM!
YESSS!
FLAIL
UMEBOSHI PASTE...
FLAIL
KATSUOBUSHI, FURIKAKE...
FLAIL
AND JAPANESE CHOCOLATE!
SHE EVEN SENT THE RABBIT PLUSHIE I KEPT BY MY BED!
WEH...
MOMMY...

HOMESICK 2

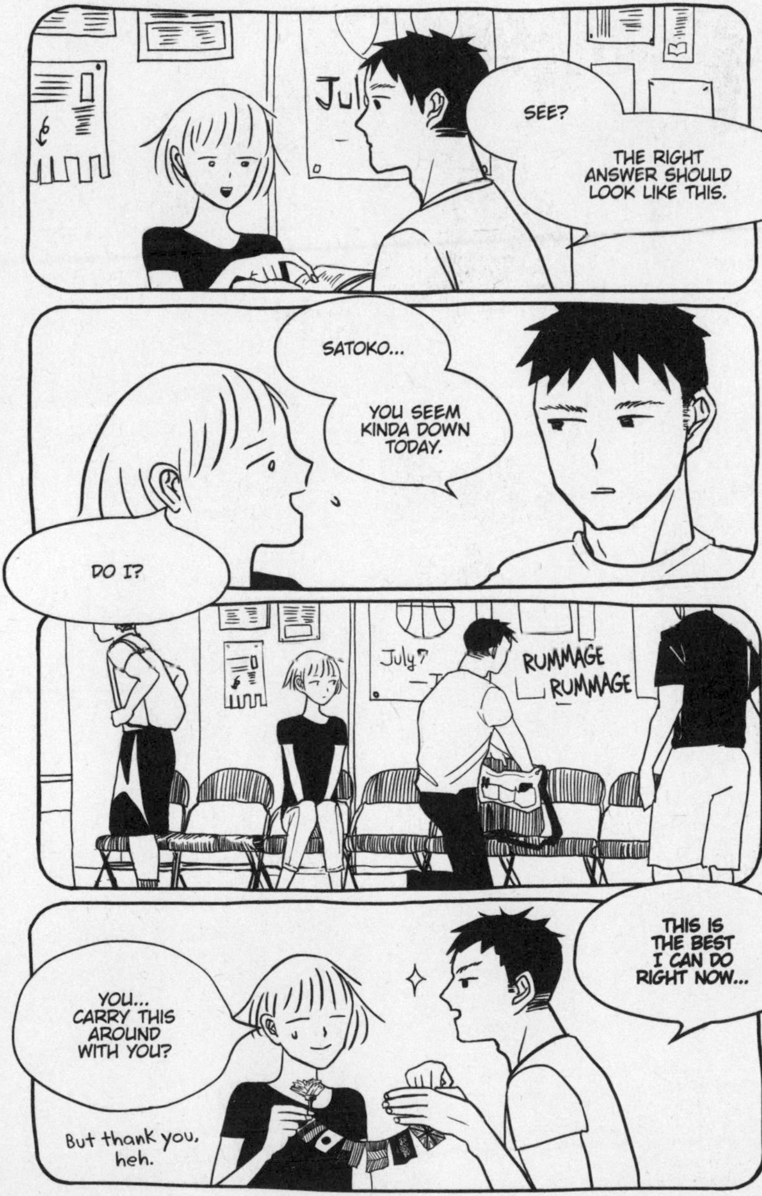
SEE?
THE RIGHT ANSWER SHOULD LOOK LIKE THIS.
SATOKO...
YOU SEEM KINDA DOWN TODAY.
DO I?
RUMMAGE
RUMMAGE
THIS IS THE BEST I CAN DO RIGHT NOW...
YOU... CARRY THIS AROUND WITH YOU?
But thank you, heh.

HOMESICK 3

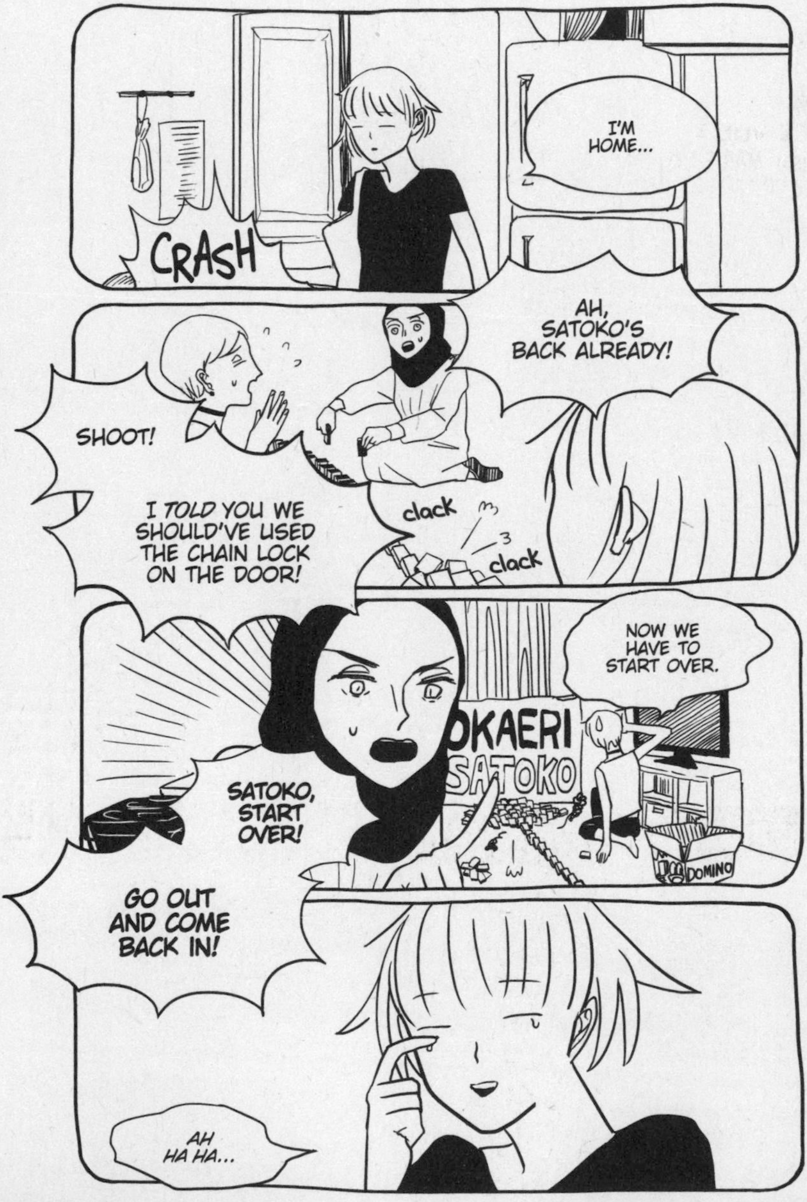
I'M HOME...
CRASH
AH, SATOKO'S BACK ALREADY!
SHOOT!
clack
clack
I TOLD YOU WE SHOULD'VE USED THE CHAIN LOCK ON THE DOOR!
NOW WE HAVE TO START OVER.
OKAERI SATOKO
DOMINO
SATOKO, START OVER!
GO OUT AND COME BACK IN!
AH HA HA...

HOLY TEXT TABOOS

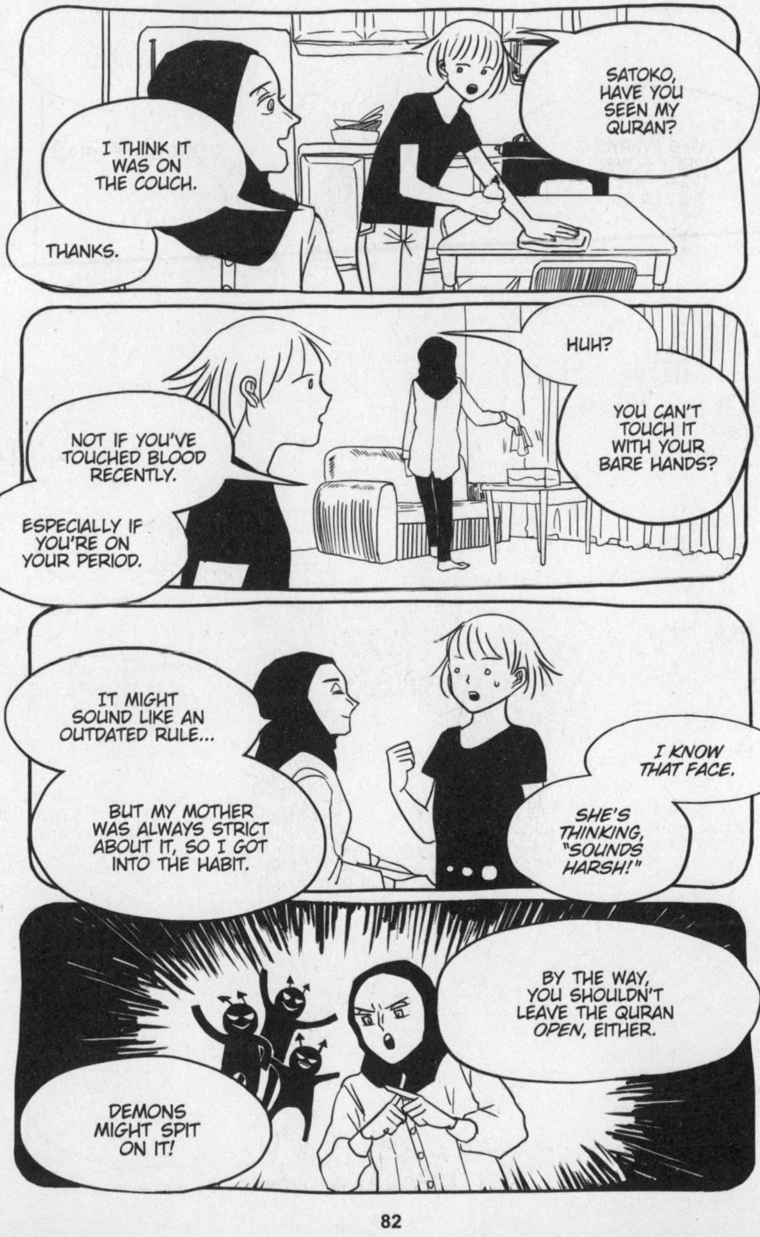
SATOKO, HAVE YOU SEEN MY QURAN?
I THINK IT WAS ON THE COUCH.
THANKS.
HUH?
YOU CAN'T TOUCH IT WITH YOUR BARE HANDS?
NOT IF YOU'VE TOUCHED BLOOD RECENTLY.
ESPECIALLY IF YOU'RE ON YOUR PERIOD.
IT MIGHT SOUND LIKE AN OUTDATED RULE...
BUT MY MOTHER WAS ALWAYS STRICT ABOUT IT, SO I GOT INTO THE HABIT.
I KNOW THAT FACE.
SHE'S THINKING, "SOUNDS HARSH!"
BY THE WAY, YOU SHOULDN'T LEAVE THE QURAN OPEN, EITHER.
DEMONS MIGHT SPIT ON IT!

MARRIAGE

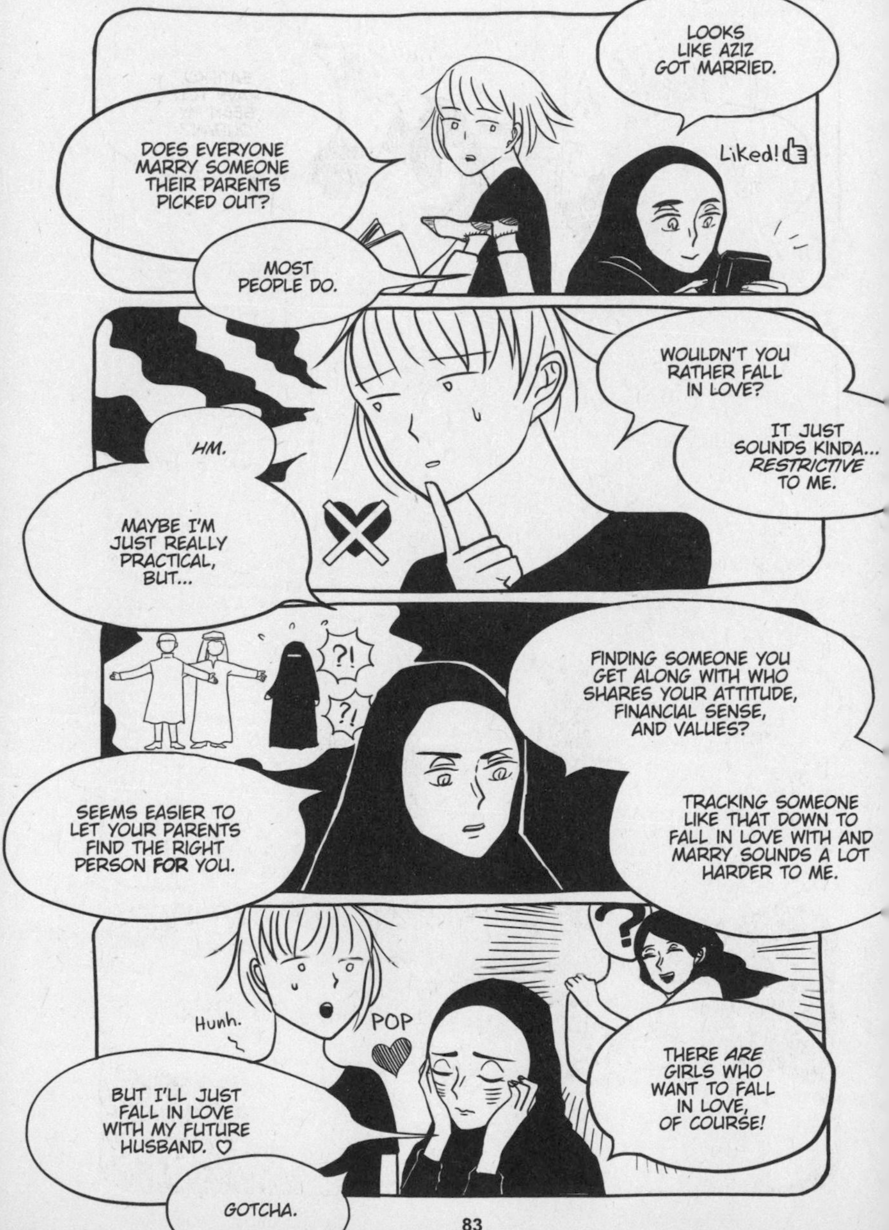
LOOKS LIKE AZIZ GOT MARRIED.
Liked!
DOES EVERYONE MARRY SOMEONE THEIR PARENTS PICKED OUT?
MOST PEOPLE DO.
WOULDN'T YOU RATHER FALL IN LOVE?
IT JUST SOUNDS KINDA... *RESTRICTIVE* TO ME.
HM.
MAYBE I'M JUST REALLY PRACTICAL, BUT...
FINDING SOMEONE YOU GET ALONG WITH WHO SHARES YOUR ATTITUDE, FINANCIAL SENSE, AND VALUES?
?!
?!
TRACKING SOMEONE LIKE THAT DOWN TO FALL IN LOVE WITH AND MARRY SOUNDS A LOT HARDER TO ME.
SEEMS EASIER TO LET YOUR PARENTS FIND THE RIGHT PERSON **FOR** YOU.
?
THERE *ARE* GIRLS WHO WANT TO FALL IN LOVE, OF COURSE!
POP
Hunh.
BUT I'LL JUST FALL IN LOVE WITH MY FUTURE HUSBAND. ♡
GOTCHA.

GETTING ALONG

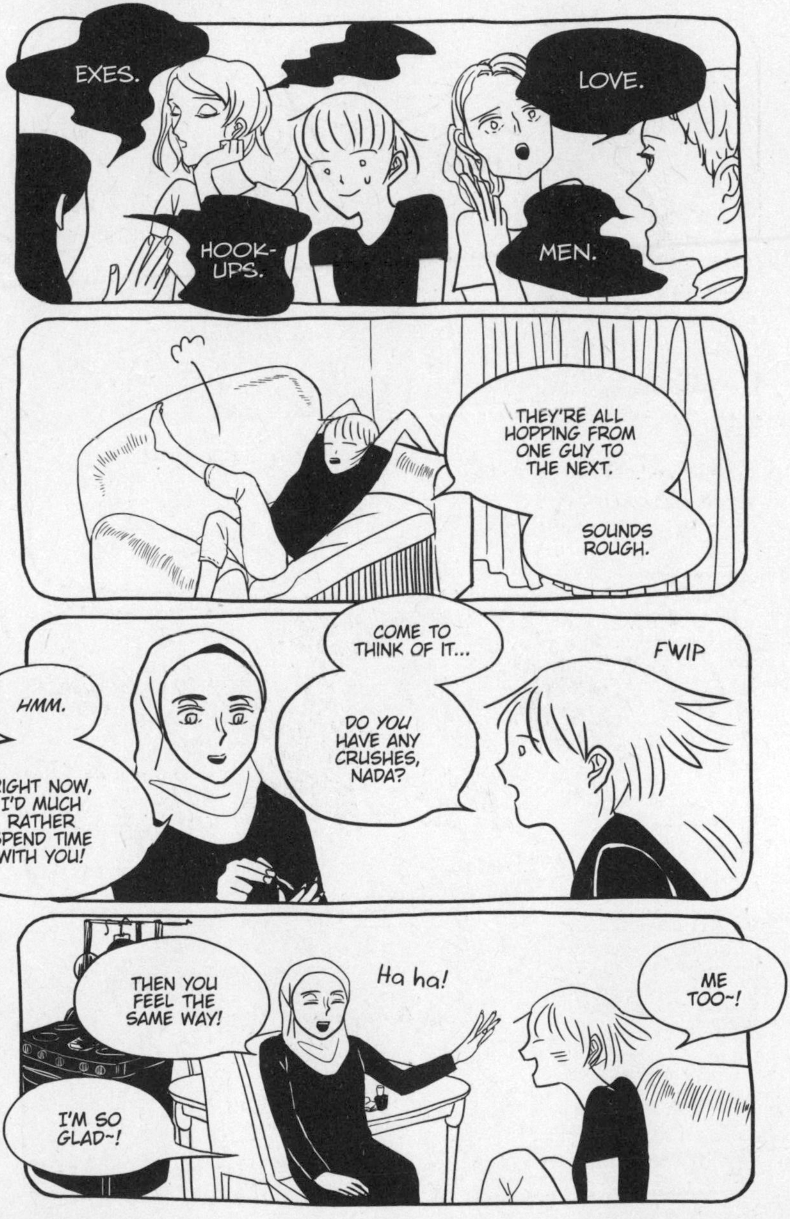

LOVE.
MEN.
HOOK-UPS.
EXES.
THEY'RE ALL HOPPING FROM ONE GUY TO THE NEXT.
SOUNDS ROUGH.
FWIP
COME TO THINK OF IT...
DO YOU HAVE ANY CRUSHES, NADA?
HMM.
RIGHT NOW, I'D MUCH RATHER SPEND TIME WITH YOU!
ME TOO~!
Ha ha!
THEN YOU FEEL THE SAME WAY!
I'M SO GLAD~!

COMPLIMENT

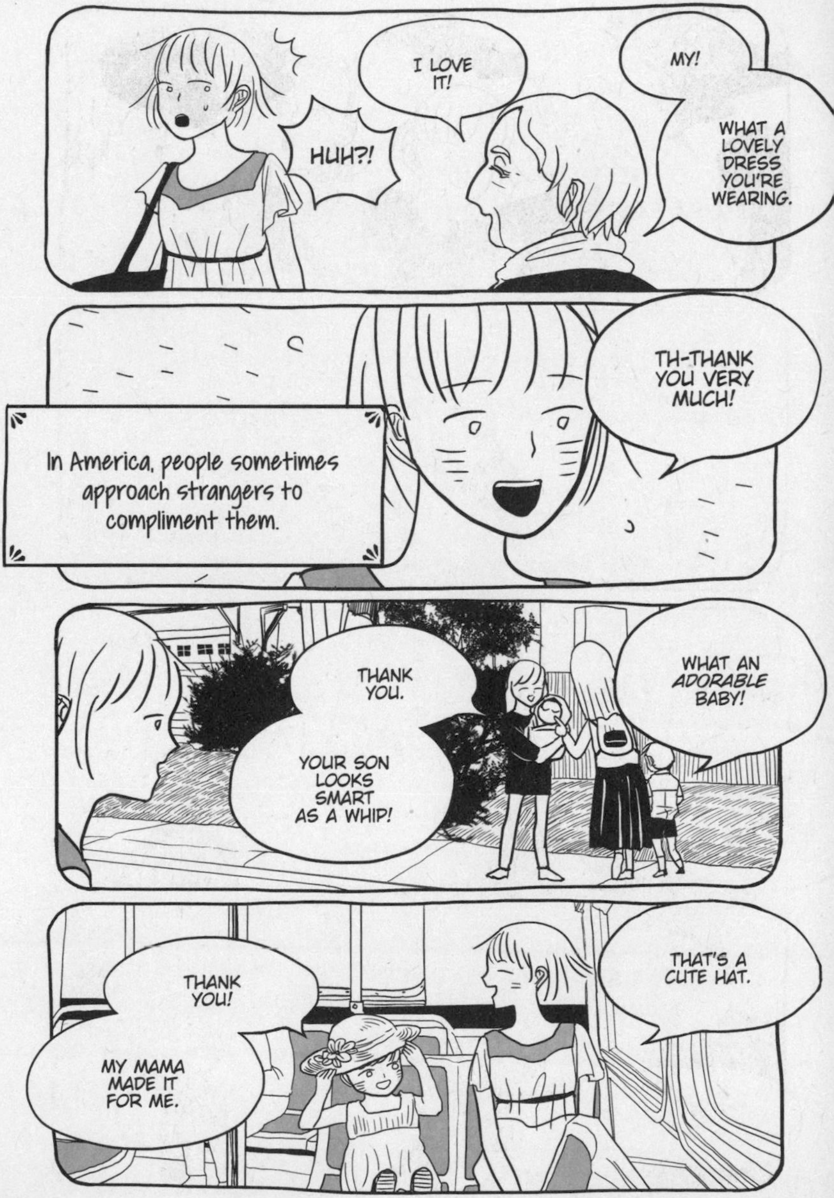

MY!
WHAT A LOVELY DRESS YOU'RE WEARING.
I LOVE IT!
HUH?!
TH-THANK YOU VERY MUCH!
In America, people sometimes approach strangers to compliment them.
WHAT AN *ADORABLE* BABY!
THANK YOU.
YOUR SON LOOKS SMART AS A WHIP!
THAT'S A CUTE HAT.
THANK YOU!
MY MAMA MADE IT FOR ME.

MASHALLAH!

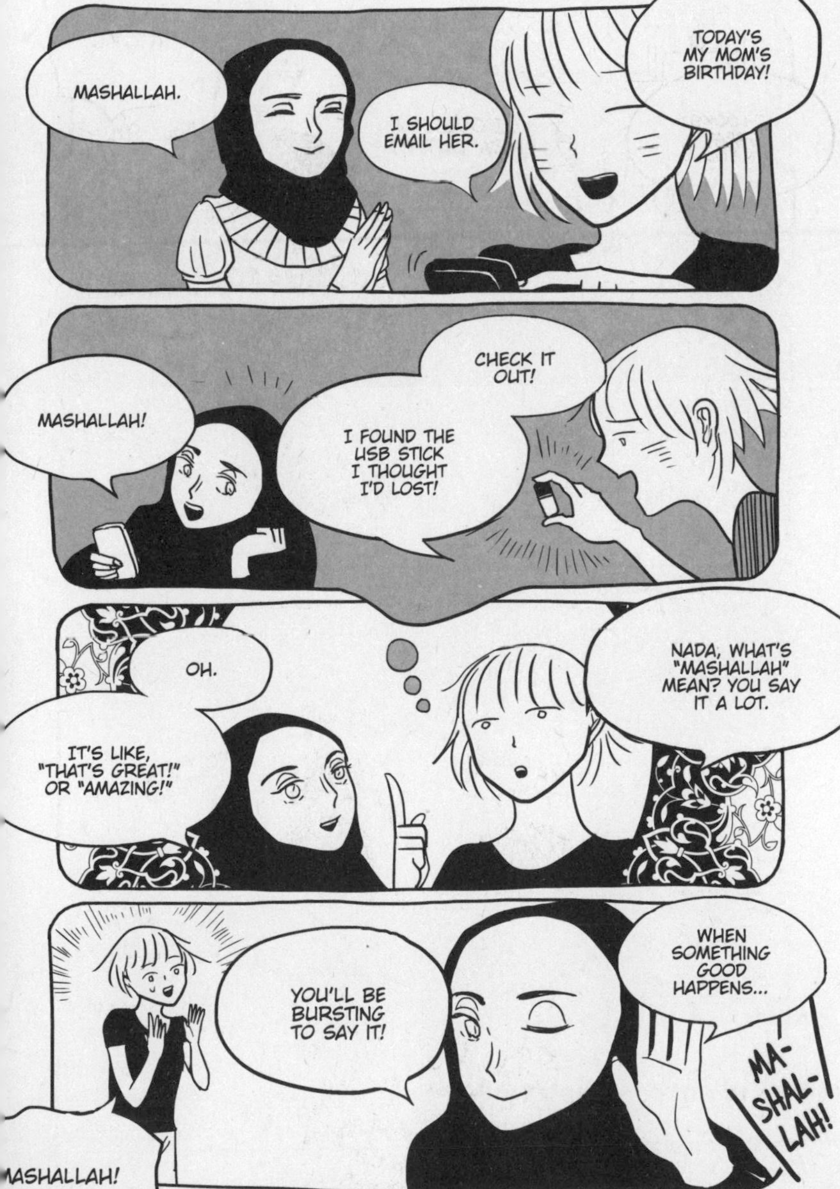
TODAY'S MY MOM'S BIRTHDAY!
I SHOULD EMAIL HER.
MASHALLAH.
CHECK IT OUT!
I FOUND THE USB STICK I THOUGHT I'D LOST!
MASHALLAH!
NADA, WHAT'S "MASHALLAH" MEAN? YOU SAY IT A LOT.
OH.
IT'S LIKE, "THAT'S GREAT!" OR "AMAZING!"
WHEN SOMETHING GOOD HAPPENS...
MA-SHAL-LAH!
YOU'LL BE BURSTING TO SAY IT!
ASHALLAH!

SAY IT!

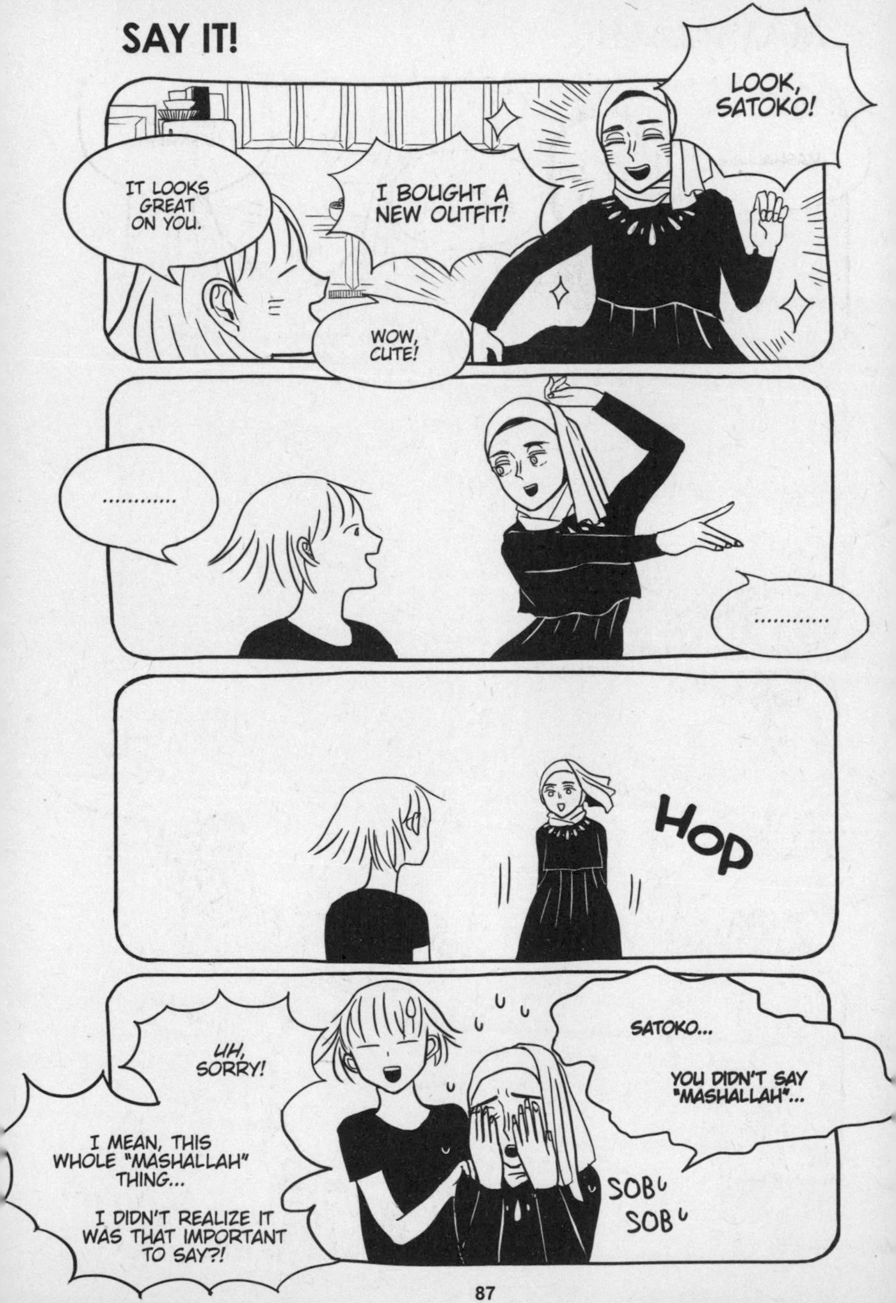

LOOK, SATOKO!
I BOUGHT A NEW OUTFIT!
WOW, CUTE!
IT LOOKS GREAT ON YOU.
....
....
HOP
SATOKO...
YOU DIDN'T SAY "MASHALLAH"...
SOB SOB
UH, SORRY!
I MEAN, THIS WHOLE "MASHALLAH" THING...
I DIDN'T REALIZE IT WAS THAT IMPORTANT TO SAY?!

THAT WORD

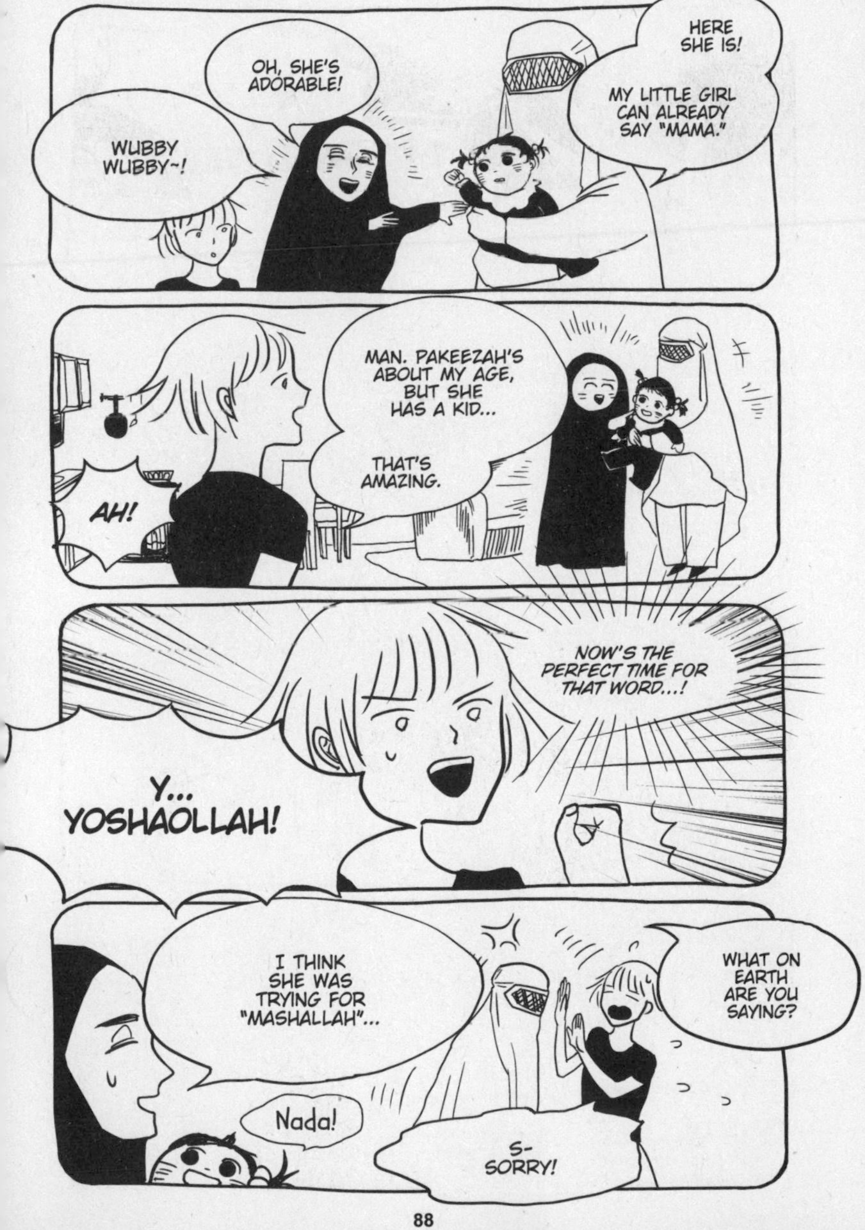
HERE SHE IS!
MY LITTLE GIRL CAN ALREADY SAY "MAMA."
OH, SHE'S ADORABLE!
WUBBY WUBBY~!
MAN. PAKEEZAH'S ABOUT MY AGE, BUT SHE HAS A KID...
THAT'S AMAZING.
AH!
NOW'S THE PERFECT TIME FOR THAT WORD...!
Y... YOSHAOLLAH!
WHAT ON EARTH ARE YOU SAYING?
I THINK SHE WAS TRYING FOR "MASHALLAH"...
S- SORRY!
Nada!

GLOOMY

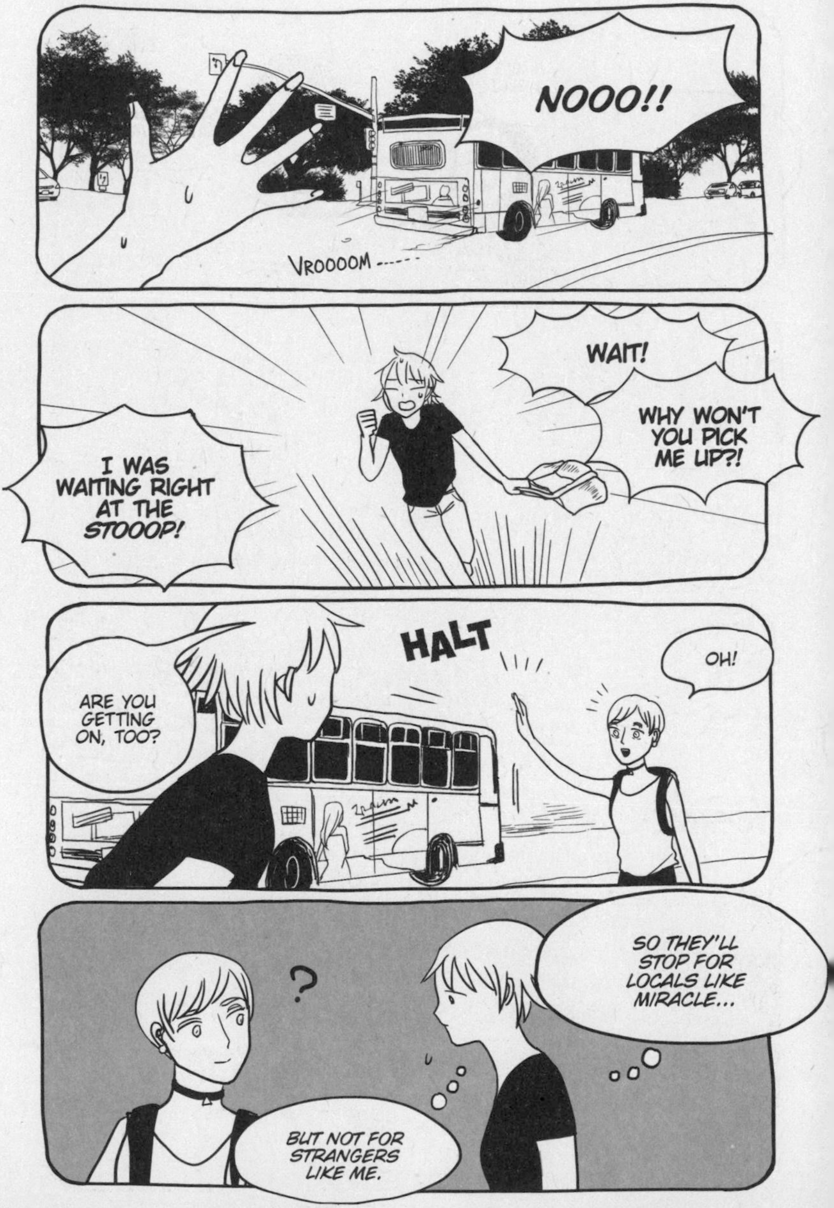
NOOO!!
VROOOM
WAIT!
WHY WON'T YOU PICK ME UP?!
I WAS WAITING RIGHT AT THE STOOOP!
OH!
HALT
ARE YOU GETTING ON, TOO?
SO THEY'LL STOP FOR LOCALS LIKE MIRACLE...
BUT NOT FOR STRANGERS LIKE ME.

OOPS

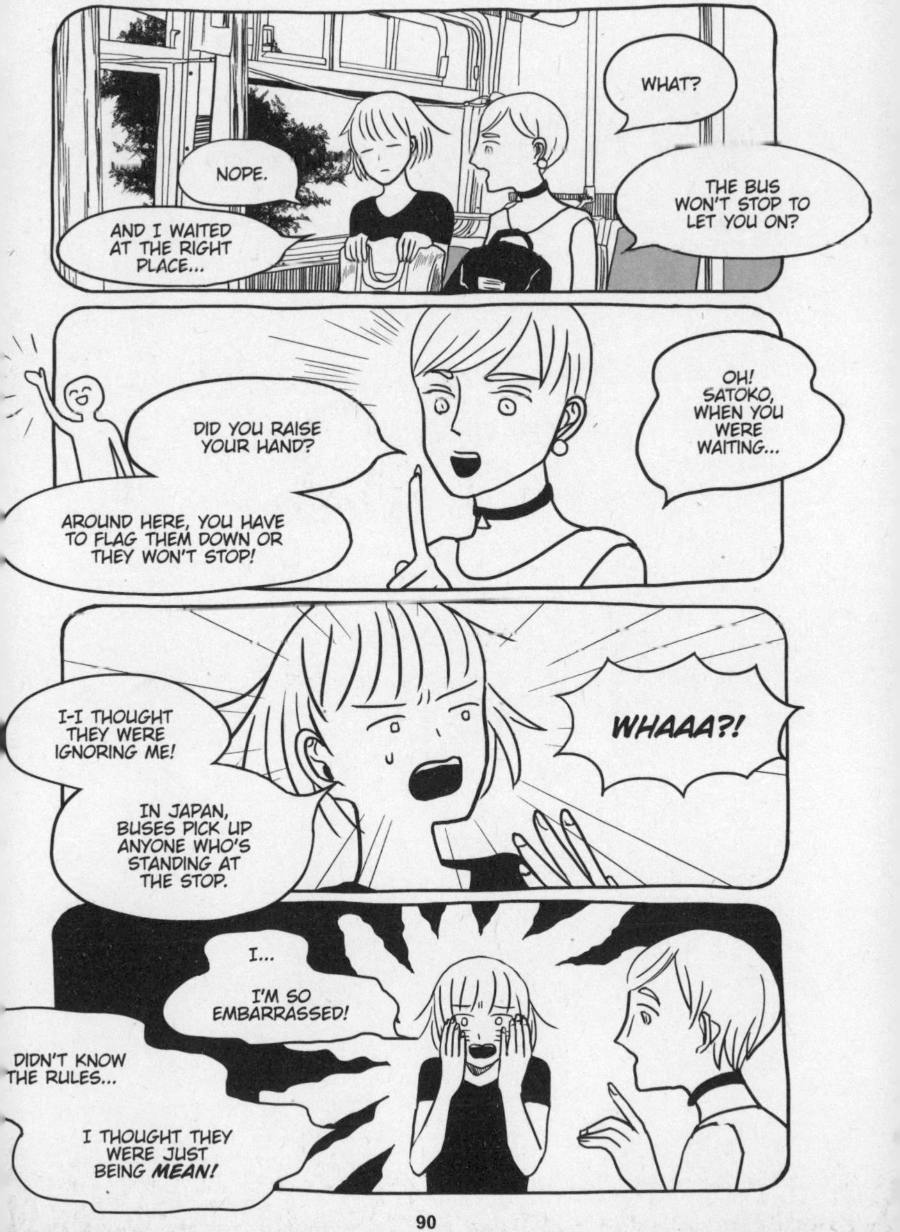

WHAT?
THE BUS WON'T STOP TO LET YOU ON?
NOPE.
AND I WAITED AT THE RIGHT PLACE...
OH! SATOKO, WHEN YOU WERE WAITING...
DID YOU RAISE YOUR HAND?
AROUND HERE, YOU HAVE TO FLAG THEM DOWN OR THEY WON'T STOP!
WHAAA?!
I-I THOUGHT THEY WERE IGNORING ME!
IN JAPAN, BUSES PICK UP ANYONE WHO'S STANDING AT THE STOP.
I...
I'M SO EMBARRASSED!
DIDN'T KNOW THE RULES...
I THOUGHT THEY WERE JUST BEING ***MEAN!***

SATOKO AND NADA

Presented by Yupechika

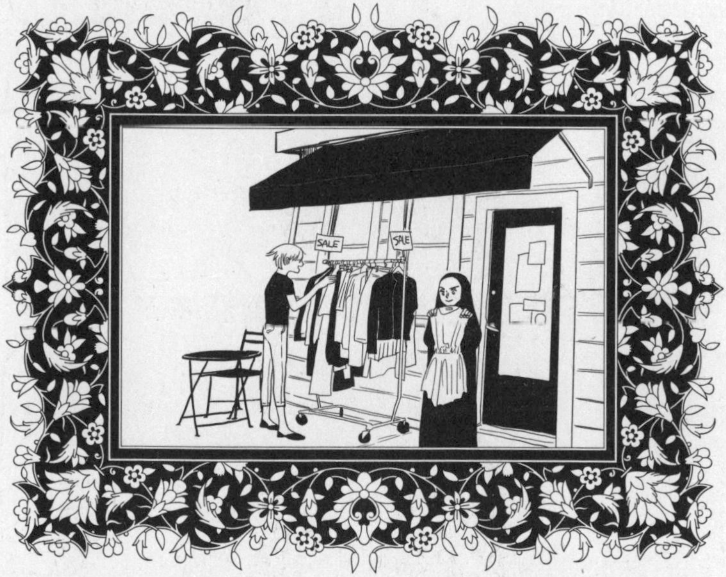
SALE
SALE

SATOKO AND NADA

Presented by Yupechika

BAGELS

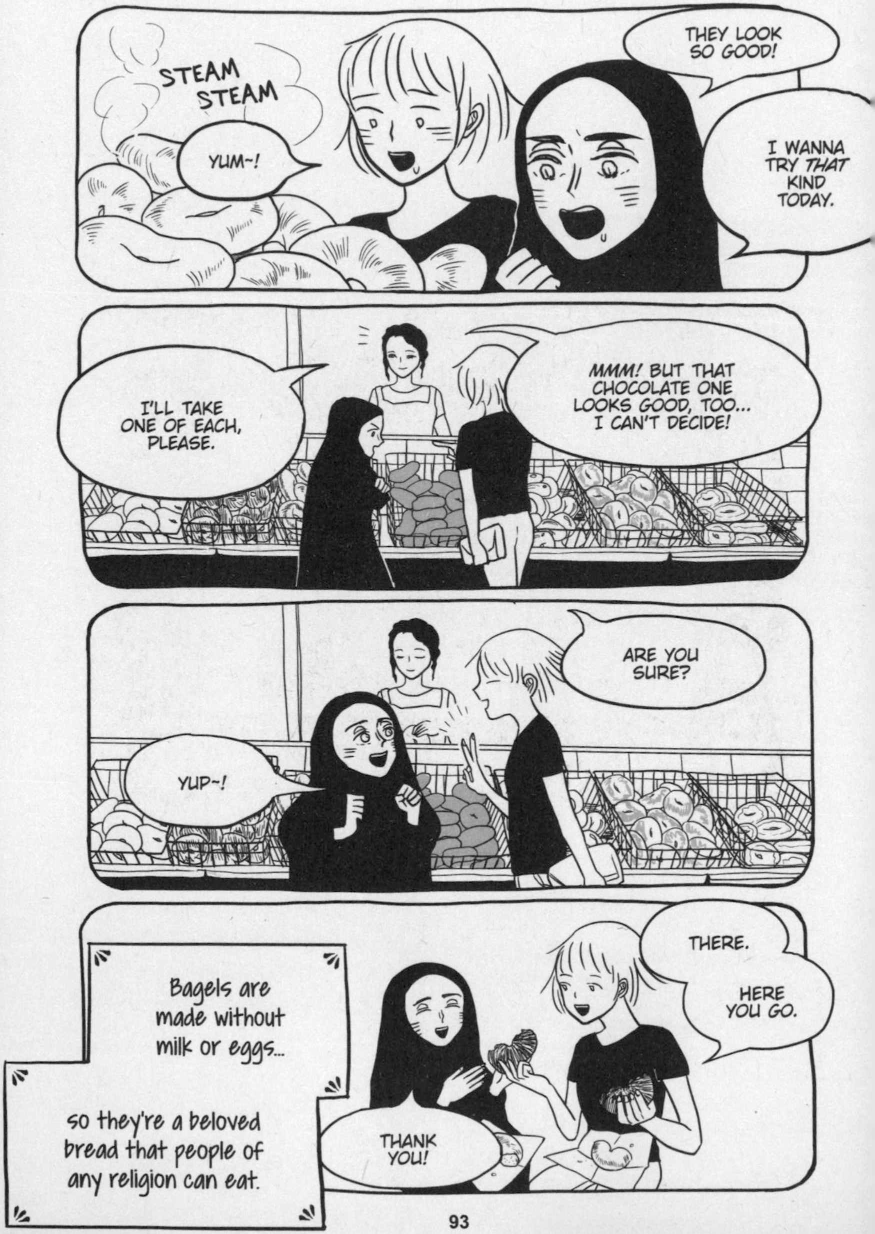

THEY LOOK SO GOOD!
I WANNA TRY *THAT* KIND TODAY.
STEAM STEAM
YUM~!
MMM! BUT THAT CHOCOLATE ONE LOOKS GOOD, TOO... I CAN'T DECIDE!
I'LL TAKE ONE OF EACH, PLEASE.
ARE YOU SURE?
YUP~!
THERE.
HERE YOU GO.
Bagels are made without milk or eggs...
THANK YOU!
so they're a beloved bread that people of any religion can eat.

PILGRIMAGE

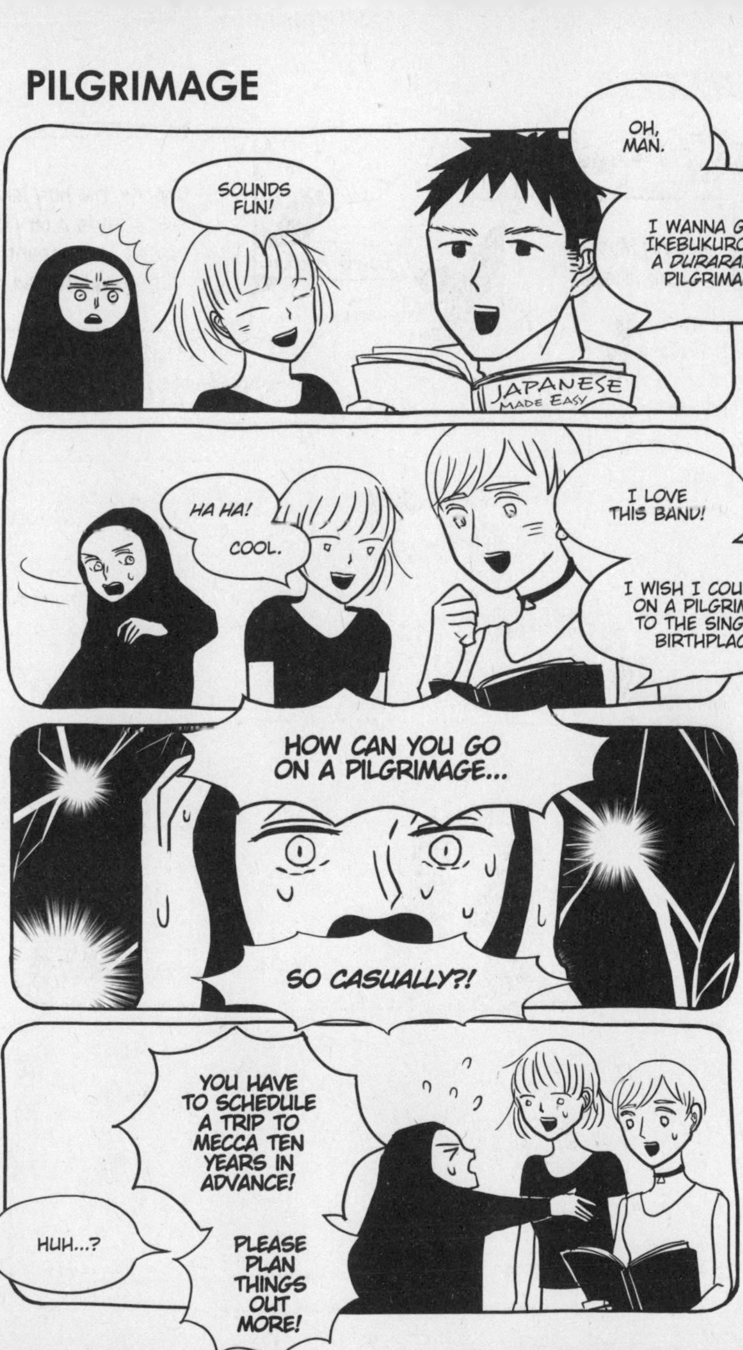
OH, MAN.
I WANNA GO TO IKEBUKURO FOR A *DURARARA!!* PILGRIMAGE.
SOUNDS FUN!
JAPANESE MADE EASY
I LOVE THIS BAND!
I WISH I COULD GO ON A PILGRIMAGE TO THE SINGER'S BIRTHPLACE.
HA HA!
COOL.
HOW CAN YOU GO ON A PILGRIMAGE...
SO CASUALLY?!
YOU HAVE TO SCHEDULE A TRIP TO MECCA TEN YEARS IN ADVANCE!
PLEASE PLAN THINGS OUT MORE!
HUH...?

MECCA

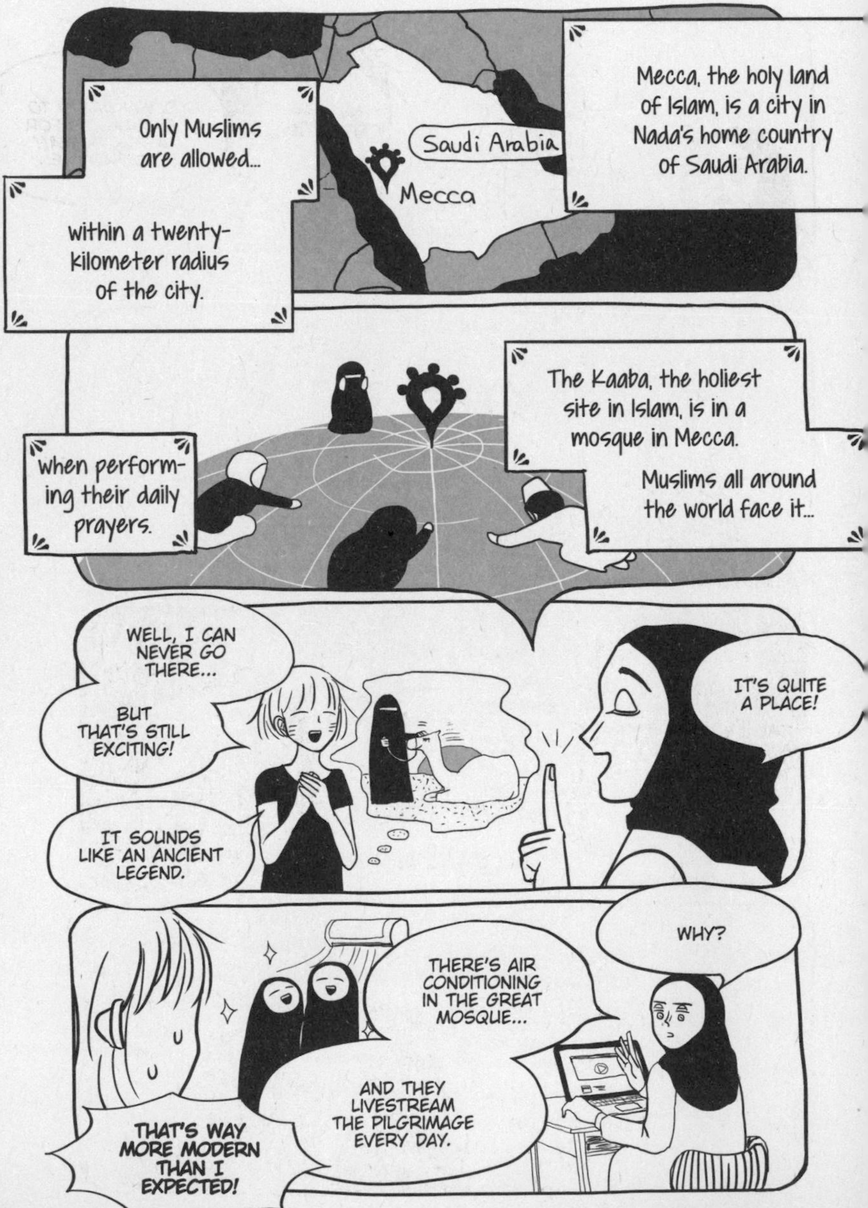
Mecca, the holy land of Islam, is a city in Nada's home country of Saudi Arabia.
Saudi Arabia
Mecca
Only Muslims are allowed...
within a twenty-kilometer radius of the city.
The Kaaba, the holiest site in Islam, is in a mosque in Mecca.
Muslims all around the world face it...
when performing their daily prayers.
IT'S QUITE A PLACE!
WELL, I CAN NEVER GO THERE...
BUT THAT'S STILL EXCITING!
IT SOUNDS LIKE AN ANCIENT LEGEND.
WHY?
THERE'S AIR CONDITIONING IN THE GREAT MOSQUE...
AND THEY LIVESTREAM THE PILGRIMAGE EVERY DAY.
THAT'S WAY MORE MODERN THAN I EXPECTED!

SECRET DEVICE

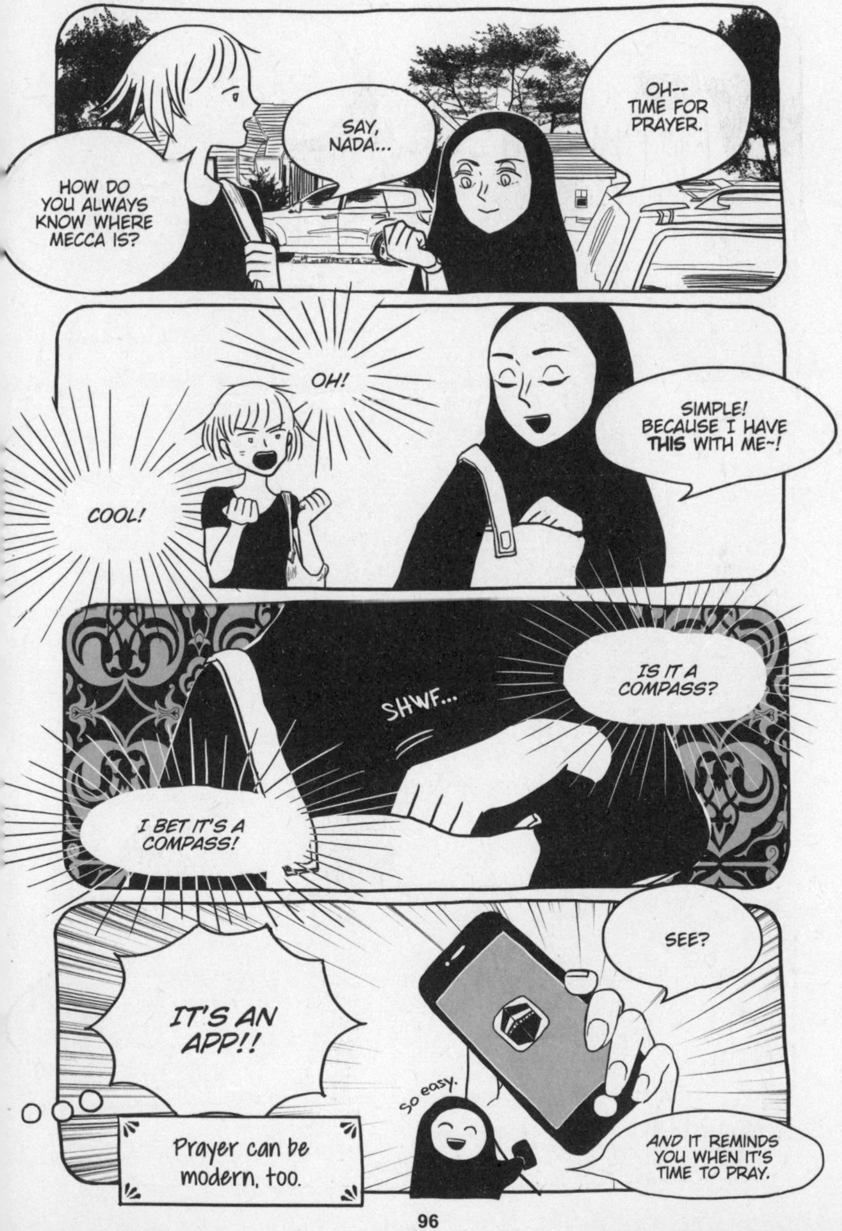
OH-- TIME FOR PRAYER.
SAY, NADA...
HOW DO YOU ALWAYS KNOW WHERE MECCA IS?
SIMPLE! BECAUSE I HAVE **THIS** WITH ME~!
OH!
COOL!
IS IT A COMPASS?
SHWF...
I BET IT'S A COMPASS!
SEE?
IT'S AN APP!!
so easy.
AND IT REMINDS YOU WHEN IT'S TIME TO PRAY.
Prayer can be modern, too.

SECRET ROOM

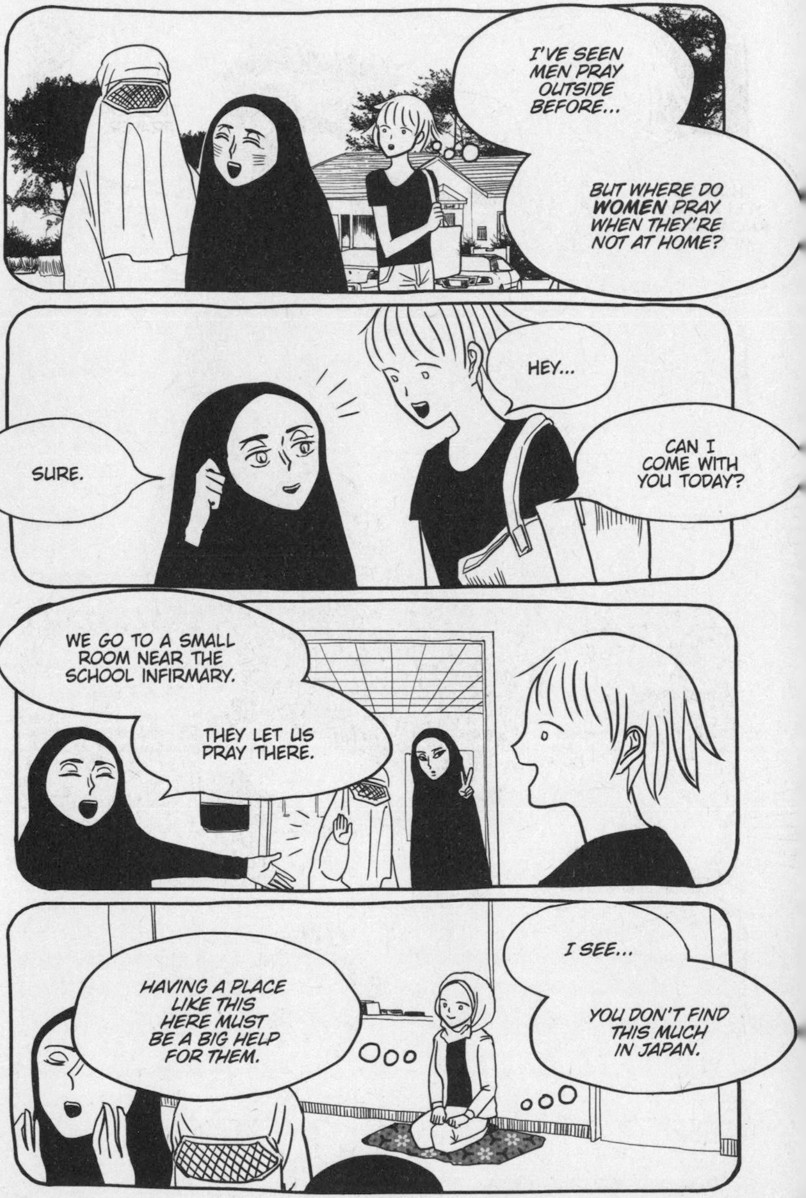

I'VE SEEN MEN PRAY OUTSIDE BEFORE...
BUT WHERE DO **WOMEN** PRAY WHEN THEY'RE NOT AT HOME?
HEY...
CAN I COME WITH YOU TODAY?
SURE.
WE GO TO A SMALL ROOM NEAR THE SCHOOL INFIRMARY.
THEY LET US PRAY THERE.
I SEE...
YOU DON'T FIND THIS MUCH IN JAPAN.
HAVING A PLACE LIKE THIS HERE MUST BE A BIG HELP FOR THEM.

COFFEE

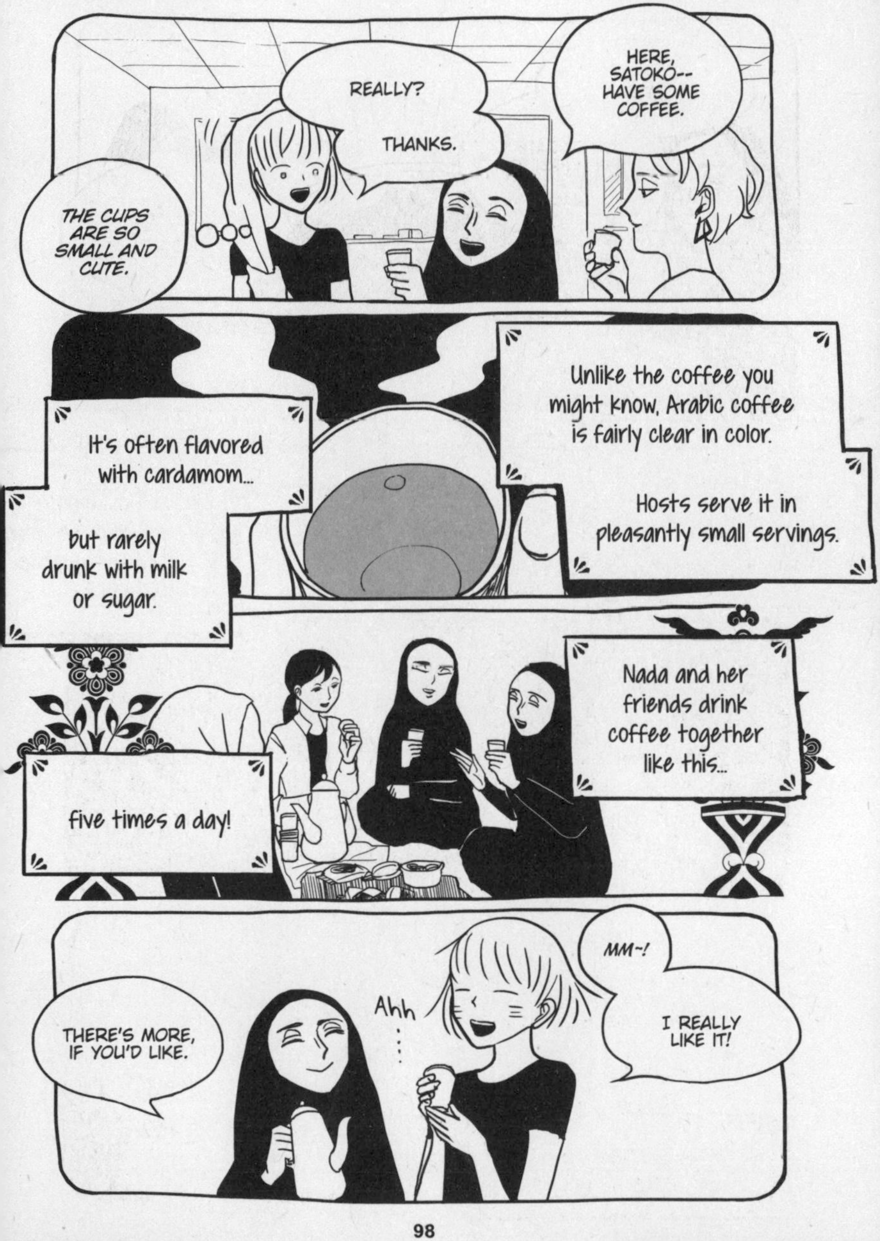

HERE, SATOKO-- HAVE SOME COFFEE.
REALLY?
THANKS.
THE CUPS ARE SO SMALL AND CUTE.
Unlike the coffee you might know, Arabic coffee is fairly clear in color.
Hosts serve it in pleasantly small servings.
It's often flavored with cardamom...
but rarely drunk with milk or sugar.
Nada and her friends drink coffee together like this...
five times a day!
MM-!
I REALLY LIKE IT!
Ahh...
THERE'S MORE, IF YOU'D LIKE.

DATES

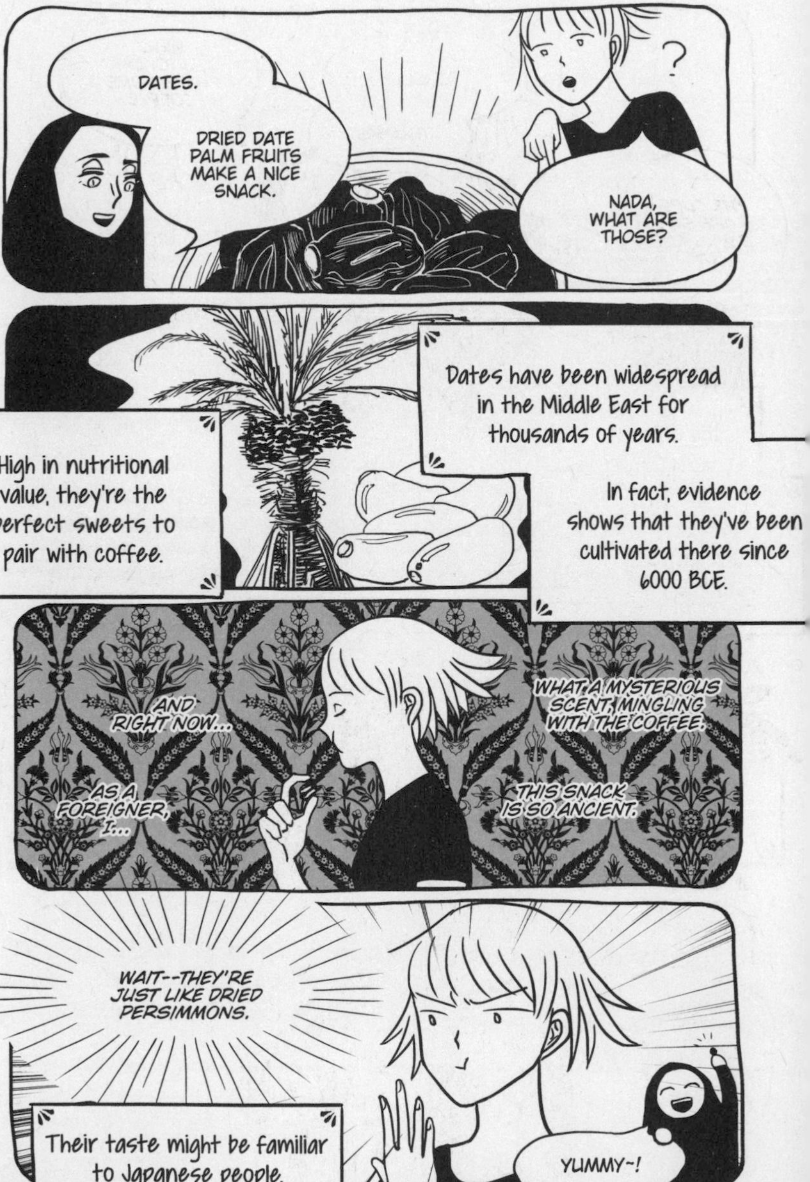
?
NADA, WHAT ARE THOSE?
DATES.
DRIED DATE PALM FRUITS MAKE A NICE SNACK.
Dates have been widespread in the Middle East for thousands of years.
In fact, evidence shows that they've been cultivated there since 6000 BCE.
High in nutritional value, they're the perfect sweets to pair with coffee.
WHAT A MYSTERIOUS SCENT, MINGLING WITH THE COFFEE.
THIS SNACK IS SO ANCIENT.
AND RIGHT NOW...
AS A FOREIGNER, I...
WAIT--THEY'RE JUST LIKE DRIED PERSIMMONS.
YUMMY~!
Their taste might be familiar to Japanese people.

NO PRESSURE

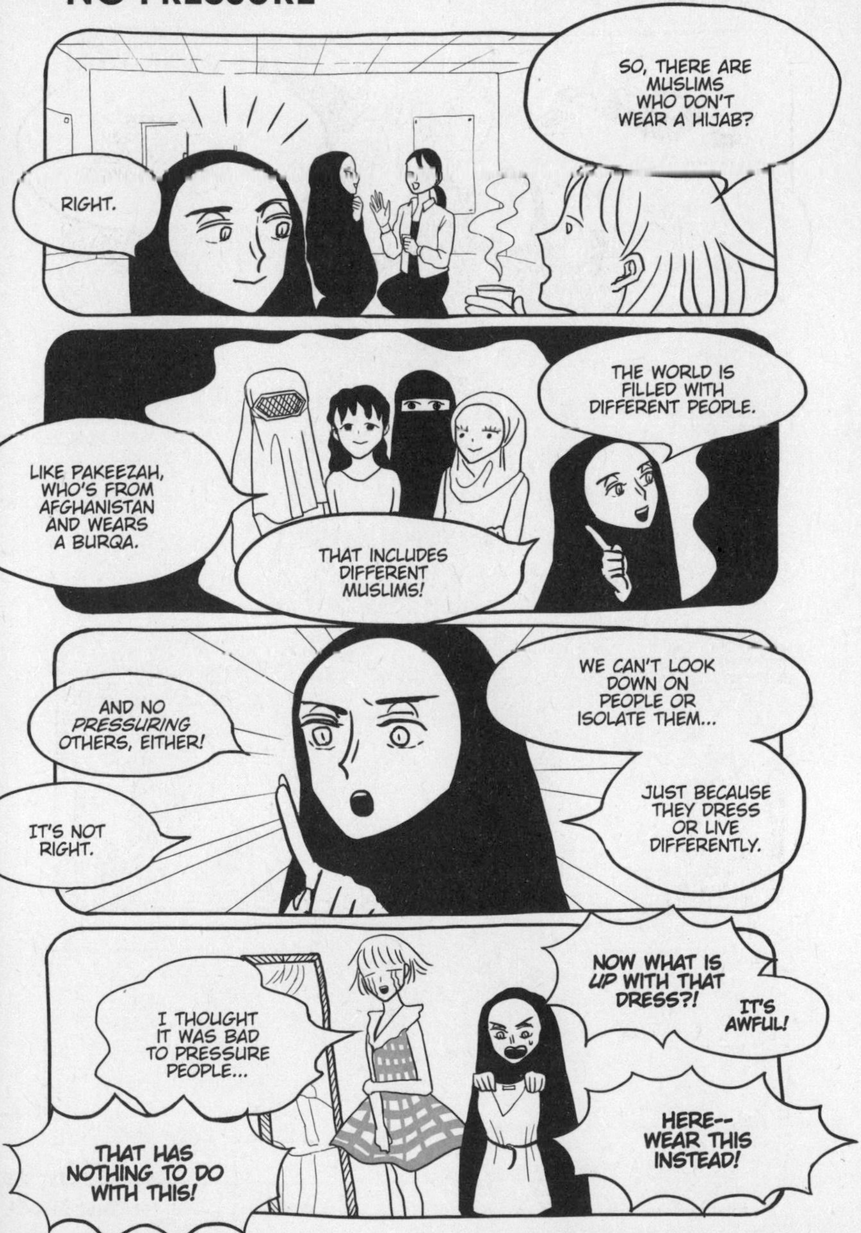

SO, THERE ARE MUSLIMS WHO DON'T WEAR A HIJAB?
RIGHT.
THE WORLD IS FILLED WITH DIFFERENT PEOPLE.
THAT INCLUDES DIFFERENT MUSLIMS!
LIKE PAKEEZAH, WHO'S FROM AFGHANISTAN AND WEARS A BURQA.
WE CAN'T LOOK DOWN ON PEOPLE OR ISOLATE THEM...
JUST BECAUSE THEY DRESS OR LIVE DIFFERENTLY.
AND NO *PRESSURING* OTHERS, EITHER!
IT'S NOT RIGHT.
NOW WHAT IS *UP* WITH THAT DRESS?!
IT'S AWFUL!
HERE-- WEAR THIS INSTEAD!
I THOUGHT IT WAS BAD TO PRESSURE PEOPLE...
THAT HAS NOTHING TO DO WITH THIS!

DIRECTION

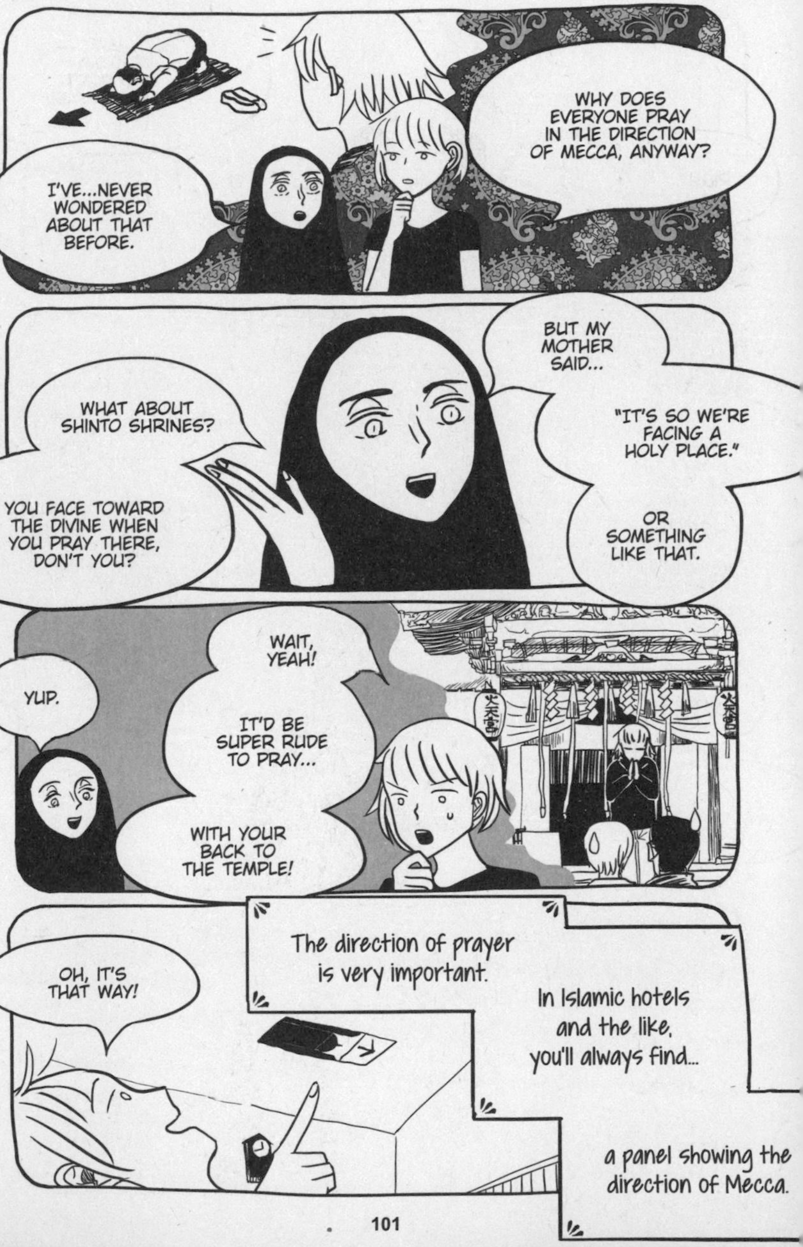
WHY DOES EVERYONE PRAY IN THE DIRECTION OF MECCA, ANYWAY?
I'VE...NEVER WONDERED ABOUT THAT BEFORE.
BUT MY MOTHER SAID...
"IT'S SO WE'RE FACING A HOLY PLACE."
OR SOMETHING LIKE THAT.
WHAT ABOUT SHINTO SHRINES?
YOU FACE TOWARD THE DIVINE WHEN YOU PRAY THERE, DON'T YOU?
WAIT, YEAH!
IT'D BE SUPER RUDE TO PRAY...
WITH YOUR BACK TO THE TEMPLE!
YUP.
The direction of prayer is very important.
In Islamic hotels and the like, you'll always find...
a panel showing the direction of Mecca.
OH, IT'S THAT WAY!

TOMATO

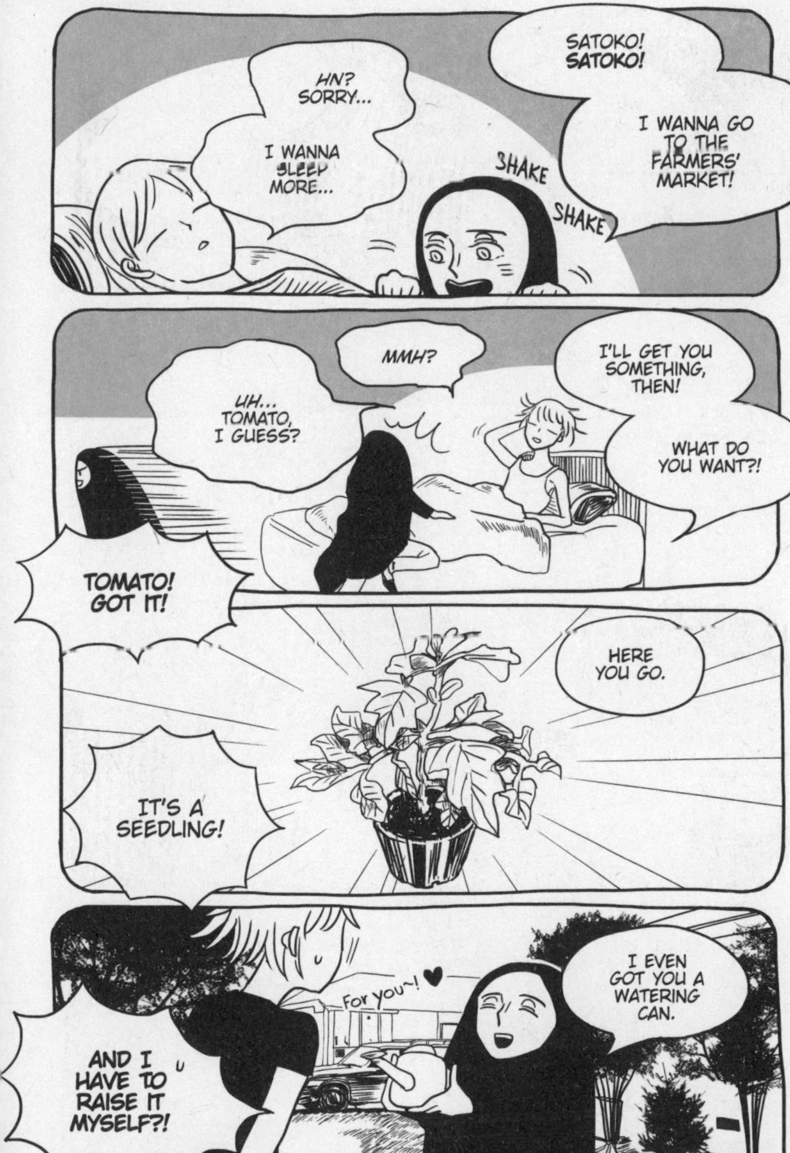

SATOKO! SATOKO!
I WANNA GO TO THE FARMERS' MARKET!
SHAKE
SHAKE
HN? SORRY...
I WANNA SLEEP MORE...
I'LL GET YOU SOMETHING, THEN!
WHAT DO YOU WANT?!
MMH?
UH... TOMATO, I GUESS?
TOMATO! GOT IT!
HERE YOU GO.
IT'S A SEEDLING!
I EVEN GOT YOU A WATERING CAN.
For you~! ♥
AND I HAVE TO RAISE IT MYSELF?!

OLD WIVES' TALE

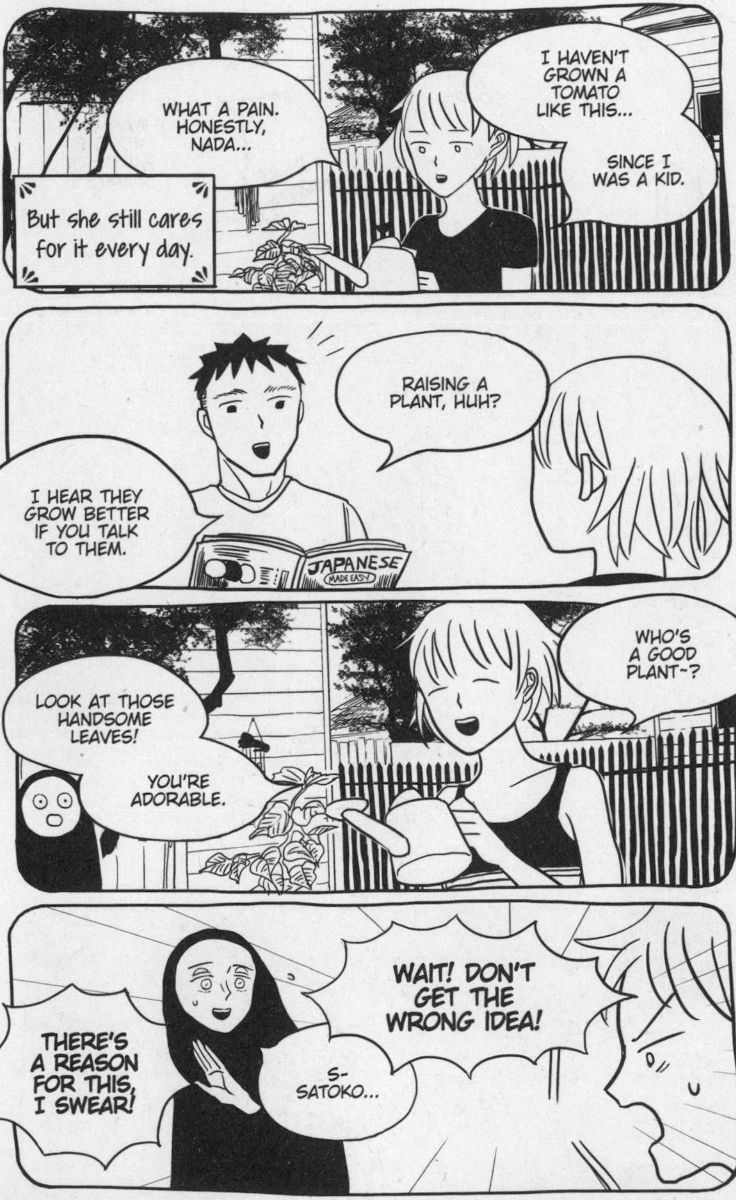
I HAVEN'T GROWN A TOMATO LIKE THIS...
SINCE I WAS A KID.
WHAT A PAIN. HONESTLY, NADA...
But she still cares for it every day.
RAISING A PLANT, HUH?
I HEAR THEY GROW BETTER IF YOU TALK TO THEM.
JAPANESE MADE EASY
WHO'S A GOOD PLANT~?
LOOK AT THOSE HANDSOME LEAVES!
YOU'RE ADORABLE.
WAIT! DON'T GET THE WRONG IDEA!
S-SATOKO...
THERE'S A REASON FOR THIS, I SWEAR!

TOP SPEED

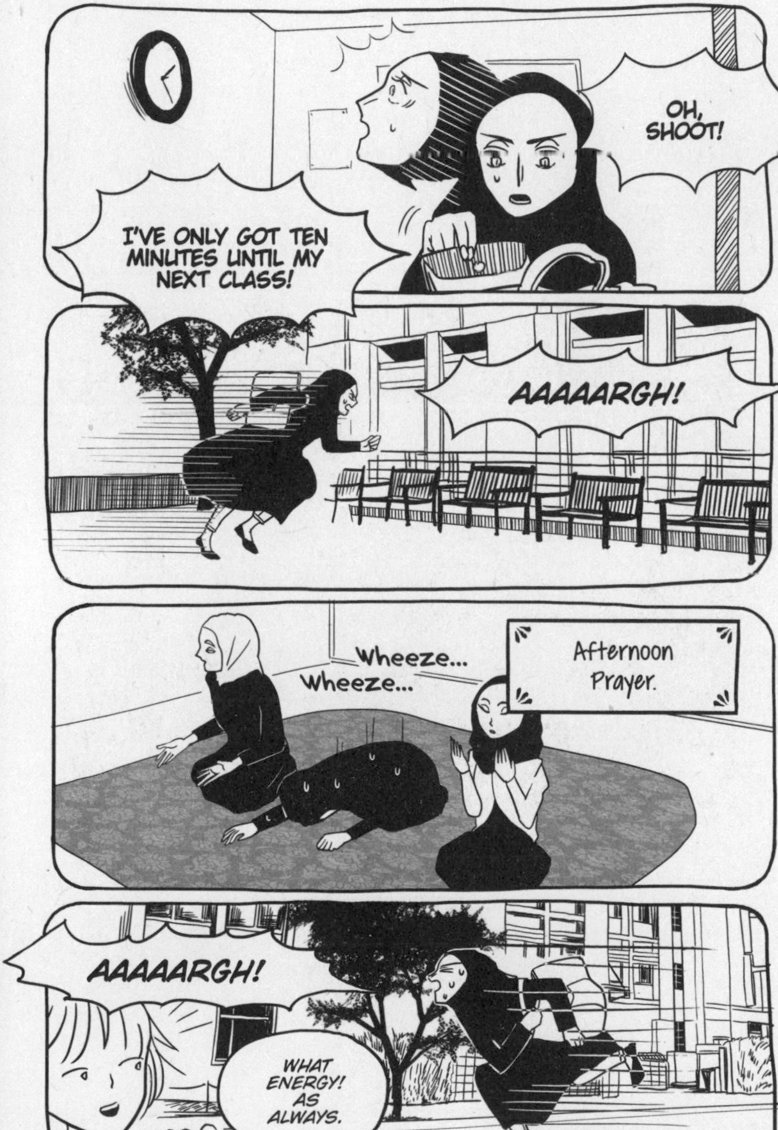
OH, SHOOT!
I'VE ONLY GOT TEN MINUTES UNTIL MY NEXT CLASS!
AAAAARGH!
Afternoon Prayer.
Wheeze... Wheeze...
AAAAARGH!
WHAT ENERGY! AS ALWAYS.
—ooO

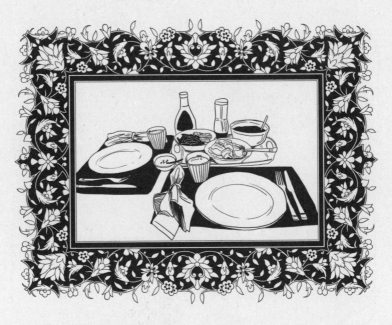

SATOKO AND NADA

Presented by Yupechika

SATOKO AND NADA

Presented by Yupechika

BIG NEWS

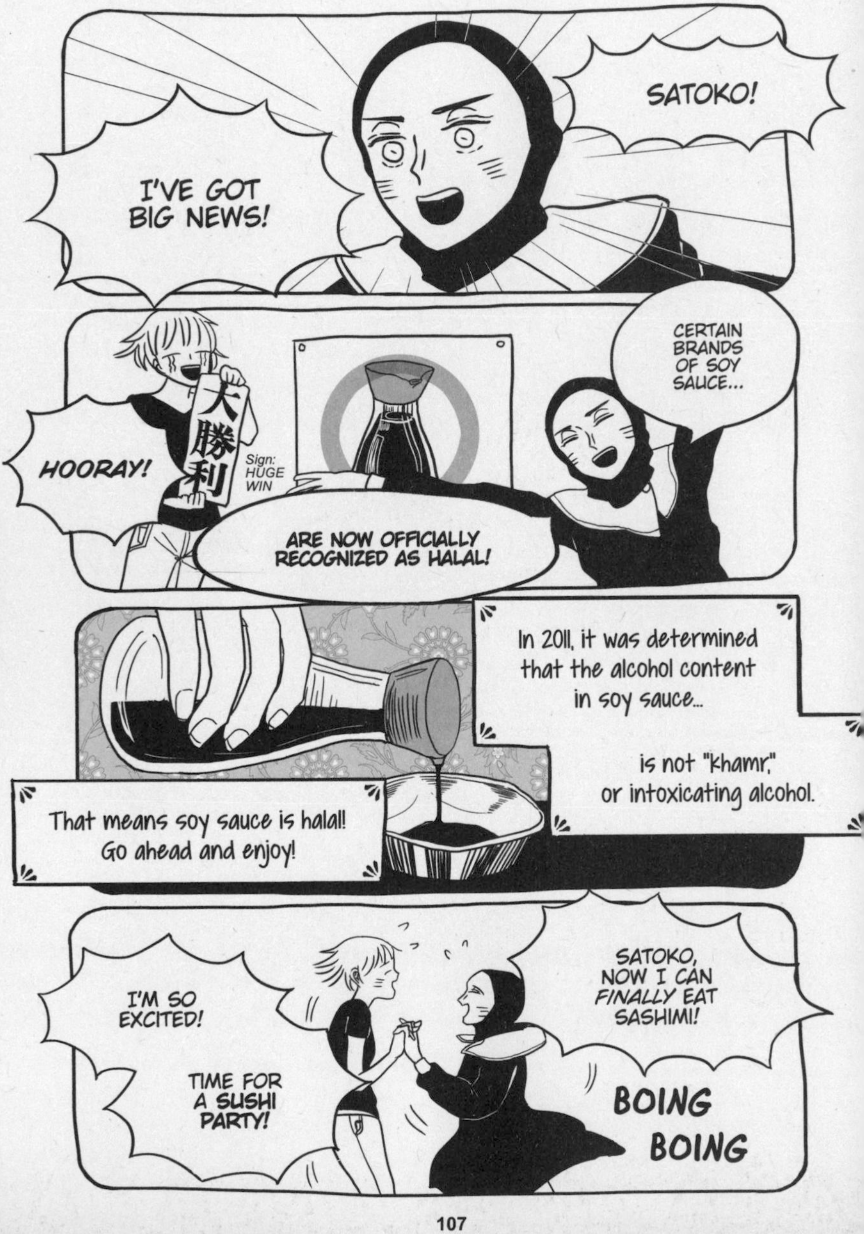
SATOKO!
I'VE GOT BIG NEWS!
CERTAIN BRANDS OF SOY SAUCE...
ARE NOW OFFICIALLY RECOGNIZED AS HALAL!
大勝利
Sign: HUGE WIN
HOORAY!
In 2011, it was determined that the alcohol content in soy sauce...
is not "khamr," or intoxicating alcohol.
That means soy sauce is halal! Go ahead and enjoy!
SATOKO, NOW I CAN FINALLY EAT SASHIMI!
BOING BOING
I'M SO EXCITED!
TIME FOR A SUSHI PARTY!

STRATEGY MEETING

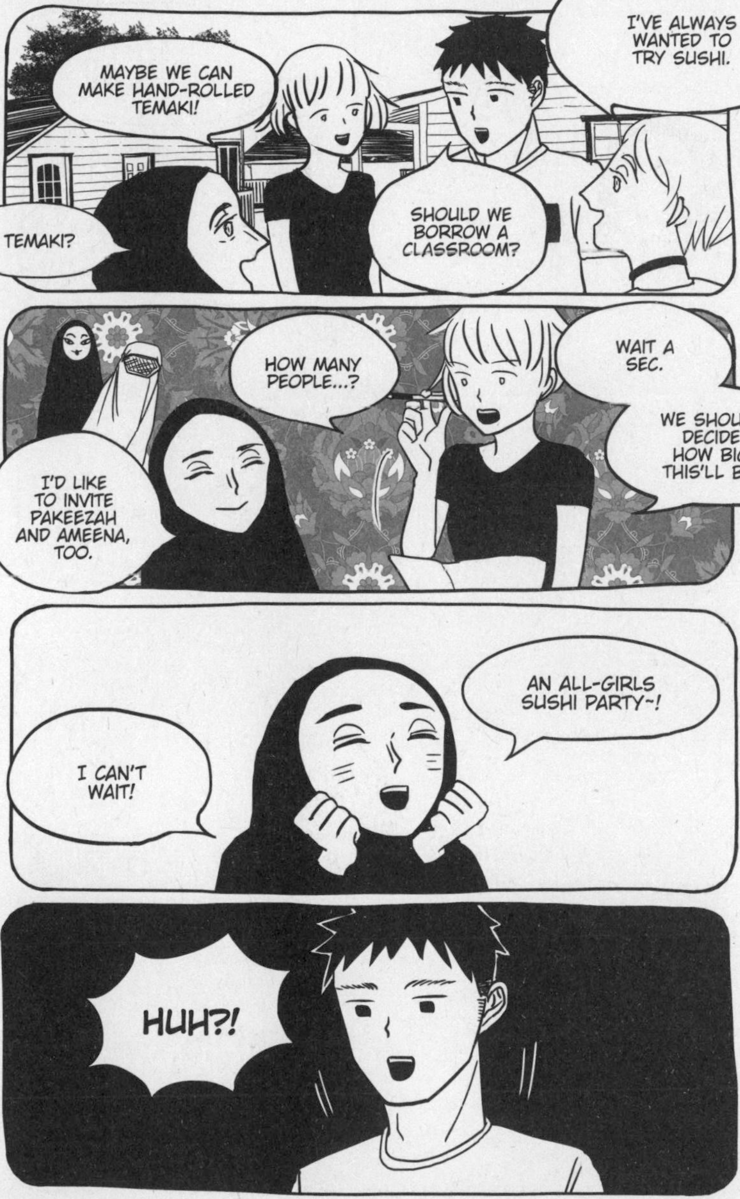
I'VE ALWAYS WANTED TO TRY SUSHI.
SHOULD WE BORROW A CLASSROOM?
MAYBE WE CAN MAKE HAND-ROLLED TEMAKI!
TEMAKI?
WAIT A SEC.
WE SHOULD DECIDE HOW BIG THIS'LL BE.
HOW MANY PEOPLE...?
I'D LIKE TO INVITE PAKEEZAH AND AMEENA, TOO.
AN ALL-GIRLS SUSHI PARTY~!
I CAN'T WAIT!
HUH?!

AMERICANIZED

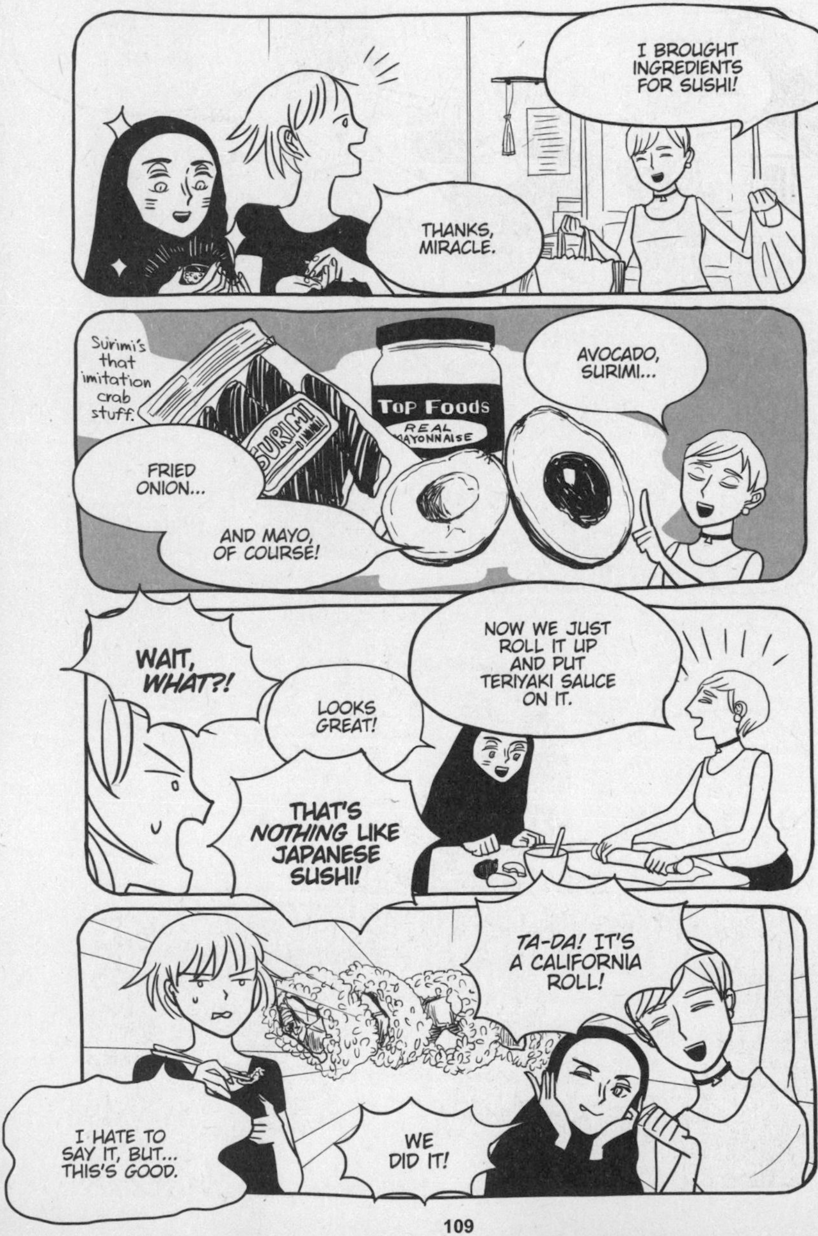
I BROUGHT INGREDIENTS FOR SUSHI!
THANKS, MIRACLE.
AVOCADO, SURIMI...
Surimi's that imitation crab stuff.
Top Foods
REAL MAYONNAISE
SURIMI
FRIED ONION...
AND MAYO, OF COURSE!
NOW WE JUST ROLL IT UP AND PUT TERIYAKI SAUCE ON IT.
LOOKS GREAT!
WAIT, *WHAT?!*
THAT'S *NOTHING* LIKE JAPANESE SUSHI!
TA-DA! IT'S A CALIFORNIA ROLL!
WE DID IT!
I HATE TO SAY IT, BUT... THIS'S GOOD.

SUSHI PARTY

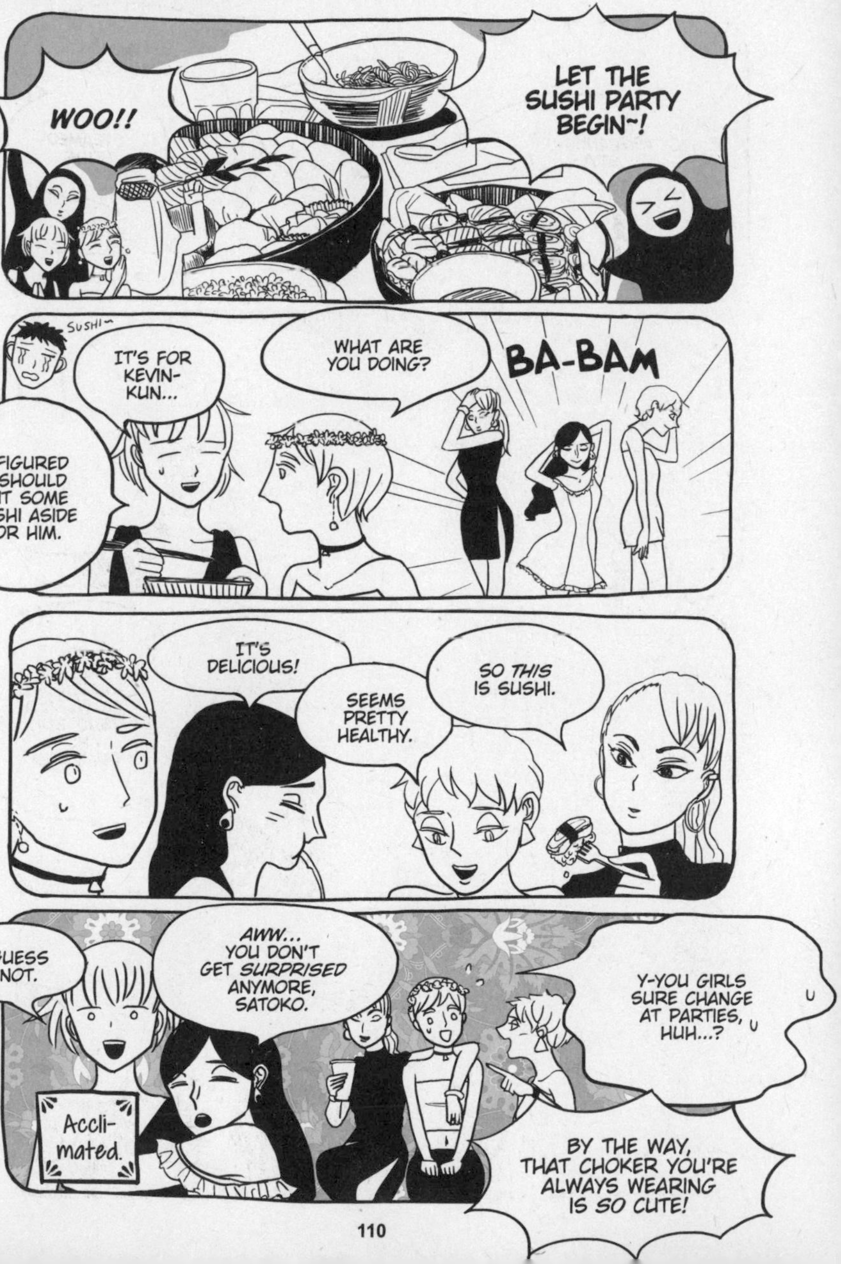
LET THE SUSHI PARTY BEGIN~!
WOO!!
BA-BAM
WHAT ARE YOU DOING?
IT'S FOR KEVIN-KUN...
SUSHI~
I FIGURED I SHOULD PUT SOME SUSHI ASIDE FOR HIM.
SO *THIS* IS SUSHI.
IT'S DELICIOUS!
SEEMS PRETTY HEALTHY.
Y-YOU GIRLS SURE CHANGE AT PARTIES, HUH...?
AWW... YOU DON'T GET *SURPRISED* ANYMORE, SATOKO.
GUESS NOT.
Accli-mated.
BY THE WAY, THAT CHOKER YOU'RE ALWAYS WEARING IS SO CUTE!

STEAMED BUNS

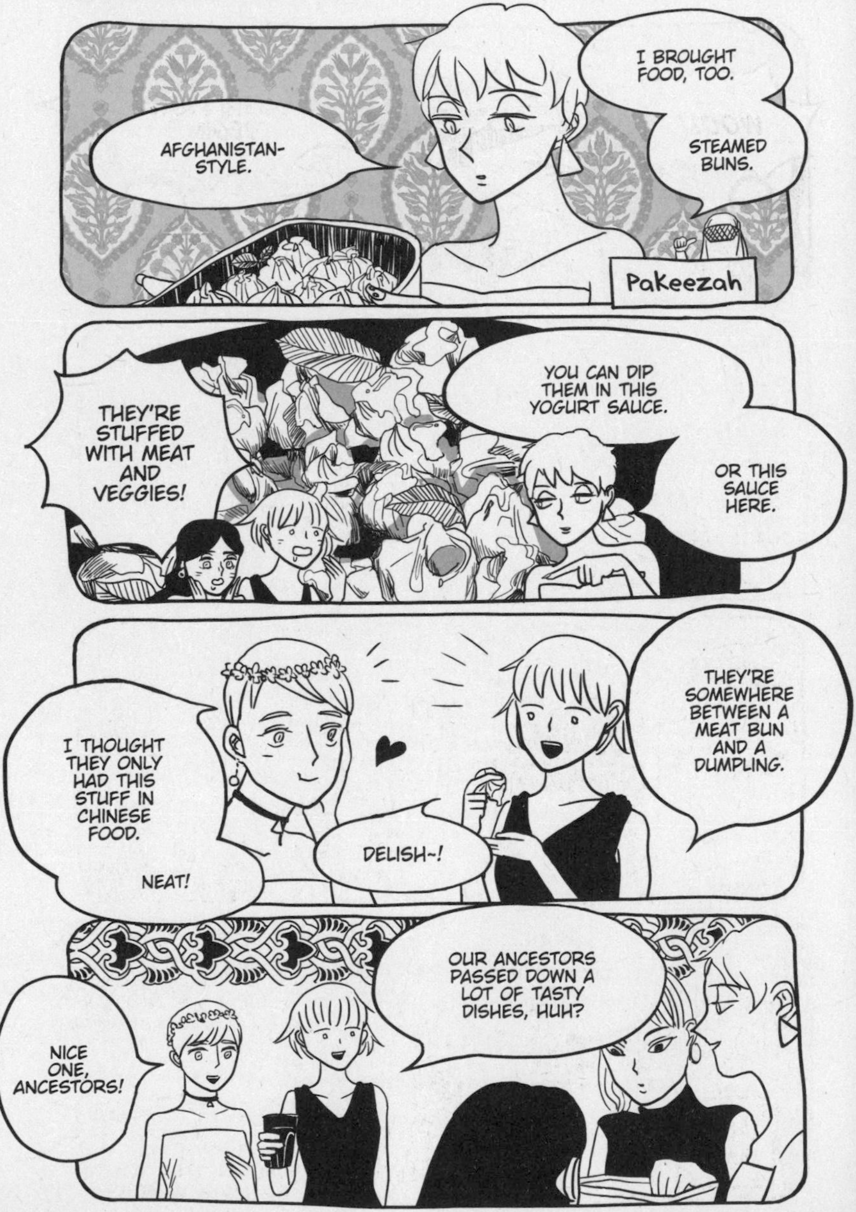
I BROUGHT FOOD, TOO.
STEAMED BUNS.
AFGHANISTAN-STYLE.
Pakeezah
YOU CAN DIP THEM IN THIS YOGURT SAUCE.
OR THIS SAUCE HERE.
THEY'RE STUFFED WITH MEAT AND VEGGIES!
THEY'RE SOMEWHERE BETWEEN A MEAT BUN AND A DUMPLING.
DELISH~!
I THOUGHT THEY ONLY HAD THIS STUFF IN CHINESE FOOD.
NEAT!
OUR ANCESTORS PASSED DOWN A LOT OF TASTY DISHES, HUH?
NICE ONE, ANCESTORS!

MEAT LOVERS

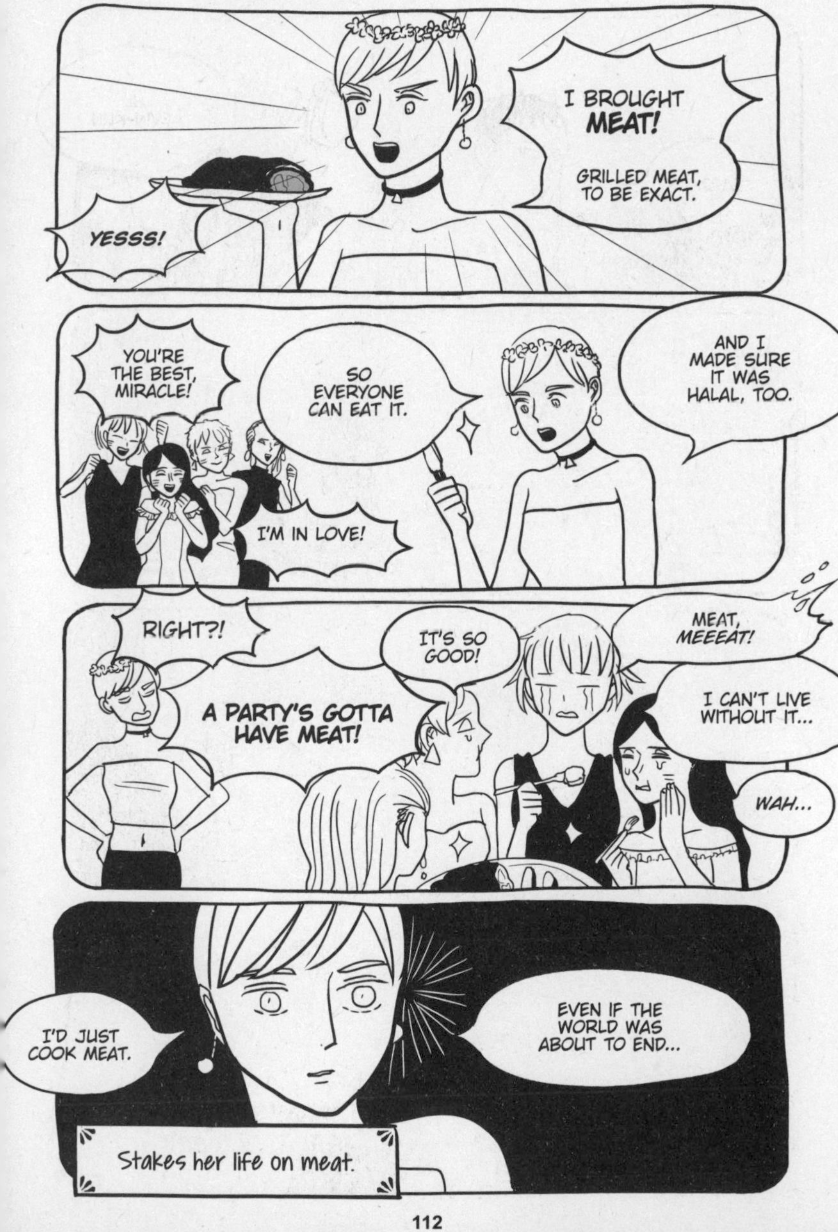
I BROUGHT **MEAT!**
GRILLED MEAT, TO BE EXACT.
YESSS!
AND I MADE SURE IT WAS HALAL, TOO.
SO EVERYONE CAN EAT IT.
YOU'RE THE BEST, MIRACLE!
I'M IN LOVE!
MEAT, MEEEAT!
IT'S SO GOOD!
RIGHT?!
I CAN'T LIVE WITHOUT IT...
A PARTY'S GOTTA HAVE MEAT!
WAH...
EVEN IF THE WORLD WAS ABOUT TO END...
I'D JUST COOK MEAT.
Stakes her life on meat.

CHEST

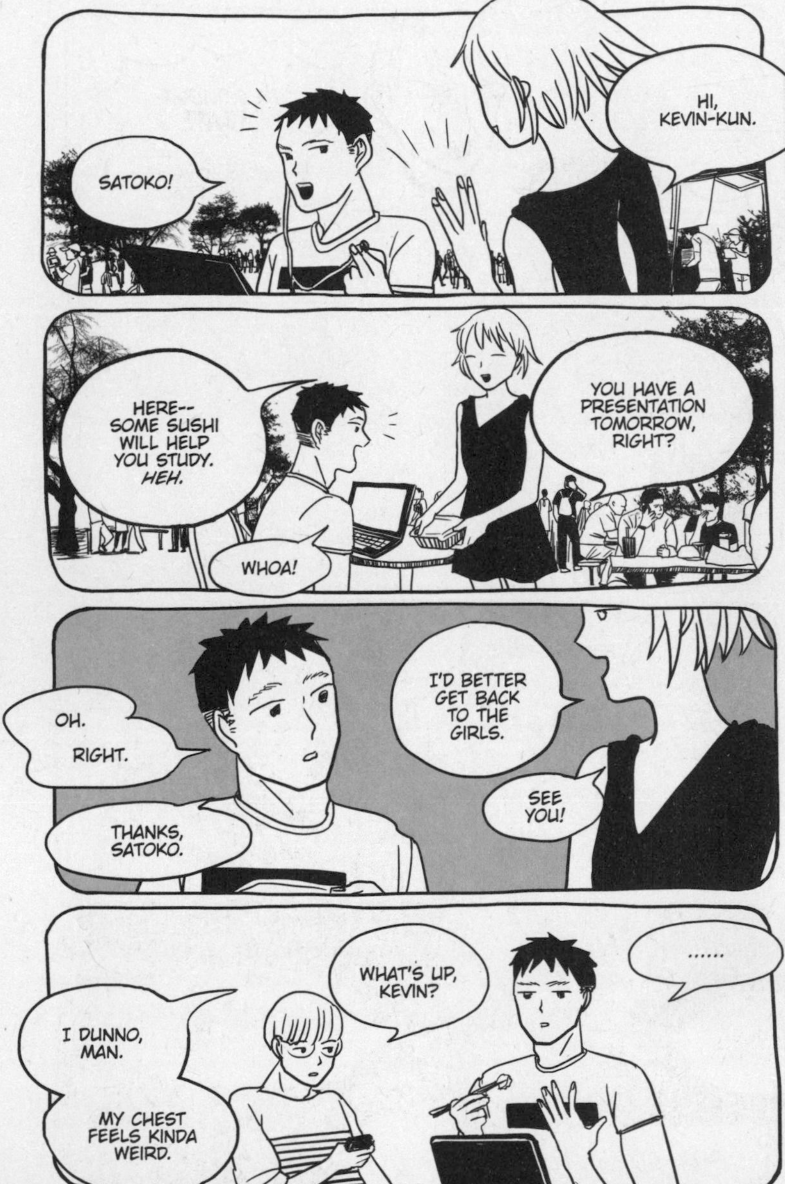

HI, KEVIN-KUN.
SATOKO!
YOU HAVE A PRESENTATION TOMORROW, RIGHT?
HERE-- SOME SUSHI WILL HELP YOU STUDY. *HEH.*
WHOA!
I'D BETTER GET BACK TO THE GIRLS.
OH. RIGHT.
SEE YOU!
THANKS, SATOKO.
......
WHAT'S UP, KEVIN?
I DUNNO, MAN.
MY CHEST FEELS KINDA WEIRD.

SENSEI

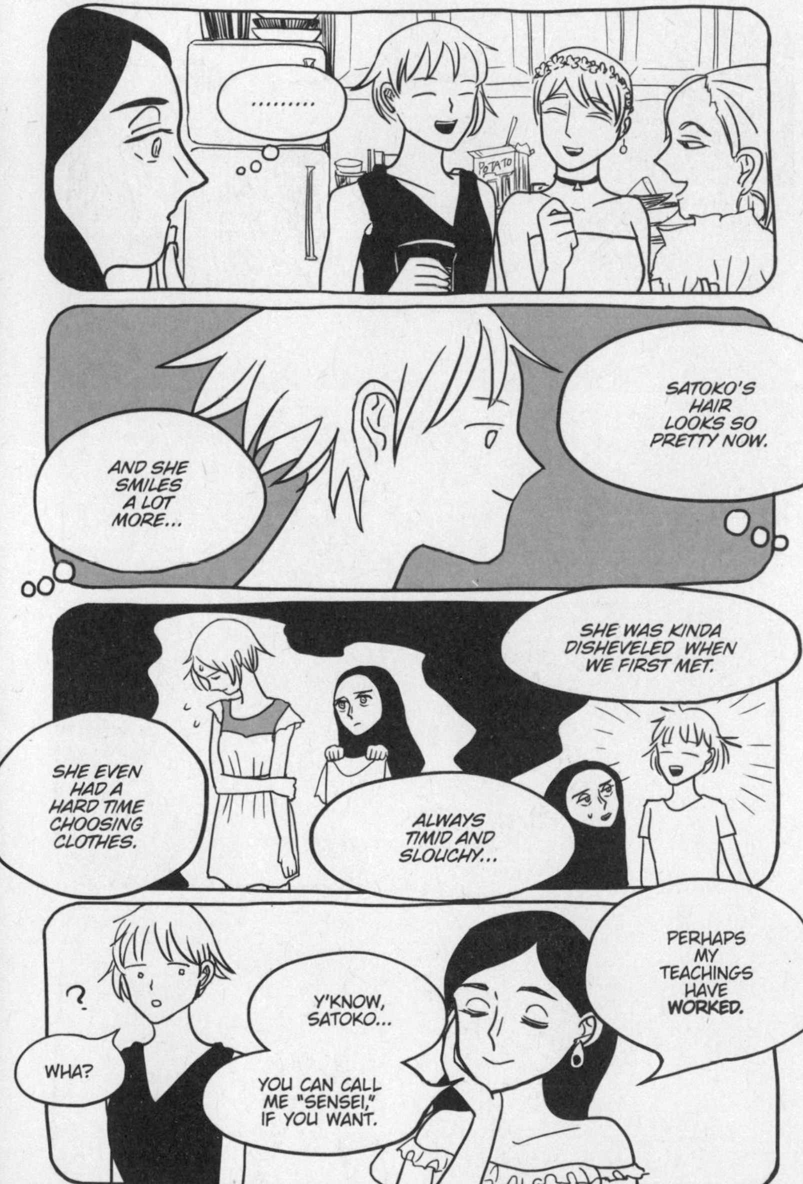
....
SATOKO'S HAIR LOOKS SO PRETTY NOW.
AND SHE SMILES A LOT MORE...
SHE WAS KINDA DISHEVELED WHEN WE FIRST MET.
ALWAYS TIMID AND SLOUCHY...
SHE EVEN HAD A HARD TIME CHOOSING CLOTHES.
PERHAPS MY TEACHINGS HAVE **WORKED.**
Y'KNOW, SATOKO...
YOU CAN CALL ME "SENSEI," IF YOU WANT.
?
WHA?

AT THE DOOR

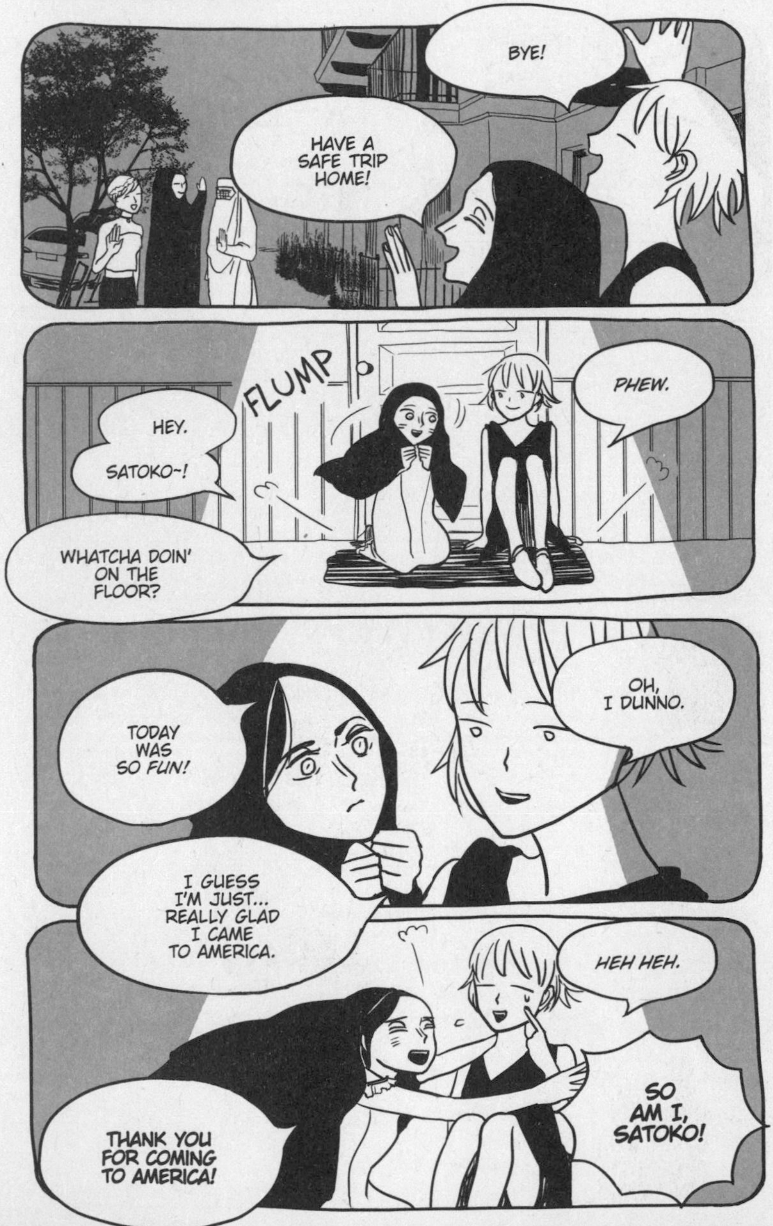
BYE!
HAVE A SAFE TRIP HOME!
PHEW.
FLUMP
HEY.
SATOKO~!
WHATCHA DOIN' ON THE FLOOR?
OH, I DUNNO.
TODAY WAS SO FUN!
I GUESS I'M JUST... REALLY GLAD I CAME TO AMERICA.
HEH HEH.
SO AM I, SATOKO!
THANK YOU FOR COMING TO AMERICA!

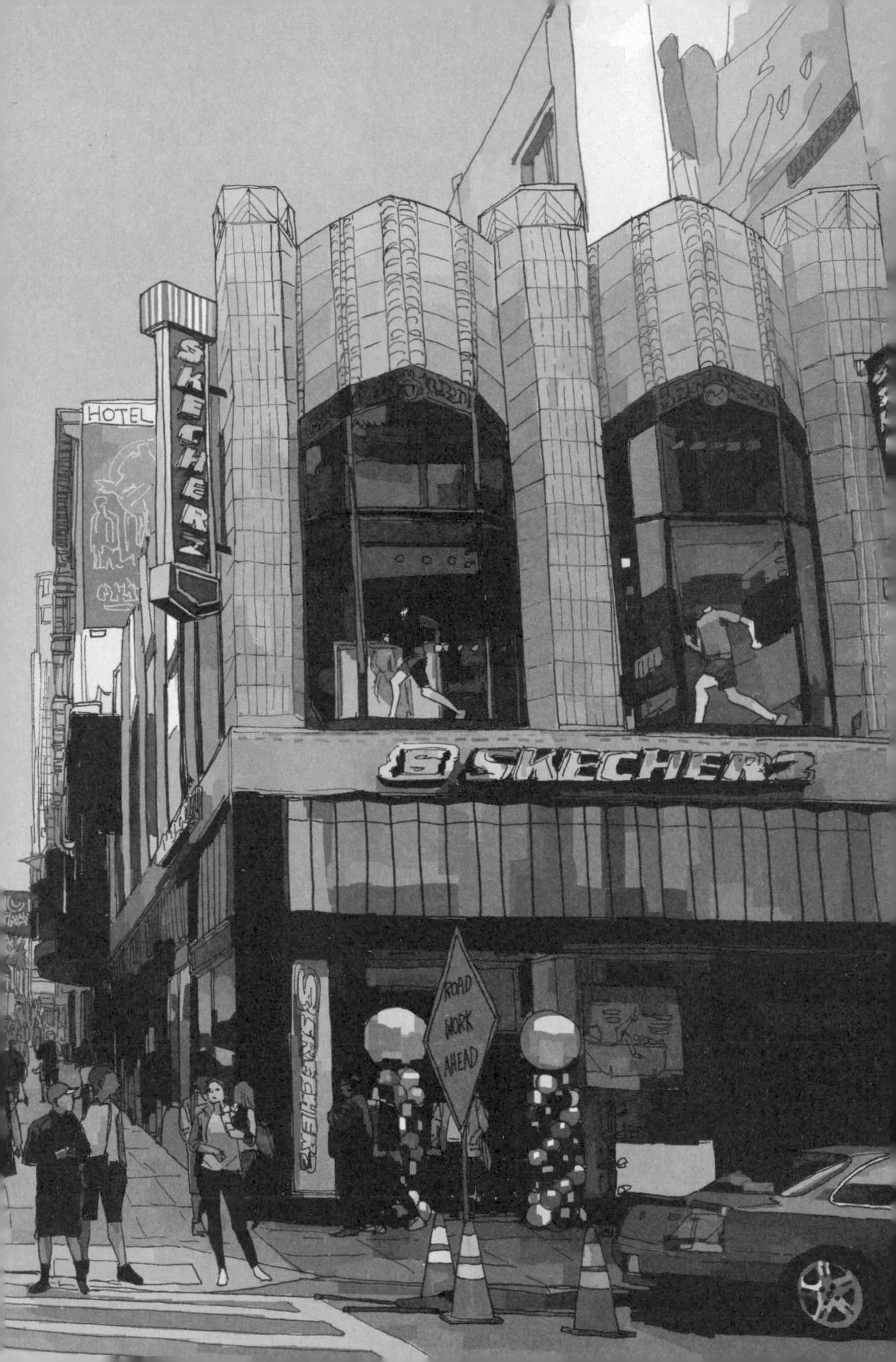
HOTEL
SKECHERS
SKECHERS
SKECHERS
ROAD WORK AHEAD

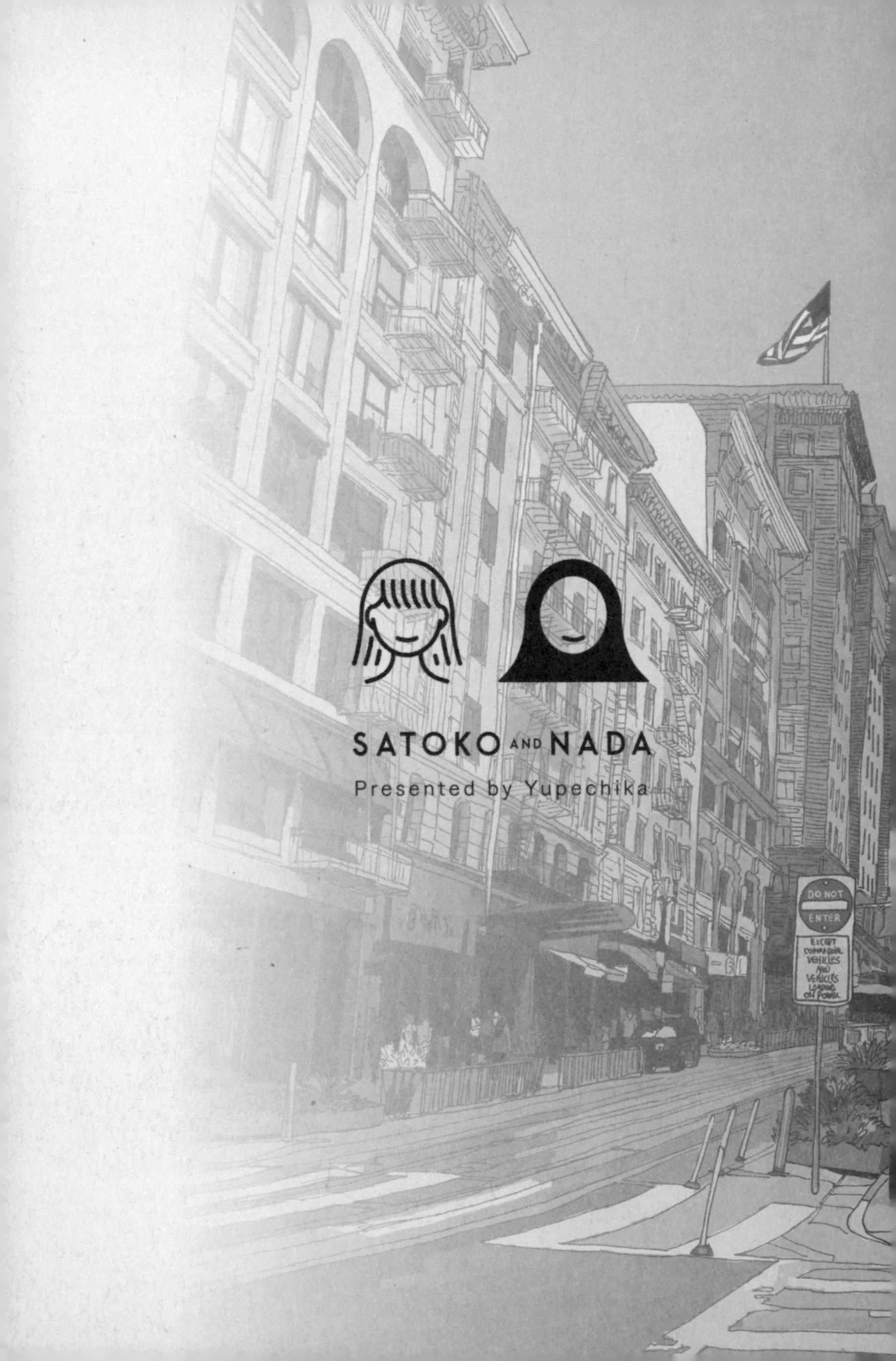
DO NOT ENTER
EXCEPT COMMERCIAL VEHICLES AND VEHICLES LOADING ON POWELL

SATOKO AND NADA

Presented by Yupechika

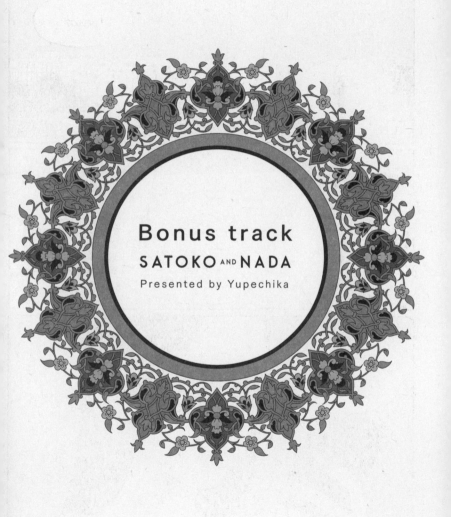

Bonus track

SATOKO AND NADA

Presented by Yupechika

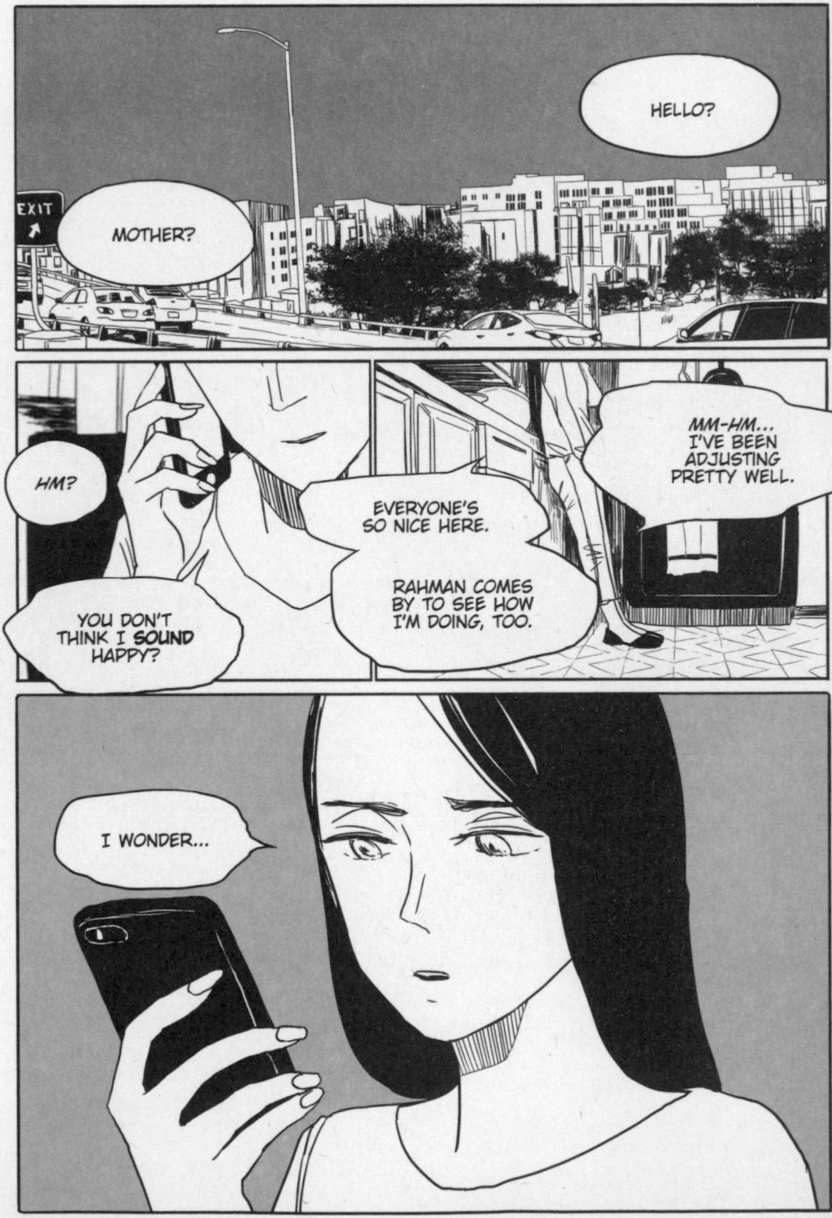
HELLO?
MOTHER?
MM-HM... I'VE BEEN ADJUSTING PRETTY WELL.
EVERYONE'S SO NICE HERE.
RAHMAN COMES BY TO SEE HOW I'M DOING, TOO.
HM?
YOU DON'T THINK I **SOUND** HAPPY?
I WONDER...

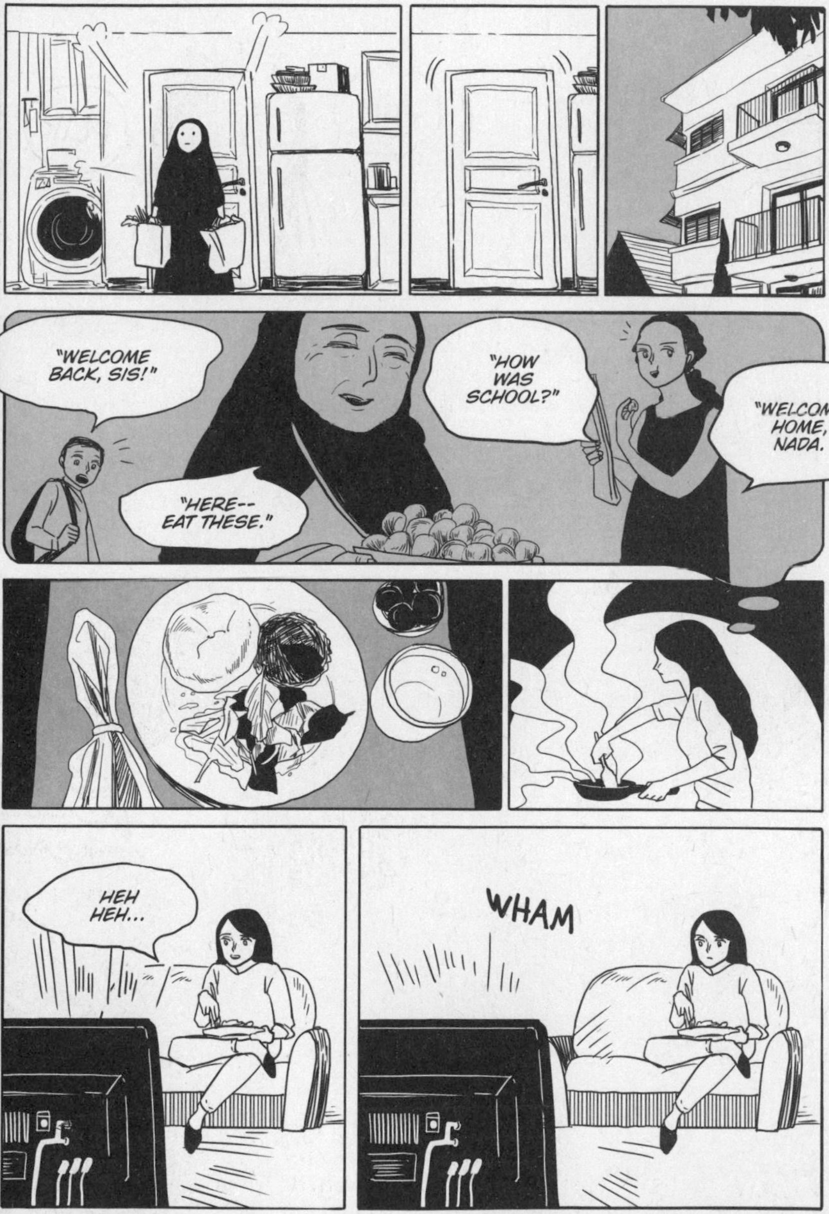
"WELCOME HOME, NADA.
"HOW WAS SCHOOL?"
"HERE-- EAT THESE."
"WELCOME BACK, SIS!"
WHAM
HEH HEH...

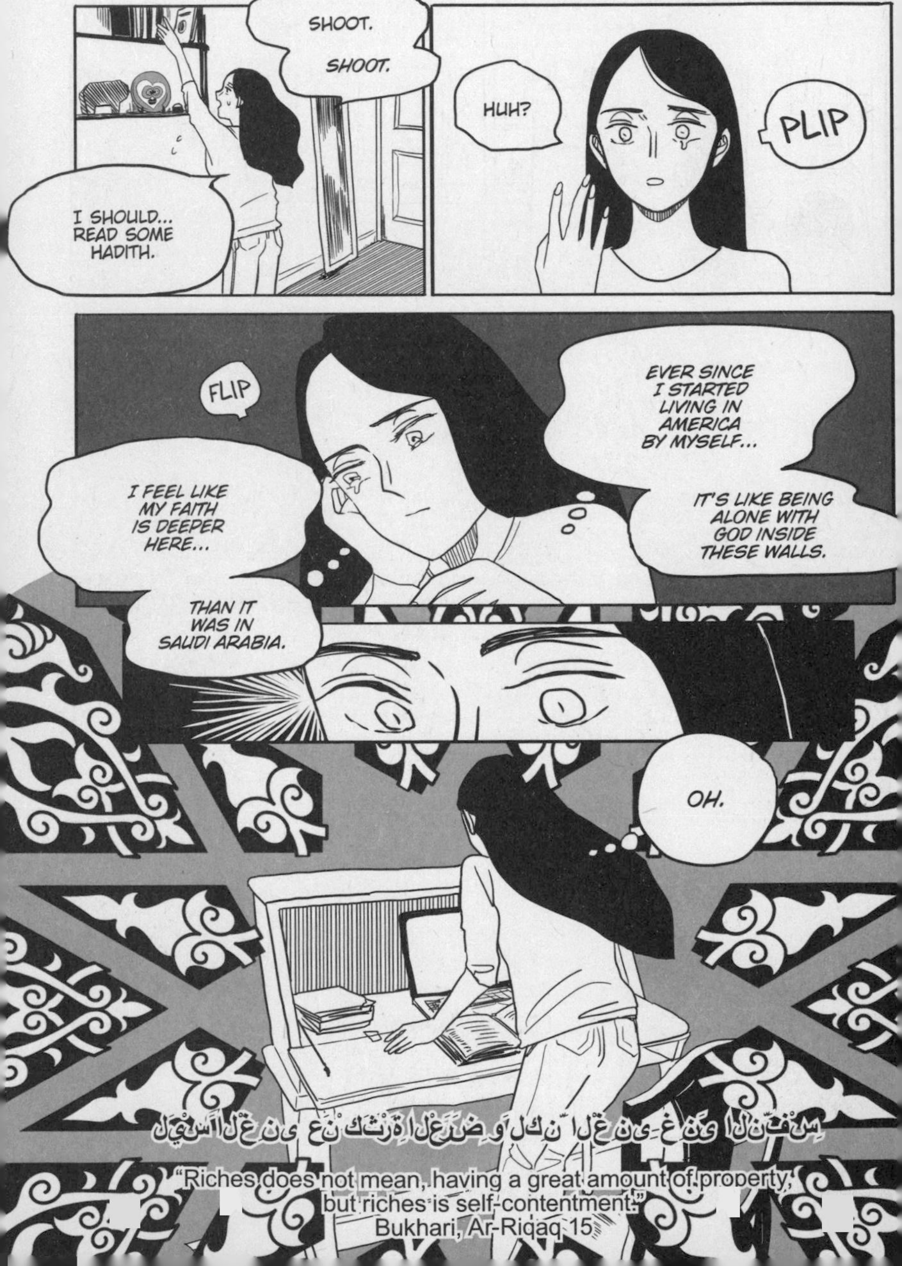
HUH?
PLIP
SHOOT.
SHOOT.
I SHOULD... READ SOME HADITH.
EVER SINCE I STARTED LIVING IN AMERICA BY MYSELF...
FLIP
IT'S LIKE BEING ALONE WITH GOD INSIDE THESE WALLS.
I FEEL LIKE MY FAITH IS DEEPER HERE...
THAN IT WAS IN SAUDI ARABIA.
OH.
لَيْسَ الْغِنَى عَنْ كَثْرَةِ الْعَرَضِ وَلَكِنَّ الْغِنَى غِنَى النَّفْسِ
"Riches does not mean, having a great amount of property,
but riches is self-contentment."
Bukhari, Ar-Riqaq 15

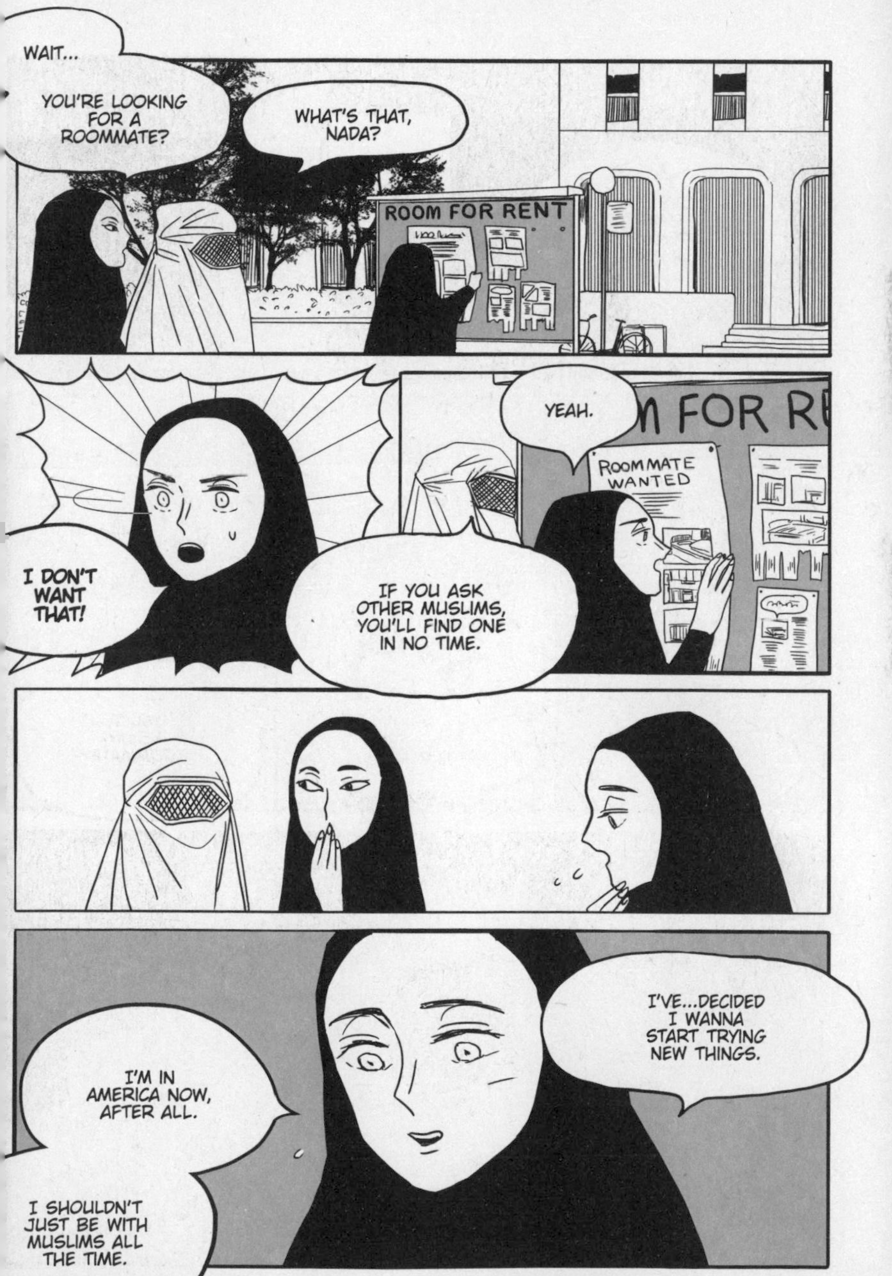
WAIT...
YOU'RE LOOKING FOR A ROOMMATE?
WHAT'S THAT, NADA?
ROOM FOR RENT
YEAH.
ROOMMATE WANTED
IF YOU ASK OTHER MUSLIMS, YOU'LL FIND ONE IN NO TIME.
I DON'T WANT THAT!
I'VE...DECIDED I WANNA START TRYING NEW THINGS.
I'M IN AMERICA NOW, AFTER ALL.
I SHOULDN'T JUST BE WITH MUSLIMS ALL THE TIME.

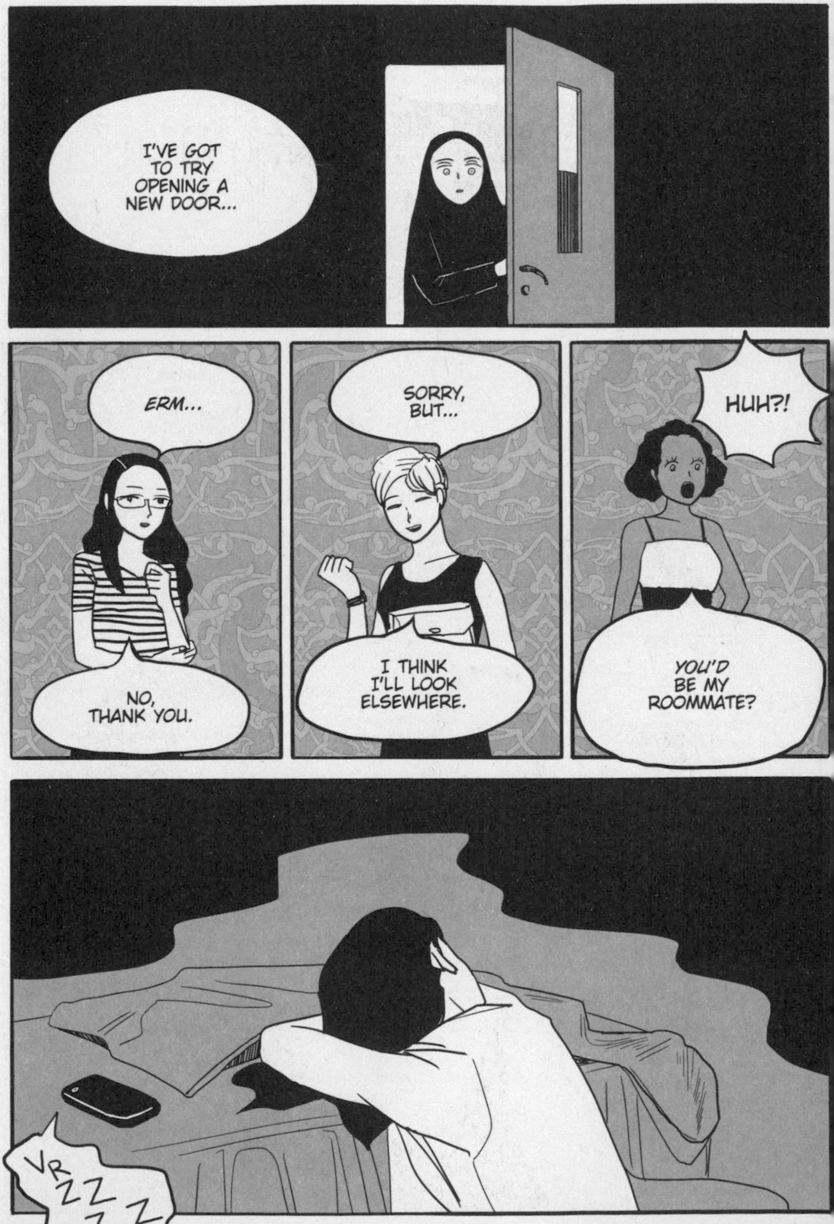
I'VE GOT TO TRY OPENING A NEW DOOR...
HUH?!
YOU'D BE MY ROOMMATE?
SORRY, BUT...
I THINK I'LL LOOK ELSEWHERE.
ERM...
NO, THANK YOU.
VRZZZZZ

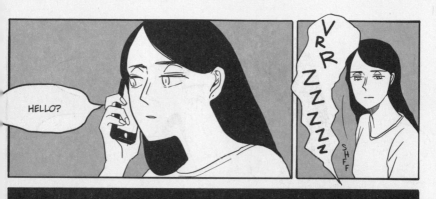

HELLO?

VRRZZZZz
SHFF

YOUR NAME'S SATOKO? I SEE...
YOU'RE FROM JAPAN?

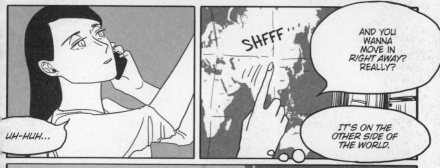

UH-HUH...

SHFFF...

AND YOU WANNA MOVE IN RIGHT AWAY? REALLY?

IT'S ON THE OTHER SIDE OF THE WORLD.

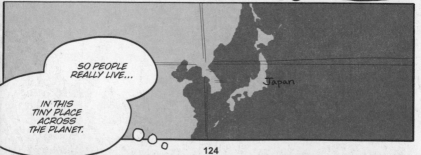

SO PEOPLE REALLY LIVE...

IN THIS TINY PLACE ACROSS THE PLANET.

Japan

124

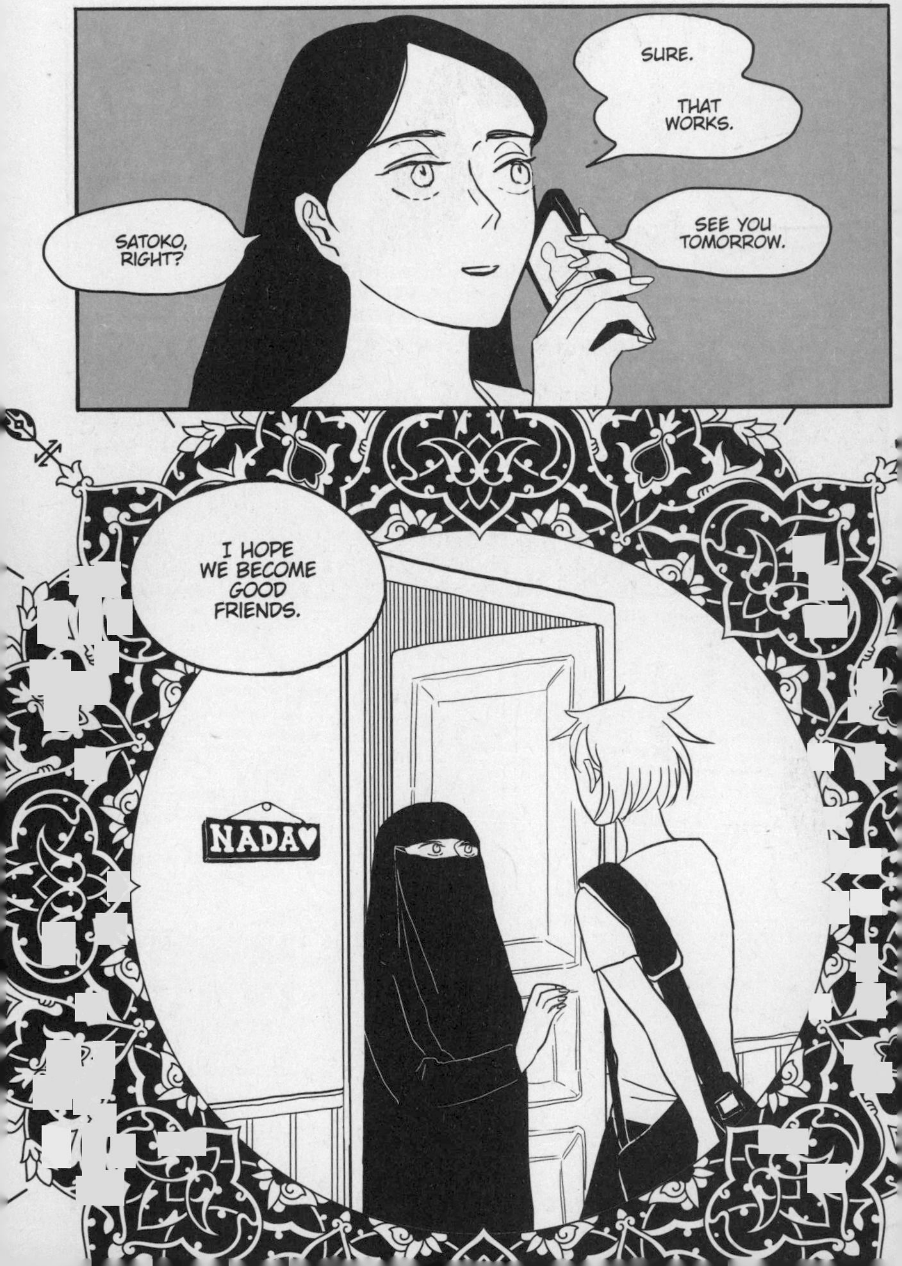
SURE.
THAT WORKS.
SEE YOU TOMORROW.
SATOKO, RIGHT?
I HOPE WE BECOME GOOD FRIENDS.
NADA♥

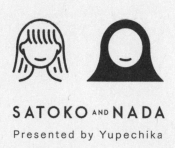

SATOKO AND NADA

Presented by Yupechika

SEVEN SEAS ENTERTAINMENT PRESENTS

SATO
AND
NAD

story and art by **YUPECHIKA** script advisor: **MARIE NISHIMORI**

TRANSLATION
Jenny McKeon

ADAPTATION
Lianne Sentar

LETTERING AND RETOUCH
Karis Page

COVER DESIGN
KC Fabellon

PROOFREADER
Danielle King
Shanti Whitesides

EDITOR
Jenn Grunigen

PRODUCTION ASSISTANT
CK Russell

PRODUCTION MANAGER
Lissa Pattillo

EDITOR-IN-CHIEF
Adam Arnold

PUBLISHER
Jason DeAngelis

SATOKO TO NADA VOLUME 1

First published in Japan in 2017 by Star Seas Company.
Publication rights for this English edition arranged with Star Seas Company through Kodansha Ltd.,Tokyo.

Seven Seas books may be purchased in bulk for promotional, educational, or business use. Please contact your local bookseller or the Macmillan Corporate and Premium Sales Department at 1-800-221-7945, extension 5442, or by e-mail at MacmillanSpecialMarkets@macmillan.com.

ISBN: 978-1-626929-09-8

Printed in Canada

First Printing: October 2018

10 9 8 7 6 5 4 3 2 1

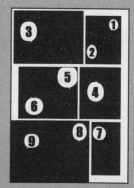

FOLLOW US ONLINE: ***www.sevenseasentertainment.com***

READING DIRECTIONS

This book reads from ***right to left***, Japanese style. If this is your first time reading manga, you start reading from the top right panel on each page and take it from there. If you get lost, just follow the numbered diagram here. It may seem backwards at first, but you'll get the hang of it! Have fun!!

1
2
3
4
5
6
7
8
9